boon Desire line
seven-time finalist for a
ters of America RITA® Award,
nor of more than one hundred romance
books regularly appear on bestseller lists and
won several awards, including a Prism Award, a
National Readers' Choice Award, a Colorado Romance
Writers Award of Excellence and a Golden Quill Award.
She is a native Californian but has recently moved to the
mountains of Utah.

Discover more at millsandboon.co.uk

THE RANCHER'S BARGAIN

JOANNE ROCK

BOMBSHELL FOR THE BOSS

MAUREEN CHILD

MIX
Paper from
responsible sources

FSC

FSC C001434

This book is produced from independently certified FSC™
paper to ensure responsible forest management.

For more information visit www.harpercollins.co.uk/green

Printed and bound in Spain
by CPI Barcelona

MILLS & BOON

First Published in Great Britain 2019
by Mills & Boon, an imprint of HarperCollinsPublishers,
1 London Bridge Street, London, SE1 9GF

The Rancher's Bargain © 2018 Harlequin Books S.A.
Bombshell for the Boss © 2018 Maureen Child

Special thanks and acknowledgement are given to Joanne Rock for her contribution to the Texas Cattleman's Club: Bachelor Auction series.

ISBN: 978-0-263-27167-6

0119

THE RANCHER'S
BARGAIN

JOANNE ROCK

One

It is okay to say no to unnecessary crazy.

Lydia Walker repeated it like a mantra while she read the digital headline from a story that had run in the Royal, Texas, newspaper earlier in the week while she'd been out of town.

Local woman boosts charity bachelor auction with $100K bid!

Seated at her tiny kitchen table with a cup of coffee grown cold, Lydia hovered her finger over the scroll button on her cell phone. She wished she could just swipe right and not worry about the "local woman" who happened to be her irresponsible sister Gail. The impulsive sibling who did *not* have $100,000 to her name. What had Gail been thinking?

In spite of herself, Lydia started reading the article again.

Gail Walker, a local entrepreneur, made the surprise bid on Lloyd Richardson, a local rancher. Ms. Walker could not be reached for comment while she is out of town on a romantic getaway with her chosen bachelor, but the Great Bachelor Auction master of ceremonies, James Harris, said he's grateful for the generous donation that benefits the Pancreatic Cancer Research Foundation. "This is what the event is all about..."

Closing her eyes, Lydia flipped the phone facedown on the table to stop herself from going over the story a third time.

Definitely unnecessary crazy.

She had just gotten back into town after a visit to her mother's home in Arkansas for Thanksgiving, a trip she'd been guilted into since she hadn't been home in almost two years. Her mom had used the time to corner Lydia about being in Fiona's upcoming wedding to a fourth husband, making the holiday a total disaster. Lydia had wanted her sister to make the long drive with her, but Gail had insisted she needed to stay in Royal and personally oversee her fledgling grocery delivery service. An excuse Lydia had accepted, proud of Gail for doing something fiscally responsible for a change.

Ha! Apparently, Gail just wanted to stay in town to bid on a sexy bachelor during the event at the swanky Texas Cattleman's Club. Had the word already gotten out around town that Gail didn't have the money? Lydia scanned the Royal paper for more news but found only stories about the auction's lone bachelorette, Tessa Noble, and her date with a local rancher. There was no follow-up article about Gail's date or her outrageous bid.

Yet.

Lydia's stomach knotted. How could Gail do something like that to a *charity*, for crying out loud? Furthermore, they shared the same last name. How did it look for the Walker women, both trying to start their own business, when they didn't pay their debts?

Anger flaring, she flipped her phone screen toward her again and dialed her sister's number. As the oldest of eight siblings, Lydia was used to high drama in the family. But for most of her life, the main perpetrator had been her mother, a woman who had parlayed her parenting experience into a successful homemaking blog, *House Rules*. Fiona Walker's online followers loved her "whimsical" approach to childrearing that Lydia viewed as flighty at best and, at times, downright dangerous. Lydia had hoped Royal, Texas, would be a fresh start for her and Gail once the youngest of their siblings was old enough to fend for himself with their mom.

But now, with the mortifying news of Gail's over-the-top bachelor auction bid, Lydia had to admit that her sister hadn't fallen far from the maternal tree.

"Lydia!" Her sister squealed her name as she answered her phone. "You'll never guess where I am!"

Frustration simmered.

"I certainly hope you're at the Pancreatic Cancer Research Foundation explaining how you're going to magically make one hundred thousand dollars appear," Lydia snapped, powerless to restrain herself. "Gail, what on earth are you doing?"

Anxious and irate, she paced around her half-finished kitchen in the house she'd been slowly renovating to one day open an in-home child care business.

She nearly tripped on the flooring samples she'd carefully laid out by the sliding glass door leading to the backyard. The toe of her slipper sent Spanish cedar and mahogany samples flying over the ash and buckthorn pieces.

"I am having a romantic holiday with the man of my dreams," her sister retorted, her tone shifting from excited to petulant. "Is it too much to ask for you to be happy for me? For once?"

Lydia covered her eyes with one hand, remembering her mother had said those same words to her—almost verbatim—just last week when Lydia refused to be in her wedding. Now, her head throbbed while the morning sunlight poured in through the back door. "I'm happy that you're having a good time. But I'm very worried about how you're going to cover the bid you placed at the bachelor auction. Have you spoken with the cancer foundation?"

"I'll bet that's why my credit card didn't work yesterday at the spa," Gail mused. In the background, music that sounded like it came from a mariachi band was growing louder. "I forgot about the payment to the bachelor auction."

"What payment?" Lydia pressed, heading back to the kitchen table to clear her plate and cup. "You don't have the kind of money you bid."

She held the phone on her shoulder, pinning it to her cheek while she set the dishes in the sink.

"And I'll figure it out after vacation, okay, Ms. Worrywart?" Her sister raised her voice to be heard over the music. "Oh, and just FYI, I'm ignoring calls from anyone I don't know this week."

"Who has been calling you?" Apprehension spiked. "The charity people?"

"No, the guy who was in charge that night. John? James?" Gail sighed. "Just forget it, okay? Right now, I've got to get back to my margarita before the ice melts!"

"Gail, wait—"

But her screen already read, "Call Ended." And she knew her sister well. There wasn't a chance Gail would answer if she phoned again.

It is okay to say no to unnecessary crazy.

The words had helped Lydia survive her teenage years. But right now, the mantra didn't roll off the tongue so well when she thought about how the local folks who had worked hard to raise money for charity were being misled. The Texas Cattleman's Club had hosted the event, and their members were a who's who list of the town's most influential people. Lydia wanted to put roots down in Royal. She'd already bought the fixer-upper property to start her child care business here. The last thing she needed was a mark against her family name because of Gail's impulsiveness.

Maybe she could at least explain the situation to someone before the news surfaced about Gail's lack of payment.

Scrolling back to the news piece, she found the name she was looking for. James Harris. The MC of the event must have been the one who'd tried contacting Gail. She'd missed seeing his photo in the margin of the story the first time, too dismayed by her sister's behavior to see beyond the text of the story. But now, Lydia's eyes lingered on the image of the man who was also the current president of the Texas Cattleman's Club.

Handsome didn't *begin* to describe him. The photo showed him in front of the organization's historic clubhouse building, a fawn-colored Stetson shielding his face from the Texas sun. Tall and well built, he wore a fitted gray jacket that skimmed impressive muscles. Broad where a man should be. Lean in the hips. An angular jaw with a great smile. She couldn't see his eyes clearly because they were shadowed by the brim of his hat, but his skin was a warm, inviting brown.

She blinked fast to banish the image from her brain since she could not afford to be sidelined by the man's potent sex appeal. Lydia was not in the market for romance. Her mother's active, dramatic love life had given Lydia a front-row seat for the way romance changed people. Fiona had metamorphosed into someone new for each guy she'd dated, heedless of how her whims affected the whole family. Lydia wasn't looking for even mild flirtation, *especially* not with someone her sister had bilked out of a small fortune.

She knew better than to try to fix things that were out of her control, but she could at least extend Mr. Harris the common courtesy of explaining Gail's situation. And, perhaps, learn possible options for compromise on the bill so she could speak sensibly to her sister upon her return. If she could still salvage some goodwill in the community in spite of Gail's fake bid, it would be a minor miracle.

Lydia had an appointment to meet with the contractor who was supposed to work on her kitchen at noon. But right after that, she'd stop by the Texas Cattleman's Club.

And hope with all her heart that James Harris was an understanding man.

"Lydia Walker is here to see you," the disembodied voice announced through James Harris's office intercom system.

He straightened from where he'd been practicing his golf swing in his office at the clubhouse. Although he'd never been much of a golfer, he had a golf tournament on his calendar and his competitive streak bristled at the idea of bringing down his foursome. Besides, focusing on a sport during his lunch break helped distract him from the knot of stress at the base of his spine. He'd never guessed the amount of work that came with his new position in the TCC, duties that ate into his time running his own ranch every day. But to complicate matters immeasurably, he now had a toddler nephew to raise.

When his brother, Parker, and Parker's wife had died in a car accident three months ago, James had been devastated. But in addition to his own grief at losing a loved one he'd deeply respected, he had been struggling with the fact that Parker's will entrusted James with the care of his son, Teddy. The weight of that responsibility threatened to take his knees out from under him if he allowed himself to dwell on it too long.

"Walker?" James repeated. The stress knot in his back tightened more at the mention of his visitor's name. Setting aside the putter, he walked closer to the intercom. "As in the woman who ran off without paying her bachelor bid last week?"

How could someone publicly bid money they didn't have? Or maybe she did have the money, but she just didn't care to give the $100,000 she promised to the Pancreatic Cancer Research Foundation. Unwilling to risk the bad publicity, especially for an event he'd supervised, he'd ended up covering the debt himself. Better to keep the club out of the papers.

That didn't mean the matter was settled.

"That was *Gail* Walker." The woman at the desk out front lowered her voice. "Maybe Lydia is a relative."

"Send her in." He kicked two golf balls under the couch near the window. Lately, he didn't mind extending his hours on-site at the clubhouse since there was a child care facility in the building and it seemed the one place his nephew was content. At home, Teddy was a handful. And then some.

James strode toward his office door to greet his guest. He hoped she was carrying a big fat check. Because while James hadn't begrudged spending his personal funds on a worthy cause, he couldn't help but resent a woman who felt no obligation to uphold a social contract.

Pulling open the office door, he could see he'd startled the woman on the other side.

Tall and slim, she had light brown hair and honey-colored skin that set off wide hazel eyes. She was dressed in khakis and a neat white blouse with a long pink sweater belted at her waist. She had one hand raised as if to knock while she nibbled at her lush lower lip. Her gaze darted anxiously to his.

A wholly unexpected attraction blindsided him.

He stared at her a beat too long.

"Lydia Walker?" He offered his hand belatedly, irritated with himself for the wayward thoughts. "I'm James Harris."

"Nice to meet you." Her handshake was cool and firm. Businesslike. "Thank you for seeing me, Mr. Harris."

"Please, call me James." Standing back, he waved her into the office, leaving the door open to the clubhouse behind her. He glanced over toward the double doors leading into the child care facility, half expecting to see Teddy banging on the window. Or a child care worker running for the hills. But all was quiet. Thankfully. Returning his attention to his guest, he said, "Have a seat."

James gestured to one of the leather chairs near the windows overlooking the garden and swimming pool. The TCC president's office had been remodeled along with the rest of the historic building. Larger windows and higher ceilings now let in more light, and there were brighter colors in the decor. But the dark hardwood floors and oversize leather furnishings retained the feel of a men's club from a bygone era. Historic photographs and artifacts from the club's storied past filled the walls.

For a few hours here each week, he could pretend his life was normal again. That he wasn't a stand-in father struggling to provide a home for an eighteen-month-old boy who surely felt the absence of his parents, yet was far too young to express himself. Dragging his fractured thoughts back to the appealing woman in his office, James focused on the here and now.

"Can I get you something to drink, Ms. Walker? Coffee or tea? A water?"

"No, thank you. And please call me Lydia." She set her simple leather handbag on the floor by her feet while he lowered himself into the chair beside hers. "I won't take up much of your time. I just came to see what I could to do in regard to my sister's debt. I've been out of town, and I only just read the news this morning."

"Ah." He nodded, admiring her frank approach. "I appreciate that, Lydia, but I'm not sure how much I'm at liberty to divulge regarding your sister's...finances."

He was no expert in the law, but he felt sure that if Gail Walker hadn't specifically asked her sister to intervene on her behalf, he shouldn't discuss the woman's bad debt with her sibling.

"I'm not asking for any information." Lydia sat forward in her seat, her expression serious. "I already know that Gail couldn't possibly pay what she promised the charity on the night of the auction. I'm sure she will contact you when she returns from her trip. But until then, I wondered about a potential compromise."

So much for his hope that Lydia Walker came bearing a check.

"A compromise?" Impatience flared. He wasn't interested in a nominal payment toward the balance. "This isn't a credit card debt where you can take out a consolidation loan and suddenly pay less than you owe."

Lips compressed in a flat line, she straightened in her seat. "And I'm aware of that. But she can't produce funds she doesn't have. So I had hoped to give Gail some ideas for what she could do instead. Perhaps donate her time volunteering for the charity in some way?"

Her hazel eyes turned greener as she bristled. The color intrigued him, even as he knew he shouldn't take any pleasure from her frustration. She'd meant well.

"I see." He nodded, thinking over her offer. She didn't know that the charity had already been paid, but he wasn't sure he wanted to share his own contribution. Instead, he found himself asking, "May I ask your interest in the matter? Why not just let your sister contact us when she returns home?"

She arched an eyebrow. "Do you have any siblings, James?"

The question cut straight through him, his grief still fresh. "Not as of three months ago."

The terse sound of the words didn't begin to convey the ache behind them.

Lydia paled. "I'm so sorry. I had no idea—"

"You couldn't possibly know." Stuffing down the rawness of the loss, James stood suddenly, needing to move. He headed toward the minifridge and retrieved two small bottles of water, more for something to do than anything else. Still, he brought one back to Lydia and then cracked open his own. "My brother and his wife died in a car crash this fall. Parker lived on the other side of the state, but we were still close."

He had no living relatives now except for his nephew. His own mother had died of breast cancer when he was very young, and his father had passed after a heart attack two years ago. The Grim Reaper had been kicking him in the teeth lately, taking those he loved.

Except for Teddy. And James would move heaven

and earth to keep that little hellion happy and safe. Even if it meant giving up the boy to his maternal grandparents—an option he was investigating since his schedule didn't allow the time the boy needed.

"I can't imagine how difficult that has been." The concern in her voice, the empathy, was unmistakable. "Most of my brothers and sisters are still back home in Arkansas, but I check in with them often. Gail moved here with me to—start over. I can't help but feel somewhat responsible for her."

He wondered why. Lured by curiosity about this beautiful woman, he almost sat back down beside her to continue their conversation. But a noise outside the office—the cadence of urgent voices speaking in low tones—distracted him from replying. He glanced toward the door that opened onto the clubhouse and saw the building's administrative assistant speaking with one of the women who worked in the child care facility.

A feeling of foreboding grew. He knew it couldn't be the boy's tree nut allergy acting up or they would have notified him. But what if Teddy had overstayed his welcome in the child care facility? James hadn't been able to keep a nanny for more than two weeks with his nephew's swings from shy and withdrawn to uncontrollable bouts of temper. James had no plan B if the TCC child care couldn't take the toddler for at least part of the time. The boy's only grandparents lived five hours away—too far for babysitting help.

"Lydia, you needn't worry about the donation," he told his guest, the stress at the base of his spine ratcheting higher up his back. As compelling as he found his unexpected guest, he needed to end this meeting so he could see what was going on with the boy. "I've already taken care of the matter with the charity, and I'll speak to your sister about it when she returns to Royal."

He remained standing, hoping his response would satisfy Lydia and send her on her way. Bad enough he'd felt an immediate attraction to the woman. But he was too strapped emotionally and mentally this week to figure out a creative solution to help her sister work off a debt that James had already paid.

"Taken care of?" Lydia sounded wary. "What does that mean?"

Tension throbbed in his temples. He would have never guessed that concerns about one tiny kid could consume a person day and night. But that's exactly where he found himself right now, worrying about the boy around the clock, certain that his lack of consistent care was going to screw up the child Parker had been so proud of.

"I paid off the bid myself," James clarified while he watched the child care worker edge around the administrative assistant and bustle toward his office door.

Damn it.

"You can't go in there," the front desk secretary called after her, while James waited, tension vibrating through him.

From behind him, Lydia Walker's gasp was followed by the whispered words, "One hundred thousand dollars?"

Damn it again.

Pivoting toward Lydia, he already regretted his haste. But he needed to concentrate on whatever new crisis was developing.

"That information is confidential, and stays between the two of us. I only shared it so you won't worry about the bid anymore."

Standing, Lydia gaped at him. She shook her head, the warm streaks in her brown hair glinting in the sunlight streaming through the windows behind her. "I'll worry twice as much now. How can we ever hope to repay you?"

He didn't have time to answer before a childish cry filled the room.

His nephew, little Teddy Harris, came barreling toward him with big crocodile tears running down both cheeks, his wispy baby curls bouncing with each jarring step. The two women stepped out of the boy's way as he ran straight into James's leg. Crushing the wool gabardine in damp baby hands, the boy let out a wail that all of Royal must have heard.

With proof of his inadequacy as a stand-in parent clinging to his calf, James had never felt so powerless. Reaching down, he lifted his nephew in his arms to offer whatever comfort he could, knowing it wasn't going to be enough. The toddler thrashed in his arms, his back arching, kicking with sock-clad feet.

James had all he could do to hang on to the squirming kid let alone soothe him.

Until, miraculously, the child stilled. The two women lingering at the threshold of his office door were both smiling as they watched. James had to crane his neck to see the boy's expression since Teddy peered at something over his shoulder, tantrum forgotten.

For a split second, he wondered what on earth that could be. Until he remembered the enticing woman in the room with them.

He sensed her presence behind him in a hint of

feminine fragrance and a soft footfall on the hardwood floor. It was James's only warning, before her
voice whispered, "peekaboo!" in a way that tickled
against his left ear.

Teddy erupted in giggles.

It was, without question, the best magic trick James
had ever witnessed. And he knew immediately that
there was a way Ms. Lydia Walker could repay him.

Two

Once the child in James's arms had settled down, the Texas Cattleman's Club's handsome president set the boy on his feet while he went to speak in low tones to the two women who hovered near the entrance of his office.

Lydia did her best not to eavesdrop even though she was wildly curious about the identity of the toddler. The brief bio she'd read of James online hadn't mentioned a wife or family, and he didn't wear a wedding ring. Not that it was any of her business. But clearly, the child was his based on the way the toddler had flung chubby arms around James's leg like he was home base in a game of tag.

For that matter, they shared the same brown eyes flecked with gold, as well.

A gentle tug on the sleeve of her sweater made Lydia realize she'd gotten sidetracked during this round of "peekaboo." She glanced back to the sober little boy in front of her, his damp hand clutching the ribbed cuff of her sweater to help him keep balance. He looked sleepy and out of sorts as he wobbled on unsteady legs, but the game was still entertaining him. Obediently, she covered her face to hide again, remembering how much her youngest brother had loved playing.

"Thank you," James said to the woman from the front desk. "I'll take care of it."

Then he turned and walked back toward Lydia.

She watched him through her fingers as she hid her face from Teddy. Tall and lean, James Harris moved with the grace of an athlete even in jeans and boots. His button-down shirt looked custom fitted, the only giveaway to his position at the club. Without the Stetson he'd been wearing in the photo she'd seen of him online, she could now appreciate the golden color of his eyes. His dark hair was close cropped, the kind of cut that meant regular trips to the barber. Everything about him was neat. Well-groomed. Incredibly good-looking.

The sight of him was enough to make her throat dry right up in feminine appreciation. She might have forgotten all about the peekaboo game if Teddy hadn't patted her knee. Belatedly, she slid her hands from her face and surprised the toddler again.

The boy giggled softly before resting his head on her knee, as though he was too tired to hold himself upright any longer. Poor little guy. She rubbed his back absently while the baby fidgeted with his feet.

"I think he'll be down for the count in another minute," she told James quietly. "He's an adorable child."

"He's normally a handful," James admitted, taking the seat across from her. "You're very good with him."

His charming smile made her breath hitch in her chest. James Harris's photo online hadn't fully prepared her for how devastatingly sexy he'd be in person, an attraction she had no business feeling for a man who had a family of his own. A man who'd bailed her sister out of a thorny financial mess that could have very well derailed both their careers. How could Lydia ever thank him?

"As the oldest of eight kids, I had a lot of firsthand experience," she admitted, accustomed to glossing over the hurtful aspects of feeling more like hired help than her mother's daughter. "I've worked as a nanny ever since and I hope to open my own child care business out of my home this year." It couldn't hurt to start spreading the word to people in the community with young families. "Do you have any other children?"

The question sounded benign enough, right? Not like she was fishing to find out more about whether or not this handsome man was married with a house full of adorable offspring waiting to greet him at the end of the day.

"No." A shadowed expression crossed his face. "Teddy is my brother's son. And up until Teddy's parents died three months ago, I was a bachelor spending every waking hour running a ranch or performing my duties here. My life has been turned upside down."

She couldn't deny the momentary relief that James was single. But just as quickly, she thought of the sadness and weariness in his voice and what that meant for Teddy. Her heart ached for all the little boy had lost. She stared down at him, his soft cheek still resting on her knee while he shifted his weight from one foot to the other, his light-up sneakers flashing back and forth at odd intervals while he rocked.

"I'm so sorry." She smoothed a palm across the back of the boy's gray dinosaur T-shirt. "For you both. I can't imagine how difficult that transition has been to deal with, especially when you're grieving such a tragic loss."

She glanced back at James to find him studying her.

His fixed attention rattled her, reminding her that he'd just admitted to being a single man. Warmth rose to her cheeks and she looked away, trying to remember the thread of the conversation.

"You could help us immeasurably." James's voice was pitched low in deference to the weary baby between them, but the tone made her think of pillow talk. Intimate conversations between two lovers who knew one another incredibly well.

Who would have guessed a whisper could be so seductive?

"I'm—um." She tried to think beyond murmured confidences and came up blank, her brain already supplying images of tangled sheets and limbs. "And how would that be?"

"You arrived at my door looking for a compromise on your sister's bid, and we've just found the perfect one." He pointed to Teddy, who had stopped moving, his eyes closed. Breathing even. "If you'll take the job of Teddy's nanny, you can consider Gail's debt paid in full."

His suggestion staggered her. Called her from her sensual daydreams.

"She bid *one hundred thousand dollars*," Lydia reminded him, wondering where she should lay Teddy down for a nap. "You'd be forgiving the cost of a home for the sake of child care. That's far too generous of you."

He shook his head, his jaw flexing. "I haven't kept a nanny for more than two weeks because he's such a handful, between the tantrums and days of being withdrawn. We could have a trial period to see how it worked out." He seemed to warm to the idea quickly, laying out terms. "If you stayed for a trial period of two months, then I'd forgive half the debt. Stick around for a year, and we'll call it even."

"You can't be serious." She got distracted around him after a few minutes. How could she ever work in his home for a year?

"I'm running out of options and I can't afford this much time away from my ranching business. You have no idea what it would be worth to me to know my brother's boy is in good hands."

She couldn't miss the desperation in his eyes. In his voice. But as much as she felt called to help him, it wasn't her debt to pay. Gail was the one who should be providing free nanny services, not her. Still, another thought trickled through, making her realize things weren't quite so simple. No matter how strongly she felt that Gail needed to clean up her own messes, Lydia recognized that without James's clearing the debt with the charity, the Walker name might have become the kiss of death for a new business in a close-knit community like Royal. While she wrestled with what to do, she turned her attention to the sleeping baby between them.

"First things first, we should find a comfortable

place for Teddy." She reached to lift him, but James moved closer.

"I can get him." He slipped his hands around the boy's waist to pick him up, his hand briefly brushing against her calf and causing a whole riot of sensations in her before he shifted the child to rest on his shoulder. "And you don't need to make a decision about my offer right now. If you're okay with continuing our meeting another time, I should be leaving for the day anyhow. I think he'll stay asleep if I put him in his car seat."

Lydia tried to ignore the residual tingling in her skin. She appreciated the opportunity he was giving her to think about his proposal. And distance from his striking good looks would give her the chance to think with a clearer head.

"You have someone to watch him today?" Lydia didn't mean to sound like she was questioning his arrangements for the child. She was just trying to keep the focus on Teddy and not the heady jolt of attraction she was feeling.

She stood to follow James toward the door.

"My foreman's daughter is home from college for the holidays, and she agreed to give me afternoon help two days a week for the next month. That's as much child care as I've got covered when I'm not here. Provided she doesn't give up on Teddy, too, when he has his next atomic meltdown." He sounded frustrated and she understood why.

James shouldered the leather diaper bag that the child care worker had set near the door to his office, then lifted his Stetson from the coat rack and dropped it into place. When she stepped out of the room, he locked the door behind them. She couldn't miss the way his large hands cradled the child so gently against his broad chest. The gesture called to her, reminding her of dreams she had for her own children one day.

Not that she was thinking of James in that way. She must be overtired and stressed to let her imagination wander like that. The sooner she made tracks out of here and away from James's tempting presence, the better.

As they left the clubhouse and strode out into the December sunlight, James tugged a blanket from an exterior pocket of the diaper bag and laid it over the sleeping boy. The day was mild, but with the holidays approaching, the temperatures had been dropping. Lydia tipped her face into the breeze, grateful for the cooler air on her too-warm skin.

"I researched the child care facilities in town when I got the idea to open a full-service business here, and I know there's a definite need." Royal was thriving, and the demographics for young families were a particular area of growth. "I've heard there are waiting lists at the most coveted places."

James nodded in response. "You've got that right. When I called one day care they said families reserve space when they're pregnant, even knowing they might not put a child into the system for a full year." He sighed wearily. "The last few months have been an education—from learning how to change a diaper to educating myself on how to avoid tree nuts for his allergy."

"He has allergies?" Lydia was accustomed to the dietary needs for children with the most common allergies. Her brother broke out in hives if he even got in the same room as a peanut.

"Just tree nuts. But I live in fear I'll leave the house

without the EpiPen." He huffed out a long breath, clearly feeling the same stress that many new parents went through. "I hope you'll consider my offer, Lydia. Maybe you can work for me, and your sister can do something to repay you."

"I'd need to figure out a way to pay my bills in the meantime." It was true she was between nanny jobs right now, but she had hoped to devote the extra time toward working on her house, doing some of the simpler labor she didn't want to pay a contractor for.

James tucked the blanket more securely around the baby's feet, a gesture that touched her all the more now that she knew he wasn't the baby's father. He was simply a man trying to do his best taking care of a child he hadn't been ready for.

"And I can't put a price on what it would mean to me to have qualified help with Teddy." He nodded at a gray-haired cowboy walking into the club. Then, once the man had passed, James turned to Lydia again. "Forget about Gail and the charity money. The universe is smiling on me by having a nanny walk into my office at a time in my life when I'm hanging on by my fingernails. Consider this a job offer for whatever you usually charge. I would have sought you out before this if I'd known about you."

"I couldn't possibly—"

"Please." He cut her off, his tone laced with an urgency—a need—she hadn't anticipated. "Just think about it. Start with the trial period and sign on for two months. See how it goes. If things don't work out, I'll understand."

Swallowing her protests, she nodded. "It's a very generous offer and I will consider it."

He seemed to relax then, a tension sliding away from him as he exhaled. "Thank you. I'll be working from the main house at the Double H tomorrow. If you'd like to stop by, I can show you around. You could see what the job would entail and take a look at the nanny's quarters before you decide."

"The Double H is your ranch?" She knew the property. It was close to the Clayton family ranch, the Silver C. The portions of the Double H she could see from the main road were all beautifully manicured. The stables and ranch house were both painted crisp white with dark gray trim, and the window boxes were refreshed year-round with red flowers.

"It is." His smile was warm. "I never knew how easy ranch work was until I tried my hand at child care. I'm very ready to return to my cattle full-time."

The idea troubled her, given that his responsibility to his nephew wasn't going to end when he filled the nanny position. But she couldn't afford to feel any more empathy for this man than she already did. She had some tough decisions ahead of her where he was concerned.

"I'll stop by tomorrow. Does after lunch work for you?"

"That's perfect." He laid a protective hand on Teddy's back. "You can repeat the trick you did today of getting him to fall asleep for his nap."

She'd been given similar compliments many times from happy clients. She was good with children. Period. And yet, somehow the thought of putting the child to sleep with James Harris looking on filled her with a whole host of fluttery sensations.

"I'll see you then." Nodding, she backed away fast,

needing refuge from the strong pull of desire. Retreating to her car, she forced her gaze away from James and shut the door behind her.

She locked the door for good measure. And then felt like an idiot if he'd heard her flick the locks. She wasn't trying to keep anyone out as much as she was trying to keep herself in check around the too-handsome rancher with golden-brown eyes.

Switching on the ignition, she pulled out of the parking lot fast, hating herself for thinking that if it wasn't for James's blatant sex appeal, she probably already would have accepted the job he'd offered.

That wasn't fair to him. And it definitely wasn't fair to the innocent boy who'd just lost both his parents.

She could help Teddy and James. And no matter what she told herself about not getting involved in her sister's mayhem, Lydia felt a responsibility to repay James in whatever way she could. By covering Gail's debt, he'd ensured both Walker women would be able to run their small businesses in Royal without censure from locals knowing that Gail had cheated the Pancreatic Cancer Research Foundation.

Lydia would just have to find a way to do the job while avoiding the hot rancher as much as possible.

Shouldering the pole pruner he'd been using to trim an apple tree, James squinted in the afternoon sunlight to check his watch at half-past noon.

Based on the number of times he'd glanced at the vintage Omega Seamaster timepiece that had belonged to his grandfather, James couldn't deny that he looked forward to a visit from Lydia Walker today. And as much as he wanted to credit his anticipation to the possibility he'd found a solution to his nanny problem, he knew that accounted for only part of it.

He wanted to see her again.

Taking his time to wipe down the blade on the pruner—an important step to prevent spreading disease—James needed to be sure Lydia agreed to his bargain. And frankly, that need was at odds with how fiercely he was attracted to her. She'd invaded his thoughts constantly since their last meeting. During the daytime, he shut down the visions as fast as possible. But during the night? His dreams about her had been wildly inappropriate and hot as hell.

Securing a nanny was his number one goal right now, and had been for the past three months. He couldn't afford to let an undeniable hunger for her confuse the issue that should be a simple business arrangement. Her sister's overbid aside, James needed Lydia. He'd spent time the night before researching her credentials and had been thoroughly impressed. Not only had she served as a nanny for two TCC members who spoke highly of her—he'd messaged them both to check—but Lydia also had an intriguing connection to the popular childrearing blog *House Rules*.

The blog was written by her mother, Fiona, but had often featured Lydia even as a teenager. There was a whole video library of Lydia, showing her mother's followers how to do everything from making organic baby food to refreshing vintage nursery furniture to meeting modern health codes. Simply put, she was incredibly qualified. But the most convincing fact for him was that he'd seen how quickly she could turn Teddy's stormy tantrums into full-fledged smiles.

That alone made her services necessary. And he'd

be damned if he allowed his unbidden desire for the woman to get in the way. Besides, if his divorce had taught him anything, it was that chemistry between people could fade fast, and made shaky ground for any relationship.

Heading toward the potting shed to stow the garden tools, James heard the crunch of car tires on gravel. Turning, he recognized Lydia's vehicle from the day before. He made quick work of putting away the tools and washed his hands at the shed's utility sink before stepping outside again.

He had almost reached her car when she stepped from it. Her long legs were clad in tall boots and dark leggings. A gray sweater dress and long herringbone-patterned coat were simple, efficient pieces. Definitely nothing overtly sexy. And yet, he found his gaze wandering over the way the sweater dress hugged her curves. But it was her smile that drew him more than anything. From her light brown hair streaked with honey to the sun-warmed shade of her skin, she seemed to glow from within. Today, like yesterday, she wore little makeup that he could see. A long golden necklace glinted as she straightened, the charms jingling gently as they settled.

"Welcome to the Double H," he greeted her, arms spread wide. "Home of the Harris family since nineteen fifty-three."

He and his brother had been born here and he took immense pride in the place, the same as his father had before his death. His brother had planned to move back to Royal one day and help expand the ranching operation. A plan that would never happen now. Strange how many ways grief could find to stab him when he least expected it.

Still, James continued to think about expanding on his own, to give Teddy the future that his father had dreamed for him.

"Thank you." She let him close the car door behind her while she spun in a slow circle to view the closest buildings. "I've always thought this was a pretty property when I've driven past here."

He couldn't help the rueful grin. "I don't know how thrilled my grandfather would be to hear that I've turned the place 'pretty.' But I've toyed with the idea of expanding the horse sales side of the business after we've had some success with recent yearlings. And traditionally, horse farms have more curb appeal since potential clients often come through the barns."

"You've done a great job." Lydia walked toward the small grove where he'd been working. "Are these fruit trees?"

He nodded, pleased she'd noticed. "I've got a dozen apple trees, a few peaches and pears. Just enough to make the ranch hands grumble about the extra work at harvest time." Although no one complained about taking fresh fruit home at the end of the day. "I was pruning these before you arrived."

"I hope I didn't catch you at a bad time." She stopped her trek through the grove and peered back at him. "I know I'm a little early, but I wasn't sure how long the drive would take."

"I had just quit when you pulled in. Your timing is perfect." He waved her toward a side entrance to the main house. "Come on in. Can I get you something to drink?"

"No. Thank you." She waited while he opened the door, then stepped inside the mudroom. "Where's Teddy? I brought him a gift." She tugged at the sleeve of her coat and he moved behind her to help.

Her hair brushed the backs of his knuckles, the silk lining of her coat warm from her body. He tried to move quickly—to keep himself from lingering too long—but he wasn't fast enough to avoid a hint of her fragrance. Something vanilla with a trace of floral.

With effort, he turned away from her to hang the coat on one of the metal hooks from the rack.

"That's very kind of you. My housekeeper took Teddy for a couple of hours while he naps so I could get the trees sprayed and pruned. I've been falling behind on every conceivable chore." He led her deeper into the house, pausing outside the kitchen. "Besides, I wanted to give my sales pitch for the nanny gig without any distraction."

Shaking her head, she gave him a half smile. "But *he* is the job, James. Your best selling point."

Skeptical, he figured he'd hedge his bets on showing off the house first. "Your three predecessors didn't seem quite as charmed by their charge."

Lydia crossed her arms as she studied him. "They don't sound worthy of the task, then."

Her defensiveness on Teddy's behalf was a credit to her character, yes. But she'd been with the boy for only a few minutes. She hadn't seen the long crying jags or the stormy rages that had caught the other nannies off guard.

"That makes me all the more eager to sign you on," he told her honestly.

After taking her on a tour of the kitchen and great

room, he took the main staircase up to the nursery where his housekeeper, Mrs. Davis, all but bolted from the room when she spotted them. Her greeting was brusque at best.

"Thank you, Mrs. Davis." James knew the housekeeper wasn't happy with the added babysitting responsibilities, but he'd shown his gratitude in her paycheck over the last two weeks. "This is Lydia Walker. She's here to discuss the possibility of taking over child care duties full-time."

"In that case, I won't keep you." She gave an abrupt nod and hurried on her way, her white tennis shoes squeaking on the hardwood in the hall as she stalked off.

"The household staff is overburdened," he explained, hoping Lydia wouldn't be put off by the woman's cool reception. "Mrs. Davis has helped me out more than once, and I've also got temporary help from my foreman's daughter. But the extra work is taking a toll."

"Understandable," Lydia murmured softly while she peered down into the crib at the sleeping baby. "Caring for a child is a huge life adjustment. Expectant parents have nine months to prepare themselves, and most of them are still overwhelmed by the transition." She smiled up at him. "You're doing well."

No doubt she intended the words to be reassuring, but the effect on him was anything but.

"You can't possibly know that," he told her flatly, refusing to accept a comfort he didn't deserve. "I can't help but think that my brother would have been far more involved with his son's upbringing than I can afford to be right now. I've reached out to Teddy's

maternal grandparents to try to involve them more."
He'd written to them twice, in fact, and hadn't heard
back. "Maybe their home will be a better place for
my nephew."

Lydia chewed her lush lower lip, looking thoughtful. The gesture distracted him from the dark cloud
of his own failed responsibilities, making him wish
his relationship with this woman could be a whole lot
less complicated.

"You're thinking about asking his grandparents to
raise him?" She stepped away from the crib, her boots
soundless on the thick carpeting as she moved.

His gaze tracked her movements, lingering on the
way her sweater dress hugged her curves. But then,
thinking about Lydia was a whole lot more enticing
than remembering all the ways he'd fallen short in his
sudden parental role.

He'd had the nursery assembled in a hurry. The
room contained all the necessary furniture but hadn't
been decorated with much that would appeal to a child.

"Definitely. I can't even keep a nanny for him, let
alone be a meaningful part of his life right now." He
wasn't sure any of this was helping his cause to convince her to take the job. But something about Lydia
made it easy for him to talk to her.

A sensation he rarely experienced with anyone.

"But that doesn't mean you'll always be too busy for
him." Her hazel eyes took on a bluish cast in the baby's room with azure-colored walls. "And your brother
and his wife must have trusted you a great deal if they
named you as his guardian."

Frustration and guilt fired through him.

"I'm sure they never believed it would come to that."

He couldn't bear the weight of failing Teddy. Failing his brother. Unwilling to argue the point, James gestured toward the door. "Come this way and I'll show you the nanny's quarters. Because no matter what happens with Teddy's future, I can't escape the fact that I need a solution for his care right now."

And that meant not letting his guard down around this beautiful, desirable woman.

Three

"I can't accept these terms." Back in the ranch's great room, Lydia stared down at the neatly typed offer James had passed her inside a crisp manila folder.

After a tour of the Double H Ranch main house, with special attention to the nursery, nanny's quarters and a potential playroom she could equip as she saw fit, James had briefly outlined very generous compensation for retaining her services. Not only was room and board included—useful for her while her contractor outfitted her home for a child care facility—but James also offered a salary, health care benefits and a recommendation if she stayed in his employ for six months. Gail's debt would be partially forgiven after the two-month trial period, and fully after one whole year.

Furthermore, there were additional pages that spelled out potential budgets for renovating the playroom and nursery, as well as a spending allowance for toys, books, equipment, outings and anything else that she thought Teddy required.

"What do you mean?" James frowned, stepping closer to glance over her shoulder at the formalized offer he'd given her. "Are there things I'm overlooking? It's all up for negotiation."

Closing the folder, she passed it back to him as they stood in front of the huge stone hearth where a fire crackled. "You haven't overlooked a thing. This is far too generous."

She'd never heard of such a well-paid nanny. And it made her heart hurt to think he was so eager to give over the boy's care that he would pay someone such an inflated fee. Especially when he was debating relinquishing the child to Teddy's maternal grandparents.

"Honoring my brother's wishes means everything to me." His jaw flexed as raw emotion flashed in his eyes, but he folded his arms, as if defying her to argue that statement.

"I understand that." Truly, she did. "But the whole reason I came to see you yesterday was to discuss options for repaying your generosity toward my sister. I can't let you give us anything else."

He was shaking his head before she even finished speaking. "You can't sacrifice your own income for the sake of your sibling. I won't hear of it." Before she could argue, he continued, "I read about you online, Lydia. You're extremely qualified."

His words pleased her. Or maybe it was the knowledge that he'd spent time thinking of her, if only in a professional capacity. Warmth crawled over her that didn't have a thing to do with the fire.

"Thank you. I already have a health care plan, so I don't need that. But if you cut the salary in half, I would be amenable."

"Half?" He shook his head. "I couldn't look myself in the mirror if you took a nickel under three-quarters of that."

"Half," she insisted. "And I'll find a way to put my sister to work for me so she's making up the difference."

Gail needed to learn that there were consequences to her impulsive actions.

He scrubbed a hand through his close-cropped dark hair. "I don't know."

She suspected he would have continued to argue the figure if a wail from the nursery hadn't sounded at that precise moment. James's gaze went to the staircase.

"I could start immediately," she offered, sensing his weakening on the salary issue.

He extended his hand. "You've got yourself a deal."

Lydia slipped her small palm into his much larger one, seized with the memory of their brief contact the day before when he'd taken Teddy from her arms. Just like then, an electric current seemed to jump between them, hot to the point of melting. Her gaze met his, and she would swear he was aware of it, too.

She was grateful for the baby's next cry, since it gave her the perfect excuse to retract her fingers. She darted from the room to escape the temptation of her new boss—and the fear that she'd just made a huge mistake.

After a brief supper shared with her new charge in the nursery, Lydia debated the wisdom of starting her new job so quickly.

She'd jumped into the baby's routine with both feet, comfortable with knowing where most things were located since her new employer had given her a quick tour. She knew the protocol for Teddy's food allergies and where the EpiPens were kept. But she hadn't clarified how or when she would go about moving her things into her suite at the Double H, thinking she'd see her new boss at dinnertime.

But James still hadn't come in from his chores at eight o'clock after she put Teddy into his crib for the night. Lydia knew because she'd peered down the stairs a few times, and twice had checked in with the housekeeper.

On both occasions, Mrs. Davis had looked at her as though she might steal the house silver at any moment. And between the woman's terse answers and general lack of hospitality, Lydia had the distinct impression that her presence was not welcomed by the older housekeeper.

Not that she was too worried. Usually, her work spoke for itself. Maybe Mrs. Davis was simply tired from the strain of caring for a little one. Lydia was more concerned to think that James might not be accessible in the coming weeks. As Teddy's parental figure, James had an important role in the boy's life even if he hadn't fully committed himself to it yet.

Then again, maybe James's disappearing act had nothing to do with his nephew and everything to do with the blossoming attraction between them.

Figuring she'd never improve things around here if she stayed hidden in her room, Lydia stepped out of the sprawling nanny suite and hurried down the hall to the staircase. The natural wood banister was polished to a high sheen, and the house's log cabin elements mingled seamlessly with more contemporary touches, like the walls painted in shades of taupe and tan. Downstairs, the stone hearth rose to a high ceiling right through the upstairs gallery walkway. A rough wood mantel and steer horns decorated the fireplace, but the leather couches and cream-colored slipper chairs were sleekly styled and inviting. Agriculture books filled the shelves in the far corner of the room, the leather spines freshly dusted.

She peered around for any signs of Mrs. Davis but didn't see the housekeeper. Before Lydia could debate her next move, the side door opened and James stepped inside.

She stood far enough away that he didn't notice her at first. He took his time hanging his Stetson and shrugging out of a weatherproof duster. Belatedly, she felt a hint of cool air that must have entered the house with him. The temperature had dropped, and she knew a storm was predicted tonight. In the shadows of the mudroom, his features looked all the more sculpted. He had high cheekbones. A strong jaw. Well-muscled shoulders that would turn any woman's head.

And yes, she acknowledged, she liked looking at him.

"Do you always work so late?" she asked as a way to reveal her presence, feeling suddenly self-conscious.

He glanced up quickly, his expression more pleased than surprised.

"Hello, Lydia. I didn't expect to see you so late."

She glanced at the antique clock on the opposite wall. "It's not even nine."

"Right. And when I've been on duty with my

nephew, I'm ready for bed before he is." He toed off his boots and lined them up on the far side of the welcome mat.

There was something oddly intimate about seeing him take off his shoes. Being in his home at this hour.

Which was a silly thing to think given that she'd been a nanny before. She'd seen parents moving around their living space while she helped out with children. Maybe it felt different with James because he was single.

And…smoking hot. Her gaze tracked him as he strode into the kitchen in sock feet. In a long-sleeved gray tee and dark jeans, he looked less like the polished Texas Cattleman's Club president and more like a ruggedly handsome rancher. He scrubbed his hands at the kitchen sink.

"Teddy went to bed fairly well for me." So far, she couldn't see any evidence of the toddler being more difficult than most children his age. "Beginner's luck, maybe."

"Or maybe you're just that good." He grinned at her while he dried off, her thoughts scrambling at the mild flirtation in the words. "Would you like to join me for dinner? I'm starving, but I'd appreciate hearing more about your day."

He moved toward the stainless steel refrigerator and tugged it open.

"No, thank you. Teddy and I ate dinner earlier." She couldn't risk spending too much time in her employer's presence based on her over-the-top physical reaction to just a handshake, for crying out loud. If she was going to reach at least the two-month mark on this trial period, she really shouldn't have late meals alone with him. "I just thought maybe now would be a good time for me to return to my house and pick up a few items to get me through the next week."

"I forgot you didn't move your things in today." He backed out of the refrigerator with a sandwich on a crusty French roll and proceeded to remove the clear plastic wrap. "There's a storm brewing that could turn nasty if the temperature drops any more."

"I'll be careful." She stepped closer to the kitchen but didn't enter it, remaining outside the granite-topped breakfast bar as she watched him retrieve a plate and glass. "I can be back in two hours."

He parted the curtain on the window over the kitchen sink, peering out into the night. "The roads are going to be dangerous if we get ice."

"As the oldest of eight in my family, I have to say it's a unique experience to have someone worry about my safety for a change." She couldn't help a rueful smile, since she was usually the one doing the worrying.

"What about your mom?" he asked, letting go of the sheer curtain to fill a water glass. "She didn't ever tell you not to go out into an ice storm?"

Even with the barrier of the counter between them, she felt the draw of his curiosity about her. She'd never experienced the pinprick of awareness all over her skin with anyone else and wondered why, of all the people Gail could have indebted herself to, it had to be a man whom Lydia found so potently sexy.

"My mother doesn't take much notice of potential dangers in the environment." To put it mildly. Lydia had saved her youngest sister from drowning in a neighbor's backyard pool while her mom led a work-shop on fostering a love of Mother Earth in children.

She'd been totally oblivious. "Fiona Walker truly believes that if you see hearts and flowers wherever you go, then the world must be a happy, safe place."

James's eyebrows lifted as he slid his sandwich into the microwave. "Sounds like you got to see a different side of the *House Rules* parenting approach."

She wasn't surprised he knew about the blog. Her mother's PR machine regularly spit out stats about how many lives the parenting website actively changed for the better—which was their highly embroidered way of reporting social media reach.

Choosing her words carefully, she replied, "Let's just say that I hope you didn't hire me because you thought I'd be giving Teddy lessons in the power of positive thinking."

"Honestly, I was just happy to read that you have CPR certification along with good references and a clean driving record." He withdrew his meal from the microwave. "But how about you let me drive you to pick up your things and we'll talk about your first day on the way?"

"What about Teddy?"

"Mrs. Davis will hear him if he cries." He picked up a key ring from a dish on the granite countertop. "Besides, we'll be back before he wakes."

She needed to speak to him about that. It didn't make her comfortable to leave her young charge in the care of a woman who seemed to resent having to watch over him. But chances were good—even if she insisted on driving herself—that James would let his housekeeper tend the child if Teddy woke anyhow.

Somehow, she had to help James feel more comfortable in a father role. And no matter that the close proximity of a car ride with her strikingly handsome boss might prove tempting, Lydia knew the sooner she discussed those issues with him, the better.

"Okay. Let me just get the nursery monitor set up for her." She had the baby monitor feed on her phone, but she knew the model in the nursery came with a physical receiver.

James nodded as he pulled out his phone. "Take your time. I'll finish up my meal while you do that." He scrolled through his screens. "Mrs. Davis's room is the first one on the left just downstairs. You can leave the monitor outside her door and I'll text her the plan. She doesn't go to sleep until after the late news anyhow."

Lydia walked upstairs to the nursery, hurrying in spite of James's assurance they could take their time. Teddy Harris had been through enough these last few months. The quicker they went, the sooner Lydia would be back here, minimizing the chance that the child would wake up to Mrs. Davis.

After retrieving the receiver, she paused near the baby's crib, gazing at his little face in the glow of a night-light. So angelic. His rosebud mouth slightly open, his fingers clutching a soft rattle in the shape of a blue puppy dog.

Tenderness filled her as she closed the door quietly behind her. Somehow, some way, she would get through at least the next two months. Not just for the way it would help Gail.

She knew she could make a difference in the baby's life. And, she hoped, in his uncle's, too.

Windshield wipers working double time, James focused on the road ahead as he navigated his pickup truck down the quiet county road that led to Lydia's place. He'd eaten enough dinner to take the edge off one hunger, but having his nephew's new nanny beside him stirred another.

He tried his damnedest not to think about that. But with her light vanilla fragrance teasing his nose when she leaned closer to switch the radio station away from some political news, he couldn't resist the urge to drag in a deep breath.

"There." She leaned back in the passenger seat once a steel guitar sounded through the surround-sound speakers. "I hope that's okay. I hate to shirk my civic duty, but some days I can't cope with even one more story about politics."

"Rainy nights and steel guitars go hand in hand." He glanced over at her profile in the reflected light of the dashboard. "But then, you're talking to a man with a lot of Texas in his blood."

"Is that right?"

He heard the smile in her voice, even with his eyes back on the road and the glare of another vehicle's bright lights.

"Yes, ma'am. My granddaddy was born on Galveston Island, but he moved here after the Korean War when an army buddy of his died and left him the care of his family farm."

"Your grandfather inherited the Double H?" She shifted her legs toward him, her knees not all that far from his.

For a moment, he cursed the size of his truck. If they'd taken her car, her leg would be brushing up against him right now. But then, he recalled that he was not supposed to be imagining his legs entwined with hers. He had no business thinking about an employee that way.

"The land wasn't really a ranch at that time. Just some farm acreage. His friend's widow was struggling to raise three kids and get the crops in, so Henry Harris Sr. moved into a trailer on the land and got to work." He'd heard the story from his father often enough, since his granddad had passed away when James was still a child.

"My house is up here on the left." She pointed to a turn ahead. "I'm sure your grandfather would be proud of how you're maintaining the property. It's a showplace."

Her words pleased him. He'd worked tirelessly for the last ten years to modernize.

"Thank you." He slowed the vehicle as he guided it into the horseshoe driveway in front of a single-story residence. Concrete-block built, the white house had what appeared to be building materials neatly stacked under tarps in the front yard. "Looks like you've got some improvements planned yourself."

"Not as quickly as I would like, but yes." She pointed toward a portico structure on the far side of the building. "If you want to park under there, we can get inside without getting too drenched."

Moments later, he followed her inside, the rain battering hard on the portico roof as she jiggled her key in a stubborn lock. He noticed the overhang leaked in a few places, with rivulets of water streaming through the gaps.

Inside, she flipped on a light to reveal a home in transit. Plastic sheeting hung on one end of a functional kitchen, an attempt to keep dust at a minimum, he guessed. But the workable section of living space that he could see showed tidy counters and cabinets, a big worktable covered with flooring samples and countertop tiles.

Beyond that, there were small touches of the woman who lived here. A bright braided rug. Heart-shaped magnets on the refrigerator that pinned a child's crayon art in places of honor. A small wall shelf contained a collection of glass and ceramic birds.

"I'll just be a minute." She headed toward an overlapping section of the plastic sheeting that divided the living space. "I need to grab some clothes."

"Can I carry anything for you?" He studied her in the light of a wrought iron chandelier over the kitchen table. "There's plenty of room in the extended cab if you want to bring any furniture or personal items to make you feel more at home."

"I don't need much—" She hesitated. "Actually, I have a few toys that Teddy might like if you want to come with me."

She held the plastic sheeting open for him and he ducked through, passing close to her. Brushing her shoulder with his accidentally. Was it his imagination, or did she suck in a breath at the contact?

He stopped too close to her in the small space, but a temporary wall had been constructed of plywood, making the hallway narrow here.

"Sorry about the mess," she said, quickly stepping ahead of him. "I've been living in a construction zone. I hardly notice it anymore when it's just me here."

His gaze roved—without his permission—to the sultry curve of her hips in her khaki slacks as she strode ahead of him. She paused to flip a light switch on one wall, and then she turned into what looked like a storage area.

"I'm glad to help," he told her honestly, not wanting to admit how much he liked spending time with her. How content he would be to linger with her here.

"Do you want to pull down those two suitcases?" she asked, pivoting in her tennis shoes to face him.

He hoped he'd lifted his gaze to eye level fast enough.

Damn. What the hell was he thinking to ogle her?

"Sure thing." He skirted around a couple of box fans to the shelves that held the luggage, and pulled down the items she'd indicated.

While he did that, she dug in a big box filled with plastic scooters, ride-on toys and trucks. He resisted the view of her tempting feminine form, concentrating on opening the first suitcase like his life depended on it.

He steeled himself for the inevitable draw of her proximity when he brought the bag over to her. In short order, she tossed in a farm set with clear plastic bags full of toy animals, fencing and tractors. She added a few other items he didn't recognize—baby gear of some sort.

"You know you can buy whatever you think he needs—"

"Babies outgrow things so quickly. It makes more sense to share." Their eyes met over the suitcase he held.

He studied her, forgetting what they'd been talking about as sparks singed between them. For a moment, they breathed in one another's air. And from the protracted pause, he knew she was as distracted by the sizzling connection as he was.

If she was any other woman, he would have set aside the suitcase and pulled her into his arms. Tested her lips to see if they were as petal soft as they looked. Wrapped his arms around her curves to see if she fit against him as perfectly as he imagined she would.

He could practically hear his own heartbeat. It rushed in time with her fast breathing in the otherwise silent room.

What he wouldn't give for just one taste…

"I'd better get my clothes," she said suddenly, pulling him out of his thoughts just in time for him to see her rush out the door and disappear down the hall.

Cursing himself up one side and down the other, James zipped the suitcase and carried it back out to the safety of the empty kitchen.

As he waited for Lydia to finish, he ground his teeth together and reminded himself that the luggage wasn't the only thing that needed to stay zipped.

Four

As the holidays neared, Lydia put all her focus on setting up happy daily routines for Teddy Harris.

She was good at her job, after all, and she needed to have something in her life that was working in her favor when she felt like she was tempted by her boss every time she turned around. Not that either of them had acknowledged the almost-kiss that happened nearly two weeks ago on the night he'd driven her to her home.

He seemed as wary as she was to cross that line since she worked for him. Because James had a high standard of ethics? Or was he simply unwilling to jeopardize his child care arrangement? Maybe a little of both. Either way, they'd been staying out of one another's way, never spending much time in each other's presence.

Now, decorating the playroom for Christmas, Lydia

hummed a carol while the toddler raced in circles, tugging a Santa sleigh pull toy behind him. She liked reading to him before he fell asleep, but some nights he was simply too wound up to sit still. He liked running, jumping and climbing stairs, although she was always careful to follow him up each step, in case he fell. But he was agile and coordinated, just very energetic.

She angled back to look at the snowflake cling-on stickers she'd pressed to the playroom windows.

A quick knock sounded on the door before it opened.

She turned in time to see James lean into the room. It wasn't fair how quickly her belly filled with butterflies when she was around him.

"May I come in?" he asked, still dressed in his work clothes, jeans and a tee with the Double H logo.

He must have left his boots and hat in the mudroom, but she guessed he'd been working on one of the fences in a northern pasture. She'd seen him repairing it earlier in the week, too, when she'd taken Teddy out for a stroller ride along one of the better dirt roads on the ranch. She'd hoped James would take some time away from the chore to visit with his nephew, but he'd barely given them a wave before returning to the task.

She'd noticed that he kept long hours, and sometimes he didn't return to the house until well past nightfall. Could he possibly be as wary of time alone with her as she was of the forbidden temptation of his presence? Or could that just be her imagination? The man might truly be just a workaholic.

"Please do. I'm sure Teddy misses you. I've been hoping you could spend some more time with him." Lydia waved James in as she climbed down the step stool. "I only had the door closed so he didn't run out of the room."

She'd placed baby safety covers in the interior door knobs in the nursery and playroom to ensure the boy didn't wander out without her knowing.

"I won't stay long," James assured her, his dark eyes lingering on her. "It must be nearing the little guy's bedtime, right?"

A shiver of awareness snaked up her spine, and she thought about how she looked with her hair falling out of its ponytail and juice stains on her shirt. She almost reached to smooth her hair, then stopped herself for making the telling motion. Instead, she pulled her gaze away from her boss's enticing stare, focusing on Teddy.

"I'm not sure there's any sense putting him in his crib just yet. Look at him." Now that she had a rhythm to the days with the little boy, she knew it was time to get James more involved with him.

To help him feel more comfortable in his new role as the boy's father figure. There was more to being a good nanny than feeding and caring for a child. Part of the job was enabling a thriving family. And so far, she hadn't seen much emotional commitment from James, let alone one-on-one time with the boy.

"He looks like he's ready to run a marathon," James observed, patting the child's fluffy dark curls as Teddy rushed past him on wobbly legs.

"Exactly." Lydia noticed Teddy had dropped the pull string to the sleigh, though, his pattern of circling more erratic now. "And I've noticed when I force the bedtime issue, he only protests loudly, whereas if I wait an extra half hour, he usually settles down faster on his own."

"Mrs. Davis says you're doing an excellent job." James stepped deeper into the room, glancing toward the bag full of holiday decorations.

Her pulse skittered faster as he approached her.

"Really?" Lydia frowned. "I find that a little hard to imagine after all the times your housekeeper has glowered at me in the past two weeks."

"I'm sorry if she's made you uncomfortable. I will speak to her," he offered, taking a seat on the cushioned bench in front of a rocking chair.

"No. I didn't mean to suggest—" She definitely didn't want to stir up trouble in the household. "She hasn't done anything to make me uncomfortable. And I'm glad to know she thinks I'm doing a good job."

Regretting the unguarded comment, she busied herself by reaching into her shopping bag to retrieve a quilted advent calendar. Farm animals peered out of the stitched barn, a new animal revealed each day until Christmas when a baby in a manger appeared in the center. She hung it from one of the plastic hooks meant to display a child's artwork.

When she turned around from her task, James had a smile on his face as he pointed to the playroom floor. Her gaze followed where he pointed to see Teddy lying on his side, a soft puppy dog rattle in one hand. Absently, the boy rubbed his fingers over the pale blue terry cloth, stroking the toy puppy's ear.

"Someone's getting sleepy." James spoke quietly. "Would you like me to carry him to his crib?"

"That would be great." Because while it was no trouble to lift him herself, Lydia had been wanting to get James more involved in the baby's daily routine. She watched as the rugged rancher leaned down to scoop up the child and cradle him against one big, broad shoulder.

James's shadowed jaw rested briefly atop his nephew's dark curls and Lydia's heart melted a little. Or maybe it was the sight of such a strong man displaying infinite tenderness toward a baby. No matter what it was that made her all soft and swoony inside, she recognized that standing shoulder to shoulder with her attractive employer in a darkened room might not be wise.

Lydia backed up a step as James headed down the hallway. "I'll be in the nursery in a minute," she assured him before darting in the other direction.

Just for a second, so she could get a handle on herself.

Instead of finding some breathing room, however, she stepped right into Mrs. Davis.

"Oh!" Lydia reached to right herself, placing a steadying hand against the wall. "I'm so sorry."

The housekeeper scowled, shaking her head. Her gray hair was down for the night, instead of in the tight twist she wore most days. Lydia was surprised to see her upstairs since she was usually in her room for the night at this hour. She tried not to react to the woman's displeased expression, remembering what James had said about the compliment she'd paid Lydia.

"I thought I heard Mr. Harris's voice," Mrs. Davis said. "I hoped to speak with him about something." The woman still wore the gray dress and apron that were her work uniform even though it was long past dinnertime.

"He's tucking Teddy into bed for the night."

Nodding, the housekeeper started to move toward the stairs and then turned back to Lydia.

"He is still grieving his brother, you know," Mrs. Davis said haltingly as she glanced toward the door to the nursery.

It was the most the housekeeper had ever said to her apart from where their duties overlapped.

"I'm sure he is," Lydia agreed. "It's only been a few months."

"And before that, he was dealing with the loss of his wife." Mrs. Davis lowered her voice even more while Lydia tried to conceal her shock.

James had been *married*?

She wanted to ask about that, but Mrs. Davis continued in her low, confidential tone. "I'm not sure he could handle getting attached to this boy and then possibly lose his nephew to the boy's grandparents. That's why I lobbied for Teddy to live with his grandparents from the start. I'm not heartless, Ms. Walker. I just don't want to see Mr. Harris hurt again."

Lydia could scarcely process all that, still reeling from the news that James had lost his wife. Had something happened to her? Had they divorced?

Before she could ask, James emerged from the nursery. Seeing the two women there, he paused.

Lydia was still too surprised to speak. Mrs. Davis straightened, and informed him, "The outdoor chest freezer needs to be replaced as soon as possible."

The two of them spoke briefly about that before resolving it to the housekeeper's satisfaction. Lydia told herself to simply say good-night and retreat.

Her boss's private affairs weren't her concern. Except what if his wife's family could make some kind of claim on Teddy? She knew that was a stretch considering the boy was James's blood relative. But still, wouldn't that have some bearing on her job? Or was she justifying her curiosity?

Before she could debate the wisdom of it, she blurted, "I didn't know you'd been married."

James braced for the inevitable pain that came from any reminder of his failed marriage.

To his surprise, it didn't come. Some resentment lingered, but not to the same degree. Had he finally put some of his past to rest? Because instead of feeling the old flare of anger about Raelynn, James only felt a surge of male satisfaction that Lydia Walker wanted to know about his romantic history.

"I didn't think it was relevant," he told her honestly. "I believe you've been as careful as I have about not getting too…personal."

He'd been working ridiculously long hours lately, not just to catch up with chores around the ranch, but to keep his distance from Lydia and their undeniable attraction. To avoid the intimacy of time together after that rainy night when he'd driven her to her house.

"It's none of my business, of course," she agreed, picking at a loose thread on the ribbed cuff of her pale green sweater sleeve.

A shade that brought out the green in her beautiful hazel eyes.

"It *is* your business. You work with my nephew, and my family status is relative to Teddy's." He gestured toward the stairs. "Let's talk in the kitchen and we can grab something to drink."

She followed him into the expansive kitchen, sliding onto one of the back-less saddle-shaped stools that pulled up to a long limestone countertop on an island. He tugged open one of the double doors to the refrigerator and chose two bottles of sparkling water and an orange. He sliced it and served a section on the rim of her glass along with her bottle.

"Thank you." She twisted off the cap and poured her own glass while he assembled some cheeses on a serving platter with a fresh baguette he found in the bread drawer.

Sliding onto the stool near her—carefully leaving a seat empty between them—he poured his own drink. The small pendant lights over the bar were on the nighttime setting, low enough to see what they were doing, but dim enough to be relaxing. He liked taking his meals here at the end of a day.

"I don't talk about my ex-wife very often since the divorce is just over a year old, and until recently, it was a source of tremendous regret."

"You certainly don't owe me any explanations." She slid a single slice of bread onto the appetizer plate along with one slice of cheese. "I just wouldn't want to be caught off guard if she came to the house, or asked to see Teddy."

"That will never happen." For so many reasons. "Raelynn never wanted children, for one thing." He'd thought about that many times since bringing his nephew into his life. If his wife hadn't left him then, she sure as hell would have bolted when she found out James was the guardian to a pint-sized tornado. "But more importantly, she's moved out of state. With her new husband."

Lydia stared at him, wide-eyed. "I'm so sorry."

"I'm not. At least we're not forced to see each other around town." He'd been hurt at first when he'd discovered how quickly she found someone new, but even he'd been able to see that she was happier in her second marriage. "I knew we were having problems, but I didn't realize how much she disliked being a rancher's wife. We agreed on a settlement, and she left. End of story."

"That still must have been painful."

"Of course. But I learned a valuable lesson. Because while I don't plan to get hitched again, I do know that I'd take a more mercenary approach next time." He dragged the cutting board closer and cut the remainder of the orange he'd used for their drinks, adding the slices to the serving platter.

The sharp tang of citrus filled the air and Lydia helped herself to a segment.

"A mercenary approach to marriage?" She lifted an eyebrow. "That just sounds wrong."

"Think about how many more successful marriages there used to be when families helped arrange the match. A wedding was for practical purposes, yes. But when a partner shares your values and interests, love can grow out of that." His gaze snagged on the sheen of juice coating her lips, and he felt a new kind of thirst.

"You can't be serious." She shook her head, a smile tugging at the corners of her lips.

She mesmerized him so much it took him a moment to remember what they'd been talking about.

"I'm totally serious. I've given it a lot of thought, and I think maybe romance is overrated."

Picking up the slice of baguette on her plate, she tore it in half and pointed at him with the ripped half. "That much we can agree on."

"Oh really?" he asked while she took a bite. "I would hate to think that you're already a cynic when it comes to love, too." He was teasing her, but he felt sad to hear it. "I hope no one's trounced your heart, Lydia."

He'd seen her tenderness with Teddy, and it made him feel protective of her.

"No. But I know not everyone views marriage as a binding agreement." She slanted a glance his way. "My mother, for example, has taken a 'trial and error' approach to finding the right guy. She was married three times before I moved out of Arkansas, and she's contemplating husband number four even now."

"That couldn't have been easy for you or your siblings." He'd read about the family on the *House Rules* blog, but didn't remember anything about a father figure in the clan.

"We managed." There was a defensive note in her voice, a hint of defiant pride. "But it certainly gave me a skeptical view of matrimony."

He wondered if that meant she'd ruled it out for herself, but wasn't sure how much to push. He was curious, though.

"What about your dad?" he asked instead, wanting to know more about her. Because even though he'd been avoiding her for the last two weeks, that didn't mean he hadn't been thinking about her most waking hours. And fantasizing about her the second his head hit the pillow at night. "Did he remarry?"

"He did." She nodded, and then took a long sip of

her water. "My father is Brazilian, and he met my mother while he was a foreign exchange student. He went back home after things fell apart with my mother. I've only seen him once since then, and I've never met his second wife."

He wondered about her last name—Walker didn't strike him as Brazilian—but maybe she'd taken her mother's surname. When he didn't respond right away, Lydia smothered a laugh, stirring her orange around her glass with a cocktail straw.

"My family has some interesting dynamics, I realize."

"Every family is unique." He understood that. "My nephew will be faced with that challenge, too. Whether I keep him with me or his maternal grandparents raise him, his childhood will be very different from what it should have been."

Lydia was quiet for a long moment. "You're seriously considering…giving him up?"

"I'm hardly equipped to raise a child by myself." Frustration simmered, not that she'd raised the question, but because he hated the situation. Hated that his brother wasn't here to be the father he'd always dreamed of being. "I want what's best for the boy."

He reached for more food, filling his plate a second time. Busying himself to dodge a sense of crushing guilt.

"That's admirable to put his needs first," she said softly, reaching a hand over to touch his forearm. Distracting him from the mixture of unhappy emotions with that spike of awareness never far beneath the surface when she was near. "But if you really want what's best for Teddy, please don't rule yourself out yet. You might make a better father than you realize."

He knew the only reason he didn't discount the suggestion immediately was because of that gentle touch on his forearm. The cool brush of her skin along his. It made it impossible to think about anything else but her. His heart slugged hard against his ribs. His gaze dipped to her lips as they parted ever so slightly.

An invitation?

Or wishful imagining?

If she'd been closer, he would have kissed her. He couldn't decide, then, if it was good thing or a bad thing that there was a vacant seat between them, keeping them apart. Instead, he covered her hand with his, watching her all the while.

Her pupils widened a fraction. Even in the dim light of the kitchen, he could see that hint of reaction. A sign of shared desire.

She didn't pull away. At least, not at first.

After a moment, she blinked fast and then withdrew her fingers slowly.

"I'd better say good-night." She rose awkwardly and backed toward the door before she turned away, her ponytail swishing as he watched her retreat.

He employed all his restraint not to follow her. Because he knew if he stood now, even just to extend their conversation, that kiss he wanted would somehow happen. It was so close he could almost taste her on his lips. And if this was what it was like between them after he'd deliberately avoided her for two weeks, what would happen if he spent more time with her and Teddy, the way she wanted him to?

He didn't have a plan for how to handle the magnetic attraction he felt for this woman, and he needed to come up with one. Fast. Because hiding out on the ranch, burying himself in physical labor, clearly wasn't working.

Five

Rose Clayton peered out her bedroom window just after dawn, not surprised to see James Harris's truck in one of the few remaining fields around the Silver C that didn't border Lone Wolf Ranch property. The Double H owner was a hard worker, no doubt, but over the past two weeks Rose had noticed James's truck at all hours in that shared pasture. The man was putting a lot of time into his place.

But then, she'd heard that his brother had died this past fall. Maybe James needed the distraction of exhausting, physical labor. She understood all too well the way grief could consume a person. She'd grieved for the love she'd lost with Gus when her father had forced her to wed Edward. She'd grieved for her mother to be married to a man who didn't care about her. Eventually, she'd even hurt for her children, who'd been raised by a hard, unforgiving man.

Rose understood the way hard work could make a person forget, for a little while at least.

Turning from the window, she took a moment to inhale the scent of bacon frying in her kitchen. For the forty years she'd been married, she'd never once awoken to the scent of breakfast being made in her kitchen. All those years wed to Ed, she'd been the one doing the cooking since he'd never managed the ranch well enough to afford much help. At least, not for her.

Pulling on a pair of old jeans and a T-shirt from a recent rodeo, Rose took her time brushing her teeth, liking the idea that she would walk into her kitchen to find Gus Slade making her breakfast.

After all they'd been through, all the ways they'd hurt each other over the years, who would have thought they could end up together? It almost seemed too good to be true. Like if she pinched herself she might roll over in her bed and find it had all been a dream. Heaven knew, she'd dreamed of Gus often enough while married to the man handpicked by her daddy when she was only eighteen years old.

Now, running a brush through her short brown hair going gray at the temples, Rose breathed in the scent of fresh coffee and headed toward the kitchen. She tugged a soft blue sweater off the back of the bathroom door and tucked her arms into the sleeves, then padded out to the kitchen in sock feet.

Her overnight guest stood in front of the farmhouse sink, sipping from a red stoneware mug while the dawn light spilled through the window onto his thick white hair. Augustus "Gus" Slade had celebrated his sixty-ninth birthday this year, but he was still well muscled,

strong enough to work the hay wagon if he was so inclined. And still undeniably sexy.

"Good morning." She couldn't help the smile that
came with the words, the unexpected joy filling her
whole body. It might not be the first time he'd spent
the night with her, but it still felt magical to wake up
to him.

Gus turned from the sink. "Good morning, beautiful." He toasted her with his coffee mug before setting it on the countertop. "Your breakfast is ready if
you want to take a seat."

"I can help," she started, stepping toward the refrigerator to get the juice and creamer.

Gus made a shooing motion with his hand, chasing
her toward the table. "I won't hear of it. I'm in charge of
breakfast, so have a seat and get used to being spoiled."

"I will never get used to being spoiled," she admitted, wondering—not for the first time—what her life
might have been like with this bold man at her side.

Would it have been this blissful every day? Or
would she have been too young to appreciate how truly
fortunate she was to have such a man? They'd been so
in love as teens, until Gus went off to make his way
in the world, promising to come back and marry her
one day. Four years later he'd returned after earning
enough money on the rodeo circuit to purchase a little piece of land nearby. Only her daddy was a cruel
man who didn't want his daughter to have anything
to do with a "nobody" like Gus. Jedediah Clayton had
considered himself—and his daughter—too good for
a Slade, forcing Rose to marry a man of Jed's choosing, threatening to kick out Rose's ill mother if Rose
didn't do as he commanded.

She'd resented her father all her life for that. But now that Ed was long gone and Gus's wife, Sarah, had died, too, Rose wondered if she would have been as good of a wife to Gus as he deserved. He was an amazing man.

Stubborn. Surly. And one hell of a ranching rival all those years that they'd been bitterly estranged, with Gus blaming Rose for marrying another man. But that was all in the past. Gus now knew that Rose had married Ed only out of fear for her mother.

"Then you underestimate me, Rose Clayton," Gus promised, stepping closer to her so he could fold her hands in his. "Because you don't know what great lengths I would go to in order to spoil you."

That joy bubbled up inside her again, making her feel like a giddy teenager falling in love with him all over again.

"Gus, all of Royal thinks I'm the toughest old bird in the county." She had spent a lifetime reinforcing the defenses around her heart and her life, trying to focus on her family and the ranch instead of all that she'd given up. "What will they say if you turn me soft?"

Gus's piercing blue eyes seemed to peer right into her soul. "They may say I'm one hell of a lucky man to win over the hottest woman in town."

She laughed. "You're too much."

The look he gave her about melted her socks off, before he kissed her tenderly on the cheek.

"Then have a seat, Rose, and let me get your breakfast."

Before she could move away, a voice cleared on the far side of the room. Rose tensed, her cheeks heating to be "caught" by her grandson, Daniel, the ranch manager of the Silver C.

Tall and well built, Daniel had turned into a formidable man who made Rose so proud. She'd gladly raised him from boyhood when her own daughter had been overwhelmed by single parenthood, turning to alcohol instead of her family for help. Rose blamed Ed for that, but she hadn't given up hope on Stephanie.

"Good morning, Daniel." She waved him over to the table. "Join us for some breakfast."

Daniel scowled. "I'll take something for the road," he muttered, stepping into the pantry before coming out with a few protein bars. "And Gran, have you thought about what you're doing, carrying on like this with this man?"

Flustered to have her own grandchild call her out, Rose was at a loss for words, her cheeks heating even though she had no cause to be embarrassed.

"Your grandmother does not 'carry on,' son," Gus told him mildly as he slid slices of bacon onto two plates. "Show her some respect."

Rose's gaze darted to Daniel's. The younger man looked as uncomfortable as she felt. Although she did appreciate Gus's easy defense of her.

"I meant no disrespect," Daniel insisted, scrubbing a hand through his dark hair. "But Gran is a well-respected member of the community. People will start to talk when they see your truck here every night."

Would people talk? She hadn't thought about that, but Daniel probably had a point. People did love gossip.

"That's no one's business but ours." Gus smiled at her as he strode closer to the table, her plate in hand. He set it in front of her while she took a seat. "But if it will put your mind at ease, I love your grandmother very much, and soon I'm going to marry her, like I should have all those years ago."

Is he serious? she thought wildly, her heart racing faster.

Her gaze went to Gus's, seeing the calm self-assurance in his blue eyes. Of course he was serious.

Just when she thought she couldn't feel any more joy in this life…boom. She felt a deep sense of happiness, as if the world was suddenly tilted right again. But she tucked those thoughts away for now, in front of Daniel, knowing her grandson didn't share her joy.

Not when his own heart was so thoroughly broken. Worse? She feared it was all her fault.

Lydia wasn't surprised when she awoke the next day to discover that James had left town on a business trip. He'd sent her a text with his contact information for a hotel in Houston in case she needed anything.

She didn't know much more than that, so throughout the week, she'd tried to look at his absence as a good thing—a favor that made her job easier. Without him in the house, she didn't have to worry about the attraction leading to anything. Except, as she went through the motions of her job, bringing Teddy for a holiday shopping outing and to have his photo taken with Santa, Lydia couldn't deny that she missed seeing her boss.

And in some ways, that felt even more dangerous to her peace of mind than the ever-present awareness between them. When he wasn't around, she found her subconscious supplied plenty of fantasy scenarios starring him.

Late in the week, shortly past dinnertime, she was in the kitchen storing some toddler portions of veggies that she'd cooked in batches for Teddy. The little boy still sat in his high chair, chasing oat cereal around his tray, tired out from the day since they'd skipped naptime while they were out doing errands.

Midway through the cooking operation, Lydia realized she'd gravitated toward the chore out of habit, an old way of coping with stress from the days when she'd lived under her mother's roof. Back then, she'd always found comfort in the ritual of work when her mother's love life got too crazy. Or her mother was too busy being romanced by her latest "Mr. Right" that she forgot to film a podcast for her blog. Lydia appreciated the way work made her feel in control.

And today, while she and Teddy had been out shopping, her mother had texted to remind her that Fiona expected a spa day before her bachelorette party—both of which were Lydia's job to organize as her maid of honor. Clearly, her mom had ignored the fact that Lydia refused to be in the wedding.

Here she was two hours later, chopping carrots and butternut squash like a madwoman, all because she hadn't found a way to make her mother listen.

Lydia heard the doorbell ring, and she assumed Mrs. Davis answered it when she heard the low rumble of voices in the front of the house. They had visitors.

And one of the voices—a woman's—she felt sure she recognized.

"Do you want to see who's here?" she asked Teddy, already unbuckling the straps on the high chair so she could lift him up.

"See here," he repeated in perfect imitation of her.

It was the first time she'd heard that combination of words, far more complicated than *bye-bye* or *cookie*, both of which he used well.

"Yes!" The sound of his clear words cheered her, reminding her that her work here was so much more than a job. More than a means to repay her sister's debt. In so many ways her involvement with children was a gift. "That's right, Teddy. We're going to see who is here."

She settled him on her hip and he laid his head against her shoulder. She couldn't resist resting her cheek on his fluffy crop of curls for a moment while she breathed in the scent of baby shampoo.

Then, she headed into the living area so she had a clear view of the foyer. She recognized Tessa Noble, a woman she'd gotten to know through her sister Gail, standing beside the tall, handsome rancher who'd bid on Tessa at the same charity bachelor auction where Gail had bid on Lloyd Richardson. Lydia recognized him only from photos in the articles she'd read online about the auction.

"Hello, Tessa." She strode closer to greet the woman who'd been supportive of Gail's fledgling grocery delivery business. Now, in simple heeled boots and jeans with her blue hoodie and a bright orange scarf, Tessa wore her dark hair loose and curly, but there was something about her that just glowed. "I don't know if you remember me—"

"Of course I do, Lydia." Tessa gave her a wide smile, stepping deeper into the room, her light brown eyes darting over the child in Lydia's arms. "But I sure didn't expect to see you here."

Before Lydia could reply, Mrs. Davis excused herself to retreat downstairs for the evening, leaving the guests to her.

Lydia waved the couple into the room. "Would you like to have a seat? James is away on business, but you're more than welcome—"

"We won't stay." Tessa exchanged a quick look with her tall, green-eyed companion. "This is Ryan Bateman, by the way. Ryan, Lydia Walker is Gail's older sister."

Lydia shook the man's hand and he gave her a warm smile.

"We just came by to thank James for encouraging Tessa to take part in the bachelor auction." He slid his arm around Tessa's waist, tucking her close as if he'd missed her in the brief moment they hadn't been side by side. "Tessa's been my best friend for a long time, but without the nudge of that night, I don't know how long it would have taken me to see that she was the right woman for me all along."

Tessa, who already glowed with happiness, brightened even more as she flashed a stunning ring on her left finger—chocolate and white diamonds set in a rose gold band. "I couldn't wait to tell James that we're getting married."

The new couple's love warmed the whole room. And while Lydia was thrilled for them, it was hard not to feel like a romantic failure by comparison.

"That's wonderful news! Tessa, your ring is gorgeous." She wished Gail was here to share her friend's engagement news. "I'm so happy for you and I know James will be thrilled for you, too." Unwilling to linger on the topic of the charity auction since she hadn't worked out what to say about her sister's exorbitant bid,

Lydia steered the conversation away from the event. "I'm working here as Teddy's nanny, by the way, so I'm sure to see James as soon as he returns."

Not that she had any idea when that might be.

With Christmas just a few days away, she wondered if he would stay away for the holiday. What if her presence in the house was actually preventing him from bonding with his nephew? The thought made hear heart ache for the boy.

Tessa ducked to peer into Teddy's face. "He's almost asleep. He looks very comfortable with you, Lydia, but please let James know that I'd be happy to help out with the baby on your days off."

"That's very kind of you. Thank you." She'd thought about taking Teddy with her the next time she had a meeting with her contractor if James hadn't returned to town by then, but it was nice to know Tessa didn't mind the occasional babysitting gig. "James worries that Teddy can be a handful, but I think it's just because he's been through so much these last few months."

"Poor baby." Tessa stroked the boy's back for a moment, her face softening. "He needs his uncle now more than ever."

The woman's words were a powerful reminder of what Lydia had thought all along.

If she wanted to be a good nanny to Teddy, she needed to recommit to bringing James more firmly into the child's routine. A task that wasn't easy if James continued to keep his distance.

So while Lydia said good-night to the guests, waving at them while they headed out to Ryan's big black pickup truck in the driveway, Lydia was already formulating a plan to bring James home for good. No matter that his presence was an undeniable temptation for her. The sweet child in her arms deserved to know the comfort of a father figure.

James sat in a luxury hotel suite in Houston, working on taxes three days before Christmas.

He couldn't decide if he felt like Scrooge for working with figures when the rest of the world was preparing for the holiday, or if should feel proud of himself for starting the Double H's tax forms before the year ended. Either way, the kind of jump start was a first for him and he owed it all to the woman who'd dominated his thoughts all week.

Lydia.

The phone rang even as he thought her name, the screen showing her as the incoming call. Not really a coincidence given that he'd been thinking of her more often than not.

He checked the antique timepiece that had belonged to his grandfather. A trickle of anxiety made him wonder if everything was okay back home when he saw it was almost nine o'clock.

"Hello, Lydia." He wished he could see her face. Know her expression right now.

"Hi." She didn't sound upset. Somehow, through that one syllable, he could tell by her tone that there was nothing wrong with his nephew. "How's Houston?"

Relief kicked through him hard, making him realize how attached he was growing to the boy in spite of himself. Pushing away from the hotel room's small desk, he tipped back in the rolling chair to peer out his window at the city skyline.

"It's quiet. I've been taking meetings with some locals who are interested in expanding the Texas Cattleman's Club into Houston, but I could wrap things up anytime now." He needed to be back in Royal, in fact, and had extended the trip this long only to make sure he gave Lydia space to get comfortable in his home.

He didn't want to crowd her with the heat that seemed inevitable when they were in the same room.

"That's good," she said in a rush. "I was calling to see if you could spend some time with Teddy this weekend."

Frowning, he straightened in the leather desk chair.

"Do you need time off?" He hadn't thought about what to do if Lydia wanted some downtime. But he recognized that her work made her on-call twenty-four hours a day.

"No. I'd be here, too," she clarified. "I just thought it would be nice for Teddy if you could spend some time with him." She seemed to hesitate a moment, before adding, "And he seems to be settling into a routine, which I think is helping with some of the behavior issues he might have had before. He's fun to be around."

James felt like a heel. Did she think that's why he'd been staying away? Because of a tantrum or two? Worse, what if she had a point? He'd been so quick to give over complete care of the child to her. And no matter what he thought about his brother's decision to appoint James as Teddy's legal guardian, he owed his brother better than paying lip service to Parker's wishes. Frustration simmered, and he rose to his feet, pacing the hotel suite.

Even if Teddy eventually went to live with his

grandparents, James always wanted him to feel welcome at the Double H.

"I will be home tomorrow," he assured her, mentally making room in his schedule. "How do you suggest we spend the day?"

"Oh. Um…thank you." She sounded surprised. And pleased. "In that case, there's a holiday ice show that he might enjoy. Even if we only get to see a part of it, I think it would be fun for him."

"Of course. I'll take care of the tickets tonight. Should we do anything else? Dinner afterward?" He couldn't deny that he was looking forward to spending time with Lydia.

"We might be pushing our luck with an active toddler," she mused aloud. "What if we bring him out to get a Christmas tree?"

"Even though we already have one?" He'd sent one of the ranch hands to the house last week to help Mrs. Davis take one out of storage.

There was a pause on the other end of the call.

"You don't like my Christmas tree?" he pressed, trying to remember what it looked like.

"It's beautiful." She seemed to be weighing her words. "But maybe we could cut down a little one for the playroom where Teddy and I could hang some homemade ornaments? You know, give him a little more buy-in?"

James couldn't help but laugh.

"By all means, a kid should have buy-in on his own Christmas." Yet even as he spoke the words, he realized there wasn't a damned thing funny about it. If anything, he found it sad to think of his nephew not being a part of a family Christmas.

The sudden punch of grief hit hard while Lydia suggested a playroom picnic afterward.

Only half listening, he was lost in his own thoughts for a moment as James recognized that he'd been screwing up his time with Teddy. He'd been so focused on providing the boy with better care than he could offer him personally, he'd ended up having very little to do with the child. His last remaining relative.

And he had Lydia to thank for helping him to see that before Teddy's grandparents got involved. He still had time to make memories with the boy. Ensure that he felt at home in the house where his father was raised.

"That all sounds good," James told her before she signed off for the night. "I've been trying to give you space. To make things easier for you while you get settled at the ranch." He hesitated. Did he need to spell out his reasons? He was pretty sure she knew all about the crackle of awareness between them. "But I'm definitely ready to spend more time with you and Teddy."

"I know Teddy will be happy to have you back home," she admitted softly, as careful as ever with her words.

His last question remained unspoken.

Would *she* be happy to have him back in the house with her every day? Every *night*?

This would be the last time he backed off that question, however. Tomorrow, they were going to face their simmering mutual attraction head-on and see what happened. No more letting it keep him from his nephew. Decision made, he felt a surge of anticipation.

"Good," he said simply. "I'm looking forward to

seeing him, and *you*, too. Very much." He let the words hover there for a moment, wanting them to linger in her mind long after the call disconnected. "Sleep well, Lydia."

Morning couldn't come soon enough.

Six

Seated beside James in a black BMW sedan the next day, Lydia reminded herself not to think about his phone call the night before. The one where he'd said how much he was looking forward to seeing her.

After all, she'd already lost sleep thinking about what he'd meant. She didn't dare lose focus on her job now that he was back in Royal, bringing her and Teddy on the special outing she'd requested.

Still, as the sleek luxury car sped toward the civic center for the holiday ice show, she couldn't help thinking how much the trip felt like a date. Especially with Teddy quietly taking in the scenery from his car seat. There was no need to entertain the baby with silly songs or toys passed over her shoulder. There was only the scent of leather seats and a hint of spicy aftershave. The sound of steel guitars muted from the speakers.

And the too-rapid beat of her heart as she smoothed the belted trench coat over her knees to cover the hem of her red sweater dress.

She was hyperaware of the compelling man behind the wheel. He wore black pants and a dark polo shirt with a camel-colored blazer and suede boots. Well dressed but not overdressed for an ice show meant for families. The tailored jacket accentuated his lean, muscular physique. No doubt she was gawking a little as he navigated easily through midday traffic for the matinee show.

Searching for a topic to distract her, she remembered the visitors from the night before.

"I'm not sure if Mrs. Davis mentioned it, but Tessa Noble and Ryan Bateman stopped in yesterday evening to thank you for encouraging Tessa to go on the auction block at the Pancreatic Cancer Research Foundation event." She remembered how starry-eyed they both looked. How glowing with happiness. "They are engaged to be married, and very much in love."

"Is that right?" James grinned as he glanced over at her. "And Tessa was always his best friend before." The deep timbre of his voice hummed right through her.

"Ryan said the auction was the nudge he needed to see her in a different light."

"I couldn't be happier for them." He frowned. "Although the last I knew, Rose Clayton was angling for her grandson, Daniel, to date Tessa."

Lydia recalled the matriarch of the Silver C only from the occasional sightings around Royal and the woman's charitable efforts in town. Everyone seemed to know about the enmity between the Claytons and the Slades, Royal's answer to the Hatfields and Mc-

Coys. As a newcomer to town, Lydia had heard only bits of gossip about old battles over property lines and water rights. The feud might be dying down now that Rose Clayton's husband was long gone and Gus Slade's wife, Sarah, had passed away. The Great Royal Bachelor Auction had been dedicated to the memory of Sarah Slade, in fact.

"Well, Tessa is most definitely taken," Lydia observed. "Rose will have to turn her matchmaking efforts elsewhere."

"After the press coverage Daniel received following the auction, he shouldn't have any trouble finding his own dates. The story calling him the 'Most Eligible Bachelor in Texas' was picked up all over the place." James pulled off the interstate onto the ramp that led toward the civic center.

Colorful billboards hung outside the arena with ads for upcoming shows, including one for the holiday ice show.

"Look, Teddy." Lydia pointed to the characters twirling on skates. "Do you see the polar bear?"

He clapped his hands once, his brown eyes wide with childish wonder. She adored this little boy.

"Bear," he said.

Clear as a bell. She couldn't help a swell of pride in him.

"Wow. Did you teach him that?" James sounded as awed as his nephew.

She flushed with pleasure, even if she couldn't take credit.

"No. Kids his age are little sponges, soaking it all in. He surprised me yesterday by repeating a phrase really clearly."

"That's incredible." He drummed his thumbs on the steering wheel while he waited for a parking space. The lot was already busy. While he waited, he glanced over at her, his gaze lingering. "And it's easy to see you've been a good influence on him. He seems calmer."

She knew the praise shouldn't feel any different from the approval she'd received from other satisfied parents in the past. Yet somehow, coming from this handsome, charismatic man, it meant more. Or maybe she just wanted more with him. The realization—that it wasn't just physical attraction between them but maybe something deeper—rattled her.

She was growing attached to James and his sweet nephew.

"Thank you," she said thickly, dragging her gaze away from his. "We've had fun together." Then, in a rush, she added, "Teddy and I."

Her cheeks felt warm. All of her felt warm from his attention. His praise. This damned awareness.

"And I appreciate you helping me to be a part of that," he said smoothly as he parked the sedan and switched off the ignition. In the quiet aftermath, he slid his hand over hers where it rested on the console. "No matter what else happens between us, Lydia, with your job or our agreement, please know that I am deeply grateful to you for stepping in to help me with my nephew. I realized last night that I was screwing up the one thing my brother asked of me."

Behind them in the backseat, Teddy made cooing sounds as he kicked the base of his car seat with one sneaker. The boy was content.

And she was completely caught off guard by James's sincerity. Not to mention his touch. She wondered if her racing heart was obvious where his finger lay along her forearm. Her breath caught as she went to answer.

"I'm glad I could help." She told herself if he moved his hand away now, then the touch was just an indication of simple human gratitude.

His hand remained.

"The last thing I want to do is complicate matters between us when you're so good for Teddy." His thumb shifted along her inner arm. Just a fraction of an inch. A tiny stroke of her wrist. Back and forth. "But I can't be with you and pretend that I don't feel drawn to you. Because I do, Lydia. That's the reason I spent this past week in Houston. And why I worked all the long hours on the ranch before I left. I tried my best to stay away."

She was spellbound by his touch. Gentle, but sure. She had no doubt he would remove his hand instantly if she asked him to. She met his eyes again, shifting toward him to meet his gaze head-on, his words sinking in.

"Because of me," she clarified, surprised that he would admit it so plainly.

There would be no taking back these words. No pretending this conversation hadn't happened. And where did that leave them, now that their mutual attraction was out there in the open? A tangible thing they couldn't hide from, especially while living under the same roof.

"Because I didn't want you to feel uncomfortable." He slid his hand under hers and then laid his other palm on top, capturing her fingers between his. "But I realized last night when you called that staying away from you wasn't good for Teddy. And I'm not interested in staying apart from you either, even if it means that we have to revisit our arrangement."

"But we only just worked out the details of how I can help Gail repay you." She opted to focus on that last part of what he'd said—about revisiting their arrangement—since she wasn't ready to think about why he wanted to renegotiate the agreement. "I don't know if I trust Gail to make an honest effort to repay you in some way, and I can't just let it go either."

"I don't want you to quit, Lydia. Just the opposite, in fact. But I guess, right now, all I really want to know is this." He stared down at the place where their hands were joined, studying the knot of fingers like a complex problem before he looked up at her again. "Could we not worry about our professional relationship so that, just for today, I could kiss you the way I've wanted to for weeks?"

They were already so close. That kiss was just a breath away, but indulging in it meant admitting that she wanted it, too. And while James had clearly already come to terms with confronting this desire, Lydia hadn't wrapped her brain around all the ways a relationship could complicate things.

Desire tightened inside her, the need for him turning into an ache.

"I wish it was that simple." She whispered her thoughts aloud, unable to move away from him.

"Do you?" He raked his gaze over her and she felt the heat of his longing as thoroughly as her own.

Her skin tingled, and it was all she could do to nod. Yes. She craved that kiss.

"Then that will have to be enough. For now." Sliding his hands away from hers, he lifted a finger to skim along her cheek. Then dragged his thumb along her lower lip in a way that did something sweetly erotic to her insides. "Knowing that you're thinking about that kiss, too…" He let the thought trail off along with his touch before he leaned back in his seat. "That's more than I had at the beginning of this day. And that's a start."

He was out of the vehicle and around to her side of the car, opening the door for her before she caught her breath. With a stern warning to herself to rein it in, Lydia redoubled her focus on Teddy. On making this a memorable day for the little boy who deserved a happy Christmas outing.

But she'd be lying if she said she wasn't thinking about kissing James, too. Every. Single. Moment.

That evening, after the holiday ice show and the trip to cut down a small Christmas tree for the playroom, James sat with legs sprawled on the red-and-green tartan picnic blanket. It was only eight o'clock, but time spent with a toddler made it feel later. Teddy had been well behaved all day. His exclamations at the ice show were no louder than the majority of the crowd made up of almost 50 percent kids. The toddler had grown weary of sitting in the seat after about forty-five minutes, so they'd slipped out during a change of scenery and brought him out on a sleigh to hike around the ranch and choose a little three-foot tree that was perfect for the play area.

They'd decorated it with only a couple of snowflakes that Lydia had made ahead of time, but she'd said they would add to it in the coming days. Besides, Teddy had set some of his toys on the branches. The rubber balls hadn't worked out as ornaments, but a couple of his stuffed toys and a few blocks still rested on the boughs. No surprise that Lydia had been correct about the boy needing a more hands-on tree. Teddy still sat on the floor beside it, now dressed in his pajamas while Lydia read a story to him from a plastic-coated book.

She glanced toward James as she read, and any sense of contentment with the day fled like smoke from a fire. Just that one shared look and his mind rewound to the intriguing conversation they'd had in the parking lot before the ice show.

When he'd been a moment away from kissing her.

He studied her now, as her attention returned to the baby and his book. With her boots off, he could see her polka-dot Christmas socks. Gold hoop earrings shone in the lamplight with her light brown hair twisted into a low braid.

Realizing how close they were to Teddy's bedtime, and the hour he would finally have Lydia all to himself, James made quick work of the picnic remains. He packed the few containers of leftover fruit and cheeses back into the straw basket that the cook had delivered earlier in the day. Then, he rolled up the blanket carefully and tucked it under the basket's handle.

"How about I tuck him in?" he offered, wanting to show Lydia he'd heard her concerns about spending more time with his nephew.

He wanted the boy to always feel welcome here, even if Teddy's maternal grandparents decided they were ready to raise him.

"That would be great. Thank you." She closed the

book and rose. "I'll bring the picnic hamper to the kitchen."

He lifted Teddy in his arms.

"The maid will get it." He had a cleaning service twice a week to help Mrs. Davis. "Why don't you head to the library and I'll meet you down there? I have a surprise for you."

"A surprise?" She leaned closer so she could ruffle Teddy's hair.

The soft vanilla scent of her lingered after she eased away. Hunger for her stirred.

"It will only take a minute. I know you've had a full day with this guy." He lifted Teddy slightly and the boy giggled. "I'll see you in a few."

Turning on his heel, he went to lay Teddy in his crib. It had gone well enough the last time he'd done it that he felt more sure of himself this time. Besides, the kid had to be tired after how busy they'd kept him all day long.

Flicking on the night-light and the nursery monitor, James made sure the crib was clear of extra toys. He was old enough for a light blanket and a stuffed rattle, but the baby seemed content to poke one foot through the slats of the crib, making babbling sounds.

Right up until he said, "Night-night."

The words clutched at James's heart, making him glad again that he'd come back to Royal today. He might not be ready for kids of his own, but he didn't want to screw up this window of time with his nephew. Not when Parker had entrusted him to care for the boy.

"Good night, Teddy," he called back to him, before shutting the door.

He carried the receiver for the baby monitor downstairs with him, his thoughts turning to the alluring woman who waited for him in his library. He hadn't dated anyone seriously since his divorce, going out a few times just to prove to himself he could.

Now? Lydia dominated his thoughts, and not just because she was good with Teddy.

She was honorable, for one thing. She hadn't needed to seek him out after her sister fled town without paying for her bachelor. But here Lydia was, trying to salvage the integrity of her family name. Doing what she thought was right.

She worked hard, for another, taking her job seriously. The difference she'd already made with Teddy was all the proof he needed.

And, as he stepped through the open library doors to see her silhouetted by moonlight streaming through the windows of an otherwise darkened room, James was reminded how incredibly sexy she was, too. The sweater dress hugged her curves, her face tipped upward. She'd slipped into the leather boots she'd worn earlier in the day, the heels making her almost as tall as him.

"You should see the moon," she said softly. "It's so huge above the tree line, it looks like a movie set. Or a honky-tonk bar."

He sucked in a breath, steeling himself for the inevitable draw of her nearness. Knowing the next move had to be hers after he'd made his intentions clear this afternoon.

"One of the benefits of living out here," he admitted. "No city lights or buildings to get in the way of the view."

He stopped short of her, since touching her again

was out of the question. Without the barrier of the baby around, he had only his own restraint to rely on. And he sure as hell wasn't going to test it for a second time today.

He leaned against the windowsill the same way she did, leaving two feet between them.

"Thank you for today." She folded her arms, one shoulder tipping against the glass pane. "For coming home and being a part of everything I had planned."

"I know you did it for Teddy." She'd been very clear about her motives. Very careful to draw boundaries. "But I had fun, too."

"So did I." Her hazel eyes locked on his.

Desire for her flared hotter. His hands itched to reach for her. To pull her against him and keep her there while he tested the softness of her lips. Tasted his fill.

Instead, he eased away from the window, needing more space from her if he was going to maintain this facade of a professional relationship. "Are you ready to see your surprise?"

Her eyebrow arched. Straightening, she nodded. "Absolutely."

"Then follow me." He headed toward the back wall of the library, to a door almost hidden by bookshelves. The room was designed that way, giving this added space an intimate ambiance. "I have a secret retreat that I thought you might enjoy some evenings after Teddy goes to bed."

He slid open the door with the antique brass handle and hit the switch for the floor lights. Inside, tiny white bulbs glowed on either side of the aisle down the center of his media room. Big leather chairs flanked the aisle in pairs, for sixteen seats in all. The screen ahead was dark for a moment until he hit a command on his phone and cued up the opening credits of a nature documentary. On the screen, the sun rose on an African savannah while birds dipped and called. He hit the mute button but let the video run.

"All this time you've been hiding a home movie theater in here?" Her fingers smoothed along the leather seat rest of a chair. "What a great space."

"I didn't show it to you that first day because I had a few clients in to look at film of one of our horses in training and there was still some electronic equipment out." He rolled aside one of the screens on some built-in shelving to show her a sample of the technology not in use at the moment. "This isn't always a good spot for a toddler. But I thought you might enjoy unwinding here sometimes."

"I will. May I?" At his nod, she lowered herself into one of the chairs as if to test it out. "This is so comfortable. Do you ever fall asleep watching movies?"

He sat in the chair beside her, only an armrest separating them in the dim room while the film showed a family of lions on the move. "Never. Believe it or not, I've only used the room for previewing racing footage or rodeo competitions since our training program involves a lot of animal analysis."

Lydia made a face, wrinkling her nose. "You remember what they say about all work and no play?"

"Guilty." He couldn't deny it. Although being around this woman made him want to be someone different. Someone more inclined to have fun. "But my life has been anything but dull these last few weeks."

Leaning deeper into the seat back, she turned to

look at him. She appeared comfortable. More relaxed than he'd ever seen her. Was she more at ease now that Teddy was sleeping? Or maybe she was simply worn out from a long day of caregiving.

"Mine, too." A smile hitched at her lips. "James, I haven't forgotten what we talked about in the car today."

Anticipation fired through him, but he didn't shift closer. Didn't touch her. He'd put the ball in her court for making the next move and he intended to be patient while she grappled with the hunger he'd wrestled since they first met. "It's been on my mind all day, too."

"I'm afraid I still don't have any more answers than I did earlier." Frowning, she nibbled at her lip for a moment as she turned her eyes toward the viewing screen where little lion cubs tackled each other. Then, she glanced back at him. "Although, I will say it's easier to contemplate a kiss when I'm not working."

The words reverberated through him like a bell, the hum of it remaining in his body long after she finished speaking. Every nerve ending acutely attuned to her.

He slid his hand under the armrest between them and tilted it up and out of the way. Removing the only physical barrier between them, but not crossing it.

"Then, solely in the interest of refreshing your memory, I'd like to remind you of my proposition."

Her shoulder angled a fraction closer to him. "Please do."

Her words were a throaty rasp of air as her fingers landed lightly on his chest.

She had to feel the rapid thrum of his heart. Wanting more.

"I thought we should shove aside all the things keeping us apart and just test run that kiss." He liked her hand on him, not just because it felt so damn good to have her touch him, but also because it freed him to touch her back.

He cradled her jaw in one hand, testing the softness of her lower lip with his thumb.

"See if it's worthwhile?" she asked.

The play of her mouth against his skin mesmerized him as she arched closer still.

"Something like that." He watched up until the last moment when her lips brushed his.

A tentative exploration. A minty breath. The tender grip of her fist twisting his shirt placket.

And then, confident he'd let her make the first move, he wrapped his arms around her, dragging her against him. She was so soft and sweetly scented, her hair fraying loose from its confining braid and her sweater dress teasing his skin.

He molded her curves to the hard planes of his body, liking the way she fit against him. Needing more, but knowing it wasn't time yet.

Knowing he'd negotiated for only a kiss. A taste.

He focused on just that—the feel of her lips and the damp stroke of her tongue. He gave and took in equal measures, exploring what she liked, breathing her in. Her hands were restless on him, gliding up his arms and down his chest.

Her touch made it impossible to pull away. She felt so damned good in his arms. So right. He adjusted the angle, deepening the kiss, telling himself it was just for a moment. She gripped his shoulders tightly, dragging him closer. Her breasts brushed his chest, and the contact made everything hotter, threatening his control.

He kissed her until his restraint stretched as thin as he dared.

Only then did he ease away carefully. Slowly.

Lydia's eyes fluttered open, her lips still parted. Damp.

With an effort, he closed his eyes. Let go of her completely.

"I should—um. Go." She sounded rattled. Or maybe she was simply as revved up as him.

But he couldn't have stopped her. Not without falling into that kiss all over again. So he just nodded tightly, remaining in his seat while she rose to her feet.

On the screen behind her, he saw night had fallen on the savannah. As for the test run of a kiss, he wasn't sure if he'd call it a success or a failure since it turned out to be the most combustible kiss he'd ever experienced.

One thing he knew for sure, though. He wouldn't try that again unless they were both prepared for it to lead to a whole lot more.

Seven

With Christmas just days away, Rose Clayton suspected she should have been prepared for the crowds of people at the Courtyard Shops just west of Royal's downtown area. This was the town's most popular shopping district, the property a reclaimed old farm where the big red barn was now an antiques store and the main house sheltered local artisans. But it had been so long since Rose had shopped for something in person—as opposed to online or through one of her ranch's administrative assistants—that she'd forgotten how much of a crush the holiday shopping outing could be. It seemed like she'd seen half the townspeople here in the last hour, from local rancher Caleb Mackenzie and his fiancée, Shelby Arthur, to the newly engaged Ryan Bateman and Tessa Noble.

Then again, maybe Rose's eye was simply drawn

to all the happy couples in town. She wanted that kind of happiness for her grandson, Daniel.

And for herself.

Taking a moment to rest in front of the live pine tree decorated with lights and oversize ornaments just outside the antiques shop, Rose soaked in the atmosphere. From the local children's choir singing carols to the scent of hot pretzels and roasted chestnuts, the outdoor venue oozed holiday cheer. Or maybe it was her who was filled with so much goodwill in the days following Gus's declaration that he was going to marry her.

Had he meant it?

Or had he just told Daniel that in an effort to keep the peace? She hadn't wanted to quiz Gus about it, unwilling to ripple the waters in this tenuous new joyful place in her life. Besides, daydreaming about a future with him made her feel like a teenager again.

Except this time, she began to think their story could have a happy ending.

"Hello, Rose." The deep timbre of a male voice sounded nearby, and she turned to see her neighbor, James Harris.

Dressed in dark jeans and a coffee-colored suede jacket, he looked more relaxed than the last time she'd seen him—working tirelessly to restring fencing near her property line.

"Nice to see you, James." She hadn't attended his brother's funeral halfway across the state, but she'd sent flowers with her condolences. The Harris family had been good to her over the years and she was sorry to see James lose a brother at such a young age.

"I've been wondering how you're doing with a toddler in the house."

"Hanging in there." He grinned as he tipped up his Stetson a fraction, juggling his shopping bags over to one hand. "I found a nanny who has really been making a difference with Teddy. Her name is Lydia Walker and I'm sure you'll see her around the ranch sooner or later."

"Mrs. Davis mentioned her to me when she came over to store some things in our extra freezer." Rose gathered the older woman wasn't thrilled with the new hire, but then Bernadette Davis had always been protective of the Harris boys. She'd been livid that James's first wife had been more interested in the Harris family fortune than her husband.

"Thank you for letting us use the freezer, by the way. I appreciated that."

The children's choir gave way to a handbell group, the ringing chimes filling the air as Rose waved off James's thanks, unwilling to accept praise for something so small.

"Your granddaddy was one of the kindest men I've ever met." Henry Harris had been one of the few people in Royal who had seen right through her act when she'd rebuffed her friends during those awful years after she'd married Edward. She couldn't bear for any of her former friends to know how Edward treated her, so she'd been cruel in the way she'd alienated everyone. But James's grandfather, a shrewd military veteran, had never bought the act. He'd kept right on being good to Rose. "You know if you ever need anything, you only have to ask. And what did you say the nanny's name was?"

She'd thought it sounded familiar.

"Lydia Walker." He lifted a hand in greeting to someone behind her as he said it. "Here she is now, in fact. She's helping me finish my holiday shopping today."

Rose turned, curious to see the woman who made James smile that way. There was a blatant male interest there that was hard to miss. And wasn't it interesting that James was out with the nanny—but no child in sight?

"Hello." The younger woman greeted her, extending her hand as she tucked a small shopping bag under her arm. Tall and slim, she wore a long skirt with boots and shawl-collar sweater, fashionable but down-to-earth. "I'm Lydia Walker, Mrs. Clayton. I recognize you from volunteering with the Family Fun Run you organized for the children's club last summer."

"Walker." Rose repeated it without meaning to, a trick that sometimes worked to jog a memory. She snapped her fingers as it came to her. "Wasn't that the name of the big bidder at the bachelor auction?" She had been stunned—along with the rest of the crowd— at the bid from the young woman. "What a tremendously generous donation to the charity."

Uh-oh. Apparently she'd stepped in it, based on the wary looks the two of them exchanged. As the awkward silence hovered, the scent of roasted chestnuts intensified with a vendor walking past with a silver concession cart. Fragrant smoke billowed to either side.

"Gail Walker is my sister," Lydia confirmed as she dodged a pair of little girls playing tag. "She definitely surprised us all with her bid."

Lydia's smile looked strained while James added, "But thanks to your grandson, Rose, the press coverage after the event really helped bring in more donations.

The Pancreatic Cancer Research Foundation couldn't have asked for a better spokesperson than Daniel."

Rose was glad to hear it. But had the added donations been worth alienating her own grandson?

"Daniel isn't thrilled about being the 'Most Eligible Bachelor in Texas,' but he's been a good sport."

Rose traded a few more words with the two of them before they left to finish their holiday shopping. Her gaze followed James and Lydia, curious about the relationship that struck her as more than just professional. It was in the way they looked at one another. The way they stood close without touching.

The way they'd gone on a shopping outing without Teddy.

Not that it was any of her business. But Rose had learned a thing or two about the ways romance could grow between unsuspecting people over the years. Maybe she had an eye for matchmaking. She'd gained a keen eye for romance since it had been decidedly absent in her own life for so long.

But now, she had Gus.

Which reminded her, she needed to finish up her shopping, too.

She was about to enter Priceless, the antiques store in the big red barn that anchored the Courtyard Shops, when her phone vibrated. She pulled it from her jacket pocket to see a text from her grandson.

I'm getting more messages and deliveries every day from nutcases who want to meet me because of that damned article. From now on, I'm forwarding everything to the main house for you since this is what you wanted. I'm done.

Knowing how frustrated Daniel was sure didn't lift Rose's spirits. She'd only meant well by having the reporter write an article about Daniel. But he seemed more miserable than ever since she and Gus had orchestrated the breakup between him and Gus's granddaughter, Alexis Slade. At the time, they'd been so sure their feud would last forever, and their grandkids didn't belong together.

But she'd gone and fallen for Gus again in spite of herself. So what right did she have to keep Daniel and Alexis apart?

Maybe she didn't have such a good eye for matchmaking after all. One way or another, she and Gus needed to make this right for their grandchildren.

Listening to James on the phone with Teddy's babysitter, Lydia walked with him to his car parked near the Courtyard Shops.

"Just make sure you have the nursery monitor with you when you go downstairs," he explained to the young woman, his ranch foreman's daughter, who was home from college for the holidays. "I'm sure Mrs. Davis left some snacks for you on the counter."

Lydia smiled to hear him, thinking he was getting the hang of caring for his nephew. Ever since she'd started at the Harris house, she could see more ease in his interactions with the boy. But would his increased comfort level with his role prompt him to raise Teddy as his own?

Clearly, that had been his brother's preference.

Weaving between parked cars, she allowed her eyes to linger on James as they neared his vehicle. Memories of their kiss still made her breathless, sparking a fresh longing in her as she admired his athletic grace and powerfully built body. She'd agreed to the shopping outing when he had urged her to take some downtime away from the ranch, and she'd thought that was a good idea. Since she had some of her own Christmas shopping to do, she'd thought it could be fun to help him purchase gifts for Teddy while they had a sitter for the boy.

And it had been.

But she hadn't been prepared to field questions about Gail's bid from Rose Clayton. Not that Rose had questioned her, per se. Lydia had simply felt uncomfortable accepting any kind of "thanks" on Gail's behalf since her sister hadn't made the donation in the first place.

James had.

He finished up his call with the babysitter a moment later and pocketed his phone.

"The sitter is set for a few hours and I've got the feed from the nursery monitor on my phone." He opened the passenger door of the black BMW sedan. He'd already loaded the shopping bags in the backseat while she'd been preoccupied. "I had hoped I could talk you into dinner."

She hadn't expected the shopping outing to lead to more. And dinner definitely sounded like *more*. But after that kiss in his home theater, she'd been thinking about him all the time.

Imagining what might have happened if she hadn't retreated to her room that night.

"Dinner?" She met his gaze.

"The timing is perfect," he told her reasonably. Before he leaned fractionally closer, his voice lowering. "And I have been forthright about wanting to know you better."

A clear invitation.

Her heart beat faster.

"You have." She appreciated that. It made things easier with their working relationship that he'd put the ball in her court about how things would advance. Or not. "Can we just commit to that much? A get-to-know-you dinner?"

"Dinner only." He nodded as she slid into the passenger seat. "Dessert optional. I'm game. I'd like to spend a couple of hours learning more about what makes Lydia Walker tick."

His words circled around her mind as he walked to the driver's side door and started the car.

"You're serious about that?" She thought of all the men her mother had dated—and there had been many. She wondered if any of them had ever taken the time to really understand the real Fiona Walker.

She couldn't help but admire James for going to the effort.

"Of course. We should play a round of twenty questions or something. Make it fun."

The idea appealed to her, especially since she knew that James had been dealing with a lot recently. Not just the death of his sibling, but adjusting to a child in his life and the demands on his time from his relatively new position as Texas Cattleman's Club president.

Her own frustrations—mainly with Gail, but also with her mom—seemed small by comparison. Gail would come back to Royal sooner or later and Lydia would help her find a way to repay James if only in child care help. As for their mom, Lydia had to make Fiona understand she wasn't going to be a part of her wedding.

"I like it. Who goes first?" She didn't ask where they were going to dinner, although she was a little curious. It had been a long time since she'd been on a date.

And there was no denying it now that the shopping outing had turned to dinner—this *was* a date.

"Lydia, you wound me. Ladies first, of course."

"Sorry." She grinned as she shifted in her seat to see him better. "My usual male companions are in the one-to ten-year-old demographic, and they don't always have the manners you do. But if I'm going first, I want to know what you do for fun."

"For fun?"

"Yes. I've seen you work on the ranch and at the club. But even a busy man like you needs to unwind. And I know you don't take in a movie in the home theater since you've only used that for work."

He took his time thinking. "I used to do saddle bronc riding," he said finally. "I quit once I took on full responsibilities as the head of Double H, but I always enjoyed it."

There was a wistfulness in his voice that made her wonder how long it had been since responsibilities had consumed all his time. She wanted to learn so much more about him.

"You deserve a new hobby," she settled for saying instead.

"Inspire me, then. What do you do for fun?" He turned her question back on her as they drove under streetlights draped with wreaths and holiday lights.

"I'm a nanny. I play all the time."

"If you needed to unwind, I guarantee you peekaboo isn't your first choice for entertainment."

She smiled. "Point taken. I like hiking. I don't get to go often anymore, but growing up I liked taking my siblings onto the trails in the Ozarks."

"Sounds nice. Although you have to admit, you might need to update your hobbies, too, if your best memories of hiking are from when you were growing up." He turned off the main road and it took her a moment to see the sign for The Bellamy.

"We can't have dinner here." She'd never been to the five-star resort inspired by George Vanderbilt's iconic French Renaissance chateau in North Carolina, but she'd seen photos and knew the place epitomized luxury.

"Of course we can. You like to visit the farmers market on Saturdays at the Courtyard Shops, right?"

She'd told him as much during their shopping outing today.

"Yes. And the farmers market is more my speed for a meal." Even at night, she could see the gorgeous, castle-like building looming ahead and all lit up. The stone turrets had huge holiday wreaths adorned with red bows, while white lights illuminated a massive poinsettia tree out front. So romantic. Anticipation heated through her.

"The Bellamy has a great farm-to-table restaurant, the Glass House. You'll love it." He was already pulling up to the valet stand.

"I'm not sure I'm dressed appropriately," she told him before he could lower the window.

"It's not overly glitzy, I promise." With the car in Park, he took her hand in his, his clasp firm and gentle all at once. "The emphasis is on great food, not decor. And you look beautiful."

She warmed at his words. She'd never been the glamorous type, but she appreciated that he saw beyond the superficial, that he saw *her*.

And wanted her.

"In that case, thank you," she said, her heart beating faster. "And based on our first round of questions, it seems like we owe it to ourselves to have some fun, don't we?"

"I'm on a mission tonight." He lifted her hand in his, kissing the back of it. "We're going to unwind and have fun."

Her skin tingled where his lips had touched her, leaving her breathless. For a moment, she forgot all about dinner, her brain stuck on the feel of his mouth on her. She'd signed on for this. Dinner. Getting to know him. A date.

And if a little shiver of nerves scuttled through her to think about what that meant—getting into a relationship with her boss—she chose to ignore it. She had worked hard. Like James, she'd taken on a lot of responsibilities at a young age. She'd always been the one to deny herself what she wanted to help out her family, while her mother and her sister certainly never thought twice about indulging themselves. Why couldn't she have a chance to do something a little wild? A little reckless?

If tonight presented her with a chance to simply enjoy herself on the arm of a handsome man intent on charming her, Lydia wasn't going to refuse.

In fact, given how much she wanted him, she might be the one to suggest they go for dessert after all.

Eight

"This is amazing." Lydia closed her eyes after a bite of the wood-roasted mushrooms midway through their dinner, clearly savoring the experience.

James hadn't eaten at the Glass House before, but he had to admit he was impressed, too. The farm-to-table restaurant had a tasting menu and he'd talked her into trying it with him so they could see what they liked best. So far, there hadn't been a bad dish in the lot, each new plate boasting locally farmed fruits and vegetables, plus cheeses made on-site and wines from an extensive cellar. Lydia professed a special love of the mushroom dish, though, even after their waiter had delivered tasting plates of smoked trout, grilled guinea hen and roasted duck.

They sat at a quiet table in the back that overlooked The Bellamy grounds, including an ornamental garden decorated with white lights for the holidays. Inside, a pianist played in the front of the restaurant, the sound pleasantly dulled for conversing thanks to the live plants and potted trees that served as the main decor. Even inside, the Glass House was full of greenery.

"It's good to see you enjoying yourself since we now know that we both work too hard." He'd been surprised to realize how long it had been since he'd taken any time for fun when she'd asked him about it earlier.

Lydia sipped her wine, a pinot noir the sommelier had paired for this course.

"I'm very fulfilled by my work," she said as she replaced her glass on the table near a tray full of white votive candles and interspersed with white poinsettia blooms. "So I'm not sure that I necessarily devote too much time to it. But I could probably balance the job with more fun outlets."

"And yet your job with the child care facility will be different from what you've been doing, right?" he asked, liking the way she'd let her guard down tonight. "Why the change?"

"I thought it would be rewarding to oversee more children. To potentially touch more kids' lives than I could as a nanny." She pushed back from the table slightly, crossing her legs in a way that had her calf brush against his for a moment.

Her gaze darted to his, awareness from that touch pinging back and forth between them. Heat rising from even that brief contact. Was she finding it as tough to refrain from more as him? That kiss they'd shared was never far from his mind.

"Yet you've been taking care of kids your whole life. Or so it seemed to me when I read your mother's blog."

That flash of heat he'd seen in her eyes faded a bit,

and he partially regretted bringing it up. But hadn't they said they were going to get to know each other?

"The *House Rules* empire is built on a whitewashed version of my family. The truth bears little resemblance to the fiction she posts online." She stopped speaking when their waiter neared to clear the plates from the meal and bring them the next round of the tasting menu, a selection of desserts.

The restaurant had grown more crowded since they'd started their meal, the muffled conversations of other diners rising though their corner of the room remained private.

Once the waiter left, Lydia dipped her spoon in the ginger ice cream while James wondered how to get their conversation back on track. He wanted Lydia first and foremost. But until she was ready for things to move forward between them, he would at least make sure he understood her more. Find out what made her tick.

"So you weren't involved with raising your siblings?" he asked, wondering how she could have faked all that knowledge she'd seemed to have in the videos online where she gave mini-lessons to parents on making homemade baby food or how to swaddle an infant.

"I was very involved," she clarified while he scooped some of the strawberry sorbet onto his plate. "But we weren't the carefree family my mother tried to pretend when she wrote blogs about our outings to the mountains or a day at the lake. While she was making daisy chain crowns with one kid for a good photo op, I was chasing six others to keep them from drowning or falling off a cliff."

He waited a beat to see if there was a follow-up to

that story. An indication that she'd been exaggerating. But she simply swirled her spoon through the ice cream and took another bite.

"Didn't anyone else from your mother's business notice? Or get involved to help?"

"For years, there was no one else in the business. It wasn't until my late teens that the YouTube videos took off and started driving traffic to her blog, expanding her reach to what it is today." She set aside her spoon and leaned back in her seat while the pianist switched to a holiday tune on the far side of the restaurant.

Lydia's hazel eyes met his, and she swept a lock of her light brown hair away from her face. She wore a long skirt and a creamy-colored sweater belted at her waist, the shawl collar parting enough to show a hint of the pink tank she wore beneath it. A long gold necklace full of tiny charms nestled at the V of the sweater's opening, her initial glinting in tiny amber-colored stones on one of the pendants that dangled between her breasts.

"In that case, your mother owes a great deal to you for her success." He nudged a plate of green apple cobbler toward her to tempt her. "Not just for watching your siblings while she worked, but also for creating all those videos."

She arched an eyebrow at him. "Please don't tell me you watched any of my videos. I sound like the world's most pompous seventeen-year-old."

"I'm not going to lie. I was too curious about how to swaddle a baby to pass that one up. But I thought you sounded like a very knowledgeable young lady."

Shaking her head, she gave a wry laugh. "I made those videos after I argued with my mother. I told her she was doing her visitors a disservice by emphasizing child-centered learning to the point where her kids were no longer being parented. I thought she should provide more practical advice."

"So she let you do the work for her, and you made the videos." From what he'd seen when he visited the blog, Lydia's videos were the biggest draw.

"It was her way of putting my experience in my own hands," she said drily. "She would say that she gave me all the resources I needed to have a meaningful childhood. And she did give me a percentage of the advertising dollars that those videos made. But I always resented not being able to attend college full-time because I was scared to leave the younger kids unattended."

How different their childhood years had been. Lydia had been raised by a woman whom many people looked up to as a role model for motherhood, surrounded by siblings. James and his brother had been raised by nannies once their mother died, their father too involved with the ranch to spend time with his kids.

"And yet you went into a profession centered on children. You must look forward to having a family of your own one day."

The observation was automatic, and maybe too personal. But he was curious.

"One day," she acknowledged, a hint of wariness in her expression.

He wanted to know more about her, to ask more about her family, but she leaned closer to him then, her fingers sliding onto his wrist where his hand rested on the table. The contact robbed him of whatever he'd been about to say while her light fragrance teased him, stirring a different hunger.

"You're getting way ahead of me on the questions," she announced, her hair sliding forward as she tipped her forehead closer to his. "It must be my turn by now."

He wanted to kiss her. Would have kissed her if they were alone. Maybe it was just as well they'd spent the day together out in public. Because without Teddy around, he couldn't help but see Lydia as a desirable woman and not as his nephew's nanny.

"By all means." His voice lowered since she was so close to him. "Ask me anything."

She stared back at him, her hazel eyes reflecting the candlelight's glow. He lifted his free hand to smooth her silky hair away from her face so he could see her better. Or maybe he simply needed to touch her in some way.

When he tucked the strands behind her ear, he skimmed his fingertips down the side of her neck. Felt the wild race of her pulse just beneath her ear. Once they were alone, he promised himself he would kiss her right there, for a long, lingering taste.

Her eyelids fluttered even now, as if she could feel the burning imprint of his lips on her skin.

"I hope you mean that." She eased back a bit, nibbling on her lower lip as her hand slid away from his wrist. "Because I've been wondering where things stand with Teddy's grandparents. You said you'd reached out to them. Have they expressed an interest in taking him in?"

The question was a far cry from what he'd expected. But he'd been honest about wanting to know more about her. So he needed to let her understand him better, too. He'd made a mistake with his wife not to give her a clearer idea of what life would be like on the Double H. It would have benefited them both to discuss their expectations.

"I get the impression they're still grieving deeply for their daughter." He hadn't wanted to push them, but their lack of response the first time had made him send a follow-up letter. "They were still struggling with the loss, even though from what Parker told me, they were unhappy with her for marrying him in the first place and hadn't spoken to their daughter after the wedding."

Lydia shook her head, her expression showing dismay while the waiter cleared plates and refreshed their water.

"James, isn't that all the more reason for you to raise Teddy instead of them? You can't let that sweet baby go to a cold and unforgiving household who will have nothing positive to say about Teddy's father."

He didn't miss the hint of accusation in her voice. In her eyes.

"Parker always thought they'd come around." James had trusted his brother's judgment of his in-laws. "They didn't necessarily dislike Parker, but they had planned for their daughter to marry the rancher with land neighboring theirs. Her marriage to my brother caused them to lose some of their acreage to the neighbor."

James hadn't remembered all the details since he'd been knee-deep in expanding the Double H at the time and marrying Raelynn. His focus had been on his own bride.

"That hardly seems like grounds for not speaking

to your own daughter." Lydia toyed with the petal of one of the white poinsettias on the table, her pink manicured fingernail tracing the outline. "What if they cut Teddy off that way? Decide to stop speaking to him?"

James reached over to squeeze her hand, needing to reassure her. "I promise I would never let my nephew go into a home unless I was certain he would be raised with love."

He owed Parker that, and more.

Her eyes searched his. And whatever she saw there must have eased her concerns somewhat because some of the tension slid from her shoulders.

"Thank you." She nodded. Accepting. "Can I ask one more thing? Since you were ahead of me in the question game?"

"Is this one going to be as dicey as the last one?" He signed the tab the waiter had left on the table, and then sat back, wanting Lydia to feel comfortable talking to him.

He wasn't going to reach the level of intimacy he craved with her if she couldn't speak freely to him. And he wanted her more with each passing minute.

"Possibly." She recrossed her legs, her calf nudging his for a second time. "Can I still ask?"

Awareness flared from the contact. Hotter this time. His thoughts about what he wanted from this night threatened to derail his focus.

"Of course." He couldn't stop himself from threading his fingers through hers.

She stared at him in the candlelight, the loveliest woman he could imagine. Not just because of her looks, but because of her giving nature. Her warm heart. He wanted to lose himself in all that beautiful inner radiance.

But before she could ask him her next question, a feminine voice trilled from behind them.

"James Harris, you gorgeous man! Where've you been hiding?"

He recognized the voice of Cady Lawson, an outrageous flirt and an old friend. He knew exactly when Lydia spotted her because her luscious lips turned into a quick frown before an unreadable mask settled over her expression. She tugged her hand from his. Folded her arms across her chest.

Standing to introduce the women, James wondered how fast he could send Cady on her way so he could get this night back on track.

If Lydia had been the jealous type, she guessed the arrival of James's lady friend could have ruffled her feathers. Dressed in sleek white leather pants and a designer white silk blouse, the woman was beautiful enough to have walked out of the pages of a magazine. Glossy dark curls spilled over her shoulders, her natural beauty not needing any adornment as she flung her arms around James.

But as Lydia listened to James's introduction to Cady Lawson, a friend from his college days, Lydia could think only how grateful she was for the woman's timing. Lydia had been about to quiz James about the fact that he'd married a woman who hadn't wanted children—a significant detail she'd caught in that first conversation she'd had with him about his ex. But with all the heated awareness between them, and his tempting touches, she'd found herself wanting to back off a question that was probably—at this stage of their relationship—none of her business.

She'd used the twenty questions game to find out enough to know she cared about him, and that she appreciated his willingness to be forthright with her. Was it really necessary to have her every curiosity about him answered before she indulged in the attraction? No doubt her mother's haste to rush into relationships had made Lydia overly cautious.

At least, she hoped it had. She never wanted to be the kind of woman who catapulted into romance.

So even though James wore a wary expression as he conducted his conversation with the absurdly beautiful—and overtly flirtatious—Cady, Lydia found herself thankful for the reprieve from a dicey conversation. Apparently Cady was from Royal but lived in Dallas now, and had met a few friends at the Glass House for dinner.

"Well, I hope you know I would have attended that bachelor auction fundraiser if you'd been on the slate," Cady teased James, winking at Lydia. "I heard it through the grapevine that's why you took the Texas Cattleman's Club job as president. To keep yourself off the auction block."

Lydia found herself smiling. That sounded like the man who preferred to work over having fun.

They spoke for another moment before one of Cady's friends waved her back to their table.

"I really should go." She made a point of squeezing Lydia's shoulder in a friendly gesture. "It was nice meeting you, Lydia. Take care of him. He's a keeper."

The woman wouldn't have heard even if Lydia had tried to reply since she hurried away on metallic silver pumps that looked worthy of Cinderella herself. Instead, she glanced up at James, who could only shake his head.

"I'm sorry about that—"

Lydia cut him off and rose to her feet. "No need to apologize for having glamorous friends. I'm ready to go home, if you are."

"Of course. I hope you didn't feel rushed."

"Not at all." She slid her arm through the crook of his elbow, grateful for the chance to redirect the evening. "I was ready to leave."

"What about your question?" He readjusted her hand on his arm, covering it with his. Tucking her closer. "You were just about to throw me back in the hot seat."

She caught a hint of his aftershave as she glanced up at him, eye level with his jaw.

"I changed my question," she confided as he opened the door for her and passed the valet his ticket.

The cool night air made her step even closer to him and he wrapped his arm around her waist, his hand an inviting warmth on her hip.

"You did?" The question was a deep vibration of sound against her ear as he kissed her hair there.

Pleasurable shivers raced up and down her spine, his voice enticing her. She half wished the valet wouldn't return with the vehicle so they could stand this way longer.

Then again, the sooner the car came, the sooner they'd be back at his home with the night ahead of them.

"Yes." She knew what she wanted, and she didn't want to be cautious about it anymore. "I just want to ask you, how fast can you get us home so we can be alone?"

* * *

As it happened, James had gotten them home very quickly.

Lydia hadn't realized that The Bellamy was so close to the Double H since they'd made a stop at the shops before dinner. A fire flamed hot inside her on the ride home, her body tense from holding back now that she'd decided to move forward with this out-of-control attraction. But before she knew it, James was steering the luxury sedan into the third bay of the ranch's main garage. The overhead door closed silently behind them.

"I just need to pay the sitter." He switched off the engine and exited the car, opening her door a moment later to offer his hand. "I'll meet you upstairs?"

She touched him only briefly, just enough to let him help her from the vehicle. If her hands lingered on him now, she feared she might not be able to pry herself away again.

As it was, his eyes dipped to her legs where her coat parted, the gaze smoking over her skin like a caress.

"Okay." She nodded, breathless from the contact. From thoughts of where tonight was going to lead. "I'll check on Teddy."

She hurried ahead of him when he let her inside the house, rushing up the stairs before she ran into one of the household staff or the sitter. She had used up all her restraint where this man was concerned, and she didn't want to risk any more delays.

Stopping by her room to shed her coat and her shoes, Lydia wondered if this was how her mother felt when she fell for a new man. Padding barefoot into her bathroom to run a brush through her windblown hair, Lydia recalled that it seemed like Fiona was in a mental fog when she met someone new. Her mom's starry-eyed attempts to get any work done were hampered by an inability to focus, an almost giddy preoccupation with the new man. Lydia had thought it looked more like a sickness than romance. But for the first time, as she stared into the mirror and her own bright eyes, she had an inkling of that sweetly off-balance feeling, a sensation no other man had ever stirred.

She hoped it was just because she'd ignored the attraction for so long. Surely that's why it felt so over the top.

Setting the hairbrush on the sleek white quartz counter beneath the rustic wood-framed mirror, Lydia left the bathroom to check on Teddy for the night.

The nursery door was slightly open, making it easy to slip into the boy's room. The new airplane night-light she'd bought for him glowed blue on the far side of the room, giving her enough light to see his face. Eyes closed, his arms rested on either side of his head, his green cotton sleeper snapped up to his neck. Lydia leaned over the crib to tug a lightweight blanket over his legs.

Turning on her heel, she almost ran into a solid wall of muscle and man.

James.

He steadied her shoulders, his hands an inviting warmth as they slid down her arms. She realized he'd taken off his shoes, too. No wonder she hadn't heard him on the plush carpet behind her.

"Sorry." He breathed the word into her ear before he glanced into the crib to see Teddy for himself. "Looks like he's down for the count."

Her heart beat too fast. James still held her hand, his fingers interlacing with hers.

"Is the sitter gone?" she asked, breathless and hoping that it sounded like she whispered on purpose.

"She is." He drew her out the door and into the hall with him before tugging her toward the master bedroom.

She hadn't seen that room on her tour of the house.

The arched double doors at the end of the corridor had been a source of intrigue for her other times during the past weeks. Now, as he turned the handle and opened them, she stepped over the threshold into his private retreat for the first time.

He let go of her hand to twist the lock, sealing them in the sitting area of the suite. Heavy linen curtains were drawn across one wall that she knew must be the bank of windows overlooking the front grounds. A stone fireplace held a stack of wood logs, and a steel-gray sectional sofa filled a corner near built-in bookshelves full of dark leather volumes. Framed paintings of stylized rodeo horses hung in a cluster above the mantel.

And, on the far side of the room, a massive four-poster bed.

James reached in the pocket of his jacket and withdrew the nursery monitor receiver. He set it on the wooden chest that served as a coffee table before returning to stand before her.

He made a point of checking his watch before he spoke.

"So, to answer your question from back at the restaurant, it seems I could have you home—and alone—in nineteen minutes." He relaxed his arms at his sides.

Stepped fractionally closer. "I have to admit I'm curious where you wanted things to go from here."

Her heart beat so loudly now she could feel the rush of blood in her ears, a vibration that drowned out everything else.

"Would you like me to be explicit?" She didn't know where she found that surge of boldness, but she smoothed the lapel of his jacket between her thumb and fingers, gliding up the fabric. "Or shall I just show you?"

She saw the flare of his nostrils. The way his pupils dilated so his eyes were almost black. She liked knowing she had that effect on him, too.

"I think I've gone past the point where I can handle anything explicit." He traced the line of her jaw with his knuckle, a teasing caress when she needed so much more. "I'll take the hands-on demonstration."

Heat tickled its way up her spine. And back down. Desire tantalizing her as her breathing grew ragged.

Arching up on her toes, she twined her arms around his neck, pressed herself to him and kissed him the way she'd been dying to for weeks.

Nine

Her kiss felt like he'd reached the oasis after a long slog through the dessert.

James let the sensations roll over him as he anchored her against him. Her vanilla-and-floral fragrance, the silky sweep of her hair feathering along his shoulders, the soft, feminine curves molding to the hard planes of his body. All of it was so damned scintillating.

And that kiss.

Her lips moved with a ravenous hunger he'd only guessed at in the weeks leading up to this moment. For so long, she'd been the consummate professional. So careful to present her capable, efficient side to the world, that seeing this facet of her reminded him that she'd trusted him with something special.

He refused to waste a second of it. Easing back to

look at her, he placed a kiss on her cheek. Each of her closed eyes.

"Come with me." Releasing his hold on her, he took her hand and led her toward the bed.

She paused a second before following him, and he realized she was reaching for the nursery monitor. Would he have forgotten? Maybe. But surely they would have heard him even from the other side of the large suite.

She'd slipped off her boots earlier, and her feet were soundless on the floor behind him. Her long skirt swished against his calf, a teasing caress as they reached the edge of the mattress. He hit the remote by the bed to dim the lights except for the two sconces flanking the fireplace.

He waited while she set the nursery monitor beside the remote on the nightstand, reminding himself not to rush this. To savor every moment of having her here with him.

But Lydia wasn't waiting. Because her fingers were already unfastening the top button of his shirt, her lips pressing a kiss to the skin she bared. Propelling him to a new tier of craving for her.

Heat flared over his skin. He skimmed a touch down her shoulders, tugging at the belted sweater, parting the shawl collar until he could see more of the silky tank she wore beneath. He bent to kiss her neck, liking the way she arched into him. He felt her heartbeat race in the soft hollow below her ear. Lingered there until he nipped her earlobe and peeled her sweater the rest of the way down.

Her soft moan coincided with her fingers' speeding up on his shirt buttons. Her hips sidled against him, a sign of the same restless ache he was feeling. An ache that had become second nature to him in the last week. The trip to Houston hadn't helped him douse it. If anything, time apart had only made him want her more.

With a fierceness he'd never felt for any woman.

Maybe that's why he was so careful not to let that hunger rule him now. Being with Lydia felt like uncharted terrain for him. An all-new experience.

"More naked," she demanded against his ear, her voice a breathless whisper he couldn't ignore.

He tugged her sweater off. Skimmed the silky tank up over her head, leaving her in the long skirt and a band of sheer lace around her breasts. The rosy peaks of her nipples tempted him, but Lydia was already sliding his shirt off.

"I meant you," she clarified, twisting to unfasten a hook on the side of her skirt that sent the pleated wool to the floor almost at the same time as his shirt joined it. "It's you who needs to be more naked."

She moved quickly now that she'd made up her mind to go through with this night, but James had been waiting so long to touch her he wanted to savor everything about her.

Sheer gray lace hugged her hips at the juncture of long, slender legs. The sight of her made him realize that taking his time wasn't going to work. Not when she trembled that way, her fingers jittery with anticipation and need.

He reeled her closer, wrapping her in his arms. Kissing her until some of that tension turned hot. Molten. She gripped his shoulders and he lifted her up, clamping an arm around her waist. He reached behind them to rake back the covers before he laid her down, her hair spilling over the pillowcase.

Lying down beside her, he kissed and touched her, finding the places she liked best. A kiss under her ear. A touch on the curve of her hip. Skimming across her belly. Cupping the lace between her legs.

The soft, whimpering sounds she made while he caressed her fueled his restraint, every throaty sigh steeling his resolve to wait. To bring her pleasure first. Ignoring the heated ache for her, he shifted all his focus on Lydia.

Ever so slowly, he rolled away the thin lace barrier over her breasts so he could tease one nipple with his tongue. She wrapped a hand around his back, palm splayed, holding him close. Drawing on the taut peak harder, he slid aside the lace between her legs, stroking her there.

Her breathing grew harsh, her short nails grazing his skin. Her back arched, her hips pushing against his hand until the tension broke in lush spasms that racked her whole body. A beautiful release that filled him with as much satisfaction as any of his own. He kissed her neck in the aftermath, holding her close until her heartbeat slowed a little.

Still a little dazed by the sweet shimmer of every nerve ending, Lydia had almost caught her breath when he slid out of bed. Before she could protest, she watched as his hands moved to his belt.

Just like that, the heat inside her flared again. That fast, her body reminded her of a new ache. The hunger for him returning. Wriggling out of her twisted lace underthings, she shed her clothes while he tossed aside the rest of his and returned to the mattress beside her.

He placed a condom on the nightstand. Gauntlet dropped.

She wrapped herself around him, arms twining behind his neck while he rolled her on top. She could feel how ready he was for her and it sent another shiver through her. Anticipation mingling with breathless desire.

When he kissed her this time, there was no holding back. No careful wait while she found release. This kiss was hungrier, a little less controlled. And she loved it.

She explored his body with her hands and mouth, reveling in the perfectly formed muscle, the taut strength evident with every flex and movement. When she kissed lower, though, tempted to give him the same kind of pleasure he'd shown her, he rolled her to her back. Pinning her briefly to the bed before he knelt up to find the condom on the nightstand.

She arched against him, hurrying him with frenzied movements of her hips. Her hands. She couldn't wait another moment.

And then, finally, he made room for himself between her legs. Entered her with a slow, perfect slide of their bodies together. The sensation stole her breath, her body slowly accommodating him while ribbons of pleasure trickled through her. She closed her eyes, savoring it, wanting to hold on to it for as long as she could.

But he started moving, and the magic of that only took her higher. Hotter. She was mindless again, all caution shredded and burnt to ashes as she clung to him, chanting her pleasure against his ear while they drove each other wild.

By the time he took her hands in his, holding them over her head while he kissed her, she was lost to everything but this moment and the man. He reared back to look at her, his dark eyes locking on her for a long moment before he lowered his head to suckle her breast.

Sending her catapulting over the edge, release sweeping through her in one exquisite wave after another.

She wasn't sure if the squeeze of her body was what spurred his release or if he'd been that close already, but their voices mingled in a hoarse song of fulfillment. His a throaty shout, hers a high cry of perfect bliss.

He rolled to her side afterward, tucking her against him while she breathed in the scent of his skin. His jaw rested on her hair, the slight bristle of whiskers catching on her hair. She nuzzled deeper into the crook of his neck, more content than she had a right to be.

But she refused to think about that now. Not when everything inside her glowed with pleasure. She planned to hold on to this feeling for as long as she could. To simply be.

As their breathing slowed and Lydia thought she might doze off, a wail erupted from the speaker on the baby monitor.

A real-world reminder that this night hadn't changed anything and that she still had a job to do. Nothing could have brought home faster the fact that she'd just slept with her boss.

But even as she righted herself to find her clothes, James gently pressed her shoulders back to the mattress.

"I'll get him." He brushed a caress over her hair. Kissed her forehead. "Don't go anywhere."

She thought about protesting, since she really didn't mind. She had missed Teddy today while he'd been with the sitter and she found herself looking forward to seeing him, if only to comfort him for a few minutes before putting him back to bed. But her nanny training told her it would be better for James to do that. To build the bond between the toddler and the man Lydia hoped would become his father.

"Okay." She smiled as James stepped into his boxers and shrugged his way into a T-shirt. "Thank you."

But as she watched him scoop up his phone and leave the room, she couldn't help but think it strange that her professional life had dictated her actions now instead of her personal preferences. Even though this evening had been the furthest thing from professional.

Tucking the covers higher under her chin, Lydia hoped she could figure out a way to balance the two sides sooner rather than later. Because she'd just experienced only her first taste of behaving with a little reckless abandon. She couldn't bear to return to her careful, cautious self just yet.

James paced around the nursery with his nephew asleep on his shoulder half an hour later, not ready to put him back in his crib quite yet.

Part of the reason was because he guessed Lydia would have dozed off by now, too, so no need to rush. But the other reason that had him still pacing? He knew that bringing Lydia to his bed tonight would have repercussions. She wasn't a woman to get involved lightly. He knew that in his bones. Yet here he was, risking losing a nanny he desperately needed just to be with her.

He tipped his cheek to his nephew's curls, stroking the baby's back while he stared at the stuffed felt figures that Lydia had strung along one wall. A bunny in a Santa hat. A couple of cats dressed like elves, one hammering a toy train and the other sewing a doll. She was so good at her job. Compassionate. Warmhearted.

She had come into James's life for Teddy's sake, but she'd brought a whole lot of happiness for both of them. Was it fair to Teddy to deprive the boy of Lydia if he went to live with his maternal grandparents? Thinking about parting with the child was getting tougher every day, but James had to do what was best for him.

Settling the baby back into the crib, James stepped out of the nursery and into the hall to check his phone. He'd seen a message from Teddy's grandmother while they'd been out shopping, but he hadn't responded to her yet. He reread it now.

We gratefully accept your invitation to spend the new year with our grandson, Samantha Mason had written in a short email. We will be arriving in midafternoon on New Year's Eve and can watch Teddy for you that evening and the next day. Thank you for opening your home to us so we can get to know our grandson.

There was nothing in the note about taking Teddy full-time. But James understood they wanted to meet the boy first. Still, it shouldn't be like a job interview where Teddy had to perform well in order for his grandparents to want to raise him.

Either they wanted the child or not.

Still, this was a step in the right direction, he hoped.

Teddy needed a more stable family than what James could provide. Plus, he deserved the tender touch of a mother figure in his life.

Opening an email screen for a response to Mrs. Mason, James tapped out a quick reply, confirming the details of their trip to Royal. The annual Texas Cattleman's Club New Year's Eve Ball was that night, and this way, Lydia would be available to accompany him.

James clicked the button to send the email and then strode back to the bedroom. He knew Lydia wanted to attend the New Year's Eve Ball for networking purposes, to find potential clients for the day care business she would open next fall. But he hoped she would be pleased to attend as his guest so they could share more incredible nights like this one.

He looked forward to thinking about how to invite her. Maybe with an extravagant Christmas present as a hint—earrings or a necklace, something beautiful to wear—could be his segue to asking her.

They had a lot of fun ahead of them. Together.

But first things first, he planned to slide back into his bed beside her. Kiss her. Touch her. Wake her slowly, in the most seductive way imaginable.

Ten

Christmas Eve day passed in a whirl of holiday preparations, and Lydia had so much fun with James and Teddy that she felt a twinge of guilt by the time the evening rolled around. She hadn't phoned her mother. Hadn't tried calling Gail.

But as she watched Teddy and James lying side by side in the living room, making "snow" angels in giant piles of cotton balls, she couldn't muster much regret about her family. They hadn't phoned her either. A fact that made her wonder why she always had to be the one to give. Was it so wrong to soak up the fun with the Harris males? One, a giggling, overtired toddler patting the cotton ball snow onto his head. The other, an exceedingly attractive rancher who had hurdled all her defenses and inspired her to start thinking about her own wants for a change.

Maybe it was high time she did just that.

Seeing how much fun her two companions were having while they played at least reassured her she'd done one thing right in helping James to be more comfortable in his father role. There was no denying he was good at this.

"Mrs. Davis is going to wonder what happened when she gets home from her holiday with family and finds cotton everywhere for the next two weeks," James observed as he sat up. Fluffy white balls rolled off his shoulders, disappearing under the sofa.

For her part, Lydia was happy to have the house to themselves for three whole days. The cook, the housekeeper and the extra part-time staffers were all on vacation for Christmas. At least now she didn't have to pretend there was nothing going on between her and her sexy employer.

"I'll vacuum it up," she assured him, her gaze wandering over him appreciatively. "It was my idea."

"You're not allowed to clean." Something heated glinted in his eyes as he leaned closer to her, kissing her hands where they rested on her knees. "I'm pulling rank on you with that one. Besides, we can turn the cotton into a tree skirt, right?" He shoved a pile closer to the fifteen-foot Fraser fir near the windows. "It will look like it snowed in here."

"What should we do with the tired little boy in the middle of the floor?" She smiled to see Teddy carefully pulling apart a cotton ball, his fingers picking at the fluffy strands before he waved a hand impatiently to remove the tufts.

James was already on his feet, scooping Teddy up in his big, strong arms. "I'll only put him in bed if I can trust you not to clean anything while I'm gone."

Lydia rose, following him so she could wipe the remnants from the baby. "It's a deal, but let me make sure he doesn't have any extra pieces on him." She picked off a few bits clinging to his sleeper, making Teddy giggle. Then she carefully examined his hands. "My little sister got a strand of hair wrapped around her toe once inside her footie pajamas, and we had to take her to the ER to have the hair removed."

"You went to the ER for a strand of hair?"

"When it winds tightly enough, it can cut off circulation." She stepped back. "But he looks good to me."

James shook his head as he spoke to Teddy. "Champ, it looks like we're going to have to change your sleeper and examine all your toes now." He glanced back at Lydia before he started up the stairs. "And I've got an early present for *you* when I'm done. Don't go anywhere."

Something about the tone of his voice sent a shiver of awareness through her. Waking up in his arms this morning had felt incredibly decadent. Making love in the shower while Teddy napped had been even more self-indulgent. Still…

She could get used to it.

Not that she'd have the chance since this window of time with James was only temporary. Soon enough, the holidays would end, her sister would return and Lydia would convince Gail to step up and take over the nanny duties with Teddy. After all, it was still Gail who owed the debt to James, and Lydia had faith her sister would do what she could to pay him back for generously covering her donation. But could Lydia maintain a relationship with James if she was no longer working for him?

The idea tempted her.

Being with James had made her take more chances, and so far, she had reaped wonderful rewards from her gambles. Continuing to see him, to date, would be an even bigger risk. She'd never wanted to turn into a woman like her mother, falling head over heels at the drop of a hat. Yet what Lydia had with James seemed so much different from that. So much more special.

Sure, she may have felt like she'd rushed into an intimate relationship. But in comparison with how fast her mom normally moved from dating to the altar, Lydia had practically proceeded at a snail's pace.

She corralled a few rogue snowballs under the tree, liking the idea of a snowy tree skirt. Teddy had so much fun playing with the fake snow anyway, he would enjoy it tomorrow, too.

James's deep voice behind her sent a thrill through her. "Remember what I said about no cleaning?"

His arms went around her a moment later and she forgot everything but being with him. About falling for him. Maybe it would be simpler if it was just about the heated connection they shared. But that didn't begin to account for her growing feelings for this incredible man. The tenderness she experienced when she watched him play with his nephew. The respect she had for his generosity and his work ethic.

She couldn't pretend what she felt was simply attraction.

"I don't think you can boss me around when I'm not technically working now," she teased. Tipping her head back to his chest, she rubbed her cheek against all that hard strength. "And I think we'll have more fun tonight if I remain off-duty, don't you?"

"Yes." He spun her in his arms so she faced him. His eyes probed hers, his expression more serious than she'd expected. "I've been looking forward to tonight all day."

His hand cupped her cheek, cradling her face. Her heart stuttered a jerky rhythm. Had Gail felt anything close to this when she ran off on a weeks-long vacation with her bachelor?

If so, maybe Lydia owed her the tiniest bit of slack. Because right now, she could almost imagine turning her back on everything to be with him.

"Me, too," she told him honestly. As much fun as she'd had preparing for Christmas and playing with Teddy today, she'd be lying if she said she wasn't looking forward to a repeat of the night before.

The chance to be in James's arms.

"But first…" He let go of her to lead her toward the Christmas tree. "…presents."

He guided her toward the big leather sofa closest to the pine branches and waited while she took a seat. She tucked the skirt of her burgundy-colored sweater dress closer to her while she watched him retrieve a small box from the back of the tree.

Wrapped in gold foil painted with white snowflakes, the paper was elegant, the package itself curiously shaped. He handed it to her, and she could feel a flat square on one side, and a heavier square against it. Almost like he'd wrapped a card.

"I only have one gift for you," she protested, wondering if she should retrieve it. "Shouldn't I wait to open this until tomorrow?"

He lowered himself onto the sofa beside her, his hand sliding around her waist. "No. This is a bonus present for tonight. Something I wanted you to have sooner rather than later."

How quickly she'd grown used to his touch. She leaned into it now while she slid a finger into the wrapping, not wanting to tear it needlessly. Inside, there was a card with her name on it along with a smaller box. But why had he wrapped the card?

She glanced over at him, but his expression gave nothing away as he waited. Opening the envelope, she saw it wasn't a greeting card, but an invitation.

"The Texas Cattleman's Club New Year's Eve Ball?" She read the embossed letters aloud. It was one of the most anticipated and prestigious events in Royal. "Really?"

"I want you to be my date," he added. "It should be fun, and I think it would really help you meet potential clients for the child care facility."

"That's very generous of you." She was touched that he'd thought of the business that meant so much to her. "I would be honored to be there."

She didn't know what the date said about their new relationship, but he must realize that taking his nanny to the New Year's Eve Ball would be a very public way to acknowledge their relationship. Surely that implied the same level of seriousness she felt about him?

"Good." He kissed her temple and squeezed her waist a little tighter, hugging her. "Then open the next part of the gift."

Excited, she opened the foil paper carefully, then lifted the lid on a yellow-and-red box. Inside, nestled on a velvet cushion, rested an old-fashioned hair comb in art deco style, with crystals outlining three tiny skyscraper buildings.

"James, it's beautiful," she breathed, already imagining how she could wear her hair to show off the piece.

"It belonged to my mother. I have a photo of her and my father on New Year's Eve with that comb in her hair, and I would like you to have it."

Overwhelmed from the magnitude of the gesture, she shook her head. "I couldn't possibly accept a family heirloom—"

"Please." He laid his hand on her forearm. "She had an extensive collection of jewelry, and I think your kindness to her grandson warrants a thank-you. I know she would be as grateful to you as I am for all you've done to help Teddy."

Blinking away the sudden moisture in her eyes, she smiled. "In that case, thank you. I will treasure it."

She felt something shift inside her. A tender place in her heart that was just for this man. Or maybe it was the last of her defenses crumbling in the face of his warmth and generosity. No one had ever put her first the way he did.

Maybe that's why it was so easy to lose herself in his kiss when he captured her chin in one strong hand. Because giving in to the heated attraction, and the simplicity of that connection, was easier than trusting the feelings for him multiplying with every moment they spent together.

James didn't waste a second coaxing Lydia up the stairs when he wanted her right here. Right Now.

The front door was locked. He had the nursery monitor feed on his phone. So he dragged the cashmere blanket from the arm of a nearby chair and spread it out on the leather sofa behind her before he gently lowered her there.

They'd been together on multiple occasions since that first electric encounter. But far from quenching his hunger for her, each time only made him want her more.

Lydia's frenzied touches were as desperate as his own, as if not touching for hours all day long drove them to this frantic shedding of clothes. His shirt. Her shoes. He didn't even bother removing her sweater dress. Between her wriggling and his greedy hands, they had the fabric up around her waist in no time.

"Condom?" she rasped against his lips, not even bothering to open her eyes while they kissed.

"Mmm." He reached in his pocket to put the packet in her hand since he didn't feel like breaking that kiss either.

He'd waited all day to have her mouth on him.

She must have set the packet aside, because her hands wandered over his fly, stroking and seeking, speeding his pulse to a drumroll. He helped her only to save himself from the zipper, but he appreciated her desire that echoed his own. The way she touched him threatened his control.

Together, they made quick work of his pants. Her panties. And, for expediency's sake, he ended up with her straddling his lap while he rolled the condom into place.

Her hands laced behind his neck, thighs bracketing his hips as he slid inside her. She tipped her forehead to his, holding herself very still for a long moment. He waited, need for her burning through him. But when she started to move, the sweetness of it made him want to give her free rein with him. She kissed her way up his neck. His jaw. All the while moving with a hypnotic grace that had him seeing stars.

It was too soon.

He'd hardly even touched her yet. But she seemed intent on her course, pinning his hands to the sofa cushion with the light press of her fingers. Her breath was a sweet brush of air along his earlobe when she told him how good it felt.

He closed his eyes, scavenging for the control he'd exercised the night before. But between her soft words, the gentle glide of her hips and the way her fingers circled his wrists, he was burning from the inside out. He kissed her deeply, then trailed his lips down her neck to her breast. He captured the peak with his mouth, feeling the answering shiver that coursed through her right before her release hit her.

He focused on the feel of it, her body throbbing all around him, drawing him deeper. Squeezing. He couldn't have held out another second, his own completion surging hard.

He banded his arms around her, anchoring her to him while the passion burned white hot. Leaving him spent and sagging into her. Strands of her hair clung to his skin as she laid her head on his shoulder. He kissed the top of her head, wanting to carry her to his bed. To wrap her in his arms and his blankets.

"That was just a warm-up," he assured her, drawing the cashmere throw up to her shoulders.

She gave a soft laugh as she disentangled herself from him and dressed. "In that case, I'm not sure I'd survive the main event. Besides, we have Christmas presents to bring downstairs. I know Teddy is young, but he will be excited to see all the packages in the morning."

James admired her commitment to making the day special for the boy. "You're a pretty great nanny." He slid on his boxers and pants. "The women who looked after Parker and me never gave much thought to our holidays."

She regarded him silently, as if waiting for more. Making him realize how self-pitying that had sounded.

Damn.

"We had great holidays thanks to my dad." It was sort of true. Christmas was one of the few days their father didn't work. "I only pointed it out to let you know you're very generous with your time and attention."

"Every child deserves happy holiday memories." She folded her arms around herself. "And Teddy is all the more special to me because he's your family."

Her words chased around his head long after they went upstairs to bring down the presents they'd wrapped from their shopping outing, distracting him. He tried picking them apart, to figure out what it was about her statement that troubled him.

It was good she cared about his nephew.

And yes, James was grateful that she cared about him, too.

But if she was already this attached to the boy, would Lydia understand if James followed through on his resolution to let Teddy's grandparents raise him?

He had a week before the New Year's Eve Ball when the Masons arrived in town to watch Teddy for the night. He hoped it would be enough time for him to find a way to tell her that if things went well with the Masons, he wouldn't need a nanny anymore.

Eleven

Christmas Day got off to a fitful start.

Lydia hoped Teddy was just teething, but he remained grumpy and unimpressed by the holidays. He'd made grouchy sounds off and on while he played with a toy train, gripping it tightly in his hand as he pushed it around and around the floor.

She hoped it was just the toddler's irritability that made the day feel awkward. At noontime, over brunch fare in the large, eat-in kitchen, she traced an idle finger over the natural wood grain in the Texas ebony slab polished into a tabletop. Yet she returned her gaze to James again and again, wondering if something had shifted between them the day before.

James had participated fully in the cooking and preparations for the meal, but as she halfheartedly nibbled a bite of her French toast, she tried to pinpoint when things had begun to feel strained. His words about his own Christmases—that his nannies hadn't participated in the holidays—had made her wonder if she'd overstepped his expectations for her role here.

She'd always been very involved with her charges, imagining a child would thrive with that warmth of connection to a caregiver. She'd received a degree in early childhood development, patching together enough online coursework for her bachelor's over the years. But her real source of knowledge about child care came from her years in Arkansas, helping to raise her brothers and sisters. But had she brought too much of her own experience with her siblings into her nannying? Too much familiarity?

Then again, maybe James's own background skewed his perception of her role here. He'd lost his mother early and hadn't been close with his caregivers. He had loved and married a woman who hadn't wanted children, after all. A fact she'd never asked him about.

Maybe it was past time she did. Because she adored children and had crafted a profession around them. One day, she dreamed of a family of her own.

Shoving aside her half-eaten plate, she sipped her sparkling water with orange and debated how to be tactful.

The doorbell's resonant chime interrupted her thoughts.

James frowned, setting down his fork. "I wasn't expecting anyone."

Teddy piped up from his high chair where he spun the wheels on his toy train. "Hel-lo?" he asked, his brown eyes turning to Lydia. "Hello?" He opened and closed his hand in a baby wave.

Her heart melted to see him make that connection, his eyes wide with curiosity as he watched James leave the room to answer the door. The small moment made her more certain of herself and the way she did her job. Forming a bond with children she cared for was only natural. Even if she didn't have strong feelings for James, his nephew would hold a piece of her heart.

"Do you want to say hello?" she asked him, getting to her feet. "We can go see who's here."

"Who. Here." He banged his train on the tray of the high chair. "Here. Here. Here."

Lydia unbuckled Teddy's safety belt and lifted him. He hadn't eaten anything besides a few pieces of dry cereal, so he was clean enough. She settled him on her hip, straightening his navy blue reindeer sweater before striding toward the living area.

"Merry Christmas!" a feminine voice trilled from the front room as James opened the door for their guest.

Lydia's sister Gail breezed right into the house, dressed in a poinsettia-printed skirt and fuzzy red sweater. Tanned and sporting fresh caramel-colored highlights in her dark brown hair, Gail wore leather boots that appeared brand-new. Worst of all? The woman who owed a hundred thousand dollars to James came with her arms full of lavishly wrapped Christmas presents.

James appeared too surprised to return her greeting. Then again, maybe he didn't even remember what she looked like since the bachelor auction had been a month ago.

"James." Lydia cleared her throat and hurried closer, mortified that her sister would think it was okay to come by unannounced on Christmas, waltzing into James's house like a conquering hero, when she'd ignored his calls and the messages from the Pancreatic Cancer Research Foundation. "You remember my sister Gail?"

"Of course." Stepping forward, he recovered himself quickly. "Let me help you with those."

"Thank you!" Gail gushed, handing over the stack of boxes and a shopping bag to James. "I don't think we had the chance to speak at the charity event. You were a wonderful MC for the auction."

Gail's hazel eyes were bright and clear, her gaze direct as she strode deeper into the living area. As if she had absolutely no conscience about what she'd done. In that moment, with her sunny smile and perfectly primped brown curls, she bore a striking resemblance to their mother. Even her voice, relentlessly upbeat as if she could deliver a House Rules podcast at any moment, reminded Lydia of Fiona Walker.

Or maybe it was simply that, no matter how much Lydia had tried to teach her siblings about hard work and practical values, Gail preferred the laissez-faire approach to life. Both Fiona and Gail were determined that things would "work themselves out." Even astronomical bids for bachelors with money you didn't have.

Incensed, Lydia couldn't seem to make her feet move from where she stood in Gail's way, blocking her from the living area where James was putting the packages under the Christmas tree.

"He wasn't just the MC, Gail." Lydia hadn't planned to confront her sister. But the realization that Gail had turned out exactly like their mother rattled Lydia to her core. Why did she keep trying to fix her family's messes when they let her down time and time again? "As the president of the Texas Cattleman's Club, James was also the main liaison for the charity when they hosted the bachelor auction."

"Is that right?" Gail stopped her forward momentum, her smile faltering only for a moment. "How nice. Mom told me you were working here now, so I hoped we could spend some family time together. It *is* Christmas."

Teddy bounced in Lydia's arms, ready to be put down.

James moved closer, reaching for his nephew. "I can take him so you two can visit."

She handed over the child, anger at her sister building as she kept her focus on Gail. "Do you know *why* I'm working here now?"

James palmed her lower back, speaking to her quietly. "Lydia, there's no need to go into that just yet."

She disagreed. Because if Gail was audacious enough to stride in here and play the benevolent sister while Lydia worked to repay Gail's debt, a conversation was warranted.

Gail's expression shifted to something that looked like concern. "I've always known how much you enjoy children, Lydia. You have since we were little girls playing with baby dolls."

"Ba-by?" Teddy asked, bouncing excitedly in James's arms.

Lydia tensed, realizing her sister's view of their shared past was too far from her own to ever be reconciled.

"No, Gail." She dragged in a deep breath to cool down the fiery frustration. "I'm working here to help repay James, who covered your outrageous bid at the bachelor auction."

"Ba-by! Ba-by!" Teddy shouted, wriggling so hard that James had to let him down to run around the Christmas tree, his light-up sneakers flashing red and blue.

She guessed James was probably glad for the chance to escape the confrontation as he chased Teddy. Lydia hadn't meant to put him in the middle of this. Then again, she hadn't expected her sister to arrive on Christmas Day, pretending nothing had happened.

"Why would you do that?" Gail studied her, shaking her head. She spared a glance for James, who'd moved to the far side of the room where Teddy had tried to hide behind a chair.

"Why?" Exasperated, Lydia paced in a circle. "Because it's the right thing to do. Because I don't want our name attached to bad debts while we're trying to get new businesses off the ground. This is a small town. Word gets around."

"But I didn't ask for help. And I told you I'd figure things out after vacation." Gail squeezed her arm. "I can tell this is a bad time. I should have known you don't like spontaneous visits."

An old dig. Her mother had always thought that the reason Lydia didn't like impulsive family outings was because she couldn't be "spontaneous." When the truth was she simply preferred to have sunscreen packed so the kids didn't end up with third-degree burns from a day at the beach. Or she liked having swimming vests for the little ones since there were too many of them to keep an eye on in the water.

But Fiona—and apparently Gail—preferred to think

Lydia was just no fun. Overly cautious. Turning on the heel of her new leather boots, Gail headed for the door. The movement shook Lydia from her thoughts.

"So you're leaving again? Without figuring out anything?" Lydia followed her sister toward the foyer, feeling as frustrated as Teddy had this morning. It was a good thing she wasn't carrying around a toy train or she would have been tempted to throw it the way the toddler had during the gift-opening.

What was it about family that could catapult a person right back to childhood dynamics?

"Why should I try to figure it out?" Gail asked over her shoulder, her hand on the big brass handle. "You'd only do a better job of it than I would anyhow." She lifted a hand to her mouth as she called back to the living area, "Merry Christmas, James!"

Lydia felt the steam hiss slowly from her ears. "Gail, we need to talk."

"You should ask James to take you to the New Year's Eve Ball at the Texas Cattleman's Club. Lloyd and I will be there." Gail grinned again, her happiness irrepressible in the face of everything. "I'm over the moon about him."

And then Gail was gone. Sauntering off to her compact car decorated with a wreath on the grill.

Something about the vehicle, her sister's joy, even her "spontaneity," made Lydia feel like Scrooge by comparison.

"Are you all right?" James's voice over her shoulder made her realize she'd been standing at the closed door for too long.

She hadn't even heard him approach.

Pivoting to face him while he held Teddy, Lydia felt

her chest squeeze with a mixture of fierce attraction and soul-deep affection. She'd come to care for him so much. So fast.

I'm over the moon about him.

Gail's comment circled around Lydia's brain, the only words her sister had spoken today that Lydia could identify with. She knew the feeling all too well. Because she felt it for the generous, hardworking man standing in front of her.

She was over the moon for James Harris. And just as quickly as Gail had plunged into her own whirlwind relationship.

The idea of sharing something in common with her impulsive sister triggered a flicker of anxiety in her chest.

"I'm—not sure." She wanted to step into the warmth and comfort of his arms. But given that she'd known James for an even shorter length of time than Gail had known Lloyd Richardson, did that make Lydia's feeling imprudent? Unwise? "I mean, I'm upset. Obviously."

She'd never had a panic attack before, but she wondered if this was how it started. She felt unsettled. Nervous. Fidgety. She swallowed fast and tried to catch her breath.

"Why don't you come sit?" James juggled Teddy in his arms and gestured in the direction of the kitchen. "We can finish our brunch. Talk."

That sounded reasonable. Because James was a reasonable, rational person, like her. She clung to the idea with both hands as she followed him toward the kitchen. At least she hadn't bid money she didn't have to win a date with him.

No, she only started an affair with her employer.

Which, for all of her mother's hasty relationships, even Fiona had never done.

"Do you think we jumped into things too quickly?" Lydia asked as James carefully settled Teddy in his high chair.

"I think *quickly* is subjective." He seemed to choose the words carefully.

"You're right." She appreciated his thoughtful response.

Some of the worry in her chest eased. James was a good man, and just because she'd developed strong feelings for him didn't mean she was turning into her mother.

She hoped.

"Can I warm up your plate?" he asked, his hand resting on her shoulder for a moment. "Or get you something else to eat?"

His touch settled her and stirred her at the same time. But she resisted the urge to tip her head against his forearm and soak in the comfort of his presence.

"No, thank you." She returned to her seat at the long table, hoping they could address some of the things that had troubled her earlier. "I'll just have some fruit."

She appreciated the distraction of Teddy banging his train on the high chair tray while she spooned a few pieces of fruit into a serving bowl.

"I thought I heard your sister mention the New Year's Eve Ball." James helped himself to more orange juice from a glass pitcher.

"She'll be attending with Lloyd," she confirmed, wishing they could rewind time. Somehow find more even footing again. "I hope that's not too awkward."

"Of course not." He sounded sincere. "Lydia, I made

the donation because handling it that way was easiest for me. I'm not worried about anyone repaying the debt."

He'd told her that before. All along, he'd been willing to forgive the debt and simply pay her to be Teddy's nanny.

"That's very generous of you."

"It also served my best interests since I was drowning in my grief and obligations, feeling like I was failing on all fronts." He took her hand in his. Stroked his thumb along her knuckles. "I am so grateful to you for getting me through these last few weeks, Lydia. But it's still my hope that Teddy's maternal grandparents will welcome him into their home and be able to give him all the time and attention he needs."

The gentle caress of his thumb was at odds with the discordant crash of his words through her.

"You still plan to give him up?" She couldn't have possibly heard him correctly.

"The Masons are driving down from Amarillo to watch Teddy on New Year's Eve so we can attend the ball," he explained. "If things go well that night, we can start discussing how to make the transition—"

"You don't want him." She wrenched her hand from his as the harsh truth smashed through her romantic hopes and the tender feelings she'd developed for James. "You never wanted children in the first place."

"That's not true." He sat back in his chair, the space between them feeling five times bigger than the physical distance. "I will keep Teddy if things don't work out with the Masons."

"Even though your brother wanted you to raise him, you're still considering giving him up?" Hurt and anger propelled the question from her even though it was a low blow. That she wasn't being fair.

But how was he being fair to Teddy, who'd so clearly bonded with James? The child had already suffered a devastating loss with the death of his parents. How would he cope with more feelings of abandonment?

James held himself very still. Calm and controlled in the face of her anger. "You of all people should understand that our siblings don't always know what's best."

Begrudgingly, she nodded, acknowledging the point even if she didn't like it. "You're right. But I'd like to ask you one more thing. Just so I understand you better."

She had to put a lid on her feelings for him. To stop them from evolving even further. Because she had been starting to love this man.

That was the only explanation for how she could be hurting so much right now.

"I'm listening." He studied her, but his gaze was shuttered, revealing nothing of his own feelings.

Making her realize how much he'd let her in over the last weeks. How much he'd shared with her. It made losing that emotional intimacy hurt even more.

But there was no going back now. No ignoring this question that she kept returning to about him.

"When we spoke about your ex-wife," she began, twisting a cloth napkin in her lap, the linen hopelessly crumpled, "you said she didn't want children." The question was highly personal, and no doubt it revealed too much about what she felt for him. But it burned in her throat and she had to ask. "Did that mean—you didn't want children either?"

His mouth flattened into a thin line. An answer all its own even before he spoke.

"I hadn't given it much thought before Raelynn. And when she told me her wishes before the wedding… it wasn't a deal breaker for me."

She nodded awkwardly, her whole body feeling clumsy and strange. Maybe it was just because she didn't know where to put the hurt she was feeling. For her. For him. For those stupid romantic hopes that weren't ever going to amount to anything.

Because even if they were just in the early stages of a relationship, she couldn't spend her time with someone who didn't have the same kind of dreams she did for a future that would always include kids.

"I see." She stood from the table, needing to escape the table. The man. "I'll put Teddy down for his nap now."

"Lydia." James said her name with a tenderness she couldn't bear, but he didn't reach for her. Didn't touch her. "I think we should talk about this more."

"I can't." She'd been so judgmental of her mother and her sister. But their foolishness couldn't compare to hers. "I'm—sorry."

She had built her life around children. Her family. Her job. Her future. Of course she had fallen for a man who didn't want them, at least not in the way she did. There was a kind of cosmic humor in it. Maybe she'd even laugh about it one day. Fifty years from now.

She fumbled with the safety belt on the high chair, her fingers not quite working. Or maybe it was because her vision was slightly blurred from tears she wouldn't let James see.

"Lydia, please." James pushed back his chair and came to help her. "I can put him down for his nap."

Ideally, she would have been able to be a professional. To still do the job she shouldn't have taken in the first place.

But right now, she couldn't even manage that.

"Thank you," she managed, before she retreated with as much dignity as possible.

She needed the quiet of her room for a few hours. To regroup. To figure out a way out of this impossible situation that wouldn't leave Teddy without a caregiver.

But one thing was certain. Now that she understood how wrong she'd been about James and the feelings she thought they shared, she couldn't possibly remain under the same roof even one more night.

Twelve

Three days before the new year, James sat in his office at the Texas Cattleman's Club and wondered if he should call Lydia. The days after their conversation had been painful, and he felt like they still didn't have any resolution yet on where things were headed between them.

Was she really ready to call it quits between them without delving deeper into what was upsetting for her? He understood why she was upset about the plans he'd made for Teddy without telling her. Because he had a different sort of life mapped out from the one she had planned for herself. Did that mean they couldn't compromise?

He feared the answer was yes. But that didn't mean they couldn't talk about it to be sure.

James hadn't wanted Lydia to leave when Teddy was clearly so attached to her, so he'd offered to work

out of his office at the Texas Cattleman's Club for a
few days. He had plenty to do with preparations for the
New Year's Eve Ball, and the rest of the staff came in
so sporadically between the holidays that no one noticed he was sleeping on his office couch.

Or, more accurately, *trying* to sleep on the office
couch. Night after night, he couldn't stop dreaming
about Lydia, and then he'd wake up feeling empty and
alone, remembering the hurt in her eyes when he'd told
her about the Masons.

Now, with the day of the ball closing in, he wondered if she even planned to follow through on their
date. Checking the antique clock on the wall, he realized it was a quarter after nine. Past Teddy's bedtime, but not past Lydia's. Pulling in a deep breath, he
punched the number for her cell into his phone. Waited
while it rang once.

Twice.

"Hello?" Her voice sounded wary.

Even so, he was damned glad to hear it. He'd missed
the sound of her, along with so many other things.
Her scent. Her touch. The sweet way she cared for
his nephew.

"Lydia." He hadn't thought beyond getting in touch
with her. Hadn't planned for how to wade through the
awkwardness. "How are things at home?"

"Good," she answered quickly. "Fine. We're both—
fine."

Right.

"I will need to meet Teddy's grandparents at the
house midafternoon on New Year's Eve to welcome
them. I wanted some time to speak with them and review Teddy's schedule."

"Of course. It's your home." Her words were clipped, her tone distant in a way that made him think of how her joy in the past had moved him. He felt the loss all the more deeply. "And I understood from our last conversation that I'm only here until your new arrangements are in place."

He ground his teeth, unwilling to tackle a complex conversation over the phone. Especially not when she was clearly still unhappy with him.

"I had hoped we could discuss that at the New Year's Eve Ball." He had been drawn to her practicality and sense of honor from their first meeting. He'd been banking on those qualities in her to ensure she showed up for their date. "Assuming you still plan to attend with me?"

She hesitated for a moment. "Do you really think it's wise for us to spend that time together when it's become obvious that…" She cleared her throat. Began again. "When it's clear now that our hopes for the future are so far apart?"

He thought it wise to at least have a discussion about what they wanted instead of assuming the worst about each other. But he clamped his tongue on that response. Besides, he wanted to be with Lydia. Being without her this week had made him realize how just how deep his feelings ran for her.

He loved her. But was he ready to risk his heart again on another woman who wasn't in it for the long haul? Regardless of the answer to that, he couldn't share how he felt about her. Not over the phone.

"I need a date for this event." He spelled it out in the only way he thought might convince her to attend. "And you could use an introduction to people who need your child care services. So the plan is practical, if nothing else."

"I recently learned there's such a thing as being too practical for your own good," she said drily. "But since I'll be unemployed again very shortly, I can't afford to turn down a good opportunity for my business. I will attend the ball with you as planned, James."

A possibility he hadn't considered hit him, something he should have thought of for Teddy's sake. What if she planned to quit even if the Masons didn't decide to take in their grandson? But he wasn't going to push for any more during an already difficult conversation. Hopefully he wouldn't need the answer to that at all. He confirmed the time for their date before he disconnected the call.

And wondered how on earth he could win back a woman hell-bent on ending things between them.

New Year's Eve was packed with Cinderella potential.

The Texas Cattleman's Club had been transformed into a shimmering silver-and-white haven. Long chains of white gladiolas were strung from the rafters, the delicate petals rimmed with hints of metallic glitter that made them shine in the candlelight. Tall candelabra draped with silver tulle and white ribbons stood atop every table in the room. A twelve-piece orchestra played along the back of the dining area, filling the room with lilting waltzes.

Lydia had splurged on a new dress for the event. Formfitting down to a little kick hem around her knees, the gown was pale green silk organza. Pairing it with an older pair of silver strappy heels, she felt as glamorous as she possibly could. Which wasn't to say she was the most beautiful woman in the room. But she looked like she belonged for at least one night. It hurt to think she'd never be a real part of this community that meant so much to James. Tomorrow, she'd return to her old life.

Alone.

Beside her, James Harris was the man everyone wanted to speak to, his job as esteemed president of the club underscoring how well liked he was. How respected. He was genuine and charming with everyone who greeted him. But despite the fairy-tale trappings of the evening all around her, Lydia had no illusions about how the night would end.

When midnight chimed, she wasn't just going back to her old life on the other side of town. She was also losing the man she'd fallen in love with, the sweet child she'd come to adore and all her illusions about herself.

She could never return to the old Lydia who used to feel good about her smart choices, her practical approach to relationships and her professionalism. Now she had to at least admit that love could rock anyone's world, skewing their perspective and making them behave in a way they normally wouldn't. She wasn't any less susceptible to that than any other woman. While she wouldn't ever get so swept away by love that she'd forget to supervise a child the way her mother had, Lydia also realized she'd been deluding herself into thinking she wasn't vulnerable to making other mistakes.

"Would you like to dance?" James bent closer to ask after he finished up a lengthy talk about yearling prospects with another rancher.

She couldn't help the shiver that tripped down her spine as he spoke close to her ear. The attraction that had been so apparent between them from day one hadn't magically faded when she'd discovered he had no intention of keeping his nephew.

"Yes. Thank you." She nodded, knowing everything she said to him sounded stilted. But she feared if she didn't carefully monitor her words, she would say something far too revealing.

So for now, she let him lead her to the dance floor and sweep her into his strong arms. His tuxedo was custom tailored, the black wool gabardine tapering to his narrow waist. There was a hint of sheen in the lapels of the jacket on either side of the crisp white pleats of his shirt. She wondered how he could appear equally at home in a Stetson and jeans as much as Hugo Boss, but some people simply seemed extraordinarily comfortable in their own skin.

"I've been wondering what you thought of the Masons," he asked as he spun her out of an easy turn, her silk organza gown flaring slightly.

As if she hadn't already been reminding herself that she was no Cinderella, the topic of conversation gave her another dose of cold reality.

Teddy's grandparents had been younger than Lydia imagined. They'd been in their early fifties, but could have passed for a decade younger. Physically fit and well dressed, they had been polite and kind. And yet… she couldn't shake the feeling that they were all wrong to raise Teddy.

"It matters more what you think," she reminded him, making the mistake of looking into his eyes. Holding his gaze made her think of more intimate moments with him. Of the ways he'd touched and kissed her. "I may be biased since I pictured something different for Teddy."

His brows pulled together. "I wish they would have responded to me sooner when I invited them to meet their grandson in the first place." He shook his head, a hint of frustration in his voice. "I realize their relationship with their daughter had been strained after she married Parker, but wouldn't you think that would be all the more reason for them to be eager to meet Teddy?"

"Yes." She couldn't stand the idea of that little boy enduring any more upheaval in his young life. "Unequivocally, yes."

"But in their defense, everyone processes grief in their own way. They might have needed that time to mourn before they came here." His grip shifted on her waist, his palm absently stroking for the briefest moment until he seemed to catch himself and still the movement.

"Perhaps." She couldn't say anything more, her senses too overloaded by that touch. By all that she would miss when she walked away from him.

She'd probably been foolish to show up tonight, to follow through with this doomed date. But she really did need the networking opportunity that it offered. Especially since she would be without a job soon.

"The comb is pretty in your hair," he said in a low, husky tone as the dance came to an end. "I'm glad you wore it tonight."

The crowd applauded for the orchestra as they took a break in their set. Lydia clapped, too, though her chest ached at the memory of James giving her the hair comb. Of how special Christmas Eve had been when they were together just one week ago. Or the long, breathless night she'd spent in his arms afterward.

Before she could respond, the microphone in front of the orchestra rang with a harsh sound. Turning, she spotted a dashing older man at the podium. He had a full head of white hair and piercing blue eyes, his skin deeply tanned. He tugged the microphone out of its stand so he could hold it in one hand, then he strode out from behind to podium to speak. The crowd quieted to listen.

James bent closer to whisper to her, "That's Gus Slade. He's a past president of the Texas Cattleman's Club."

She recognized the rancher from around town, the feud between the Slades and the Clayton family one of the bits of Royal history she'd picked up through local gossip. She welcomed the distraction for a moment to gather her defenses against leaning into the temping man beside her.

"Sorry for the feedback, folks." Gus Slade spoke into the microphone as he strode into the center of the raised platform near the orchestra. "We'll get back to the music in a minute. But first, I hope you'll indulge me. I have an announcement to make, and I want you all to be my witnesses."

The crowd settled into an even deeper silence. They all seemed to collectively hold their breath. Lydia peered over at James to see if his face gave any indication he knew what was about to happen since he'd helped put together the event. James must have felt her gaze since he glanced her way and shrugged.

"The new year is a time for a fresh start," Gus said,

his voice strong and certain. "And more than anything, I want a chance to begin again, with the woman I love at my side." He paused for a moment, before someone turned a house spotlight on. The white-and-blue light fell around Rose Clayton seated at a table in the back. "Rose, would you do me the honor of becoming my wife?"

Rose and Gus?

The rest of the crowd seemed as stunned as Lydia felt, a shocked murmur reverberating through the well-heeled guests while Rose covered her surprised gasp with one hand, her eyes getting teary before she nodded quickly.

"Yes!" she called out across the room, standing up in her sparkly silver dress. "I will marry you, Gus Slade."

The microphone shrieked as Gus dropped it, forgotten, on the platform. He charged toward Rose with his arms open. The crowd clapped and there were a few cheers, although everyone still seemed taken aback by the proposal.

Behind her, Lydia heard a man say, "But I thought they were sworn enemies?"

Moved by the romantic gesture, Lydia felt her heart in her throat. The orchestra played a refrain from a popular country love song while someone turned off the microphone and the party got back under way. James guided Lydia from the dance floor, the romantic moment reminding her of all that was missing in their relationship.

It took her a moment to realize that she was following James out of the building into the garden, her thoughts still on the couple inside and all the love shining in their eyes. The night air was warm for December, but still a refreshing break from the crowded party rooms. It was quiet out here, where a few landscape lights gave the bushes and ornamental trees a silvery glow. More white lights outlined the walkways of smooth, decorative stone.

Here, there wouldn't be any networking opportunities for her child care business. Under the moonlight with James, there was only the two of them. Why would he bring her out here? And more important, how would she hold strong against his powerful allure?

He turned to her, his expression serious. "Seeing Gus and Rose in there made me all the more determined to speak to you about what's happening between us, Lydia."

"There's nothing else to say," she reminded him, unwilling to hurt any more than she already did. It would already be tough enough living in the same town with him. "I can't be with someone who doesn't want to have children in his life."

"But it's not that I don't ever want them," he clarified. "I'm just not ready right now. Today."

A whisper of hope swirled through her. And just as quickly, she tamped it down.

"I understand that's the right decision for you." She wondered what had made him so certain he wasn't ready to welcome a child into his life. "But in the meantime, a confused little boy who already lost one father is going to lose another man he's grown attached to."

"A child deserves to have a family in place. A family that's going to stay together." He spoke with passionate conviction. "The Masons have that, Lydia. I don't."

"You have me." She had thought that meant something to him.

"And look at how ready you are to walk out at the first sign of trouble." He shoved his hands in his pockets, his shoulders tense. "As soon as I brought up the idea of bringing the Masons to town, you shut down the discussion."

Surprise stole any response she might have made. Is that how he saw it? Perhaps she hadn't understood how deeply wary his failed marriage had made him. For that matter, maybe he hadn't known how incredibly gun-shy her past made her either.

"I'm sorry, James." She didn't know what else to say. The knowledge that he was hurting, too, didn't make the breakup any easier. If anything, it only increased the ache in her chest. She hadn't wanted things to end this way.

The vibration of a cell phone cut through the awkward silence, the soft hum emanating from James's breast pocket.

"I'd better see if it's the Masons," he muttered, reaching into his jacket. Stabbing at the screen. "Hello?"

He must have hit the speakerphone button because Samantha Mason's panicked voice cut through the quiet.

"Teddy's having an allergic reaction," the woman sobbed in a rush of words. "We're on the way to Royal Memorial Hospital, James. Please hurry."

Thirteen

James wasn't surprised when Lydia insisted on riding with him to the hospital. She might be done with him, but her attachment to Teddy was undeniable. Whatever her reason to be in the passenger seat with him, and then rushing into the emergency room with him fifteen minutes later, James was grateful as hell to have her at his side.

"I told them where the EpiPen was." James knew he'd said it more than once on the way to the hospital.

But the thought kept circling around in his brain after he'd hung up from Samantha Mason's frantic first call.

"You did. You showed it to them," Lydia reminded him again as they wound through the triage area to the desk. "Maybe the shot didn't help. Maybe they weren't able to give it to him fast enough."

He hadn't asked what happened when he got the call. He'd been too shaken up, too terrified. What if something happened to his brother's son, when protecting Teddy had been the only thing Parker had asked of him?

"We're here for Teddy Harris." He willed the nurse at the counter to give him good news. Tell him his nephew was okay. "I'm his legal guardian."

"He's in room three." She pointed to a door behind the nurse's station. "The doctor is in with him now."

James was already moving. Lydia's high heels tapped a quick beat to his longer strides and he slowed a fraction to give her his arm. His movements felt wooden, his body on autopilot.

She accepted his help in silence, her expression mirroring the fear that chilled his insides.

"He's going to be okay." He told himself as much as her. Needing it to be true.

The hospital room was quiet, after all. Surely there would be all sorts of noise and staff in motion if the worst was happening.

Still, dread filled him as he pushed the door open. Teddy's grandparents stood on either side of the toddler. Between them, Teddy lay in a hospital crib. Around him, monitors beeped quietly and an IV bag hung by the bed, giving some kind of fluids into the boy's tiny arm. An oxygen mask covered the lower half of his face. His eyes were closed, but James wasn't sure if that was because he was sleeping or because of the swelling around his eyes.

His skin was pink and splotchy.

James didn't know how he remained standing upright. But he thought it helped that Lydia squeezed his arm hard for a moment before she hurried to the baby's side. Her hands fell to his little knee through the white blanket that partially covered him.

"Is he—" James felt his throat close up tight.

Death had stolen everyone from him. *Everyone*. He could not lose Teddy.

His eyes burned.

"He'll be fine, Mr. Harris." A shorter man in a white lab coat stepped between James and the crib, offering his hand. "I'm Dr. Voss."

"He's okay?" James shook the man's hand, though half his attention was still on the other side of the room where Lydia leaned over the crib wall to stroke Teddy's dark curls.

A swell of love for her filled his chest, easing some of the fear. He turned back to the doctor, needing the rest of the story before he could believe Teddy would make a full recovery.

"He's stable now. The EMT crew faced the worst of it on the way over here." Behind Dr. Voss, Mrs. Mason released a quiet sob, a ball of tissues wadded up in one hand.

Teddy's grandfather moved around to the other side of the bed to be by his wife, sliding an arm around her shoulders.

The doctor continued, "We're still giving him some cortisone and antihistamines intravenously, and we wanted to keep him on supplemental oxygen for a little while. But we're monitoring him carefully just in case he exhibits any more signs of distress."

"What about his face?" Lydia asked from the bed-side. "He's so swollen."

"We'll get some ice on that," the doctor assured her,

backing toward the door. "I'll ask a nurse to come in and remove the oxygen in about thirty minutes, and we'll start some ice for the swelling. But it should go down on its own in time."

"He already looks better than—" Teddy's grandfather, George, interjected "—before."

"Don't be too hard on yourselves, folks." The doctor paused with the door half open. "You did the right thing coming in. Even if you had administered his EpiPen, we would have wanted to see him after that kind of a reaction."

Samantha Mason let out another sob behind her tissue as she sat down.

Relief flooded through James. "He's going to be okay."

"James, I'm so sorry." Samantha straightened from where she'd been slumped in a metal chair near the bed. "George had a snack pack of cereal that he eats sometimes when his sugar is low. We'd never give Teddy anything like that after what you said about the nut allergy, but we think he must have eaten a piece that fell on the floor. Right?" She turned to her husband for confirmation.

George shrugged. "I don't remember dropping any, but maybe I did. I was feeling a little shaky. But the next thing we knew, Teddy was wheezing."

James understood mistakes happened. It could have been him who'd dropped a piece of food that Teddy ate. Or Lydia. Still, he couldn't help a spike of frustration. "So what happened with the EpiPen?"

The couple exchanged looks before George answered, "When you showed it to us, I thought you took it from the top kitchen drawer in the island."

James shook his head. "I keep it in the diaper bag."

He knew the bag had been sitting on top of the island when he'd shown it to them. But it didn't matter now. He'd make sure the hospital sent them home with another. While he spoke with the Masons, Lydia rose and let herself out of the room.

His gaze followed her. Was she leaving for good? Or just getting a nurse? Maybe she simply didn't want to hear all the ways the Masons had endangered Teddy. Truth was, he found it tough to hear the story, too. Especially since their babysitting had ended with Teddy in an oxygen mask, hooked up to an IV.

Guilt swamped him. He should've done so much better by his brother's child. Teddy was the only family James had left, and he hadn't taken that responsibility seriously enough.

Was this some kind of cosmic payback for almost giving up custody of the boy? He'd been a fool to ever consider it.

Samantha shivered, rubbing her arms as tears welled in her eyes again. "I was pulling out all the drawers in the island. I just kept thinking how we'd already lost Mandy, and now we were going to lose her little boy, too."

"I called 911 right away," George offered, shaking his balding head. "It all happened so fast."

James had heard enough. He really wanted to be with his nephew. "Anyone would have been scared to see that happen," he reassured them since there was nothing to be gained in arguing with them. "You must be exhausted after going through that. If you want to go back to the hotel, I can call you if there's any change in his condition."

He also really hoped Lydia hadn't left. But Samantha Mason was still visibly upset as she continued telling him about her daughter, Parker's wife. Between tears, she said, "And we never did see Mandy again. Never had a chance to heal our differences. Little Teddy is all we have left of our beautiful daughter now."

Something about the way she'd phrased it made James uncomfortable. Did they really see Teddy as a replacement for their dead daughter? James tried to offer some comforting words if only to speed the Masons out the door.

Teddy wasn't a replacement for anyone. He was an innocent boy who'd lost too much in his young life, and he deserved the best that James had to offer.

From now on, he needed to focus on his family.

That meant Teddy. He saw that all too clearly now. Teddy was his, now and always.

And, if he could find her, he wanted to tell Lydia that he finally understood what she'd been trying to tell him all along. That Teddy was his family. But the part that Lydia hadn't figured out yet was that she was his family, too. Because he was ready to claim Teddy as his son, and he wanted Lydia to be at his side when he did.

Lydia couldn't sleep when she got back to the house.

She put the kitchen back in order so Mrs. Davis wouldn't return from her New Year's holiday to find spoons and papers on the tile floor, but after that she went upstairs to pack her things.

Seeing Teddy in the hospital bed had been devastating. Rationally, she knew his exposure to tree nuts could have happened to any babysitter. Yet it upset her to think the Masons not only let the substance into the house where their grandson had a serious allergy, but then they hadn't even been able to locate the medicine that could have slowed the reaction and possibly prevented anaphylaxis. Every second would have counted for that first responder team when they arrived on the scene.

They could have lost Teddy.

Although as much as she'd grown to love the little boy and his uncle, Lydia knew she had no claim on them. They weren't hers to love. So she had phoned her sister in the predawn hours, asking Gail to act as a babysitter if Teddy needed one when James returned from the hospital with him.

Gail might be financially irresponsible, but Lydia trusted her to watch a child. Even a severely allergic child. That certainty in her gut made Lydia realize she needed to make peace with Gail. Because they were still family, and Gail had never asked her to cover for her with the bachelor auction bid.

Lydia had involved herself in that situation on her own. She was a caretaker. A fixer. And she could tell herself that it was okay to say no to unnecessary crazy as many times as she wanted, but she kept jumping in to help. She'd realized in this last painful week without James that she needed to take ownership of her own life.

She had changed for the better because of knowing him. Lydia had a newfound acceptance of her family— and the pieces of herself that had been shaped by them. She would have to appreciate those changes, since they would be all she had left of her time with James. She understood herself too well to try to accept the path he chose, a path without Teddy.

When she heard the low hum of a car engine outside, she hurried to the front door, expecting to see her sister. She twisted the knob, tugging the double panels open, and was shocked to find James's black sedan rolling to a stop in the driveway.

A lump rose to her throat. The tug of emotions in her belly was nothing new around him, but it hurt far more now that she couldn't act on those feelings. Now that she had to find a way to forget about him.

The thought twisted sharply inside her, reminding her that wouldn't ever happen.

James stepped from the driver's side door, his gaze locking on her. "I'm glad you're here."

Opening the rear door, he leaned into the vehicle to unfasten the restraint on the car seat.

Lydia moved closer, wanting to see Teddy even though she knew every moment she spent with him only made it harder to leave. She needed to know he was okay.

"My sister's coming over," she told James while he lifted the baby in his strong arms, his shoulders blocking her view of Teddy. She closed the door behind them, then heard another car turning into the driveway. "That might be her now, in fact."

She reminded herself it was for the best to turn over her nanny duties to Gail for however long James still needed help with Teddy. Lydia didn't want to be in the house when they packed his things to send him to Amarillo with the Masons.

"I know. I spoke to Lloyd a few minutes ago."

"Lloyd?" Lydia followed James as he strode toward

the house, trying to peek around his shoulder to see
Teddy's face.

She'd changed into jeans and a sweater, but James
still wore his tuxedo from the New Year's Eve Ball.
The bow tie hung around his neck, the top button of
his shirt undone. He still looked too handsome for his
own good.

Too handsome for hers, at least.

James paused on the front mat, glancing down at
her. "The bachelor she fell head over heels for, remember?"

"Right." She found it hard to think about her sister's drama with too much of her own crowding her
thoughts and breaking her heart. "Of course."

Glancing back at new vehicle in the driveway, she
realized it wasn't Gail's compact. There was a man in
the driver's seat of an exotic-looking sports car, but
from the passenger side, Gail gave Lydia a wave.

Confused, Lydia waved back, then hurried after
James as he stepped inside the house.

"Lloyd wants to give me a check to cover your sister's bid. I told him it was not necessary, but he was
so insistent, we agreed he'd donate the money to the
Pancreatic Research Cancer Foundation."

"Really? That's amazing." She couldn't fully process that news and the implications it might have when
she really just wanted to see Teddy's face first. Distracted by worries about the baby, she stepped closer to
James again. "May I just see him? Is he really okay?"

"He's still a little groggy." James dipped his shoulder so Lydia could have a better view of the boy. "The
doctor said to just let him rest for a few hours and the
last of the swelling should dissipate by evening."

"Thank goodness." Relief rushed through her, so strong it made her weak in the knees. She couldn't resist a final, gentle squeeze of Teddy's arm. A stroke of his fluffy dark curls. "I'm so glad he's okay."

"Me, too." James's gaze held hers for a moment, making her aware of how close they stood.

Heat grazed her skin, the pull of attraction so strong in spite of everything. Stepping away from him was downright painful.

"Hello!" Gail called through the front door, knocking gently before cracking it open a sliver. "Can we come in?"

"Please do." James invited them inside. Gail and a tall, blond-haired man with a square jaw and aviator sunglasses.

Gail had the same "in love" glow that Tessa Noble had when she'd stopped by with Ryan earlier in the month. Gail introduced Lydia to Lloyd while James excused himself to put Teddy in his crib.

"Nice to meet you," Lydia said automatically as she shook Lloyd's hand, although her eyes followed James's progress up the main staircase.

"You, too," Lloyd said, tugging off his shades. "And we're going to stay out of your hair. We're only here for babysitting duty." He grinned. "You get two for the price of one with us."

Lydia tried to smile, charmed in spite of herself by Gail's new boyfriend. But it was hard to make small talk when her heart ached.

Once Gail and Lloyd went to watch over Teddy, there was nothing to keep Lydia here. Her gaze fell on the suitcases she'd already packed and set near the front door.

"There's a playroom near the nursery," she told them, thinking of all the hours she'd spent there in the last weeks, delighting in Teddy's accomplishments as he lost himself in playtime and forgot to be the confused, fractious little boy she'd met that first day at the Texas Cattleman's Club. "It has a sitting area—"

"We'll be fine," Gail assured her while Lloyd tugged her toward the stairs by the hand. Behind him, she mouthed silently to Lydia, "He's so hot!"

If there'd been any doubt what she was saying, Gail fanned herself before she had to focus on the steps.

"But—" She had hoped to speak with her sister longer. At very least, to apologize for intruding in Gail's business when clearly she had addressed the situation herself.

The couple holding hands were too far up the stairs now, however. They passed James, who pointed out the door to the nursery and the playroom on his way down.

Toward her.

Her throat closed right up at the thought of saying goodbye to him.

"Lydia, wait." He'd taken the time to change into dark jeans and a long-sleeved white T-shirt. He tugged one of the ribbed cuffs higher on his forearm as he strode into the living area. "Can we talk?"

"I was just—" She pointed to her suitcases, not sure what else there was to say. "I called my sister to take over for me until the Masons—"

"There will be no Masons." He took her hands in his, surprising her with his touch as much as his words. She looked up into his light brown eyes flecked with gold, and, as always, warmth tripped down her spine at the mere sight of him.

Sunlight spilled over her shoulders through the big windows, the holiday decorations casting rainbow reflections around the room.

"I don't understand." Unless…a horrible thought occurred to her. "Did they decide not to take him because of what happened? Is he too much trouble?"

"No." He shook his head. "Nothing like that. They love Teddy and feel terrible about triggering the allergy."

She relaxed slightly as the maternal defensiveness eased. "Then what do you mean?"

He squeezed her hands tighter, his thumbs stroking the insides of her wrists. "I can't describe the fear I felt last night when we walked into that emergency room. Not just a fear that I'd messed up my brother's one wish for me that I keep his son safe." He hauled in a long breath. "I knew I'd be devastated to lose him, too. Because I love that child, and I'm not going to ever let him go."

"Oh, James, that's wonderful." She was thrilled for him. For Teddy. "You'll make such an amazing father."

She was overwhelmed with the urge to hug him, so she did. Even though it hurt to feel so much love for him, to feel so close to him, and not be able to share in the future he painted.

Because even though it was almost everything she could have wished for, the picture he painted hadn't included her.

The reality of that brought her back to earth in a thud of awkwardness over how she'd thrown herself into his strong arms to hug him. She tried to ease back.

Only he kept on holding her tight, burying his head in her hair.

"Lydia. I've missed you so much," he spoke into her hair, the scruff on his jaw snagging the strands.

Her heart pounded harder. She hardly dared to hope...

"I'm—" She'd already told him how she felt. So she clamped down on the thought now as she pulled away. "I know Teddy will be so happy to grow up here. Where he belongs."

Her eyes stung a little. Happy tears, she told herself.

"You belong here, too, Lydia. With me." His voice hit that deep note that rumbled right through her, even though it was softly spoken.

"I—" Blinking, she tried to focus on what he was saying. She couldn't afford to misunderstand when she was already holding together the pieces of herself from the heartbreak of the past week. "I can't be his nanny anymore, though. Not when—"

"Not as a nanny." He drew her closer again, curling a finger under her chin to look into her eyes. "As my wife." He let the words sink in. Holding her gaze with his. Canting closer to speak softly against her cheek. "Marry me, Lydia Walker. I can't get through another day without you in my life. I love you too much."

Happiness stole her breath, filling her with a shiny new hope that made her feel lighter. So light she might float right away with it.

"Really?" She closed her eyes, swaying into him, needing to hear it again.

"Every day without you has been painful. But I knew it was wrong to ask you to come back when I wasn't sure about Teddy. I think I was still grieving for Parker. Still feeling like I'd never have enough to offer a child of my own." He cupped her face in both hands, his gaze steady, certain. "But I've got everything he needs, because I love him."

"That's true." She arched up to brush her mouth along his, knowing she could help the Harris males find happiness. But more than that, she was going to love them, too.

"And it felt so right when I figured that out." He kissed her eyelids. Her cheeks. "But then, it got even better when I realized that I might still be able to win you back. Because it's not a family without you."

"Consider me won." She wrapped her arms around his waist, fitting against him like she was made for him. "I love you, too, James."

His expression lit up at her words. "I don't have a ring yet." He stroked her shoulders and peered down at her. "And I'm not going to rob you of a special proposal—"

"I'm not worried about that." She wasn't the kind of woman who needed a splashy display. It was enough to have her "over the moon" love.

"I can't let Gus Slade outdo me in the romance department." He arched a teasing eyebrow at her. "I want to give you the fairy tale, Lydia. You deserve that."

"I just need you." She smoothed her hands over his chest, feeling all that delicious male strength. Feeling the steady beat of his heart. "Everything else is a bonus."

"It's a new year today." He kissed her lips. A slow, thorough kiss that promised so much more, a lifetime of more. "A new start. And I can't imagine a happier way to begin it than having the woman I love in my arms."

She wasn't ever going to get tired of hearing him say that. A shiver of pleasure tickled her neck. Anticipation hummed through her.

She stepped away from him so she could lace her fingers in his. Leading him toward the staircase.

"Actually, I can think of one way that might add to our happiness." She felt breathless with new love. New hope. And a whole lot of desire. "Especially since we have babysitting help."

"I've heard that new parents need to make the most of their alone time." He caught her up in his arms, kissing her again until they were both breathless.

They stared at each other for a heated moment before their feet were moving again. Up the stairs, straight for the master suite.

Sometimes, no other words were needed.

Epilogue

Four weeks later

Rose Clayton Slade could have danced all night.

She and Gus had invited half of Royal to the wedding ceremony and reception held in one of the restored barns at the Silver C. They'd brought in patio heaters and obtained special permission from the local fire commissioner so they could celebrate their night in a place close to their hearts. She twirled under her groom's arm as he spun her in a country waltz they both knew all too well. Gus had hummed the same tune to her many, many years ago when he'd asked her to dance with him in this very barn.

She'd never forgotten the steps. And she wanted to repeat them with him a thousand more times at least.

When the music shifted to a more upbeat piece,

Rose relinquished her new husband to one of his daughter's friends who wanted to claim a dance.

"I want a two-step when I come back," Rose whispered in Gus's ear before he kissed her on the cheek.

"I want that and a whole lot more," he told her with a wink.

How was it he could make her feel like a girl again, all blushing and flirtatious, when they'd argued like cats and dogs for so many years? Rose tried not to question it. She wanted to just be. To let this beautiful wedding reception unfurl all around her like an endless summer day. They'd paid the fiddler and his band to play as long as there were guests still in the barn, since all their friends from the Texas Cattleman's Club came out in force to celebrate.

It did her heart good to see all the couples together having fun, even outside the barn in the cooler night air where you could still hear the music. They'd put up a canopy strung with white lights, decked with more greenery and patio heaters. She was surprised so many people had made use of it in the cool evening. But James Harris and his new fiancée, Lydia, were so wrapped up in each other as she strode past them, she was sure they didn't even hear her say hello.

Which was the lovely thing about a wedding. Everyone could celebrate their love. If only her grandson had that in his life.

Ducking behind a rose-covered archway they walked through earlier, Rose breathed deep and looked up at the moon, savoring a peaceful moment alone before she went back inside. She was about to return to the barn when a familiar voice on the other side of the flower-covered arch stopped her.

It sounded like Gus's granddaughter, Alexis, was speaking in hushed tones to someone.

"No, I'm not worried," the woman was saying. "I'm pregnant, not helpless! I'll manage. It will be fine."

Rose nearly fell over straining to hear more, but the voice outside must have moved farther away. Not even remotely concerned about eavesdropping, Rose rushed outside to see if it really had been Alexis.

Pregnant?

It couldn't possibly be.

Except there, walking fast toward the front lawn of the main house, she caught a glimpse of Alexis Slade clutching a cell phone to her ear. Her back was to Rose, but the pink floral lace dress was unmistakable in the outdoor lights.

Rose felt faint.

She walked as fast as she dared in her tiered white wedding dress and turquoise-colored cowboy boots. She was not surprised to see her grandson, Daniel, charging toward Alexis, too, a look of determination on his chiseled features.

Not many women would have dared stop him with that look on his face. But those rules did not apply to grandmothers.

"Daniel." She double-timed her step to intercept him, tugging his arm.

His gaze stayed on Alexis for a long moment before he focused on her. "Yes?"

"Daniel, is it true?" She kept her voice low, mindful of guests even though they weren't close to anyone here by a stack of hay bales left out in case anyone needed an impromptu seat. "Is Alexis pregnant?"

His jaw jutted. "How did you find out?"

Her heart sank. She didn't need to ask if he was the father. She remembered seeing them together before. The spark between them was impossible to miss. Breaking them up had brought her and Gus together, and now Rose felt sick about it.

"Daniel, you have to—"

"I have." His dark brown eyes flashed fire. "I asked her to marry me, and she said it was too late. That I was only asking because of the baby."

"Were you?" She couldn't help but ask. But, seeing his expression and his patience worn thin, she changed tactics. "I'm sorry, Daniel. I—"

"Gran, you know I'd do anything for you. And I'm happy for you today. But I really need to go."

She nodded, seeing the way his shoulders bunched. His hands flexing into fists at his sides. She understood the way feelings could drive you to dark, unhappy places. She'd feuded with Gus for most of her adult life because she loved him and couldn't be with him.

It hurt to see him walk away. Not toward where Alexis had been, but toward his truck, parked close to the main house.

"Where's my bride?" Gus's voice called her from her worries.

She watched him stride toward her across the grass, so handsome and vital. A wave of love steadied her despite the ache in her chest.

"Sweetheart, what's wrong?" he asked as he came closer, pulling her into his arms. "You don't look like the happy bride who promised to meet me on the dance floor."

"I know." She nodded, gripping his hand. Needing his strength. "I just overheard that Alexis is pregnant."

Gus lifted a weathered hand to his face, covering whatever he might have said. She could see the shock in his eyes.

"The baby is Daniel's," she continued, wishing she'd found a gentler way to break the news to him. She leaned into him, wrapping her arms around his waist. "I asked him about it, and he said he asked her to marry him, but she won't because he's only proposing for the baby's sake."

Gus stroked her back, hugging her closer. Until that moment, she hadn't realized how chilled she'd grown outside. She was shivering.

"What a mess we made," Gus said gruffly, tucking her against him.

"It was hard enough seeing them so unhappy. And now this?" She heard the music pause inside and she worried it might be time to cut the cake. "Gus, we need to go back. But promise me we'll figure out a way to get them together?"

She would gladly delay the honeymoon so they could put their heads together and figure something out.

Gus nodded. He took her hand and squeezed. "I've got an idea. So don't you worry about it for even another instant, Rose. I'm going to fix things this time. For good."

And at the strength of the conviction in his voice, a strength she wished she'd trusted in decades ago, she believed him. She tucked her fingers into the crook of his arm and started walking back toward the barn where their guests, their community, their future waited.

* * * * *

BOMBSHELL
FOR THE BOSS

MAUREEN CHILD

To my cousin Timarie—steadfast and strong,
beautiful and brave. She faced the dragon and won.
We're all so proud.

One

"We already talked about this." Ethan Hart leaned back and stared across the desk at his younger brother. Elbows propped on the arms of his chair, Ethan steepled his fingers and narrowed his gaze. Irritation simmered inside him. How often did they have to go through this? Not for the first time, Ethan wondered if having his little brother on the board was a good idea.

Gabriel Hart pushed up from the visitor's chair and shoved both hands into his slacks pockets. "No, Ethan. *We* didn't discuss anything. *You* commanded."

One eyebrow winged up as Ethan lifted his gaze to meet Gabe's. "Since you remember our last conversation so well, I wonder why you're here trying to go over it all again."

"Because even as stubborn as you are, Ethan, I keep hoping that I'll manage to get through to you."

"I'm stubborn?" Ethan laughed and shook his head. "That's funny, coming from you."

"Damn it, I'm trying to do something important," Gabe argued. "Not just for me, but for the company."

And he believed that, Ethan knew. Gabriel had always been the one to try new things, to push envelopes. Well, that was no problem for himself. But for this company? Trying something new wasn't worth risking a reputation it had taken generations to build.

This was an old argument, getting older by the second. Ever since Gabe had taken his place in the Hart family chocolate company, the brothers had been doing battle. Ethan regretted that, because he and his younger brother had always been close. But the bottom line was Ethan was in charge and it was Ethan who would make the final call about the direction their company would take. And Gabriel was just going to have to find a way to live with that.

Standing up, he faced his brother. "Reality is, Gabe, we sold thirty-one *million* pounds of chocolate last year. The company is doing fine. We don't need to take risks."

"Damn it, Ethan, taking risks is how our great-grandfather started this company in the first place."

"True. Joshua Hart started the business," Ethan said tightly. "And each generation has kept our reputation a sterling one. We're one of the top five chocolate companies in the world. Why in the hell would I want to take risks now?"

"To be number *one*," Gabriel snapped. Clearly frustrated, he shoved a hand through his black hair. "Times change, Ethan. Tastes change. We can keep making the same great chocolate *and* we can add to our lists. Bring in new tastes and textures. Attract different customers, younger customers who'll stick with us for decades."

Ethan looked at his brother and felt twin tugs of affection and irritation. It had always been like this between them. Ethan had been looking out for his younger brother most of their lives. Gabriel was the wild one. The one who wanted to try new things, see new places. He was a risk taker and Ethan had rescued him from more than one escapade over the years. And that was fine, Ethan supposed, until it came to business. There, Ethan wasn't going to buck traditions that had built his family company into a worldwide giant.

"You want to start your own company," Ethan said softly, "and sell oregano chocolate or whatever, help yourself. Heart Chocolates will remain at the top of its game by giving our customers exactly what they want and expect from us."

"Very safe," Gabriel muttered, shaking his head. "And boring."

Ethan snorted. "Success is *boring*? We do what works, Gabe. We always have."

Gabe slapped both hands down on Ethan's desk and leaned in. "I'm a part of this company, Ethan. We're brothers. This is *our* family business. Dad left it to both of us. And I want a say in how it runs."

"You get a say," Ethan said, as irritation simmered even hotter, becoming a ball of anger in the pit of his stomach.

"And you get the final vote."

"Damn straight I do. The company was left to both of us, but I'm in charge." Ethan met his brother's gaze and tried to ease the hot knot of fury that settled inside him. He understood what was driving Gabriel. His

younger brother wanted to make his mark on the family
company. But that didn't mean Ethan was going to gam-
ble everything they'd built on his brother's risky ideas.

Yes. They could introduce new flavors, new types
of chocolates with strange fillings and flavors that
bucked every traditional norm. But their current customers wouldn't be interested—they knew what they
wanted and counted on Heart Chocolates to provide it.

"Never let me forget that, do you?" Gabriel pushed
off the desk, then stuffed his hands into his pockets.

"Look, Gabe, I get what you're trying to do, but it's
my responsibility to protect the reputation we've spent
generations building."

"You think I'm trying to wreck it?" Gabe stared at
him, astonished.

"No. You're just not considering all the angles of this
idea." Ethan's patience was so strained now he felt as
if he were holding on to the last remaining threads of
a rope from which he was dangling over the edge of a
cliff. So he tried a different tactic. "Introducing a new
line of chocolates, hoping to reel in new customers,
would require a huge publicity campaign well beyond
what we already have in place."

"Pam says the campaign could be run within the plan
that we're already using."

One of Ethan's eyebrows lifted. "Pam, huh? Who's
she?"

Gabriel took a deep breath and looked as though he
regretted letting that name slip. "Pam Cassini," he said.
"She's smart as hell. She's setting up her own PR firm
and she's got some great ideas."

"And you're sleeping with her," Ethan added for

him. Did this explain Gabriel's latest attempt to change things up? Was his new girlfriend behind it all?

"What's that got to do with anything?"

Before he could answer, Ethan heard a brisk knock on the door, then it swung open and his assistant, Sadie Matthews, poked her head inside. Her big blue eyes shifted from him to Gabe and back again before she asked, "War over?"

"Not even close," Gabriel said.

Ethan scowled at him. "What is it, Sadie?"

"The shouts are starting to drift out onto the floor," she said, stepping into the room and closing the door behind her.

For just a second, Ethan took a long, hard look at her.

Sadie had been his executive assistant for five years. Tall, she had short, curly blond hair, dark blue eyes and it seemed to him that a smile was always tugging at her mouth. She was efficient, beautiful, smart, sexy, and completely off-limits. Over the years, he'd actually had to train himself to not react to her as he would if she didn't work for him. It wasn't easy. Hell, one look at her curves would bring any red-blooded man to his knees.

Her mouth was a temptation and that spark of barely restrained rebellion in her eyes had always intrigued him. Early on, he'd even considered firing her just so he could try for a taste. But she was too damn good at her job.

Walking toward his desk, she said, "I actually heard a couple people placing bets on which one of you would win this round."

"Who?" Ethan demanded with another hard look at his brother.

She looked surprised at the question and shook her head. "I'm not going to tell you."

"What the hell, Sadie…"

She ignored him and looked at Gabriel. "The new distributor is waiting in your office for that meeting you have scheduled. If you'd rather, I could tell him you're in a heated battle with your brother…"

Gabriel gritted his teeth, but nodded. "Fine. I'll go." He looked at his brother. "But this isn't over, Ethan."

"Never thought it was," he said with a sigh.

When Gabriel was gone, Ethan asked, "Did you bet on me?"

She grinned. "How do you know I placed a bet?"

"You're too smart *not* to bet on me."

"Wow, a compliment for me and a pat on your own back all at the same time. Impressive."

"Is the distributor really in Gabe's office or did you do that just to break up the war?"

"Oh, he's really there," she said, walking toward the bank of windows. "But I did want to break up the argument, so I would have made something up if I'd had to."

"He's driving me crazy." Ethan turned and moved to stand beside her at the windows overlooking the Pacific Ocean. January could be cold and gray in Southern California, but winter seas had their own magic. The water was as dark as the sky, with waves rolling relentlessly toward shore. Surfers posed on their boards, waiting for the perfect wave, and a few boats with brightly colored sails skimmed the water's surface. The scene should have calmed him—it usually did. But this thing with Gabriel was getting more irritating every time it came up.

"He still wants to make some changes to the chocolate line, doesn't he."

Ethan glanced at Sadie. "And now he's got some woman helping him wage his campaign."

"It's not a completely crazy idea," she said with a shrug.

He stared at her. "Not you, too."

Sadie shrugged again. "Change isn't always a bad thing, Ethan."

"In my experience, it is," he argued. He took her shoulders, ignored the leap of heat inside, then turned her to face him. Once she was, he released her and stepped back before saying, "People always talk about changing their lives. New car, new house, new hair color, hell, new beliefs. Well, there's something to be said for stasis. For finding what works and sticking with it."

"Okay, but sometimes change is the only route left open to you."

"Not this time," he muttered. Turning his back on her and the view, he headed to his desk, sat down and reached for the latest marketing report. He gave her a quick glance. "Sadie, if you're going to side with Gabriel on this, I don't want to hear it. I'm not in the mood to have another argument for change."

"Right. Well, we all have to do things we don't want to do."

"What?" He looked up at her.

She blew out a breath and handed him a single sheet of paper. "I'm quitting my job."

"You can't quit. We have a meeting in twenty minutes."

"And yet…"

Ethan just stared at her, not really sure he'd heard her correctly. This was coming out of the blue and made absolutely no sense. "No, you're not."

She waved the paper. "Read the letter, Ethan."

He snatched it from her and skimmed the neatly typed lines. "This is ridiculous." He held it out to her. "I'm not accepting this."

Sadie put her hands behind her back so she wouldn't be at all tempted to take the letter and pretend none of this had happened. Oh, she had known quitting was going to be hard. Had known that Ethan would fight her on this, and she was a little worried he might convince her to stay. Because she didn't really want to leave Heart Chocolates.

But, she reminded herself, she really didn't want to spend the next five years of her life as she'd spent the previous five. Hopelessly in love with a boss who saw her as nothing more than an efficient piece of office furniture.

"You can't quit," he argued. When she refused to take back her letter of resignation, he tossed it face-down onto his desk, as if he couldn't bring himself to even see it again. "We've got the spring campaign to finalize, the rehab at the factory—"

"And all of it will get done without me," Sadie said, and hoped he didn't hear the nearly wistful tone in her voice.

"Why?" he demanded, scowling at her. "Is this about a raise? Fine. You have it."

"It's not about money, Ethan," she said tightly. She already made more money than she would at any other job. Ethan was generous with his employees. That wasn't the issue at all.

He stood up. "All right, an extra two weeks of vacation a year, *plus* the raise."

She laughed at the idea and suddenly relaxed her guard. Really, for being such a good boss, he was also completely clueless sometimes. "Ethan, I don't take my vacation *now*. What good is two more weeks to me?"

"You're being unreasonable."

"I'm being pragmatic."

"I disagree."

"I'm sorry about that," she said, and she really was. Sadie didn't *want* to leave. Didn't *want* to never see him again. In fact, that thought opened up a dark, empty pit in the bottom of her stomach. Which told her she simply had no other choice.

"Then what's this about?"

"I want a life," she said, and hated how desperate those four words sounded.

But she'd spent the last eight years of her life working for *Heart* chocolates, the last five of which she'd been Ethan's assistant. She worked outrageous hours, hardly ever saw her family, and the houseplants in the condo she'd purchased the year before were dried-out sticks because she was never there often enough to water them.

She wanted romance. Sex. Maybe a family of her own before she was too old to get any of that.

"You have a life," he said, clearly affronted at the accusation that he'd somehow cheated her. "You're integral to this business. To *me*."

If only.

The real problem here was that she'd been in love

with Ethan for years now. It was empty, completely one-sided and guaranteed to leave her a bitter old woman one day. Nope. For her own sake, she had to quit.

Shaking her head, she said, "That's work, Ethan, and there's more to life than work."

"Not that I've noticed," he complained.

"That's part of the problem," she argued. "Don't you get it? We work hideously long hours, come in on weekends, and last year you even called me in from my cousin's wedding to help you cover that mix-up with the Mother's Day shipment."

"It was important," he reminded her.

"So was Megan's wedding," she told him, shaking her head. "No, I have to do this. It's time for a change."

"Change again," he muttered, standing up and coming around the desk to stop right in front of her. "I'm really getting sick of that word."

"Change isn't always bad."

"Or good," he pointed out. "When things are working, why screw it up?"

"I knew you'd hate this and maybe it was bad timing coming in to talk to you right after your latest battle with Gabe. But yes. I need a change." She stared up into his grass-green eyes and felt a pang of regret that she was leaving. His dark brown hair was mussed, no doubt because he'd been stabbing his fingers through it again while arguing with Gabe. His tie was loosened and that alone was so damn sexy, her breath caught in her throat.

What was it about this man that hit her on so many levels? It wasn't just how gorgeous he was or the way he made her yearn with just a glance. He was strong and smart and tough and the combination was a constant temptation to her. So resigning was really her only choice.

How could she want him so badly and stay in a position that guaranteed she'd never have him?

"Damn it, Sadie what is it you want changed, exactly?"

"My *life*," she said, looking up into his eyes and willing him to see *her*, not just his always professional assistant. But he never would. She was like the fax machine or a new computer. There to do a job. "Do you know my brother, Mike, and his wife, Gina, just had their *third* baby?"

Confusion shone in his eyes. "So? What's that got to do with you?"

"Mike's wife is two years younger than me." She threw her hands up in disgust. "She has three kids. I have four dead plants."

"What the hell does *that* mean?"

She sighed a little. She'd known going in that quitting wouldn't be easy. That Ethan would try to keep her by offering raises, promotions, vacations. But she hadn't realized how hard it would be to tell him what was bothering her. What was driving her to leave. Heck, she'd only recently figured it out for herself.

"I want a family, Ethan. I want a man to love me…" *You*, her brain whispered, but she shut that inner voice down fast. "I want kids, Ethan. I'm almost thirty."

"Seriously?" He pushed the edges of his jacket back and stuffed both hands into his pants pockets. "That's what this is about? A biological clock moment?"

"Not just a moment," she told him. "I've been thinking about this for a while. Ethan, we work fifteen-hour days, sometimes more. I haven't been on a date in forever and haven't had *sex* in three *years*."

He blinked.

She winced. Okay, she hadn't meant to tell him that. Bad enough that *Sadie* knew the pitiful truth. Downright embarrassing for Ethan to know it. "My point is, I don't want to look back when I'm old and gray and all alone—except for a cat and I don't even like cats—and have the only thing I can say about my life be, *Boy, I really was a good assistant. Kept that office running smoothly, didn't I?*"

"Doesn't sound like a bad thing."

Exasperated, Sadie stabbed her index finger at him. "That's because *you* don't have a life, either." Yes, it had been forever since she'd been with anyone. But he was no better. "You bury yourself in your work. You never talk to anyone but me or Gabe. You own a damn mansion in Dana Point, but you're never there. You eat takeout at your desk and pour everything you have into charts and ledgers, and that's not healthy."

One dark eyebrow arched. "Thanks very much."

Sadie took a step back, mostly because standing so close to him was hard on her nerve endings. He smelled good. His jaw was tight, his eyes flashing and he looked…too tempting. Not for the first time, she wondered what would happen if she threw herself at his chest and wrapped her arms around his neck. Would he hold her back? Kiss her senseless?

Or would he be horrified and toss her to one side?

Since she was quitting, she could easily find out the answers. But the truth was, she wasn't sure she wanted to know. Sometimes a really good fantasy was way better than reality.

"This isn't about me and my life," he pointed out.

"In a way it is," she said. "Maybe if you hire an assistant who insists on a nine-to-five schedule, you'll get out of this office once in a while."

"Fine." He jumped on her statement. "You want nine to five, we can do that."

Sadie laughed. "No, we can't. Remember Megan's wedding?" Her cousin had been hurt that Sadie had slipped out of the chapel and missed the whole thing. And Sadie hadn't liked it, either. "I'm really sorry, Ethan, but I have to quit. I'll stay for two weeks, train a replacement."

"Who?" He crossed his arms over his chest and dared her with his eyes to come up with a suitable replacement.

"Vicki in Marketing."

"You're kidding."

"What's wrong with her?"

"She *hums*. Constantly."

Okay, she had to give him that one. He wasn't the only one to complain about Vicki. Worse, Sadie was pretty sure the woman was tone deaf. "Fine. Beth in Payroll."

"No." He shook his head. "Her perfume is an assault on the senses."

Typical, she thought. Of course he would find something wrong with everyone she suggested. He might be young, gorgeous and a sex-on-a-stick walking fantasy, but he had the resistance to change of a ninety-year-old.

Good thing she'd been prepared for this. "How about Rick? He's been working here for two years. He knows the business."

If anything, his jaw got tighter. "Rick agrees with

Gabriel. I'm not going to spend every day arguing with my assistant."

True. So it came down to this. To *him* suggesting her replacement. "Who do you suggest, then?"

"You." He was frowning and somehow that only made him look sexier.

What was *wrong* with her?

"We're a team, Sadie. A good one. Why break that up?"

Though she loved the fact that he didn't want her to leave, she knew she had to go for her own peace of mind. How could she ever look for love somewhere else when she was too wrapped up in Ethan Hart? God, how pitiful did that sound?

"I'll find someone," she said firmly.

He didn't look happy at that, but he jerked a nod. "And you agree not to leave until a replacement is trained."

She narrowed her eyes on him, because she saw the trap. If he never agreed to a replacement, she'd never get that person trained and thus, never leave. "And you agree to accept the replacement."

He shrugged. "If this nameless person can do the job, of course."

"You sound so reasonable." Sadie tipped her head to one side and watched him closely. "Why don't I believe you?"

"Suspicious nature?"

His eyes flashed and her insides skittered in response. Seriously, from the moment she'd taken this job with Ethan Hart, Sadie had been half in love with him. And over the years, she'd taken the full-on tumble. She still wasn't sure why. Ethan wasn't anywhere near her ideal man.

She'd put a lot of time and thought into what she wanted. Yes, Ethan was gorgeous. Really way *too* handsome. Women were always tripping over themselves trying to get close to him. Yes, he was successful, but he was driven by his work to the exclusion of everything else in his life. She didn't know if he liked children because he was never around any. She didn't know if he was an amazing lover—though she'd had quite a few dreams in which he was the ultimate sex god. He had a sense of humor but he didn't use it often, and he was entirely too spoiled. Too used to getting his own way.

No, Ethan Hart was not the man for her and if she ever hoped to find that elusive lover, then she had to leave this job.

"I have reason to be suspicious," she said.

"Why would I lie?" he asked, feigning astonishment at the very idea.

"To get what you want."

"You know me so well, Sadie," he said, shaking his head. "Just one more reason why we make a good team."

They really did. Damn it. She hated having to leave and couldn't stand staying.

"Ethan, I'm serious," she said, lifting her chin and meeting his gaze squarely. "I'm quitting."

He looked at her for a long, silent minute. "Fine."

Just like that, his walls went up and his eyes went blank. "Wow, you're good at that."

"What?"

"Going from hot to cold in a blink."

"I don't know what you're talking about."

"Of course you do," Sadie said, staring into those beautiful eyes of his. "It's your signature move. Whenever a conversation or a negotiation starts going in a direction you don't approve of, up come the defenses. And now that I've officially resigned, I can tell you that I don't like it when you do it."

He frowned. "Is that right?"

"Yes." Sadie planted both hands on her hips. "You know, it's pretty great being able to just say what I'm thinking."

"I've never known you not to," he pointed out.

"Oh," she said with a laugh, "you have *no* idea the restraint I've shown over the years. Well, until now."

Those grass-green eyes narrowed on her. "Feeling pretty sure of yourself now, are you?"

"I'm always sure of myself, I just don't usually tell you everything I'm thinking. I have to admit," she added, "this is very freeing." Sure, she'd miss her job. And she'd *really* miss Ethan. But this was the best thing for her, and since she had to leave anyway, she was going to allow herself to enjoy her last two weeks with him. She'd be completely honest and hold nothing back. *Well, she wasn't about to admit she loved him or anything, but other than that...* "Also, I hate your coffee."

Now he looked insulted. "That's the world's finest Sumatra blend. I have a supply flown in every two months."

"Yes, and it's awful. It tastes like the finest Sumatran dirt."

"I don't think I care for this new blunt honesty policy."

Sadie grinned. She'd surprised him, something that was nearly impossible to do because Ethan Hart was always thinking two or three steps ahead of everyone else in the world. "Well, I think I like it."

"I could just fire you and be done with it," he warned.

"Oh, we both know you won't do that. You don't like change, remember?" She shook her head. If nothing else, she was completely confident in saying, "Never going to happen."

When a knock at the door sounded, they both turned and Ethan ordered, "Come in."

She was going to miss that bark of command.

"Mr. Hart? Ethan Hart?" A woman walked into the room carrying a baby that looked about six months old.

Instantly, Sadie's heart melted. The tiny girl was beautiful, with big brown eyes and wispy, black hair. She was chewing on her fist as the woman holding her crossed the room.

"Yes, I'm Ethan Hart. And you are?" The icy king-of-the-universe tone was back in his voice.

"Melissa Gable." She swung a black diaper bag off her shoulder and dropped it onto the visitor's chair. Digging into it one-handed, she came up with a manila envelope and handed it to Ethan. "I'm from Child Services. I'm here to deliver Emma Baker to you."

"Who's Emma Baker?" he asked warily.

"She is." And Ms. Gable handed the baby to Ethan.

Two

Not too long after his argument with Ethan, Gabriel was at his girlfriend Pam Cassini's house and his frustration felt as if it had a life of its own.

After the futile meeting with his brother, he'd hated walking back to his office, knowing everyone there had heard the argument and had known he'd lost. Gabe hated that Ethan wouldn't listen to reason and he hated having been born second. If Gabe had been the older brother, things at Heart Chocolates would be done differently.

"Instead," he mumbled, "I'll always be the little brother."

The junior partner, forced to fight for every scrap of recognition. Maybe he should have just gone home to the penthouse apartment he kept in Huntington Beach. He rented out half the top floor of the best hotel in the city and enjoyed the views and the convenience of twenty-four-hour room service and housekeeping.

Today he was in a foul mood, so he should have gone off by himself. But he didn't want to be alone, either.

"Oh hell, just admit it. You wanted to see Pam. Talk to her."

In the last six months, Pam Cassini had become more important to him than Gabriel was comfortable admitting. He hadn't been looking for any long-term relationship when he met her. And maybe that's why he'd fallen into one. He was no stranger to women wanting to hook up with one of the Hart brothers. But Pam was different. She was strong and smart and ambitious. She had her own career and she was as passionate about it as he was about his. He admired that.

Pam's tiny condo on a quiet street in Seal Beach was warm, welcoming, even to its bright yellow door flanked by terra-cotta pots filled with cheerful splashes of pink and white flowers. You could fit the whole damn place inside his apartment twice over, but there was something here his own place lacked. Pam.

He knocked and stalked the small porch while he waited. When she opened the door, Gabe blurted out, "My brother has a head like concrete."

Pam sighed, gave him a sympathetic look and opened the door wider. As Gabriel stomped past her, she asked, "He's still not willing to try a new line?"

He walked right into the living room and stopped in front of her small, white-brick gas fireplace, hissing with a few flames dancing over artificial logs. "He reacted like a vampire to garlic."

Shaking his head, Gabe turned around to face her in the narrow living room. He hardly noticed the comfortable furniture or the fresh coffee scenting the air. But as she walked toward him, even his fury with Ethan couldn't keep him from taking a moment to simply enjoy the view of *her*.

Pam was short, with a lush and curvy body that drove Gabe mad with hunger. Today she wore a tight, white T-shirt that clung to her breasts, and a pair of black yoga pants that defined every line of her butt, hips and legs. Her feet were bare and her toes were painted a deep scarlet.

She also had long black hair, the warmest brown eyes he'd ever seen and a wide, full mouth that had tempted him from the moment he first met her, more than six months ago. That was at a chocolate convention. He'd been there representing Heart Chocolates, of course, and Pam was handing out cards for her burgeoning PR business.

They'd had dinner that night, and by the end of the week they were inseparable. They'd been together ever since. In that short amount of time, Pam had become a kind of touchstone to him. She listened to his plans, liked his ideas and encouraged him to stand up to Ethan and fight for his own plans and ambitions. For all the good it was doing him.

She put one hand on his arm and looked up at him. "Trying to convince Ethan to change his mind isn't working. I told you, Gabe, all we really need is the chocolate recipe."

She'd been saying that for weeks now, and still Gabe hesitated. A chocolate recipe was sacred to a chocolatier. As ridiculous as it sounded, there actually were corporate spies out there, eager to steal a competitor's recipe. They could use it themselves, sell it, post it on-line or simply find a way to ruin it.

The Hart family had guarded their basic recipe for generations, just like every other chocolatier. And Gabe was hesitant to be the first member of the Hart family to trust an outsider with it.

"Think about it, Gabe," Pam was saying. "I know a great chocolate chef we can trust. With the recipe, we can have my guy make up samples of the new fla-vors and present them to Ethan as a done deal. Once he's tasted them, he'll see you're right and he'll jump on board."

A nice fantasy, Gabriel conceded, but hardly based in reality. He snorted. "You don't know Ethan."

"But I know you," she said softly, her voice dropping to the deep, breathless, sultry tone that always drove him crazy. "You're determined and when you believe in something, you just never quit. You don't give up, Gabe. You get what you go after. You got me, didn't you?"

In spite of everything, he smiled. How could he not, with this gorgeous woman looking up at him with hun-ger in her eyes? "We got each other."

"Ooh, good answer." Pam licked her lips, gave him a slow smile as she wrapped her arms around his neck and laid that luscious mouth over his. He went hard as stone instantly and gave himself up to the need she quickened inside him. He'd never known a fire like he felt with her. And a part of him wondered just how long that fire could last.

Then he stopped thinking entirely. Frustration, anger, everything else in the world simply faded away at the touch of her mouth to his. And as they moved together, in a rhythm that seared his blood and stole his breath, he knew there was nowhere else he wanted to be.

"Um," Sadie said, looking at the baby in Ethan's arms. "Is there anything you want to tell me?"

"It's not mine, if that's what you mean." He glared at her. He'd always been careful. He had no children and didn't plan on any. "I think I'd know if I'd made a baby. Besides, you just told me I don't have a life. How could it be mine?"

Sadie sighed. "First, not an 'it'. It's a girl."

"Fine. *She's* not mine."

"She is now," Sadie reminded him. Glancing through the paperwork the social worker had left behind, she said, "Bill and Maggie Baker were her parents. Ring a bell?"

He frowned and then frowned deeper when the baby kicked impossibly small legs, screwed up her face and let out a howl a werewolf would have been proud of. "What's wrong with it?"

"Being called *it*, probably," Sadie muttered, and snatched the baby from him. Positioning her on one hip, Sadie bounced and swayed in place until the child stopped crying.

Ethan took a step back just for good measure. The damn social worker had done her job. She'd handed off the baby, a car seat and a diaper bag, then left so quickly he hadn't had time to argue about anything. But he was ready to now. He couldn't take care of a damn baby. The idea was ludicrous. Who would have made *him* a guardian? Ethan had never been around a baby. He didn't even own a dog.

Baker. Bill Baker. Why did that sound familiar?

Ethan glanced at Sadie and, in spite of the situation, felt a hot rush of heat jolt through his system and settle in his groin. He'd worked with this woman for five years and he'd been fighting his instincts about her for every second of that time. It hadn't gotten any easier.

Hell, there she was, holding an infant and he *still* burned for her. She smiled at the baby, then kissed her forehead, and Ethan's belly jumped. He wanted her badly, and now that she'd resigned, he could have finally made a move on her. But if he did that and then was able to coax her into not quitting her job, after all, there'd be nothing but complications. So no move. He gritted his teeth, hissed in a breath and wished to hell for a cold shower.

Deliberately pushing thoughts of hot, steamy, incredible sex out of his mind, he went back to "Baker. Why do I know that name?" Then it hit him. Ethan stared at the baby, then Sadie. "Hell. I did know him. In college. We were roommates, for God's sake." As more of the past rushed into his mind, Ethan cursed under his breath and slapped one hand down on his desk. "We made a deal. A stupid deal."

"Involving children, I'm guessing."

"Funny." He glared at her, noticed the child watching him through wide, watery eyes, and looked away quickly. What was that ribbon of panic? Nothing scared him. But one look at that child and he was ready to run for the hills. That realization was humiliating.

"Yes," he said tightly, as memories crowded his mind. "It did involve children, obviously. Bill didn't have family. He and Maggie were engaged and she had been a foster child herself, so no family there, either. He asked me to be legal guardian to his kids if anything ever happened to him."

"And you did it?" The surprise in Sadie's voice jabbed at him.

The fact that he now regretted what he'd done so long ago didn't come into it. Instead, he was insulted that Sadie was incredulous that he would offer to help a friend. Did she really think so little of him? And because he *was* regretting it, Ethan had to ask himself if she wasn't right. Irritating.

"He was my friend." Offended at her tone, and the insinuation, he snapped, "I was twenty. Of course I agreed." Looking back now, faced with the consequences of that promise, Ethan couldn't believe he'd agreed. But in his defense, he added, "I never thought anything would come of it. At that age, you pretty much think you're immortal, anyway. Hell, he's the same age I am. Who would expect him to die?"

"Certainly not him, I think," Sadie said, skimming the paperwork again. "They were on a road trip to Colorado. The car went off the road, hit a tree. The authorities believe Bill fell asleep driving. Bill and Maggie were killed instantly." She turned to look at the baby. "It's a miracle she didn't die, too."

"Miracle." He pulled in a breath and blew it out again. From where he was standing the baby's survival looked like a damn tragedy. She'd lost both her parents in a blink and now found herself with a stranger who didn't have the first clue what to do with her. "What the hell am I supposed to do now?"

Sadie gave him a quizzical look, as if she couldn't believe he'd even asked the question. "You raise her."

"You say that like it's so simple."

"Ethan," Sadie said patiently, "she doesn't have anyone else. She needs you."

Well, that didn't sound good. He didn't want to be needed. Hell, he'd gone out of his way all these years to *avoid* any kind of connection with anyone. Except for his all-too-brief marriage. But that had turned out to be an excellent life lesson. Ethan had learned that he sucked at being a husband. He simply wasn't the *hearth and home* kind of man.

"You just told me I don't have a life," Ethan argued fiercely. "How am I supposed to give her one?"

At his rising voice, the baby started whimpering and Sadie rocked her a little more firmly. "I guess you're going to have to make some changes, Ethan."

There was that word again. Change usually screwed everything up. He liked his life just the way it was. He worked hard to keep his life unencumbered, rolling along on an expected road. And now…change.

Shaking his head, he backed up farther, as if he could actually maneuver his way out of this. And even as he argued for it, Ethan knew he couldn't. Stupidly or not, he'd made a promise, and when he gave his word he damn well kept it. When the blind panic lifted enough that he could begin to think clearly again, he said, "I don't need a life. I need a nanny."

"Oh, Ethan."

"What else should I do?" he demanded. "Get *married*? No. A nanny is the answer. All I have to do is find the right person. Someone qualified—" He broke off, checked his watch. "We're supposed to be in a meeting on the Donatello acquisition right now."

"Yes, well, we can't be." She looked at the baby as if to remind him of the hell his life had suddenly become.

"I can tell you that Richard Donatello hasn't changed his mind about selling out to you."

"He will," Ethan said. "You could take care of her while I handle business."

"No." Sadie shook her head firmly. "I'm not your babysitter, I'm your assistant. Plus, I just quit, remember?"

"I remember you gave two weeks' notice. So you're still on the payroll."

"As an assistant."

"So assist me!" That came out as a desperate shout and he hated it. So did the baby. She started howling again and Ethan winced.

"Shh, shh," Sadie whispered, bouncing the baby and patting her back. Firing Ethan a hard look, she said, "Cancel the meeting, Ethan."

Damn it. She was right. The meeting had to wait. Fine. Meeting canceled. Sadie quits. Baby arrives. *Change is not good*, he reminded himself. And sometimes you simply had no choice but to adjust. Still, he told himself as something occurred to him, that didn't mean he couldn't help himself out. At least, temporarily. Before he could think better of it, Ethan blurted out, "I'll pay you one hundred thousand dollars if you stay for an extra month."

"What?" Her eyes went wide and her jaw dropped.

Of course he'd surprised her. Hell, he'd surprised himself. "A hundred thousand dollars," he repeated, then added, "on the condition you help me with…" He waved one hand at the baby.

"Her name is Emma," Sadie said wryly.

"Good. You already know that, so you're ahead of

the game." Nodding to himself at the brilliance of his solution, he demanded, "Well? What do you say?"

"I think you're crazy," Sadie said. "But yes, I'll stay for a month. Help you find a nanny."

"And help me take care of it until then."

"Her."

"Right. *Her.*" He reached for his phone, punched a couple buttons and waited for a second. "Kelly. Tell the team the meeting's postponed until tomorrow. Something's..." he looked at Sadie and the baby "...come up." Huge understatement.

When he hung up, he looked at Sadie and deliberately shoved his hands into his slacks pockets so he couldn't be forced to hold the baby again. "Call Alice at the house, tell her what's happened. Have her get a room ready for the kid—order whatever she needs and offer a big cash bonus for quick delivery and setup."

"Ethan—"

"You still work for me, Sadie. Get it done." Then he walked to his desk, sat down and started working. He avoided looking at Sadie again and told himself it was for the best. Hell, the baby wouldn't want to be held by him, anyway.

A few hours later, Sadie and Ethan, along with the baby, were at Target, staring at a wall of baby supplies.

"How does anyone know what to get?" he asked of no one in particular.

"Well, here I've got a little experience," Sadie admitted. "On those rare Sundays off, I've been shopping with Gina, my sister-in-law."

"You're elected as guide, then."

Sadie noticed that he looked completely out of place

in the perpetually crowded store. In his elegantly cut
suit, he would have been much more at home in his
meeting, or in a five-star restaurant, or even just sitting in his sleek black convertible. But here in Target,
Ethan Hart was enough out of the ordinary that every
woman who passed him paused to stare. Of course,
that happened everywhere. The man practically oozed
sex and success.

But at the moment, he was devoting himself to
staying as far away from the big red cart and the baby
strapped into it as humanly possible. Sadie gritted her
teeth. She'd promised to *help* him with the baby, not do
everything herself. Not even for a hundred-thousand-
dollar bonus. This was Ethan's chance to step outside
the carefully built path he'd designed for himself, and
Sadie wanted to see him do it. But now wasn't the time
for that argument. Pretty soon, the baby would be hun-
gry. Or wet again. Or tired. Sadie would rather avoid
the inevitable meltdown that she'd witnessed with her
infant nephew just a couple weeks ago.

"Okay," she said abruptly. "First, we need diapers."

"Right." Ethan instantly turned to the task at hand.
"But what size? There's a million of them." He scanned
the shelves, looking like a blind man trying to feel his
way through a forest.

"You held her. How much do you think she weighs?"

He pushed one hand through his hair. "Twenty
pounds?"

"Okay," she said. "Start there. I'll get some formula
and bottles and...*everything*."

Yes, she'd been shopping with Gina, stocking up on
baby supplies, but that was just adding a few things to
an already well-stocked house. *This* was starting from

scratch, and she was overwhelmed with deciding what Ethan might need to care for Emma. He was right—there were just too many *things*.

While the baby slapped her hands on the cart and Ethan stayed at the end of the aisle, reading the descriptions on every bag of diapers, Sadie loaded in whatever she thought might be useful. Toys, a stuffed bear that Emma grabbed hold of and refused to release, bottles, bibs, nipples, pacifiers… The cart was pretty much full when Ethan turned and dropped a single package of diapers on top of it.

"One?" she asked, stunned. "Really? You think one package will do it?"

"How the hell do I know? You're the expert here."

"Ooh," Sadie said with a grin. "That had to have been hard for you to say. Ethan Hart, the man who's never wrong and must be obeyed at all costs."

He scowled. "I don't remember you being this sarcastic over the last five years."

"That's because I muttered most of it," she admitted. "Get two more packages to start and that should hold us."

"For what? The apocalypse?" He stared at the cart. "She doesn't really need all of that, does she?"

The baby frowned, as if she understood what Ethan had said and disapproved. Sadie almost laughed, but she was afraid it might sound hysterical, so she swallowed it. Busy shoppers rushed past them as music pumped through the store speakers. "Do you really want to find out in the middle of the night that you need something and you don't have it?"

"Oh, hell no. Fine. We'll take it all." He started to walk away, but Sadie stopped him.

"She needs clothes, too, Ethan."

He goggled at her. "This is incredible. How do people do this?"

"Well, most people don't have to do an entire stock-up run all in one day…"

"Right." He looked over the aisles they had just been picking clean and said, "You know, the chocolate business makes billions, but turns out, that's just peanuts. The *real* money is in baby junk. How can someone who can't even talk possibly need so much stuff?"

She almost felt sorry for him. Almost. This was a huge disruption in the placid lake that was his life. But hey, sink or swim. "It's a mystery. Come on. Baby clothes."

He followed after her, grumbling under his breath, and Sadie looked into Emma's eyes and grinned. In the five years she'd worked for the man, Sadie had never seen Ethan completely out of his element. And it was sort of endearing. She didn't need another reason to be drawn to him, though, so she really tried to dismiss what she was feeling.

Then he did it to her again when he picked up baby pajamas and discarded the penguins in favor of the ones covered in teddy bears. When he caught her looking at him quizzically, he shrugged and tossed the jammies into the cart. Then, pointing at the baby now chewing fiercely on the stuffed bear's ear, he said simply, "She likes bears."

Sadie took a deep breath to still the jolt of her heartbeat. He didn't want the baby, but he was doing everything he could to make sure she was cared for. He didn't like change, but he was so far accepting a huge one in his life. He didn't belong in Target, but here he stood. And God knew he shouldn't look so damn sexy, but there it was. Even as she thought it, she spotted a woman staring at Ethan with open admiration.

Sadie told herself to get past it. Get over it. She was going to leave Ethan behind so she could find the right man for her. No matter how she felt about Ethan, no matter how her blood burned when she looked at him, going after him was a catastrophe waiting to happen.

He wasn't the man for her and trying to pretend otherwise was just setting herself up for a crash. So she busied herself by concentrating on the shopping and promising herself that one day, she'd be doing this for her own family.

The sad part of that dream was Ethan wouldn't be a part of it.

Three

By the time they were finished and checked out, Sadie was stunned by just how much Ethan had bought—and that wasn't even counting the baby furniture ordered and hopefully already delivered to his house. Sadie took Emma in her car while Ethan loaded all the bags and boxes into his. They'd taken both cars so Sadie could leave once he was settled in with his new charge.

With Emma in her car seat, Sadie headed for Dana Point, barely keeping up with Ethan as he hurtled down Pacific Coast Highway. If she hadn't known better, she would have thought he was trying to lose her. But that couldn't be true, because she already knew where he lived.

Sadie had been to Ethan's house before, bringing him papers or running one of the parties he threw for distributors, but today felt different. They weren't there for business and it sort of colored how she looked at the house itself.

It was Spanish-style and gigantic, even by mansion standards. The red tiled roof made the white walls seem even brighter than they normally would have. The grounds, from the sweeping lawns to the flower beds and climbing roses over the pergola in the backyard, were lovingly tended by a team of gardeners and the floor-to-ceiling windows glinted in the winter sunlight. Behind the house, she knew, was a sloping yard that ran down to the cliffs where waves beat a constant rhythm against the rocks.

The view was majestic and the house itself was breathtaking. Every room was huge, open and appealing in an earthy, masculine way. Brown leather furniture and burnished wood decorated every room and the dark red ceramic tiles in the halls were a dramatic statement. Sadie's favorite spot was the Spanish-style, enclosed courtyard. Three sides of the house surrounded an outdoor living area, complete with comfortable furniture, a bar and kitchen. Terra-cotta pots held a wide variety of plants and the area provided a wonderful view of the ocean.

Today, though, she really didn't have the time to luxuriate in the place itself. She had a cranky baby in the backseat and a ton of things to unload.

Ethan came around and opened her car door. The baby chose that moment to scream her fury and Ethan winced. "How does she hit those notes?"

"It's a gift."

"Why don't you take her inside? I'll get the gardener and some of his guys to empty out the cars."

Huffing out a breath, Sadie accused, "You're just trying to avoid touching her, aren't you?"

"See why I hired you?" he countered. "You're smart."

"Right." This did not bode well for Ethan and Emma. If he avoided the baby every chance he got, he'd never adapt to the new situation. Yes, he'd paid Sadie a lot of money to hang around until he got things settled. But she was going to make sure that he did at least half the baby care.

She got the little girl out of the car seat, plopped her on one hip and headed for the front door. Ethan wasn't too far behind her, but when she opened the front door and walked inside, they all stopped dead.

Alice, Ethan's housekeeper, was standing in the entryway, arms folded across her abundant chest and a frown etched deeply into her features. Really, Alice defied stereotypical logic. Looking at her round body and bright blue eyes, most people would have guessed her to be as kind as Mrs. Claus. Nothing could be further from the truth. Sadie had never understood why Ethan kept such an unpleasant woman working for him. It probably helped that he was rarely at home and so wasn't exposed to her much.

Alice's eyes narrowed accusingly on the baby. "I'm the housekeeper," she said flatly. "I don't take care of children."

"Fine," Ethan said, pushing Sadie farther inside so he could step past her.

"I mean it." Alice lifted her chins and sniffed. "I've got my routine and I won't have it upset by an infant."

Sadie had never really liked Alice. No surprise there, since the woman was cold and distant. On those rare occasions when Ethan was here, in his own house, Alice behaved like he was an interloper. Normally, she had the run of the mansion on the cliffs. She was alone here more often than not and Sadie had a feeling it was only Ethan's inherent hatred of change that had kept him from firing the woman.

"I said fine," Ethan repeated. "Fernando and some of his guys are bringing the baby's food and—" he waved a hand to indicate everything else they'd dragged along "—stuff to the kitchen. Did the furniture for her room show up?"

"It did," Alice said, her mouth flattening into a grim line of displeasure. "Those men tracked dirt all over my floors and made a racket for nearly an hour."

Ethan just looked at her. "So her room's ready."

"It is, just don't expect me to clean up after an infant."

Sadie took a breath and clamped her mouth shut to avoid telling Alice exactly what she thought of her. Holding the baby a little closer as if to protect her from the nastiness, she watched Ethan and saw a flash of anger in his eyes. It was a wonder Alice didn't bother to notice it, as well.

"I'm a housekeeper, not a babysitter," Alice said again.

"I heard you the first time," Ethan said, and Sadie heard the warning in his tone.

"As long as you remember it," the woman snapped. "Now, I'll be having my dinner in my kitchen. As I didn't know you'd be home, or bringing along company—" her gaze swept over Sadie and the baby dismissively "—I didn't prepare a meal for you. I'm not a babysitter and I'm not a cook."

"Here's something else you're not," Ethan interrupted. "Employed."

"I beg your pardon?" Alice bleated.

"You should," Ethan retorted, "but I doubt you really are. You're fired. Get your stuff and get out."

"What?" Sadie said.

She couldn't believe this. For years, she'd thought he should get rid of Alice. But to do it today? When everything was already in turmoil? What had happened to "change is bad"?

Alice's whole body stiffened as if someone had shoved a pole down the back of her grim black dress. Clearly indignant, she lifted her chin and glared at Ethan. "I see no reason for this—"

Ethan took a step closer to her and the woman backed up. Alice was in no physical danger and she had to know that, but seeing Ethan's temper was so rare, it was startling when it finally appeared.

"This is my house, Alice. Not yours," he said. "Something you seem to have forgotten over the years."

"I don't know what you mean..."

"Yes, you do." Ethan loomed over her, using his height as an intimidation factor. "Do you really think I haven't noticed that you've crowned yourself queen of *my* house?"

The woman's eyes darted from side to side as if looking for an escape—but she didn't find one.

"I've been willing to put up with your attitude because, frankly, you didn't matter enough to make a change. But that ends now," Ethan told her. "This is *my* house. And I'll run it however the hell I want to run it. And I'll hire someone who's more concerned with her job than she is with pretending she's the lady of the manor."

Alice sputtered and Sadie ducked her head to hide a smile. She really shouldn't be pleased about this, but Alice had had this coming for a long time. Plus, Ethan was the sexiest show she'd ever seen. Anger rippled off him in hot waves, yet he spoke so quietly, so coolly. It was the contrast, really, that was making Sadie feel as if her nerve endings were electrified.

Well, that and the look in his eyes. The man was so hot that smoke should have been lifting off the top of his head. He was definitely her weakness.

"You owe me two weeks' salary," Alice snapped.

"You're right." Ethan started for the stairs, already putting the awful woman in the past. "Leave an address on the entry table and I'll mail you a check and a severance bonus."

"A bonus?" Sadie said quietly, as she followed after him.

"It's worth it," Ethan muttered.

"See?" Sadie countered, her voice as quiet as his. "Like I told you. Not all change is bad."

He shot her a look. "Save it."

By the time they got the baby settled in her room, Ethan was even more on edge. He'd fired his housekeeper, been saddled with a baby and his assistant had resigned.

"Hell of a day," he muttered.

"A long one, anyway," Sadie agreed. "At least the baby's room looks beautiful. Well, except for that beige paint. That should be changed to something a little more girlie."

"I'm not having a pink room in my house," he argued, walking down the stairs behind her. His gaze dropped to the curve of her butt and his hands itched to grab hold and squeeze. Actually, what he really wanted to do was get her out of her work clothes, stretch her out on the floor in front of the fire and explore every square inch of that tidy body.

"I didn't say pink," she said, tossing him a look over her shoulder. "That's a little sexist, don't you think?"

"I didn't know a color *could* be sexist."

"Well," she quipped, "now you do. I was thinking something cheerful, bright. Pale yellow, maybe, or a soft green. With pictures and maybe a mural. Something to stimulate her."

He snorted a laugh. "The way she screamed when you put her in the crib tells me she's already plenty stimulated."

At the bottom of the stairs, Sadie stopped and turned around to look at him. "She's lost her parents, been thrown at people she doesn't know and forced to sleep in a bed she doesn't recognize. I'd like to see how well either of us would handle that situation."

There were actual sparks in her eyes as she glared at him. Ethan held up both hands. "You're right."

Astonishment flashed across her features. "Wow. I'm right. A banner day indeed."

"There's that sarcasm again. What does it say that I'm starting to enjoy it?"

"That you're a glutton for punishment?" She grinned, turned around and marched across the foyer to the front table, which held a massive crystal vase and a fall flower arrangement. She picked up her brown leather bag and slung it over her shoulder.

Suspicion washed over him as he demanded, "What are you doing?"

"I'm going home."

A feeling he didn't want to describe as "panic" washed over him. He glanced down at the baby monitor in his hand as if it were a live grenade. "You can't leave."

"Sure I can." She gave him a smile that punched at his insides. "Don't worry, thanks to that bonus, I'm staying for an extra month, remember? I'll see you tomorrow."

He threw a quick look at the stairs behind him. There was a baby on the second floor and if Sadie left, *he* was the only one here to take care of it. *Her.*

Unacceptable.

How had this happened to him? He, who so carefully regimented the world around him. This morning, his life had been just as he wanted it. A successful business, an efficient assistant, no bumps or twists on a road that lay before him, straight and narrow. And now...everything was a tangled mess and damned if he'd suffer through this alone. "Stay."

"I am."

"No," he said tightly, knowing she was referring to staying on at the office, and helping him find a damn nanny. He meant so much more. "Stay here. At the house."

A flash of something interesting darted across her eyes and was gone again in a blink. "You want me to stay the night?"

"No," he corrected, making sure she understood. "I want you to stay here at the house with me. Help me with that baby until I find a damn nanny or hire a housekeeper who isn't allergic to children."

She laughed a little and shook her head hard enough to send those loose blond curls into a dance around her head. "Not a chance."

Her laughter was both erotic and extremely annoying. Sadie was about to walk out that door, leaving him alone in the house with a child. Cowardly or not, Ethan had no problem acknowledging that he did *not* want to be alone with that baby.

Earlier that day, he'd given Sadie a lot of money to get her to stay an extra month. Maybe all he really needed to do here was offer even more. Hell, money was easy for him—asking for help wasn't.

"I'll pay you fifty thousand dollars extra to move in here temporarily."

"What?" She stared at him.

"You heard me." At least he had her attention. She hadn't left yet, and that was good.

"I did. I just don't believe it."

"Well, believe it." Ethan pushed one hand through his hair briefly. "Look, I don't like admitting this, but when it comes to that baby I'm out of my depth. I need your help."

Her head snapped back and a small smile curved her mouth. At any other time, he would have enjoyed that soft smile.

"You're saying that there's something Ethan Hart can't handle."

He scowled at her. "You're enjoying this, aren't you?"

"A little."

This was new territory for Ethan. He was self-sufficient. In charge. Yet now, an infant had reduced him to admitting his failings. "Fine. Yes. I need your help. So what do you say?"

She tipped her head to one side and her short blond curls fell lazily with the movement. "For fifty thousand dollars, of course I'll stay."

Pleased, but a little surprised that she'd given in so easily, he wondered why money was such a motivator for her. Was there something going on in her life that he didn't know about? "I didn't expect you to agree so quickly. Who knew you were so mercenary?"

She laughed shortly. "Mercenary? That may be how it looks to you, but I've got news for you. Maybe it's not the same for gazillionaires, but the rest of us peons have to make mortgage payments, car payments, buy, you know, *food*. This money will let me take my time finding a new job. Help me get a new car, maybe fix the plumbing in my condo..."

He didn't much care for the "finding a new job" thing, but for the rest, he realized he hadn't taken any interest in Sadie's life before now. He should have. The car she had strapped the baby into was a nearly fifteen-year-old sedan. Why was she driving such an old car? And her condo had plumbing issues? Hell, until today he didn't know she *owned* a condo.

They'd worked together closely for five years and she was a mystery to him. His own fault, he told himself. He'd been so attracted to her that he'd treated her as if she were invisible. He hadn't taken an interest in her because he couldn't *afford* to. Since she'd turned in her resignation a few hours ago, it was as if he were meeting her for the first time.

The desire was there and stronger than ever—but

there was also something new. Damned if he didn't *like* her.

Well he felt like an ass. It didn't happen often, thank God, but Ethan could admit to it when it did. At least to himself. Offering her money had been a last-ditch effort for him to keep her in her job. To keep her here, where she could help him out with that baby. He hadn't even realized how important that money could be to her. He paid his employees well and never really thought about it otherwise. He'd grown up wealthy and intended to stay that way. So when you were used to a lot of money being readily available, you didn't often stop to think that money might be an issue for someone else.

She was still watching him. Waiting. Finally, he said, "Fine. I admit it. You're the hero of the working class and I'm a cold money grubber."

"That sounds about right." She grinned and that smile punched him in the solar plexus so hard he had to fight for air. "I mean, come on. You're paying me a hundred and fifty thousand dollars to help you out for a month. Normal people don't do that."

"Now I'm not normal?"

She laughed again and it irritated him just how much he enjoyed the sound.

"Of course you're not."

"Thanks very much," he muttered darkly.

"I didn't say you were *abnormal*," she said. Digging into her purse, she pulled her keys out and jangled them in her palm. "For example. Most people don't live in mansions."

"I know that."

"Do you?" She tipped her head to one side again and Ethan realized just how often she did that when talking to him. And he also realized how fascinated he was with those loose blond curls and how they moved. He wondered how they would feel sliding across his skin.

"You realize the bonus you offered me today is more than most people make in a year."

He frowned and shook himself out of the distraction of her hair. Focusing, he said, "I'm not completely clueless, Sadie." Then he noticed the car keys in her hand. "Where are you going? You just agreed to stay *here*."

"Not without clothes."

Okay, that short sentence opened up a world of images in his mind. Sadie, walking through his house naked. Sadie in the shower, water sliding down her skin. Sadie stretched out across his bed, holding her arms up to him. Sadie beneath him, crying out his name as he slammed his body into hers.

Ethan swallowed hard, took a breath and blew it out again. Man, once he'd unleashed all the sexual thoughts about her he'd been suppressing for years, they were almost too much to take. He came back to the present in time to see her headed for the door. She paused and looked back over her shoulder. "I'm going home to pack a bag. I'll be back."

He couldn't stop himself from shooting a worried glance at the staircase that led to the ticking time bomb upstairs. Shifting his gaze back to Sadie's, he said, "An extra twenty-five thousand if you make it back before she wakes up and starts screaming again."

"Stop throwing money at me." She laughed and the sound bubbled through his bloodstream like champagne. "You're really off your game, aren't you?"

"Will it get you back here fast if I say yes?"

"Relax. I'll be back in an hour or so." She opened

the door, stepped onto the porch, then added, "Emma's not going to kill you, Ethan."

When she left, closing the door behind her, Ethan muttered, "Don't bet on it."

"I'm still not sure about this."

Gabriel stood outside the Heart Chocolates offices and looked up at the building as if he'd never seen it before. He'd done a lot of thinking about this plan and he was still torn about what to do.

Not surprising, really. He was a Hart, after all, even if he was the younger brother. He'd grown up with the same family stories Ethan had heard. He'd been taught to respect what had come before and build on the traditions already set in stone.

But wasn't that what he was trying to do? Build on what had been left to them? If they went Ethan's route, they would continue to be successful—at least in the short term. But if they didn't grow and build on what had been left in their care, would they be doing justice to the great-grandfather who had started it all?

Behind him, on Pacific Coast Highway, traffic whizzed past in a never-ending stream. He turned to watch the life pulsing on the street and the cold, January wind slapped his face. Winter nights came early, but that didn't mean people avoided coming to the beach. Out on the sand tonight there would be flames dancing in fire pits, barbecues and music pumping into the night.

When he was a kid, he'd been a member of the never-ending party at the beach. But right here, right now, all Gabe could think about was what he was about to do.

For generations, his family had guarded their chocolate recipe like the Holy Grail. Was he really willing to be the first Hart to share that recipe with an outsider?

"Gabe..." Pam took his hand and gave it a squeeze, as if she could sense his uncertainty. "You're not betraying anyone. You're trying to help. To make a difference."

"Yeah," he mused wryly, "not sure Ethan would see it like that."

"This isn't about Ethan," she said softly. "But honestly, if you don't feel right about this, then don't do it."

He looked down into her brown eyes. The streetlights threw shadows across her face and made her eyes seem even deeper, darker, than they usually were. Gabe held on to her hand like a lifeline. "No, I have to. But trust me, once Ethan finds out what I did. This could tear us so far apart we might never find our way back to each other. And yeah, I know he's a pain in the ass, but he's my brother."

A cold, damp wind rushed past them, lifting Pam's hair into twisting black strands. A rush of heat and something more filled Gabe, and he held on to it, to distract him from what he was about to do. He read the sympathy on her face and held on to that, as well.

He tried to make her understand how he was feeling about all of this. As much as Gabe wanted to try out his ideas, to push his brother into stepping into the twenty-first century, it went against everything he was to sneak into the office and take that recipe. His whole life, he'd been raised with the notion that family was more important than anything. That their family legacy was to be honored. Defended. But essentially, wasn't that what he was trying to do?

Rubbing one hand across his eyes, Gabriel murmured, "You know, Ethan's been the head of the family since our dad died. He's taken care of everything. Put me through college and worked here, running everything by himself until I was ready to come on board."

"And the minute you did, his thumb came down on top of you," she reminded him. "I can't remember how many times you've told me about Ethan squashing your ideas."

Gabe winced. It did feel like that sometimes, but he knew what Ethan dealt with. It wasn't just about maintaining the Hart family legacy... It was dealing with buyers, merchants, marketing, and God knew what else, just to keep moving forward. If Gabe went through with this tonight, what else could it be but a betrayal?

"Maybe I made it sound worse than it is," he mused.

"I know all about family, Gabe. And yes, my brother drives me nuts, too. But really, this comes down to you. You're having second thoughts," Pam said, holding his hand between both of hers.

"And third and fourth," he said, agreeing with her as he took an even longer look at the building that held his family's heritage.

It was brick, which made it stand out in the middle of Newport Beach. Probably not a good idea to build with brick in earthquake country, Gabe silently admitted. But his grandfather had insisted the brick looked sturdy. Dependable. As he wanted their then-fledgling company to be. And Gabe had to admit he must have been onto something because but for a few falling bricks and a couple cracked windows in the last big quake, the building was still standing. Just like the Hart family itself.

But would the family connection survive Gabe going behind Ethan's back to prove a point? And if he didn't go through with this, see his own ideas through, would Gabe eventually resent Ethan enough to destroy their relationship completely?

Questions he wished he had answers to.

"Gabe?" Pam's voice cut into his thoughts and he could have kissed her for it.

"Yeah?"

"You're not doing this *to* Ethan. You're doing it *for* Ethan."

His mouth quirked briefly. He knew damn well his big brother wouldn't see it like that.

She wasn't finished, though. "Like I said before, I understand family loyalty, Gabe. I really do. But sometimes, you have to do what you know is right, whether the family agrees or not. This is your chance to prove something—not just to Ethan, but to yourself."

Pam was right and Gabe knew it, though he wasn't thrilled about it. Still, if he didn't try making up those new flavors, following through on his idea, he'd always regret it. He had to know that he'd done what he could to make his own vision a reality. After all, if *he* didn't have faith in his vision, how could he hope to convince Ethan?

Pam reached up and cupped his cheek in the palm of her hand. "But if you don't want to do this…"

"I really don't," he said, bending down to give her a quick, hard kiss that scrambled his brain cells even as it steadied him. "But I also don't have a choice."

"Are you sure, Gabe?" she asked, biting her bottom lip in a sure sign that she was anxious. "I'll back you either way. You could even wait for a better time. I didn't mean to rush you into this by suggesting we take the recipe to a chocolate chef I know."

"You didn't push me into this," he assured her. "Don't think that. The idea to make up some of the new flavors was a good one. But I'm doing this for me, Pam. If I don't try, I'll never know."

She studied him for a long minute, then nodded. "Okay, then. I'm with you."

"Yeah," he said, smiling. "You really are."

He slung one arm around her shoulders and hugged her tight before steering her toward the glass doors. Gabe already knew Ethan wasn't at the office. His car wasn't in the parking lot, so the coast, as they said in old movies, was clear.

The security guard in the foyer leaped to his feet to unlock the door as Gabriel approached. Once they were inside, the door was closed and locked again. Light streamed down on the gleaming, honey-toned wood floor. The walls were splashed with colorful pictures of their chocolates.

"Evening, Mr. Hart," the guard said. "Didn't expect to see you back here tonight."

"I won't be long, Joe," he said, and guided Pam to the elevator. "Just have to go get something from the office."

"Yes, sir." The older man went back to his desk and wasn't even looking at them when the elevator doors hissed closed.

The office was too quiet. It felt as if they were walking through an upscale abandoned building. Their shoes on the hardwood floors clacked noisily in the stillness. The lights were dimmed and in every shadow, Gabe imagined he could see his great-grandfather and all the other Harts who'd come before him watching with disapproval. But he shook that off and continued into Ethan's office.

The original recipe had, of course, been scanned into the computer and was kept in an encrypted file that only Ethan and Gabriel could access. It was also stored on flash drives kept in several different places, for security's sake. And because he was Ethan, Gabriel's big brother kept the original recipe in a bank box, and a copy of it in a wall safe. He did it because their father had done it that way, too. As if keeping that recipe close would continue the company's growth.

Though it wasn't a plea to the universe for luck. It was more of a family talisman.

And Gabriel was about to set it free.

Four

Sadie was running late, but she stopped at her brother's house, anyway. She told herself it was sort of on the way to Dana Point from her condo in Long Beach, so it wasn't as if she'd gone very far out of her way. Fine, it was *way* out of the way. But the truth was, she just wanted to talk to Gina.

Mike and Gina's house was in a subdivision in Foothill Ranch. The houses were big, but rooms were small. The neighborhoods were laid out in curving, twisting streets and the houses sat practically on the curb. No room for a front yard or a driveway. The backyards were small, too, but the streets were crowded with herds of children. Which was really why her brother and his wife were still in the house they were outgrowing.

Still, every time she turned onto their street, with the cookie-cutter houses lined up like pale beige soldiers, Sadie thought of the opening shots of the old movie *Poltergeist*.

"Hey! Nice surprise!" Gina opened the front door, reached out to hug her, then dragged Sadie into the house. "How did you escape your captor?"

Sadie laughed. Mike and Gina were not big fans of Ethan. "There've been a lot of surprises today. That's why I'm here. Had to talk to you about it."

"Oh, now I'm intrigued." Gina grinned and tucked her shoulder-length black hair behind her ears. She wore faded jeans, one of Mike's long-sleeved white shirts that, on Gina, hung down past her thighs, and she was barefoot. Her daughter was only three weeks old and already Gina looked fabulous. "Come on in, sit by the fire and spill your guts."

"Lovely invitation." Sadie glanced at the stairs. "The kids in bed already?"

"Don't jinx me," Gina warned, holding up one finger to her lips. "I wore the boys out at the park today and the baby's in one of her four-hour sleep jags. So let's take advantage of it. You want some wine?"

"So much." Sadie dropped her purse on the dining room table and followed Gina into the kitchen. Through the wall of windows behind the sink, Sadie looked out at the greenbelt and the yellow lab, Einstein, who was sprawled across the grass, taking a nap.

The house, this place, was cozy. There were toys on the patio, a trampoline in one corner of the yard and tiny sneakers kicked off beside the back door. It was family. It was exactly what Sadie wanted for herself. And finally, she'd set herself on the path toward getting it.

"What's going on?" Gina handed her a glass of wine,

took one for herself, then led the way to the couch lined up in front of a gas fireplace that was hissing merrily.

Sadie told her. All of it. As she talked, she watched Gina's reactions and was glad to see that most of them matched what she'd been feeling herself.

"I don't know what to comment on first," Gina finally said, when Sadie ran down.

"Dealer's choice." Sadie took a long sip, then got up to grab a bag of chips from the pantry.

"Okay, *wow* on the money front. I mean, whether he knows it or not, Ethan just helped you quit."

"I know." Sadie plopped down beside her friend. "I don't think he realizes that yet."

"Eventually he will and he won't be happy." Gina reached out and patted Sadie's hand. "But honey, this is great. You'll be able to take some time before you jump back into another job. And get a new car before the one you have breaks down around you and you're left sitting on the street clutching a steering wheel."

Sad, but true. "That's what I was thinking."

"Plus you won't be held hostage at a chocolate factory anymore, so maybe we could set you up with Mike's friend Josh." Gina grinned and winked at her. "He's really great. Gorgeous. Beautiful eyes, fantastic butt."

"Aren't you married to my brother?"

"Please. Was I struck blind lately?" Gina rolled her eyes. "Anyway, Josh joined the fire department a month ago and Mike really likes him."

Mike was a firefighter, which meant he was gone for four days, then home for four days. Since they all spent so much time together, Mike got to know the guys at his station really well. But this was the first time he and Gina had tried to set Sadie up with one of them.

"Wow. A setup. That's a first."

"Well, come on, what would have been the point before?" Gina shook her head slowly. "You were always working. Why bother setting you up? Heck, you walked out of Megan's wedding for your job."

Sadie winced. "I just reminded Ethan of that today."

Gina curled her legs up under her and leaned back on the couch. "Sweetie, this is your chance to have a life. What're you looking so worried about?"

"Do I?"

"Your forehead's all wrinkled up. You should stop that."

Instinctively Sadie reached up and smoothed her fingers across her brow. "I'm not worried. I'm…" She sighed. "I don't know what I am. It's been a weird day."

"You could say that," Gina said with a laugh. "Resigned, helping take care of a baby, poor little thing, and lots of cash."

"And," Sadie mused, "once I quit, Ethan looked at me differently."

Gina snorted. "You mean he noticed you were female?"

"Exactly." Sophie took another sip of the cold white wine. "It was…exciting."

Gina slapped one hand to her forehead. "Oh, God."

"What?"

"Sadie, the whole point of quitting was so you could find a life, right?" Gina reached out, grabbed her hand and shook it. "Didn't you tell me two weeks ago that you want to find the right guy for you and give up on the fantasy of Ethan?"

God, it was humiliating to have her own words tossed back at her. But this was why she'd come to Gina. To get the truth. Hard as it was to hear. Mike and Gina had the kind of relationship that Sadie wanted for herself. They were partners. They laughed. They fought. They loved and always had each other's back. And Sadie wasn't blind. She'd seen the looks her brother gave his wife when he thought no one was watching.

She wanted to be wanted like that.

"Yeah, I did." Sadie looked down into her wine. "But…"

"Do you still have your list?" Gina asked.

"Of course." Sadie had been working on that list for the last two years.

"How many qualifications are on it now?"

"Five," Sadie said, staring down into her glass. When she first made up the list of what she wanted in a man, there'd been more than twenty items on it. Over time, though, she'd whittled it down to the top five.

"Let's hear them."

Sadie knew what her sister-in-law was up to. She wanted to remind Sadie that Ethan was *not* the man for her. And maybe Gina was right. Today had been fun. Watching Ethan's panic, sharing things outside the job with him. Seeing him fire Alice and take charge of a child he hadn't wanted. It was as if they'd been a team of a different sort today. Not the work thing, where they each knew their roles and acted them out effortlessly.

This had been different. Today they'd been simply Ethan and Sadie. Man and woman. And she'd enjoyed it way too much. So it would probably be a good thing if she reminded *herself* about her list.

"Fine." She ticked them off on her fingers. "Sexy.

Adventurous. Sense of humor. Spending time with me. Loves kids."

"Uh-huh," Gina mused. "And how many of those fit Ethan?"

"Sexy…" Her voice trailed off, because she couldn't say more. "Okay, fine. He's not the man on my list."

"Thank you." Nodding at her, Gina said with some sympathy, "Sadie, I know you're nuts about the man, but you deserve someone to be nuts about *you*."

"Yeah. I know. But—"

"No buts," Gina interrupted, holding up one hand to keep her quiet. "Ethan's not going to give you what you want."

"What if all I want is hot sex?"

Gina laughed and set her glass down. "Who doesn't want that? But it's not *all* you want."

"No, it's not." But oh boy, it was a great idea. Just imagining hot, wild sex with Ethan set off tiny fires inside her. She took a drink of the cold wine, hoping to smooth things out. It didn't work.

"Still, not a bad idea." Gina shrugged and took another sip of her own wine. "If you think it'll help, get the hot sex from Ethan, then when you finally leave your job, you walk with no regrets. No what-if's running through your head. Sadie, it's long past time to look out for yourself."

More heat rushed through Sadie at the thought of hot sex with Ethan. But then, she'd been feeling that rush for five years. Was Gina right? Should she take advantage of her "resigned but still with him" situation? She *really* wanted to. Even if her future wouldn't include the man she'd loved for so long…the present could be pretty great.

"Good," Gina said. "You're thinking about it. And from what I can see, you like the idea. But don't think too long," she warned. "Sometimes you think yourself right out of doing what you want to do."

Sadie fell back against the couch. "It's really annoying that you know me so well."

"That's so sweet."

Sadie laughed just as a baby's wail drifted through the monitor sitting on the coffee table. Gina sighed. "Playtime's over. You sure you don't want to stay here tonight and go rescue Ethan in the morning? Mike's shift won't be over for two more days and I could use the company."

"Tempting," Sadie said, "but Ethan offered me another twenty-five thousand if I made it back before Emma woke up."

Gina's laugh rolled out loud and hard. "The man's really desperate, isn't he? Okay, fine. But once you're really out of a job, your nephews would love to spend some time with you."

"Disneyland trip on me," Sadie promised, then leaned in to give Gina a hug. "Then I'll camp out here with you when Mike's on shift."

"Good, that sounds great."

"Thanks," Sadie said. "Seriously."

"I didn't do much."

"You married my dumb brother just because you knew I needed a sister," Sadie teased.

"Yeah, that's why I did it. And the hot sex, of course."

"Well, naturally."

If she hadn't been so damn efficient, Sadie could have been on the road toward Ethan's house. Instead, she was stopping by the office to pick up the file on the Donatello acquisition. Since the meeting had been postponed until tomorrow, she and Ethan could go over the basics again tonight.

Joe let her in the front door and she headed straight for the elevators. Time was ticking. She'd stayed too long with Gina, but it had felt good to have her sister-in-law back her up. Of course, no surprise there. Gina had been after Sadie to quit her job for the last two years so she could have a life outside the office.

And Gina was right. Sadie knew it, even though she didn't like it. Stepping off the elevator, Sadie looked around the place that had pretty much been her world for the last five years. It wasn't the first time she'd been in the building long after everyone else had left for the day. She couldn't count how many times she and Ethan had worked late, just the two of them in the quiet.

This time, it felt different to her. Not only because she was here alone, but because now she knew she wouldn't be here much longer. In another month or so, she'd be gone from her job, this office, Ethan's life. She felt a small pang of regret at that thought, but leaving was really her only choice if she wanted more for herself than a good-paying job.

She started walking toward Ethan's office. The lights were dim, cubicles quiet and the air still smelled of the day's coffee. It was empty, of course, but for the memories that crowded around her. "It's going to be weird to not come here every day," she whispered, and shivered a little as her voice dissolved in the silence.

Sadie shook off the thought and her own mixed feelings as she opened Ethan's office door and said, "Gabe? What're you doing here?"

Startled, Gabriel jumped, then laughed shortly. "God, you scared the hell out of me."

The woman with him was pretty, with long black hair and big brown eyes. As Sadie watched, she moved in closer to Gabe, standing beside the bank of wide windows. "Hi," she said. "I'm Pam. Pam Cassini."

"Right, sorry." Gabe shook his head and dropped one arm around Pam's shoulders. "Seriously, Sadie, you move so quietly I didn't hear you coming in. What're you doing here?"

"I wanted to pick up a file to take to Ethan's."

He looked confused. "You're going to Ethan's house?"

"Yeah," she said, walking across the room to the wall of wooden cabinets. Opening the top one, she flipped through the files inside until she found Donatello's and pulled it out before shutting the cabinet again. Sure, they had all the files on computers and backed up by the cloud, and any number of other security measures. But they still kept hard copies, too. So much easier to read through.

"It's a long story," she said, "so I'll let Ethan tell you about it. But bottom line, he's been named guardian of a six-month-old girl."

"Ethan?" Gabriel's shock was understandable. Ethan wasn't exactly father-of-the-year material. "My brother's taking care of an infant?"

Sadie laughed a little. "With my help. But why are you guys here?"

Gabe looked at Pam briefly, then shrugged and said, "I wanted to show Pam around and Ethan's office has the best view."

It did. But not at night. Odd, but it wasn't her business why one of the owners might be in the office after closing. After all, *she* was there, right?

"Okay. Well," she said, waving the file, "I'd better get moving. I'll see you tomorrow, Gabe. Nice meeting you," she added to Pam, who smiled and nodded.

She was in the lobby, still wondering what was going on with Gabriel, when her cell phone rang. "Thanks, Joe," she said, slipping out the door before glancing at the phone screen.

Grinning to herself, she answered. "Hello, Ethan."

"Are you on your way back?" he demanded. "She's making noises. I think she's waking up."

"On my way." This situation was really far more entertaining than it should be. But Sadie couldn't help enjoying seeing the man who was always calm, cool and in charge suddenly thrown off balance by a baby. She unlocked her car, slid in and fired it up. "Be there in twenty minutes, and don't offer me more money if I can get there in fifteen."

"Just get here."

Still smiling to herself, Sadie shook her head and steered into the never-ending traffic on Pacific Coast Highway.

"She's asleep again," Sadie told him a half hour later. "I just patted her back for a while and she drifted off."

"Good." Ethan grabbed a beer out of the fridge. "Do you want anything?"

Oh, so many things, Sadie thought. Starting with, of course, that hot sex she'd been talking about with Gina. Looking at him now, she found it astonishing to realize just how sexy the man looked in a pair of jeans and an untucked blue dress shirt. She'd only ever seen him in one of the elegant suits Sadie had sort of assumed he had been born in.

God knew he was sexy as sin in one of his suits, but seeing him here, dressed so casually, put a whole new spin on her fantasies. Her mouth watered and her heartbeat kicked up a notch. Then she took a breath, pushed her fantasy aside and said, "Food, Ethan. I want food."

He nodded. "I had Chinese delivered. It's in the oven."

"Perfect." Sadie got it and set everything out on the table, then opened a half-dozen cabinets before she found plates.

Ethan found silverware, opened a bottle of wine and got each of them water besides. In a few minutes, they were sitting opposite each other in the soft, overhead light. The kitchen, like the rest of the house, was huge.

It was white—boring—with gray cabinets and a mile and a half of black granite counters. They were so tidy it looked as though no one used the room at all, and that was probably true. Alice had said herself she wasn't a cook, and Sadie was willing to bet that though he could order takeout, Ethan wouldn't have the first clue how to cook for himself.

The table sat in front of windows that overlooked the backyard and the ocean beyond. At night, though, like now, there were solar-powered lights shining beneath bushes, under trees and along a path that led down the slope toward the cliff's edge.

As she thought of that, Sadie said, "You're going to have to put a fence in at the end of the yard. Once Emma starts getting around, it won't be safe the way it is."

"Already thought of that," he said, helping himself to a serving of cashew chicken. "While you were gone,

I called the contractor who did the remodel here a couple of years ago. He's coming out tomorrow to do the measurements."

Impressed, Sadie said, "That was quick."

Wryly, Ethan responded, "I may not know how to diaper a child, but I do know how to keep it safe."

"Her."

"Her." He took a bite, glared at Sadie and said, "What took you so long?"

She dived into her beef and broccoli—that was a point for Ethan. He remembered her favorite from all those times they'd had dinner in his office while they worked. "After I got my stuff, I stopped at my brother's house to talk to Gina."

"To tell her you resigned?"

"Yes," she said, "and other things." She wasn't about to admit to him that Gina had suggested using him for hot monkey sex. Although now that the thought had settled into her mind again, the suggestion was sounding better and better.

"And was Gina happy to hear it?"

Sadie looked up and met his eyes. The overhead lamp shone down on his face, creating shadows, but strangely, it also illuminated. Everything inside her turned upside down. It had always been that way with Ethan. One look from him and she was quivering inside. It was humiliating to admit, even to herself, since he seemed completely unaware of her as a person—let alone a *woman*.

"Yeah," she finally said, taking a sip of wine before digging into the fried rice. "She was glad I quit."

"Nice that your family's happy about you being unemployed."

Her eyebrows lifted. "That's because she knows I

won't be for long. What they're happy about is that maybe now they'll get to see me occasionally."

He dropped his fork and it clattered onto the fine china plate. "You make it sound as if you were an indentured servant. It wasn't that bad."

"Megan's wedding," she said.

"One time," he countered.

"Hardly. I couldn't get to the hospital for any of Mike and Gina's kids' births, either," she reminded him.

"And this is all my fault." His tone clearly said he didn't think so.

"Partly," Sadie said, reaching for her glass of water. She took a long drink, then said, "Mostly mine, though." Meeting his gaze across the table, she continued. "I could have said no to you. I could have told you that I wouldn't work all hours. Or that I wouldn't leave Megan's wedding."

He studied her and she wished she could tell what he was thinking. But he'd sat back in his chair and now his eyes were shadowed, too, hiding what he was feeling.

"I didn't, though, because I liked my job, Ethan." Well, that was true as far as it went. But it wasn't what had caused her to come running whenever Ethan called. That was something else.

Wanting to be with him, around him, working and talking with him.

She didn't mind the late nights because she and Ethan were together, solving problems, making plans for the company's future. She'd fooled herself into believing there was more between them than there was. Her own imagination and desires had convinced her that one day he would notice her.

Well, that had never happened.

"And," she went on, "since I liked it, I sort of let it take over my life."

"Thanks for that, anyway," he muttered.

"Wasn't finished," she added, waving her fork at him. "You do the same thing, Ethan. You don't have a life outside the business."

"So you said earlier." He pushed the plate in front of him to one side. "But my life is just how I like it."

She looked around the kitchen, which was so tidy it could have been in an empty model home. "Really? You like being one man living in a house big enough for ten or twenty people?"

"I like the quiet."

"Right." She laughed shortly and pushed her own plate aside. Here in the darkness, it felt intimate, sitting so close to him. With no one to interrupt, she felt as though she could actually say a few things that she'd wanted to over the years. "You're hiding, Ethan."

"Hiding? From whom?" A bark of laughter shot from his throat. "That's ridiculous."

She shook her head slowly. "No, it's not. Ever since your divorce, you shut yourself off from everything."

Even in the dim light she could see his features freeze up. His laughter abruptly ended, and his mouth flattened into a grim line. "We're not talking about that."

"Of course not. You never have." Forearms braced on the table, she leaned toward him. "This time, though, you don't have to. I will," she said with a shrug.

"You're full of yourself after turning in that resignation," he said.

She nodded. "That's fair. Like I said, it's very freeing."

He didn't smile. "Think you can say anything you want, and I suppose you can. But I don't have to listen."

Her head tipped to one side. "Hiding again?"

"Not hiding," he said shortly. "Just not interested in *sharing*."

She sat back. Picking up her wine, Sadie took a sip, then asked, "What are you interested in, Ethan?"

"My company."

"And?"

"And what? That's it," he said, and stood up. He carried his plate to the sink, turned around and looked at her. "My family started this business more than a hundred years ago and it's up to me to keep it at the top. To protect it. And since when do the two of us talk about this stuff?"

"Since I quit and I don't have to worry about my boss firing me." Sadie carried her plate to the sink, too, and stood beside him.

"I can still tell you to get out."

"But you won't." She pointed to the baby monitor standing in the center of the black granite island.

He gritted his teeth so hard the muscle in his jaw twitched. "Think you're safe, do you?"

"Actually, yes, I do." Turning around, she leaned back against the counter, bracing her hands on the cold, hard edge. She tilted her head to one side and noticed a brief flash of something in his eyes.

"You realize you're still working for me for the next month…"

"Sure," she said, "but that's unofficial."

"I'm paying a lot of money for 'unofficial'."

"I'm worth it," she quipped, and saw that flash in his eyes again. However briefly it had appeared, it set off a similar flash inside her. Sadie felt heat puddle in the pit of her stomach and then slide slowly south. A deep throbbing began at her core as she stared up into his eyes, and it took every bit of her self-control to keep from moving to try to ease that ache.

"I suppose you are." His words came in a whisper and his eyes looked suddenly deep, dark and filled with emotions she couldn't read.

Sadie would have given a lot to know what he was thinking, but in the next moment, she got her first clue.

"It's strange," he said.

"There's been a lot of strange today," she said softly. "Can you be more specific?"

"Okay. I think this is the first time I've ever seen you out of your work clothes…"

Sadie glanced down. She wore black jeans, a long-sleeved red T-shirt and black ballet flats. Hardly an outfit worth putting that look of interest on his face, but there it was.

"And you're barefoot, wearing jeans. I didn't know you *owned* jeans," she said. God, he was barefoot. That was sexy, too. *Get a grip, Sadie.* "It's the first time we've been together when we're *not* working."

"Not true." He put his hands on either side of her and loomed in close. "There was that trip to Dublin last summer."

"A business trip," she murmured, and felt his heat drifting toward her. He was doing this on purpose. Why was he doing this? And oh, she hoped he didn't stop.

"What about when we had a drink in that pub after the meeting?"

"Still work," she said, and she had to look up to meet his gaze as he loomed over her. Her brain instantly painted another picture where he would be looking down at her. Where his body would cover hers. Where his mouth would be on hers as they came together in the most intimate way possible.

"And the singing?" he asked, and she dragged her focus back to the conversation at hand.

"Work but fun," she said, remembering that night in Ireland as one of the best out of the last five years.

"So you can at least admit you had fun that night."

"Never said I didn't."

"Uh-huh. Are you having fun *now*?" he asked, bending his head a little closer to hers.

"I could be, if I knew what you were up to," Sadie admitted, staring into his eyes and trying to decipher what was behind all this. "But I think *you* are having fun."

"Oh, I am," he assured her, as his gaze moved over her features.

"Why are you doing this?" she asked, and could have kicked herself. Did it really matter *why*? Having his mouth just a breath from hers, having his gaze locked on her, was something she'd thought about for years, and now that it was happening she questioned it? What was *wrong* with her?

"Am I making you nervous?" Ethan asked in response.

"If you were?"

"Then I'd stop."

"Then I'm not nervous."

"Glad to hear it." Suddenly any trace of humor was gone from his eyes. His features were taut as he stared at her as if seeing her for the first time. When he leaned in closer, so did Sadie.

Her breath was gone. And she didn't care. She could hear her own heart pounding, felt it hammering in her chest, but breathing was simply off the table. Her blood rushed through her veins, then headed south to set up camp in her groin. Heated throbbing took over, along with an ache she knew all too well. She wanted him, and now it looked like she might have him, and her body was reacting with bursts of internal joy.

"I've thought about doing this," he whispered.

"Me, too," Sadie said softly.

"Yeah?" One corner of his mouth lifted. "I didn't because you worked for me. But now you don't."

"Good point," she agreed. She stared into his eyes, lowered her gaze to his mouth and then back up again. "So, are you going to kiss me or what?"

"Stop talking, Sadie." Then he kissed her.

Five

That first touch of his lips to hers was electric. Sadie's whole body lit up like a neon festival. He cupped her face with his hands, tilted her head and took more. He parted her lips with his tongue and she met that intimate caress with eagerness. It was everything she'd thought it would be and more.

Pulling her close, Ethan held her pressed against his chest as his hands moved to stroke her, touch her. Everywhere. He grabbed hold of her behind and squeezed, sending new tendrils of excitement scattering through her cells.

She moved in even closer to him, twined her arms around his neck and held on while their mouths met and danced and promised each other more.

Hot sex with Ethan.

That one thought blazed across her mind and she

groaned as Ethan tore his mouth from hers to drag his lips and tongue along the line of her throat.

This was really going to happen. She was going to have sex with Ethan. She was going to actually live out her fantasies.

And then it ended with a screech.

Breaking apart, they stared at each other while they struggled for breath. Ethan looked down at her and his expression told Sadie he was as stunned as she felt. Even in her wildest imaginings, Sadie had never expected to react to him as she had. It wasn't like she was a vestal virgin or something, either. She'd had sex. Plenty of times. But even the best of those nights couldn't hold a candle to what she felt when Ethan kissed her.

Then the baby cried again, that shriek coming through the baby monitor on the counter. Emma was demanding attention and there would be no ignoring her.

"I should go check on her," Sadie said brokenly.

"Yeah. Yeah, we should." Ethan let her go and took a step back.

Sadie had never felt colder in her life. Strange how the heat enveloping her dissipated instantly the moment she wasn't being held against him.

And strange that she didn't know whether to be disappointed or grateful that the baby had interrupted them.

Hot sex, sure. But now that her blood was cooling off, she could think about the possible pitfalls of this. He'd paid her to stay for another month. If they were having sex all month—and didn't *that* sound great—would it be too weird? Did she care? And that was why she should be grateful, Sadie told herself. Her brain was confused enough already.

Little Emma had unwittingly given Ethan and Sadie more time to think. To look at every angle of what might happen and really decide if this was what they wanted— oh boy, she really wanted it. And she hoped he did, too.

"Okay, we'll…"

"Talk about this," he finished for her.

Nodding, she walked out of the kitchen, headed for the stairs and Emma. Ethan was right behind her and she was almost surprised that he was willing to do his part in taking care of the baby.

But a bigger part of her was wondering if their "talk" would turn into something else.

A few days later, they were already settling into a "routine." One that Ethan had never wanted. Having an infant in his house was unsettling enough, but seeing Sadie every day and every night was harder to deal with than he'd imagined. He'd been thinking about that kiss for days. Wanting more, knowing he shouldn't have it.

And still, he knew exactly what he wanted.

Sadie.

Funny how a few days could change everything. And this was one change he could completely get behind. Sadie was living in his house, in the room across from his. He'd tasted her and hadn't been able to sleep since for thinking about it. About *her*.

Neither of them had talked about it since, but the tension was there and building. Need pumped through him with a vengeance almost constantly, and damn it, it showed no signs of fading away. If anything, his desire for her had only grown since that one seductive kiss.

Five years. Five years he'd worked with her, known her and had never guessed what he might find if he kissed her. Just as well, he told himself. If he'd had any idea at all, he would have fired her years ago and seduced her on the spot.

Shaking his head, he tried to turn his mind back to work, but it was surprising how little the Mother's Day marketing campaign interested him at the moment. "Which is why you need to concentrate on it."

There were too many damn distractions in his life right now. They'd interviewed two would-be housekeepers and neither of them were right for the job. He and Sadie were bringing Emma to the in-house day care every day, but that couldn't keep going on. Ethan wasn't going to be driving a child back and forth to work every morning and evening. He needed space. Time to think. He needed his life to get back into order.

As much as he wanted Sadie, as much as he wanted this day to be over and the two of them alone together back at the house, Ethan knew that being with her would open up all kinds of problems. What if she took sex the wrong way? What if she expected a relationship? What if she started looking at the two of them plus the baby as a family? No, he wasn't going down that road again.

He'd tried marriage once, completely screwed it up and had learned his lesson. He was no good at it. He liked his space and wasn't interested in being seen at the "best" parties, either. His ex-wife had made it plain when she walked out that he was less-than-stellar husband material.

When they married, Marcy had thought marrying a billionaire would mean great trips, big parties, celebrity friends. But that wasn't Ethan, and she hadn't bothered to hide her disappointment. He hadn't fought the divorce. What would have been the point? Marcy had been unhappy, so why try to keep her where she didn't want to be?

Besides, that brief marriage had taught Ethan an important lesson. He was better off on his own. He didn't like failure and so had no plans to set himself up for another disaster. He liked women, but he didn't want one permanently. Not even one who could make him feel what Sadie had.

As much as he burned to have her—under him, over him; didn't matter, he wasn't picky—he'd seen Sadie's eyes when she looked at the baby. When she held Emma, Sadie got a soft look about her, as if she were wrapping herself emotionally around that child. She clearly wanted kids. A marriage. A family.

What he wanted could be solved in a few hot, steamy nights.

"That does it," he muttered, and lunged out of his chair. He couldn't keep thinking about this. About *her*. It would drive him even crazier than he was feeling at the moment. Walking to the bank of windows behind his desk, he stared out at the ocean, hoping the view would ease the knots tightening inside him. He pushed one hand through his hair and wasn't the least bit surprised when Sadie's image rose to the front of his mind again.

When someone knocked, then opened his office door, he didn't bother to turn around.

"Ethan?"

He closed his eyes briefly. Even the sound of her voice now hit him with a visceral punch. "What is it, Sadie?"

"I just wanted to bring you the Donatello file. The meeting's in an hour, so…"

He glanced at her over his shoulder.

She shrugged and walked toward his desk. She dropped the file on top, then said, "You know, I stopped by here that first night to pick up the file, thinking we could review it before the meeting… Then it got postponed again and I just forgot about it. Well, to be honest, I forgot about it that night. At the house. When we…"

He knew why, too. Hell, looking at her right now, he'd come up blank if anyone asked him anything about business. His gaze locked on hers and he felt a quick jolt of white-hot need that shot from his suddenly tight throat down to his groin, where it flashed into fire that felt as if it would consume him.

"Guess we both forgot things that night."

"And we haven't talked about why, yet."

He laughed shortly. "You really think *talking* is going to solve this?"

"I didn't know anything needed solving."

"Sadie…" He took a breath, blew it out and said, "You know damn well that what happened that night changed things."

"I do." She bit her lip and he flinched.

But he didn't want to talk. He wanted to taste. To touch. To explore. So he turned back to his desk, glanced at the file and added, "Thanks. I'll look it over before the meeting."

"Sure." She didn't leave.

"Is there something else?"

"Yes." She walked closer to the desk and stood opposite him. "What's going on?"

"I don't know what you mean." Yes, he did.

"Yes you do." She was wearing black slacks, a white shirt and a short red jacket that managed to draw his attention straight to her breasts. He'd almost had his hands on them last night and his palms itched to do it right now.

"Just leave it alone, Sadie," he ground out through gritted teeth. "This isn't the time."

"I don't think so. We said we'd talk. It's been days. It's past time. And I'm ready to talk."

"Here?"

"It's where we always are, Ethan," she pointed out.

"We can talk at the house tonight."

"Tonight we'll have the baby to take care of. At the moment, Emma's in day care, so we don't have any interruptions."

She folded her arms across her chest, lifting her breasts even higher, and Ethan wondered if she was doing it on purpose just to keep him off his game.

"Fine." He came around the desk, then perched on the edge of it so that they were nearly eye to eye. "Talk."

"Okay," she started, letting her arms fall to her sides. "I've done some thinking the last few nights. Actually, I did a *lot* of thinking."

"Me, too." Especially since he hadn't been able to sleep. Sadie's image had kept rising up in his mind. Her taste had lingered in his mouth, flavoring every breath.

"Good. I think that's good." She looked not nervous, but as if she were searching for every word. "So what I need to know is if you're thinking what I'm thinking."

"Which is?" He held his breath. If she said no to sex, he wasn't going back to the house. How the hell could he live across the hall from her and *not* have her?

"It's probably a really bad idea for us to sleep together."

"Wasn't thinking at all about *sleeping*," he told her.

"Yeah, me, either." She took a breath, licked her bottom lip and unknowingly sent arrows of heat darting through him. "But—"

There was a "but."

"—it's probably not a good idea," she said.

"Yeah." His chest felt tight. "That's what I think, too."

"Oh." She looked disappointed. "But the thing is, I also think we should do it, anyway."

He came off the desk in a blink, had her wrapped up in his arms and pressed along the length of him in seconds. "I agree," he said, then took her mouth with all the hunger that had haunted him through what felt like forever.

It was just like the first time. Ethan half expected to see actual flames licking up his body. He'd never known this flash-fire need before. Ethan had tried to tell himself that his reaction to Sadie was simply because it had been too long since he was with a woman. Any woman. He devoted so much of himself to work, there was rarely time to think about anything else.

But the truth was it was Sadie doing this to him. He'd never experienced such a mindless rush of desire before. Ethan wanted to believe his hunger for her would be eased by having her, but something told him it was only going to build. He didn't care.

Tasting her, stroking his tongue against hers, feeling her breasts crushed against his chest… This was all about *Sadie.* And beyond satisfying what he was feeling at the moment, he didn't want to think about what that might mean.

He couldn't touch her enough. Feel her enough. Her mouth joined to his, her tongue stroked his and Ethan felt those flames rising, growing more powerful. He had to have her. Her hands swept up his back to his shoulders, where her fingers curled in and held on. That simple action went straight to his groin and tightened his erection to the point of pain. Desire pumped wildly through his system, shutting down all thought beyond this moment. This had never happened to Ethan before. This complete loss of control. All he could think about was getting his hands on her.

With that thought in mind, he tore his mouth free of hers, looked down and quickly opened that bright red jacket. Then the buttons on her shirt.

"Ethan…"

"Have to feel you under my hands," he murmured.

"Oh, good…"

He gave her a quick grin, pleased that she was as torn up as he was. Relieved that she hadn't said "stop." Stopping now might kill him. Ethan spread the fabric of her shirt apart and looked at her pale pink bra. "Pretty. But in my way."

"It unhooks in the front."

"Good news." He flicked the hook and eye open and her beautiful breasts spilled into his waiting hands. At the first touch of his skin to hers, she inhaled sharply. His thumbs and fingers worked her nipples as they jumped into life, going rigid with the need swamping her.

Ethan watched her eyes glaze over as he tugged on those twin sensitive points. He felt her reaction as if it were his own. She rocked her hips helplessly against him and he smiled again. Desire was alive and burning in the room, heat swirling around them like hot air from a blast furnace.

He did a quick turn, lifted Sadie and plopped her on the desk, then bent his head and took first one nipple, then the other into his mouth. Her taste filled him, her scent surrounded him and his mind was a fog from the physical demands crowding his body.

"Ethan…" Her voice was a strained whisper as she threaded her fingers through his hair, her short, neat nails scraping along his scalp. He licked and nibbled and suckled at her breasts, drawing her deep into his mouth as the rush of heat building between them became all encompassing.

This. This was what he'd needed. To indulge himself in her. For years, he'd fought to ignore her, to bury his desire for her, until now it felt as if he were breaking free from the chains he'd wrapped around himself.

"Ethan," she choked out, "whatever you do, don't stop."

"Not the plan," he answered in a murmur. Again and again, he drew on her breasts, his mouth working her tender skin until she was writhing on the desk, helpless against the rising tension inside her. And he knew what he could do to help that.

He dropped one hand to the junction of her thighs and cupped her. At his first touch, she gasped, threw her head back and moved into him. Her slacks were in his way… That was all he could think. He wanted to touch her heat. Push his fingers inside and stroke her until he felt her climax pump through her.

But he couldn't stop long enough to give either of them that gift. For now, he stroked and rubbed and tasted and nibbled until she was a writhing mass of desire. Her response fueled his own. They both fought for air as the most basic of needs overtook everything else.

The first ripples of release hit her and Sadie leaned forward, burying her face in his shoulder. He heard the harsh, keening sound she made, but he knew she'd muffled it purposely so no one else in the building would guess what was happening here. Finally, she stopped, and Ethan took a breath and straightened up. Pulling away from her, he stepped back. Her eyes tracked him as she fought for air.

"What're you doing?"

"I'll be right back," he ground out, and congratulated himself silently on being able to speak at all.

"You're *leaving*?" She sounded outraged and he couldn't blame her. Hell, he could barely move for the pain in his hard, aching groin.

"No." He walked across the office, flipped the lock on the door and came back to her in a blink. "I'm making sure no one's going to walk in before we're finished."

"Oh, good. We're not finished."

"Not even close."

She nodded, licked her lips and sent a jolt of electricity to his dick. "Then locking the door was a good idea."

"I thought so." He walked to the other side of his desk, pulled open a middle drawer and took out the box of condoms he'd bought that morning when they'd stopped to get more diapers for Emma. Sadie was still watching him, and this time, she smiled. "I love a man who's prepared for any situation."

He disregarded the *L* word and went with what they were both feeling. "I bought these today. In case we actually did what we were working up to."

"Good call."

"But I don't want to wait until tonight." It cost him,

this fight for control. His voice was thin, strained as he looked at her.

Her curls tumbled around her face. Her breasts were displayed in all their glory and her delicious lips parted as she slowly, deliberately, licked them again. This time, he could see, in anticipation.

"Neither do I." She scooted off the edge of the desk and shrugged her shirt and bra off. "Now, Ethan. We can talk later, but right now, I need you inside me before I explode."

"It's *when* I'm inside you that you're going to explode."

"Show me."

He tore the box, grabbed a condom and ripped the foil package open.

"Let me help," she whispered, holding out one hand for the sheer latex covering.

He moved in closer and handed it to her. Her nimble fingers undid his slacks, pulled the zipper down, then reached into his shorts to free him.

The minute her fingers curled around him, Ethan groaned. *Too long*, he told himself. It had been too long. Instantly, he realized that he was doing it again. Trying to explain away what he felt with Sadie by dismissing it. The truth was, he'd *never* reacted like this to a simple touch. Sadie's fingers curled around his length and stroked him slowly in a tantalizing motion that had him reaching for the ragged ends of his control.

Her thumb traced the tip of him, wiping away a single bead of moisture before sliding that, too, along the length of him. Her gaze was locked on his, so he saw the flash of desire burning in her eyes. Felt a similar burn within himself. "Put it on me, Sadie. I can't hold out much longer…"

She smiled at his admission and he saw that powerful look all women got when a man was at their mercy cross her features. Then it was gone and there was only desire again. She smoothed the condom down his length, making sure her fingers did another long tease of him as she did. By the time she was finished, Ethan was breathing hard and aching in every inch of his body. Need was a pulsing beast crouched inside him. And Ethan was done holding it back.

"That's it," he said, in what was more a growl of frustration than a simple statement. He undid her slacks and pushed them and her pale pink panties down her legs. She kicked them and her shoes off.

Then he dropped one hand to her hot, damp core again and she trembled, groaning out his name. One finger, then two, slid inside her, stroking, rubbing, exploring. His thumb smoothed across her core and she jolted in his arms, spreading her legs farther apart to accommodate him.

Ethan stared into her eyes, watching emotions flash and burn one after the other as she rocked her hips into his hand wildly. Then she came again in a sudden, hot rush of satisfaction. She bit down hard on her bottom lip to keep from crying out—still keeping quiet to protect them both from discovery.

He admired her control, but he wanted to break it. Wanted to hear her crying out his name, screaming it. He wanted—needed—more.

When the last of the tremors died away, Ethan reached out and swept everything off his desk to fly out and land on the hand-tied rug that lay across the wooden floor. Then he turned her around, laid her out across his desk and whispered, "Hold on."

He looked at her like she was a feast laid out before a starving man. And that was how it felt. Sunlight poured through the wall of windows and made her skin seem to glow. Ethan kept his gaze locked on her as he stripped his own clothes off and tossed them aside.

She curled her fingers around the edge of the desk, glanced back over her shoulder at him and parted her thighs. Then she whispered, "I'm ready, Ethan. I mean, *really* ready."

So was he. Ethan filled his gaze with her. Her bare butt was beautiful and waiting for him. He rubbed her behind hard, squeezing her flesh until she moaned and twisted her hips in response. She threw him a hot look and muttered, "Ethan, *now*."

"Now," he agreed, and pushed his body home. In one long stroke, he was buried deep inside her heat. Her body moved and rocked to accommodate him and Ethan groaned at the satisfaction rippling through him.

He lost himself in the rush of finally joining with her. Of feeling her take him in. Her hips moved as her breath crashed in and out of her lungs. He couldn't stop looking at her. Looking at *them*, together.

Heart racing, Ethan felt her response, deep inside as her muscles contracted around him. Her climax hit hard and Sadie bit down on her lip again to keep from crying out. But he'd seen her reaction. Knew what they were doing to each other, and a moment later, Ethan gritted his teeth to muffle the sounds of his own surrender as he gave himself up to her.

A few minutes—or hours—later, when his heartbeat stopped thundering in his ears, Ethan was stunned at what they'd just done. Hell, he'd *never* had sex in his office before. Five minutes alone with Sadie and that record was smashed. Hell, he didn't know how he'd ever get any work done in here again. He would forever be seeing her stretched across his desk, deliciously naked.

Shaking his head, he carefully stepped back from Sadie, then helped her up. She moaned a little as she stood, and Ethan winced. "Damn it, Sadie, did I hurt you?"

She threw those blond curls out of her eyes and looked up at him with a wide grin. "Are you kidding? I feel fantastic!"

Just like that, he wanted her again. How had he not guessed all these years what kind of woman Sadie Matthews was? He'd thought of her as efficient and she was. But she was so much more, too.

This was going to be trouble.

She scrambled to get back into her clothes, so Ethan did the same. Once they were dressed, though, he took hold of her shoulders. "That was crazy."

"I know," she said, still giving him that wide smile. "Honestly, it was crazy *and* amazing."

He scrubbed one hand across the back of his neck and watched her. "That talk we were supposed to have? I think it's time we had it."

"Okay." She stared up into his eyes and Ethan's mind went blank for a long second or two. Hell, he'd completely lost focus. Another first.

All he could think about was what had just happened between them and how badly he wanted to do it again.

"You start," she said, and walked around him. She squatted down to pick up the scattered papers and pens he'd pushed off his desk.

Irritated somehow, Ethan snapped, "You don't have to do that."

She glanced up at him. "I do still work here, Ethan. Relax."

His brain was racing and she was telling him to relax. Not going to happen. When she'd gathered everything, he reached down for her arm and helped her up. She set it all down on the desk, then gave the wood a soft pat.

"I'm going to have real affection for this desk from now on."

He didn't know what to make of her. They'd worked together closely for five years and Ethan felt like he didn't know her at all. She wasn't horrified or regretful or even embarrassed. She reveled in what had happened between them and Ethan envied that. Because he wasn't at all sure they hadn't made a huge mistake. He really hated this uncertain feeling. Ethan always knew what to do, what to say, in any given situation. This off-balance sensation was unsettling.

"You're still worried and you don't have to be," she said softly. Walking up to him, she laid one hand on his chest and looked up into his eyes. "What happened here is because we both wanted it to happen. You don't owe me anything and I'm not asking for anything, so you can get that slightly panicked look off your face."

Offended somehow, he instantly smoothed out his features. "I'm not panicked. I just don't want you to think that this means more than what it was."

Now she laughed shortly and gave his chest a pat. "Ethan, I've known you for five years. If anyone knows you're not a relationship person, it's *me*. Besides, I quit, remember?" She threaded her fingers through her curls, then said, "In four weeks, I'll be gone and you won't have to worry about any of this."

Then she walked across the room and opened the door. Giving him a finger wave, she slipped through and he was alone again. The room was still humming with sexual energy and all Ethan could think about was what she'd said.

In four weeks, I'll be gone.

And damn it, he already knew that four weeks wouldn't be enough.

Six

Gabriel had it all worked out.

A chef at Heart Chocolates would be making the samples of the new flavors. This was the best idea all around. Not only did Jeff Garret already work for him as an assistant chocolate chef, he was looking to advance his career. Plus, Gabriel didn't have to take the recipe out of the company fold. A win—win. All he had to do was find a professional kitchen he could rent for a couple nights.

"I still don't understand why you didn't use the chef I arranged," Pam said, anger clear in her tone.

And Gabe didn't understand why she was so pissed. But she had been ever since he'd told her the new plan. "Because I don't know him."

"I do," she argued.

"That's great," Gabe said, "but Jeff's a chef with my

company. He's studied with the top chocolatier in Belgium and he wants more responsibility at the company. This is his chance to prove himself." Gabe stopped, laughed a little and said, "I guess Jeff and I have a lot in common in this."

She scowled at him. "This isn't funny, Gabe. Not to me."

"Yeah, I can see that." He studied her for a second or two. "What I don't know is *why*?"

She shook her head, obviously thinking about it briefly, and said, "We were doing this together, and now all of a sudden we're not. What am I supposed to tell my friend?"

Now she was concerned that her chef friend would have his feelings hurt? His professional pride? Well, that really wasn't one of Gabe's big concerns.

"Tell him the truth," Gabe countered. "That this is my family's recipe and I can't trust it to just anyone."

"I'm 'just anyone'? Good to know." Pam whirled away so fast her long dark hair swung out around her shoulders like a cape. Then she spun back to look up at him. "You weren't trusting my chef, Gabe. You were supposed to be trusting *me*."

She turned again and this time walked away from him.

Gabe caught up with her quickly. Grabbing her arm, he whirled her around and looked down into her big brown eyes. "I do trust you."

"Sure." Her gaze slid from his. "I'm convinced."

He was getting more confused by the minute. Ever since he'd told her about using one of the Heart chefs, she'd been irritated and hadn't bothered to hide it.

They were in his penthouse apartment at the hotel.

They were supposed to be celebrating with a great dinner and an icy cold bottle of champagne he'd ordered from one of the best restaurants in the city. But the dinner was uneaten and the champagne was rapidly going flat.

This was not how Gabe had thought the evening would go. He'd planned the great dinner and then figured on having some celebrational sex when they were finished. Looked like that was out the window.

When Pam stormed through the living room and out onto the balcony overlooking the ocean, Gabe followed her. This was the first time he'd ever seen her temper. And though it was impressive, he also found it sexy as hell. He liked a woman with fire in her eyes. He'd just like to know what had caused all this.

"I don't understand why you didn't stick to the plan," she said.

"Because this plan's better. I told you. This way the family recipe stays in the family." He looked at her, and even in profile he could see the suppressed anger on her face. Well, he wasn't too far behind her on that front.

"I'm sorry," she said suddenly and just like that, his own temper drained away. "I was just surprised, Gabe. You didn't even tell me you were changing the plan."

"Hey." He took her arm, turned her around to face him. "Honestly, I didn't think it would bug you so much. This isn't about trust, Pam."

"Isn't it?" She pulled free of his grasp and took a step back. Holding on to the wrought-iron railing with one hand, she pushed her windblown hair out of her eyes with the other.

He threw both hands high in exasperation. How did this go sideways so fast? "We're a team, Pam. Nothing has changed."

"Doesn't feel like it." She shook her head. "Not anymore."

"What the hell, Pam?" He shoved his hands into his jeans pockets. "Where's all the fury coming from? I don't know your chef from a hole in the ground. Why wouldn't I use one I already know? The guy's insanely talented. And he already works for me."

"Fine." She waved a hand at him, effectively dismissing that argument. "But now I have to explain to my chef why he can't be in on the ground floor of a new chocolate line."

"He wouldn't have been, anyway," Gabe argued. "He was going to make samples. That's as far as his involvement went. But if this goes well, then Jeff will get a promotion and I'll have the satisfaction of hearing Ethan apologize and admit he was wrong for the first damn time ever."

She didn't look like she cared much.

"This is making zero sense," Gabe said, his own frustration building. "And damned if I'm going to apologize for protecting my family even while I'm sneaking around behind their backs."

"Hey," she said quickly. "Nobody's *forcing* you to do anything. You *wanted* to do this," she reminded him. "I didn't talk you into it. In fact, I told you that you didn't *have* to do it at all."

He stepped up closer, laid both hands on her shoulders and could practically feel her vibrating with anger. The woman was making him crazy. "Babe, I know that.

This whole thing is on me. Which is why I'm doing it my way. You said you understood family loyalty."

"I do."

"Then you should get why I'm doing it like this."

She considered that, then took a breath and huffed it out again. "I get it, Gabe. I just don't know why you kept it from me."

"I only finalized it today," he argued. "Hell, I didn't see you until a half hour ago. When was I going to tell you?"

"When you started thinking about changing the plan?"

There was more going on here than anger over a plan changing. Something else was bugging her. He just had no idea what it was. "What's really going on here, Pam?"

Below, the ocean was dark, but the waves were topped with froth that stood out in the moonlight. Couples strolled the sand at the water's edge and a few bonfires winked in the blackness of the beach.

"What do you mean?"

"This is about more than using a different chef," he said, as suspicion slipped through his mind. He didn't like the feeling. But what the hell else was he supposed to think when her reaction to all of this was so damn irrational?

Pam was the one he could count on. Talk to. She'd been his sounding board for months. Always supportive. Always ready to listen. If something had changed, he wanted to know what it was. "So tell me what's happening."

"There's nothing to tell," she said, then pulled her phone from her back pocket to check the time. "I've got to go. It's my father's birthday and the whole family's gathering at their house."

"You didn't say anything before."

"Well, I am now," she murmured.

"But we've got dinner. Champagne."

"Yeah, I don't feel much like celebrating."

She slipped out of his grasp and his hands felt empty, cold. "Damn it, Pam, tell me what's going on with you."

"It's nothing."

Before he could say anything else, she was walking back into the main room and snatching her purse up off the couch. The table, set for an intimate dinner, complete with candles, was ignored. "Pam."

She stopped, turned and looked at him. In her eyes he could see disappointment still shining there. Her mouth was tight and flat, and her spine was stiff. "What?"

He didn't know what had gone wrong here, so he didn't know how to fix it. That was an irritation, too. Looking at her now, he could see that though she was standing right there, she was miles away emotionally. But until she was willing to talk to him about what was bothering her there wasn't a hell of a lot he could do about it.

"Are you going to be there when we make the new chocolates?"

Her mouth curved though her eyes remained the same—dark, closed off. "Of course I will. I want to see this through with you."

"Good," he said. "I'll call you tomorrow."

"Sure, Gabe. Tomorrow." Then she left and he wondered if this idea was going to ruin his and Pam's relationship as surely as it would his and Ethan's.

* * *

"They're holding out for more money." Ethan sat back in his desk chair a few days later and looked up at Sadie.

Her breath caught in her throat. Not so long ago, she'd been sprawled across that desk like the main course at a feast. And the memory of it sent a quick ripple of excitement along her spine. Hard to keep your mind on work when all you could think about was…

"Sadie? Are you listening?"

"What?" She snapped back. "Yes. Of course. They want more money."

"I thought we were close to finalizing. The old man, he wants to sell, but his adult children are making him have second thoughts." Ethan tossed a pen onto his desktop and pushed himself to his feet. "The lawyers, ours and theirs, are trying to hammer out a deal, but—"

"Why don't you do it personally?" Sadie asked.

He shifted to look at her. "I don't do the negotiating. That's why I pay the lawyers."

She chuckled and shook her head. "That's the way we usually do it, yes. But Donatello's might be different."

"How?"

He'd tucked the edges of his suit jacket back and had his hands tucked into his pockets. He looked the epitome of the high-powered businessman. And yet, looking at him, she could see him as he was when they were together, and that sent heat waves rocketing through her body.

"Sadie?"

Wow, she really had to concentrate. "Okay, um, I mean that Donatello's is a family business."

"Yeah, I know. I just told you. It's the kids who are

fighting this buyout. They're the ones demanding more money, and at the same time, telling their father not to sell at all." He scowled fiercely. "If they'd just butt out, we could have this done. I don't know why they're being so difficult, anyway. We're offering a fair price."

Funny that he couldn't see the similarities between the Hart family and the Donatello family. Richard Donatello's adult children were fighting for their legacy, their own family's traditions, just as Ethan was. As important as the chocolate company was to him, he should understand what the Donatello kids were going through.

"Right." Sadie shrugged. "Well, you know how you feel about the Hart family business. We both know you would do whatever it took to keep this company thriving. So just for a minute, put yourself in their place."

He snorted. "Not the same. Not by a long shot. Yes, Donatello's has a great reputation, but they're still a small, one-shop business."

"Just how Heart Chocolates started."

"A long time ago," he pointed out.

Honestly, sometimes Sadie felt like beating her own head against a brick wall. It would certainly be more satisfying than trying to convince Ethan that he was wrong about *anything*.

"Donatello's has been around for almost fifty years." He frowned.

"And it's successful enough that you want to buy it."

"Well, yes," he argued. "Because they have a great web presence, an excellent location in Laguna and their customer list is phenomenal."

"All good points," she said, wondering why he still wasn't getting it. Really, was it possible that once you reached success, you actually *forgot* how it had happened? "What I'm saying is that the Donatello chocolate shop is where yours started out a hundred years ago. Hardworking. A family. Building a reputation."

He frowned again, but she could see that he was considering what she was saying. It was a start, Sadie told herself, so she went on.

"Is offering him more money such a horrible thing?" she asked. "Hasn't he earned it? Richard Donatello built a company that you badly want. Maybe if the kids see that you treated their father well, they'll back off."

"Maybe." He nodded thoughtfully.

"And think about it, Ethan…you paid me an extra hundred and fifty thousand for one month."

"Yeah," he said tightly, "that was personal. This is business."

He had the wide windows behind him, where gray, January clouds scuttled across the horizon, hovering over a sea the color of steel.

"Not completely," she argued, and watched one of his eyebrows arch. "Business, sure. But it's also about family. Their family, Ethan. A legacy as important to them as yours is to you."

A couple long, tense seconds passed before he nodded again. "All right. You've made your point. I'll give it some thought."

Sadie knew when to leave well enough alone. "Okay, good. Now back to the personal front—"

"I don't have time for a quickie today, Sadie."

She blinked and her head jerked back as if she'd been slapped. Staring at him, she could see that he wished he hadn't said that, but it was enough to know that he was thinking it. "I don't remember asking for one."

"No, you didn't." He sighed, shook his head and rubbed the back of his neck. "I'm sorry. That didn't come out right."

"Oh, I don't know. You made yourself pretty clear," she said stiffly. And she'd really love to know what had brought on such an insult to her—to both of them. What they'd shared had been far more than a "quickie." There'd been emotions involved as well as their bodies, but apparently, Ethan didn't want to admit that to her or himself. "As it happens, I wasn't talking about sex, Ethan. I was going to tell you the agency is sending over another housekeeper to be interviewed tonight."

"Oh." He frowned. "Fine."

Apparently he was going to pretend he didn't say anything, and she was supposed to pretend she hadn't heard it. Well, fine. She could do avoidance and pretense as well as anyone. Hadn't she been hiding her love for this idiot man for five long years?

"Her name is Julie Cochran. She's a single mother of a five-year-old. She's a good cook, has no issues with also looking after a baby, and she really needs the job."

His jaw dropped and his eyes went wide. "You want to move *another* child into my house?"

Sadie almost sighed. She'd really thought they'd been making progress over the last few days. Hearing him now was more than disappointing. "I'm sure the little girl doesn't have the plague or anything, so you should be safe."

"That's not funny."

"No," she agreed. "None of this is funny. But Julie is a single mom who needs work. The agency says she's one of their best—"

"Then why is she out of work?"

"Because the woman she worked for was elderly and recently died."

He frowned. "Oh."

"Ethan, you want someone good with kids. Well, Julie is. The housekeeper's quarters are big enough for her and her daughter, *and* she's a cook, as well." She shouldn't have to work so hard to sell him on this. "She pretty much hits every point you needed."

"I didn't need another child," Ethan ground out. "Hell, I didn't want the one I've got."

"Wow." Sadie just stared at him. For some reason, she'd thought he was coming around a little. He was helping take care of Emma. He'd fed her and bathed her the night before. The two of them together had tucked the baby in for the night. So what was the problem?

"Damn it, don't look at me like that."

"How?" she asked. "Horrified? Disappointed?"

"Either," he muttered. "Both."

"I don't know who I'm more insulted for," she admitted. "Me or Emma."

"I'm not trying to insult either one of you."

"Well, congratulations then," she said tightly. "You appear to be so gifted with insults you don't need to try."

"Damn it, Sadie—"

"I'm not talking about me now, Ethan. This is about Emma. You've only had her a little more than a week," she said, reminding herself as well as him of that fact. Maybe he'd need more time to get used to having Emma in his house. But what kind of excuse was she supposed to make to cover the insult he'd delivered to *her*? "Give it a chance."

"I am, aren't I?"

"Are you?" she countered. "Honestly, I thought you were. You're really good with Emma, but hearing you now, I don't know if you're doing the right thing in keeping her."

He stared at her, surprised. "What else can I do? I promised her father I'd be her guardian."

"A guardian is more than a place to live and a housekeeper to make sure the child is fed and clean." Sadie stared him down. "A decade-old promise isn't enough reason to keep her, Ethan. Emma needs more than your duty. Heck, she *deserves* more than that. She deserves to be loved. If you can't do that, maybe you should consider giving her up for adoption to some-one who can."

Now he looked stunned. "You really think I'd do that?"

"Before the last five minutes, no," she admitted. "But listening to you complain is pretty convincing."

"That's great. Thanks." He paced behind his desk and she thought he looked like a tiger in a too-small cage. "Good to know I have your support."

"Like I have yours?" she countered just as hotly. "What was that you said about a *quickie*?"

He stopped pacing and threw her a look that was both apologetic and irritated. Amazing that he could conflate the two. "You know damn well I didn't mean anything by that."

"Do I?"

"You sure as hell should," he snapped. "We've known each other too long for you to take one stupid comment and build a case on it."

There was more going on here than just the baby and

the housekeeper and the constant change in a life that had been so rooted in routine that it was more of a rut than a path forward. And maybe it was time he told her what was bothering him.

"What's going on with you, Ethan?" she asked quietly.

"Nothing."

"Right." She crossed her arms over her chest. "You've barely spoken to me since we were together. You leave every morning without a word, and when you are forced to talk to me at work, you're cold and distant. And let's just add, as of today, insulting."

"I said I was sorry."

"Well, all better then." She uncrossed her arms, then set her hands at her hips. "Why are you avoiding me?"

"I've been busy."

"Hey, me, too," she said, walking toward him. "And I'm also the one who took Emma to the day care. The one who checked on her at lunch, and I'm guessing I will be the one driving her back to the house. You've been ignoring both of us, Ethan. Why?"

He glared at her, then looked away. "Because things are different since we had sex."

Surprised, she asked, "Different how?"

He snapped her a look. "Hell, it changed everything. I've thought about it and realized that what we did was a mistake."

Sadie flushed and felt both rage and embarrassment rise up inside her. Strange, she hadn't been embarrassed at all while she was laid out in front of him. But hearing him dismiss what they'd shared was enough to color her own memories of it. "Is that right?"

"It is," he said tightly, and locked his gaze on hers. "There's too much going on right now and I don't think we should let that happen again."

"How long have you been working on that speech?"

"What?"

Sadie was furious. This was why he'd been ignoring her? He had regrets over what they'd done, and like the lord of the manor, he was going to put everything right again. Men were just idiots sometimes. He thought insulting her, ignoring her, would be enough to keep her at a distance. Clearly, he didn't know her as well as he thought he did.

"*You* don't think," she said, keeping her voice as calm as possible. "You've decided. Thank you, Ethan. How very kind of you to figure all of this out without any input from me."

He winced a little. "If you'll just listen…"

"Now you're ready to talk and I should just, what? Sit down and listen as you lay out your plans?"

"I didn't say that…"

"Let me ask you, Ethan, do I get a vote in any of this?"

"Of course you get a vote," he practically snarled, and came to a stop behind his desk, as if he needed that heavy piece of mahogany furniture as a barrier between them.

But only a few days ago it had been so much more than that.

"Well, that's very democratic of you, Ethan."

He frowned and watched her warily. "The words sound right, but the tone is off."

"Good catch," she said. "But the real question is,

why didn't you talk to me about this before you made up your new rules?"

He scrubbed one hand across his jaw. "It's complicated."

"No, it isn't." Sadie was frustrated and her fury was beginning to ease back down into extreme irritation. "For heaven's sake, Ethan, it doesn't have to be complicated unless you make it so. Whatever you're thinking, just stop it."

He laughed shortly. "Sure. I'll stop thinking."

"You overthink, Ethan. That's the problem." Shaking her head, Sadie stepped forward, laid both hands on the edge of the desk and said, "We had each other, right here."

His eyes flashed.

"Why can't you just let it be what it was?" she asked. "Two adults enjoying each other."

"You said that then."

"And will again tomorrow if I have to," Sadie said, folding her arms across her chest again and giving him a hot stare. "And I probably will, because you don't seem to be listening. I didn't ask you for anything, Ethan, remember? You don't owe me anything and I don't need you to protect me from big bad you."

He reached up and shoved both hands through his hair. "I don't want this—whatever it is we've got going on here—getting messy."

"It will."

His head snapped up and his eyes fired.

She sighed. "Life gets messy, Ethan. It just happens. But relax. I won't be crawling at your feet, begging for scraps of attention."

"I never said you would," he said in his own defense.

"And you're perfectly safe from a proposal, too," Sadie reassured him. "Trust me when I say you are not the man for me."

He actually looked offended. "What's that supposed to mean?"

"It means," she told him, "that I have a list of qualifications for the man I want and you only meet one of them." She stopped, thought about the impromptu hot sex on the desk in the middle of the day and had to admit that he was not only *sexy*, but had proved himself to be *adventurous*, too. "Okay, two. But that's not enough."

"How many points are on this dubious list?" he asked, frowning.

"Five," she said. "And two out of five is not nearly good enough for me. So believe me when I say you're completely safe."

"Great." He was still frowning, and if anything, the offended expression on his features had deepened.

Not a bad thing, she told herself. Maybe it was good that Ethan find out he wasn't the prime catch he thought he was.

"So, if you're okay now, I'm going back to work." She turned for the door and stopped. "You will be at the house tonight to interview Julie?"

"Yeah."

"Good. And once you've completely recovered from this conversation, maybe we could try out a bed next time…"

She didn't wait to hear his answer.

She didn't need to.

She left and stood with her back to the closed door. The office was bustling, phones were ringing and fingers clacked on keyboards. But she wasn't paying attention to any of it.

Instead, her mind was on the man she would soon be walking away from. Forever.

Seven

"So what do you think?"

Ethan looked over at Sadie and saw the gleam of triumph in her eyes. He couldn't blame her. "I think you were right. Julie will work out."

"Wow. *I was right*. I like hearing that."

One of his eyebrows lifted. "Don't get used to it."

She laughed and, God, the sound of it slammed into the center of his chest and tightened everything inside him. After their conversation that afternoon, he would have bet every penny he had that Sadie would make him pay, by dishing out silence and cold, hard stares. It was how every other woman he'd ever known had gone about payback. About making sure he understood just how wrong he'd been in whatever personal situation was happening at the time.

He should have known that Sadie would be different here, too. She was behaving like they hadn't had an argument at all.

"I don't know," she said with a grin. "I think I'm on a roll. You're offering Donatello's more money. You hired Julie in spite of her little girl…"

True, he had upped his offer for the Laguna chocolate shop. He hadn't heard anything yet, but Sadie had made a good point that he hadn't thought about before. Donatello's was a small shop, but they'd been in their location for forty-five years. They'd built a family business just as his own family had. That was something to respect, and a part of Ethan was ashamed that until Sadie spoke up, he hadn't noticed. Hadn't *let* himself notice. And that admission was a hard one to make.

As for Julie, that had turned out to be the easiest damn decision he'd ever made. Yes, there was now *another* child in his house, but even Ethan had to admit, at least to himself, that Alli was a cute kid. Didn't mean he was getting soft. Only that he had eyes, he assured himself.

"It was her chicken dinner that sold me," he admitted.

"Can't blame you for that. It was delicious. Now you know why she insisted on cooking for us. To prove she knows her way around a kitchen." Sadie leaned back on the couch and propped her feet up on the low table in front of her. She had tiny feet. Why was that sexy? He shook his head to clear out distracting thoughts.

"Yeah," he said, remembering the dinner Julie had fixed for them. "Makes me wonder why I put up with Alice all those years."

"Because you hate change?"

He looked at her and caught the impish gleam in her

eyes. "Must be it," he agreed. Though for a man who hated change as much as he did, there'd been plenty of it in his life lately.

Most of it revolving around the woman smiling at him. But then, so much of his life over the last five years had revolved around Sadie. She'd been a constant in his daily life. At work, which was really the only life he had, she was irreplaceable. And he was only just now figuring that out. So what did that say about him?

Frowning, he glanced around the empty room, then back to where Sadie was reclining on the deeply cushioned couch. Suddenly, he realized that they were alone in the house but for baby Emma. Julie and her daughter wouldn't be moving in until the following day.

And in spite of everything he'd said only that afternoon, he wanted Sadie so badly it was an ache inside him. To hell with rules. Plans. If she wanted him, too, why shouldn't they have each other again?

"So with Julie willing to watch Emma, I guess you don't really need me to stay the full month, right?"

Startled, he realized *that* hadn't occurred to him. The firelight streaming from the hearth danced across her features and shifted in shadows that seemed to settle in her blue eyes. Why hadn't he thought of that? He had almost three more weeks to go with Sadie and damn it, he wanted them.

He'd already wasted too much time, worried about consequences when she clearly wasn't.

"We still need to find a nanny," he said firmly.

"Yes, but Julie will be able to watch Emma until you do, so…"

Ethan pushed up off the far end of the leather sofa and walked over to her. Reaching down, he pulled her from the couch, and when she was standing right in front of him, he said, "Yeah, I paid you to stay a month. I still need you here."

"Why?" She looked up into his eyes and he found he couldn't look away.

He told her the honest truth. "Because I'm not ready for you to leave yet."

"Why?" She smiled and that simple curve of her mouth tugged at something inside him.

He gave her a reluctant smile. "Going to make me say it?"

She tipped her head to one side in that move he was so fond of, and said, "Yes. I think I am."

"Fine." He nodded, swallowed hard and let the desire pumping inside him have free rein. His body tightened; his heartbeat thundered in his chest. "You're right about this, too. I want you, Sadie. I want you all the damn time. Every time I have you it only makes me want more."

"And that's a good thing, right?" she asked, and made her only reference to what they'd talked about just that afternoon.

Best thing that had ever happened to him, not that Ethan was going to be admitting that anytime soon.

"It's a damn gift is what it is," he ground out.

She wrapped her arms around his neck and said, "Well, what're we standing here for?"

"Good question."

He swept her up into his arms and Sadie felt a bone-deep thrill rush through her. He held her close to his chest, looked down into her eyes, and she read the hunger shining there. Clearly, he was done trying to pretend that what was between them could be ignored or pushed aside. That hunger radiating from Ethan fed what she was feeling, making her tremble with reaction.

It had been days since they'd been together and Sadie had wondered if they ever would be again. She knew Ethan so well and had realized that over the last few days, he'd questioned himself, what had happened, and tried to work out every possibility, up to and including never touching her again. He was a man with a hard inner line that he didn't cross on a whim. But here he was, holding her, looking down at her with a promise of what was to come, and Sadie silently acknowledged that she still loved him. Would always love him. And it wouldn't matter if she left. Didn't matter if she tried to find someone else to make a life with.

A part of her would always be here. With Ethan.

"You accused me of overthinking, but I can see the wheels in your mind turning," he said as he walked toward the stairs. "Changing your mind?"

"Not at all." Caught, she scrambled for something to say that wouldn't give away what she was feeling. So she went with humor. "I was just wondering how quickly you could take the stairs…"

"We're about to find out," he said with a grin, and made it to the second floor in seconds.

"Impressive," she said, and dragged her nails against the back of his neck.

He inhaled sharply and turned toward the master bedroom. "I'm just getting started impressing you."

A sizzling knot of anticipation settled in the pit of her stomach and made her blood fizz like champagne. Reaching up, she stroked his cheek and he gritted his teeth in response.

There was no sound from the baby's room, thank goodness, because Sadie didn't want an interruption. Not even from the cutest baby in the world. All she wanted now was Ethan. She would always want Ethan.

When he carried her into his bedroom, Sadie took a moment to look around. In all the time she'd known him, she'd never seen it before. Over the years, when she'd come to his house, it was for business, and she'd worked with him in his office downstairs or in the main room or even outside on the patio.

Now, it was personal, and she felt as if she were being given a glimpse into the man.

The room was massive, of course, as she'd expected for being in a mansion. There was a huge TV hanging on the wall opposite the bed. A wide bank of windows looked out over the backyard and the ocean beyond. She guessed that in daylight, the view would be gorgeous. Now, though, she saw only the dark with the pale wash of solar lights on the lawn.

Beneath the TV was a fireplace, cold now, and twin comfy chairs pulled up in front of it. There was a long, low dresser on another wall and tables on either side of a gigantic bed that was covered in a navy blue duvet and mounded with pillows in shades of blue and gray.

"It's nice," she said, and knew that sounded lame, but really, she'd been lucky to squeeze those two words out of her tight throat. The room was lovely, but impersonal. There were no hints to the inner thoughts of Ethan Hart. It was as if this were a palatial hotel room. And actually, that's what it was. Though Ethan owned this beautiful home, until the last week or so, he'd spent almost no time in it. At most, it was a place to sleep and to store his clothes.

There were no family photos in the room, no scattered coins on the dresser or keys casually discarded. Sadie realized that outside of his office, his company, Ethan had less of a life than she'd guessed. But maybe she could help him change that while she was there.

"Thanks," he said, "glad you like it." He gave her a wry smile, walked to the bed and dropped her onto the mattress.

Sadie yelped in surprise, then grinned as she bounced. "Very suave."

"Again. Thanks."

She toed off her shoes and let them hit the floor with a thud. Then her fingers went to the buttons on her shirt. He was watching every move she made and Sadie loved the flash of heat she saw in his eyes.

"Trying to make me crazy by undoing those buttons extra slowly?"

"Is it working?" She knew it was. She could feel his impatience building as quickly as her own. It felt like forever since she'd touched him. Since he'd been inside her.

"Way too well," he said tightly, and tore off his own shirt, sending buttons skittering across the hardwood floor.

She drew in a fast, deep breath. He must have a gym somewhere in this palace, Sadie told herself, because the man's body was sharply defined muscles that made her fingers itch to touch him. He undid his slacks, stepped out of them and his shorts, and then he was standing in front of her and her heartbeat jumped into a gallop. His chest wasn't the only impressive physical trait the man possessed.

"You're overdressed," he murmured, leaning forward

to unhook her jeans and pull them down and off her legs. Then he gave her a smile of appreciation. "If I'd known you were wearing black lace, it might not have taken us so long to get here."

In the heat of his gaze, Sadie felt beautiful. Powerful. Her stomach swirled as she sat up, undid her shirt and shrugged it off to display the matching black lace bra.

"You are a picture," he whispered. "But you're still overdressed."

She smiled up at him. "Why don't you see what you can do about that?"

He reached for her and she rose up to meet him. His fingers flicked the clasp of her bra free and his eyes fired even as he filled his hands with her breasts and rubbed her pebbled nipples with his thumbs.

Sadie's head fell back as a buzz of awareness swirled through her, tightening into a coil in the pit of her stomach. It felt so good. *He* felt so good. His hands were strong and gentle and oh so talented.

She opened her eyes to look up at him and saw her own desire reflected in his gaze. "I've missed you," she admitted.

"I missed you, too," he said softly, "and I didn't want to."

Sadie almost laughed. That was so Ethan. "Then it's twice as nice to hear," she said, and took his face in her palms to kiss him.

Instantly, he levered her back onto the bed and covered her body with his. His mouth latched on to hers and their tongues twisted together in a sensual dance that began slowly and in seconds became breathless, frenzied. Sadie ran her hands up and down his arms, up to his broad shoulders. She curled her fingers in, holding on to him as if to keep him right where he was. His hands swept up and down her body; his fingers hooked around the thin elastic of her panties and pushed them down. She lifted her hips, helping him. She wanted nothing between them, not even that tiny scrap of lace.

He dipped his head to her breast and Sadie took a harsh breath at the sensation of him drawing her body into his mouth. He suckled her, drawing and pulling until it felt as if he would tear her soul from her and into him. And while she sighed and writhed beneath him, he touched her core, dipping his fingers into her heat as he had once before, and this time it was even better.

Because they were here, in his house, and she could shout if she wanted to? Because she'd finally accepted that the love she felt for him wasn't going anywhere?

Did it matter why? No. All that mattered was his next kiss. The next touch. The next breathless antici-pation. In the next instant, she pushed every thought aside. Nothing mattered but this moment. She wanted it to go on forever. The feeling of his body against hers. His hands on her skin.

"God, you smell good," he whispered, tracking his lips and tongue along her skin, up to her throat, where he nibbled at her pulse beat.

She tipped her head to one side to give him better access and slid her hands up and down his back. "And oh, you feel good."

He lifted his head, looked down at her and smiled. "I really do feel good, thanks."

She laughed and realized that until this time with him, she'd almost never seen his sense of humor. Sadie enjoyed this closeness between them. Beyond the sex, beyond their bodies coming together, this link was everything she'd ever hoped for. This easiness between them was worth everything.

The smiles, the laughter, the shared sighs and the breathless need all combined to make Sadie feel as if she and Ethan really were connecting on a much deeper level than simply physically.

He sat up and pulled away then, reaching for the bed-side table. She knew what he was doing and she was all for it. "Hurry up, Ethan."

He shot her a grin. "We have all night, Sadie. No need to hurry."

All night. Didn't that sound wonderful? But for now, she had an ache demanding to be satisfied. She went up on her elbows and tossed her hair back out of her face. "Hurry now, take our time later."

He sheathed himself with a condom, turned back to her and said softly, "Yes, ma'am."

Grabbing hold of her butt, he pulled her closer, lifted her legs and draped them over his shoulders. Sadie shifted, writhed, wiggled her hips, anything she could do to entice him to get on with it. She felt as if she were wired so tightly she might just explode, and nobody wanted that.

Then she almost did, the moment his mouth covered her core. She was helpless in his grasp. All she could do was moan and shout and beg for the release he kept just out of reach. Sadie watched him, reached down and ran her fingers through his hair, then held him to her. He licked her, nibbled at her, scoring her center lightly with the edges of his teeth. Again and again, his tongue claimed her, stirring that one sensitive bud until it felt as if it were electrified.

She rocked her hips because it was the only move

available to her. He took her higher, faster, than he had before, and Sadie fought for air. She didn't want to pass out and miss anything about this moment. She couldn't tear her gaze from him.

His hands kneaded her butt while his mouth tormented her. He didn't stop, not even when her climax erupted and turned her into a writhing, screaming mess, trying to hold on to the world so she wouldn't fall off.

Before the last ripple had coursed through her, Ethan dropped her to the mattress and claimed her body in one long, hard stroke. Sadie felt shattered. As if she'd come apart and now he was tormenting the jagged pieces. And she moved into him to make him go faster, deeper.

He set a rhythm designed to drive her insane. Caught, held in place by his strength, she lifted her hips, rocking high to take him deep. Sadie curled her fingers into the silky duvet and held on tight.

"Ethan!"

"Come on," he ordered harshly, his voice hardly more than a scrape of sound. "Come again, Sadie. Come for me."

She shook her head. If she climaxed again, she might never be put back together again. And yet there was no stopping it. She screamed his name again and relished the feeling of his body slamming into hers, over and over again.

She felt it coming, so she opened her eyes so she could look at him when he pushed her over the edge. His eyes burned as his gaze locked on her. He moved faster, harder, and Sadie rushed to meet that crashing release. And when it claimed her, she shouted his name like a prayer.

Once again, Ethan didn't give her body time to stop shaking, shivering, before he moved and changed the game again. Smoothly, he shifted to lay on his back, taking her with him. Sadie straddled him then and braced her hands on his hard, sculpted chest.

He was embedded so deeply inside her now, she wanted to savor that feeling, keep it with her always. His hands came down on her hips and Sadie smiled at him. "Your turn, Ethan."

She moved on him, and this time it was *her* setting the pace, her driving the action and creating a rhythm that drove Ethan to the edge of madness. She watched him, saw his eyes glaze with passion, felt the strength of his hands tighten on her hips. She swiveled on him, deepening their contact, driving them both now. Sadie knew another orgasm was coming and she held it back, wanting to reach that peak with Ethan this time.

And when he was ready, she took his surrender and gave him her own. Seconds, minutes, maybe hours ticked past as their bodies exploded in tandem. Then she crashed down onto his chest and was cradled in his arms.

"That was…" Sadie said with an exhausted, yet exhilarated sigh.

"Yeah, it was." Ethan dragged his hands up and down her spine, keeping her right where she was, sprawled on top of him.

"I don't think I can move," she admitted. Never in her life had Sadie experienced anything like what she had with Ethan.

He was the man she'd looked for her whole life. And he was the one man she couldn't have.

Her heart broke a little even though her body was content, practically humming.

"That's good," Ethan said. "I really don't want you to move."

She laughed a little and turned her face into his chest. "We can't stay like this, Ethan. We'll starve."

"We can call out for pizza," he said. "I can reach the phone from here."

"And the delivery guy will bring it to us here?" She lifted her head and looked into his eyes. "A little embarrassing, don't you think?"

He grinned. "I'll toss the duvet over your excellent ass."

Her heart turned over in her chest. "Excellent? Thanks."

"Absolutely," he said, as he dropped one hand to her behind and squeezed. "Nobody sees that ass but me."

She thrilled to that and her too eager heart started celebrating. But she knew he didn't mean anything by it. He wasn't talking about permanence. Heck, he might not even really like her butt. It could all be the kind of things he said to every woman he took to bed. It would be foolish to build something out of nothing. And yet…

Sadie pushed those thoughts aside to examine later. For now, she kept her gaze fixed on his. "Your bed's a lot more comfortable than the desk."

She saw a flash in his green eyes and his hands on her butt tightened. "I've got a real fondness for that desk, now."

"Me, too," she admitted, then shivered.

"You cold?"

"A little," she said, then whooped when he rolled them over, covering her body with his.

"Better?"

"Better," she assured him, then gasped when he bent his head to taste one of her nipples again. "Okay," Sadie whispered, "not cold anymore."

He lifted his head to wink at her. "Glad to hear it. Now, let's get even warmer."

She swallowed hard, told her heart to slow down so it wouldn't simply explode out of her chest, and let herself slide into the feelings Ethan engendered in her. His hands were everywhere. He moved and she sighed. He touched and she moaned. He kissed and she hungered.

With her eyes closed, it was strictly a sensory world. She heard the bedside table drawer open again. Heard foil being ripped. Heard him sigh as he sheathed himself, and then he was turning her onto her belly, lifting her hips and pushing her legs apart. She turned her face to one side as she reached up to hold on to the padded, gray leather headboard. Then Sadie looked over her shoulder at him, saw him poised at her center and felt everything inside her melt into a puddle of need and love and desire so thick and heavy, her body ached with it.

How could she need him again so quickly?

She licked her lips and whispered, "Do it, Ethan. Take me."

His green eyes burned. His jaw was tight. Desire rippled off of his body in waves that washed over her and nearly took her under. Then he pushed himself home and she forgot everything.

She moved back into him, rocking, pushing. He ran his hands over her butt, then swept one down to touch her core as he drove into her from behind. Again and again, he was relentless, tireless. He pushed her, demanding she give him all she was, while he gave and took all at once. Their bodies slapped together and the heat in the room was breathless.

He was all. He was everything. What he could do to her. What she did to him. The magic they created together shone around them like fireworks raining down from the ceiling. He stroked her hard, pushing down on that tight, hard nub with his thumb, and Sadie shattered again. She screamed his name and only moments later, he shouted in triumph and emptied himself into her.

Bodies burning, hearts crashing, they curled up together, her back to his front, and dropped into exhausted sleep.

For Ethan, the next few days were…challenging. Not only did he have a new housekeeper and her five-year-old daughter living at the house, but he and Sadie had crossed the barriers separating them. She spent every night in his room, because what was the point of going in and out of the guest room?

Every night, they made love with a frantic fierceness that seemed to only get stronger. He couldn't stop touching her. Wanting her. He woke up in the middle of the night and reached for her. She'd become…essential. Ethan wasn't sure when that had happened or even *how* it had.

He'd wakened this morning to realize there were lotions and makeup lined up like tiny soldiers on his bathroom counter. In the shower, her shampoo sat beside his and made the whole damn room smell like lemons. Her clothes were in his closet, her shoes lined up alongside his, and when he'd finally noticed all this, he'd had one brief moment of panic.

It had been a long time since he'd shared any part of his home, his life, with a woman. And that had ended so badly, he'd promised himself he would never risk it again. But this was different, he assured himself. This situation with Sadie was temporary. This wasn't a mark of a relationship beginning, but of a business partnership ending.

"And I don't care for that, either." They still had almost three weeks on their deal and neither of them had spoken again about the fact that now that Julie was working for him, and willing to care for the baby, he didn't really need a nanny. At least, there wasn't a huge rush for one.

So why had he asked Sadie to stay? Why hadn't he told her that she could move out of his house?

"Because," he muttered, turning in his chair to stare out at the ocean, "you don't want her to leave."

Sure, it worried him to see how much she was settling into his home, his bedroom. But the nights with her were addictive. The more he had her, the more he wanted her. If she left, he might never get her back in his bed again, and Ethan wasn't ready to give that up yet.

And then there was Emma.

The tiny girl was carving out a place for herself in his heart and that was shocking, as well. He'd never expected to feel something for the baby. Care for her, sure. He owed Bill and his wife that. Ethan had made a promise and he intended to keep it. But he'd never been around kids much and he'd liked it that way.

Now Emma was opening his eyes to the idea that just maybe he'd been…wrong. It didn't happen often, which was why he hadn't recognized it right away. But he was a big enough man, he hoped, to admit when the unthinkable happened.

Only the night before, he'd been struck by just how the changes in his life had affected him. He'd heard Emma stirring on the baby monitor and got up before Sadie could wake. In the dark, quiet house, he'd walked into Emma's room and crossed to the crib. The little girl opened her eyes, looked up at him and *smiled*. She knew him. Trusted him. Was happy to see him.

And in that instant, a bubble of warmth had spread through his chest and settled around his heart. He hadn't expected it, wasn't prepared for what it was going to mean to his life, but he also couldn't deny it.

Emma. Sadie. They were changing everything and it was quickly coming to the point where he couldn't remember what it had been like without them in his house. In his mind.

All he had left of his once orderly world was work. His company. And even that was under constant assault from Gabriel, though Ethan hadn't heard another word from his brother about changes. Which should worry him, he supposed. On the other hand, he'd take the break where he could.

Then a knock on the door sounded and Sadie poked her head inside. "Ethan. Ms. Gable from Child Services is here."

Well, that break didn't last long. He wondered if this was a routine check or if the woman had some idea of taking Emma from him. If that was her plan, she would be disappointed.

Emma and Sadie were his and Ethan wasn't ready to give either of them up.

Eight

"Send her in, Sadie."

Melissa Gable walked into his office with long, purposeful strides. Ethan silently gave her points for an intimidating presence. In her black suit jacket, starched white shirt and knee-length black skirt and sky-high heels, she looked all business. He supposed most people might wither and quietly panic beneath her steady stare. But Ethan wasn't worried. Ms. Gable wouldn't get anything he wasn't willing to give.

She carried a black bag the size of Montana on her left shoulder, and as he rose to greet her, Ms. Gable reached into the bag and pulled out a manila file folder.

They shook hands, then she took a seat opposite his desk. He sat down, too, studied her, waiting. He didn't wait long.

"I've already been to your day care here in the building to check in on Emma, see how she's doing."

"How did you know she wouldn't be at home with a nanny?" Just curious, he told himself.

"I didn't," she said. "But it's my job to be thorough, so I checked the day care first."

"And?" He offered nothing. He'd learned long ago that the secret to successful negotiations was remembering that he who speaks first loses power.

"She appears to be happy and healthy," Ms. Gable allowed. "And as a side note, I have to commend you on your in-house day care, as well. Unfortunately, there aren't enough employers farsighted enough to realize that a well-run day care is imperative in this day and age."

"Agreed." He nodded. "It pays to keep your employees happy, and when they don't have to worry about their kids, they're more productive." Well damn, that sounded cold even to him. Maybe that *was* why he'd begun the day care in the first place. But since Emma had arrived in his life, he'd realized just how important it was for people to be able to check on their children during the day. He'd been downstairs a few times himself.

"Yes. Well." She checked her notes, then looked at him again. "I've spoken to the day care operators, who tell me Emma is well fed, clean and obviously well cared for."

That irritated him beyond measure. "You expected she wouldn't be?"

"No, but even the most well-meaning people don't often pull things together as quickly as you seem to have." She flipped through to another page, scanned it, then said, "I went by your house earlier and your house-keeper showed me Emma's room. I approve of what you've done there and…" She checked again. "Julie, is it? She assured me that the baby is cared for and happy."

"Again," he said, tapping his fingers now against the desk. The desk where he and Sadie had taken each other for the very first time. Odd, but that stray thought eased the temper building within. "You're surprised?"

Ms. Gable closed the file, tucked it into her bag and said, "Forgive me, Mr. Hart, but you seemed less than happy when you discovered Emma had been left in your charge."

He winced internally at that, because she made a good point. He hadn't wanted the baby. Had resented that Bill had remembered that long-ago promise Ethan had made. But whether he'd wanted them to or not, things had changed. That baby girl had started out as nothing more than his responsibility. Now she was more. Now she was *his*.

Just then, he recalled Sadie telling him, "If you can't love Emma, maybe you should give her up to someone who can." And he thought about that. Thought about that tiny girl. How it felt when she curled her fingers around his. How *he* felt when she laid her head down on his shoulder. How right it was when he checked on her at night and saw her smile at him with delight.

He did love her.

Might not have wanted to. Might not have counted on this ever happening to him, but Emma was important to him now. And he'd give her up to no one.

"Mr. Hart?"

"Emma stays with me," he said flatly, coming out of his thoughts. "I'm looking for a nanny now and until

I find one, my housekeeper, Julie, is helping us care for her."

"Us?"

"My assistant, Sadie Matthews, is assisting me with Emma, as well."

"I see." Nodding to herself, she stood up, held out her hand and waited for him to shake it. "Well then, from what I can see, you have this situation well in hand. I'll make my report to my superiors and recommend the guardianship become permanent. If you care to eventually legally adopt Emma, I'd be happy to help you in any way I can."

Surprised, but pleased, Ethan stood up and nodded. "I appreciate that."

Once the woman was gone, Sadie slipped into the room and closed the door, leaning back against it. "Well? What did she say? Do? Think?"

He laughed a little. Sadie's enthusiasm was contagious.

"Emma stays with me," he said.

"Really?" Sadie smiled at him and approval shone in her eyes. Strange how good it felt to know she was proud of him and what he'd done.

"I'm glad, Ethan."

"Why?" he asked, his gaze sliding over every square inch of her.

"Because I think Emma's good for you."

One eyebrow arched. "More direct honesty?"

Sadie shrugged. "A little late to change that now. Besides, would you prefer lies?"

"No," he said, his gaze locked on her. She was wearing what he'd always thought of as her "work uniform." Black slacks, dress shirt and short black jacket. And she looked sexier than any other woman would have in diaphanous lace or a skimpy bikini. Just looking at Sadie hit him on so many levels he couldn't have counted them all.

He wanted her.

As he did every moment of every damn day.

It didn't matter if she was laughing with him or her eyes were snapping with fury. Sadie Matthews was the one thing in Ethan's world he couldn't predict. Couldn't control. And he enjoyed knowing that more than he would have thought possible.

"It's not as scary as you thought, is it?"

Could she read his mind now?

"What's that?"

"Love."

The way she said that word sent a chill along his spine. He stiffened and his voice went deep and gruff as he demanded, "Who said anything about love?"

Her head tipped to one side, delighting him, even as her expression screamed disappointment. "I did. But you should. Ethan, you love that baby."

"I care for her, sure," he hedged. He wasn't going to use the *L* word because it didn't matter. He'd made Emma a part of his world, his life. He would take care of her, make sure she was happy. Wasn't that enough, for God's sake?

"Is it really beyond you to admit you know how to love?"

"It's not that I don't know how," he said tightly. "It's that I choose not to."

"And that's immeasurably sad."

He ground out, "Thanks so much."

"Ethan…" She took a step toward him and stopped.

"I'll only be here a couple more weeks. When I leave, what then?"

A couple more weeks. Well hell, he didn't want to think about *that*. Time was moving too quickly. It wasn't only Emma who had invaded his life, it was Sadie, as well, and knowing she would be gone soon was like a thorn constantly jabbing at him. Ethan wanted to find a way to keep her with him; he just hadn't come up with anything yet. But damned if he'd lose Sadie now.

Marriage was, of course, out of the question. He'd already failed spectacularly at that institution and he had no interest in repeating the mistake.

"You don't have to leave."

"We've been over this, Ethan."

"I don't want you to leave," he said abruptly.

"What?" She stared at him, shocked. "What are you saying?"

"I'm saying we're good together, Sadie." He came forward, took both her hands in his and held on tightly, stroking his thumbs across her knuckles. "We're a hell of a team. Why should we end it?"

"Ethan..." Her eyes shone and she licked her lips as if they'd gone suddenly dry.

"Things have changed between us, Sadie. You know it as well as I do. We have more together now." The thought of losing it was unacceptable. "You don't have to go, Sadie."

She looked as though she might be considering it, so he continued. "In the last couple of weeks, we've been more flexible with work time, right?"

"Work time." She frowned.

"Yes." He held her hands tighter when she tried to pull free. "You can work whatever hours you want. You can take your vacations and I won't call you out of family gatherings."

"I see…"

"And we can be together," he finished, pulling her up against him.

"Like we have been," she said softly.

"Exactly." He looked down into her eyes. "Sadie, the last couple of weeks have worked for both of us, haven't they?"

"Yes."

"So why change it?"

She gave him a small smile and shook her head. Ethan didn't like what he was reading in her eyes.

"Because I want more in my life than great sex and work," she said.

"What else is there?" Ethan demanded, though he knew damn well what her answer would be.

"*Love*, Ethan," she said, meeting his gaze with an intensity that almost slapped at him. "I want someone to love. I want to *be* loved. I want a family of my own."

"You have Emma," he countered, thinking of how close she'd become to the baby over the last couple weeks. "We both know you love that baby. I can see it whenever you hold her."

"I do. I really do. But she's not mine, Ethan," she said, shaking her head again. "She's a darling, but she's your baby. To her, I'll never be more than someone who comes and goes from her house. Like a visiting aunt."

"Then live there with us," he argued.

She took a breath, blew it out and said, "You want me to live with you, have sex with you, help you raise Emma and work here for you."

"Is that so bad?" The demand rolled from him in

deep, tight tones. "For God's sake, Sadie, we're doing all of that now. Why not keep doing it?"

"Because it's not enough."

"It is for me," he countered.

"Not for me." She swallowed hard and added, "If I'm going to have my own life, have what's important to me, I have to leave. To you, I'll never be more than your lover."

"And that's bad?" He released her hands and didn't let himself think how empty his hands felt.

"For me, yes," she said. "I need more, Ethan. I deserve more."

He couldn't argue with that, because she did deserve everything she wanted. But he couldn't give it to her. Wouldn't get married again.

"Fine." Nodding, he stepped back behind the desk, as if pulling on a suit of armor. "Well then, you'd better get busy finding your replacement here. And I'll still need a nanny for Emma."

"Ethan, I wish—"

He ignored that. "Get me marketing, will you? I want to have another look at the Mother's Day campaign before it's set in stone."

"All right."

"And bring me some coffee when you get a minute."

"Sure." Her heels tapped against the floor as she left the office.

When she was gone, he sat back in his chair and told himself to get used to that empty sensation. It was going to be with him for a long time.

"You had sex."

"I did," Sadie said, and picked up the wine Gina had poured for her. "Many times."

"Finally." Gina sighed happily, took a sip of her own wine and demanded, "Who's the lucky guy?"

"Ethan."

Gina choked on her wine, slapped one hand to her own chest and coughed until her eyes ran. Feeling a little guilty, Sadie tried to help, but Gina shook her head and waved one hand at her. When she could finally breathe again, she cried, "What do you mean, many times? Are you crazy?"

Sadie had been asking herself that for almost two weeks now. And the answer was still the same. If she *was* crazy, she didn't care. "No. He's—"

"Don't. Don't even say it," Gina told her, and took a cautious sip of her wine. "Honey, I know I told you to have sex with him, but that was to get him out of your system, not to dig him in even deeper."

That's just what had happened, though. Even after the scene this afternoon at the office, Sadie couldn't regret what she'd had with Ethan. Yes, he'd made it plain that he wasn't interested in love. That he didn't want to give more than he had or risk more than he dared. And maybe she could understand why, even though she wanted to throttle him to make him see what they could have together if only he'd believe.

She'd left the office right after their…*meeting* and come to Gina's. Ethan was perfectly capable of driving Emma home and seeing that she had dinner. It would be good for him to do it himself. To see what it would be like without Sadie around to help. And oh, that thought broke her heart. She wouldn't be there to watch Emma grow up. Wouldn't be sleeping with Ethan. Or having sex with him. Or waking up snuggled next to him. She wouldn't even be working with him anymore, and boy, his absence in her life was going to leave a huge, gaping hole.

"I need cookies." Gina got up to rummage in a cupboard and came up with a bag of chocolate-covered marshmallow cookies. "This is my private stash. None of the kids know. Not even Mike has found them yet. But I'm willing to share with you."

"You're a saint." Sadie grinned and took a cookie for herself. Biting in, she took a quick look around. Gina's kitchen was bright and cheerful. White walls, red cupboards and black granite counters. There were sippy cups on the drain board and a row of baby bottles waiting to be filled. It was homey and cozy and light-years from Ethan's showplace kitchen. But, Sadie reminded herself, now that Julie was working at his house, she'd made some changes to the sterile atmosphere that could almost make it this warm.

"If I were a saint I wouldn't have told you to sleep with Ethan."

Sadie looked at her sister-in-law. "You couldn't have stopped me, either."

"Well, don't tell Mike that. I have him convinced I'm all powerful."

Sadie laughed and took another bite of cookie. "I can't help what I feel, Gina."

"But you're hoping this is going to turn into a fairy tale or something," the other woman said. "I can see it in your eyes."

"Well, that's annoying," Sadie admitted. Because of course that's what she'd been hoping for. Even knowing the chances of it happening were practically zip. And today had pretty much tied that up in a bow. Yet still, she hadn't completely given up. "Okay, yes, I'm hoping, but the more rational part of me knows this isn't going anywhere. But Gina, he's hitting most of the points on my list now."

"Really…" Gina ate another cookie and washed it down with wine.

Sadie ticked them off. "Sexy, oh yeah. Adventurous…" Thinking of the night before in the shower, she flushed with pleasure. "Boy howdy. He's spending time with me and he loves Emma."

"Has he actually said so?"

"No, but I can tell." He didn't want to say the word, but that didn't mean he wasn't feeling the emotion. The more time Ethan spent with the baby, the easier he was with her. Emma had wormed her way into the man's heart against his will and it was wonderful to watch. Whether Ethan knew it or not, he was opening up to the world. To possibilities. Why couldn't one of those possibilities be *her*?

"And sense of humor?"

"He has that, too," she insisted. "He doesn't show it often, but it's there."

"Sadie, that list was there to prove to you that Ethan wasn't the man for you. Instead, you're fiddling with it to make sure he meets all the criteria you have. That's not a good thing."

"I know." Restless, Sadie set her wine down and walked across the kitchen, picked up one of the baby's bottles and turned it in her hands. She wanted children of her own. A husband. A job she loved. Was that really too much to ask?

Not looking at Gina, she said, "We're still hunting for a nanny. When we find one, I'll go."

"I know you don't want to," Gina said.

"I really don't." Looking at her from across the room, Sadie gave her sister-in-law a sad smile. "I just love him. Like you love Mike."

"I know. But sweetie, setting yourself up for heart-break isn't the smartest thing you've ever done."

"True. But honestly, if there is no happy ending here, at least I had this time with him."

"It won't be enough."

Sadie set the bottle down. "It'll have to be."

Gabriel watched as the chef made up the samples that they'd present to Ethan.

Making fine chocolates was more a science than an art, though most people didn't realize it. Of course, there was plenty of art involved, as well.

Tempering the chocolate itself to the right temperature, where it would set up glossy and hard enough to *snap* when you bit into it. Mixing the ganache to the perfect texture before infusing it with the flavors Gabriel was hoping would convince Ethan to open his mind and try something new. Once the ganache was ready, the truffles and other assorted fillings had to be hand rolled into a uniform size and perfectly rounded or squared. Sometimes they used molds to get the right shapes, but here, in this rented kitchen, Jeff Garrett would be rolling the chocolates by hand.

As an assistant chef at Heart, Jeff was talented and eager to move up the ladder. Tonight was his chance at excellence, as well as Gabe's. Jeff already had the chocolates—milk, white and dark—tempered and waiting. The cold marble slab held rows of perfectly rounded truffles and ganache and were just waiting for Jeff to hand dip them and then stamp and decorate. Now that most of the basics were done, the chef as artist would take over. With talent and style, a good chocolate chef would make his creations shine like jewels.

"It smells great in here, doesn't it?" Gabe murmured, not wanting to disturb Jeff as he mixed the last of the spices into the final ganache.

"It does," Pam whispered, her gaze never leaving the chef and the chocolates laid out on the marble slab in front of him. "Do you still have the recipe with you?" she asked. "Just in case he has to start over, I mean."

"Don't even say it." Gabe shuddered and checked his watch. "Jeff's already been at it for hours. If we have to start over…"

"But the recipe's safe, right?"

He looked at her. "Yeah. Of course. Don't worry so much."

"I just…know how much this means to you, that's all." Pam watched as Jeff used a candy fork to hand dip a lavender truffle into the white chocolate melt. He carefully lifted it out, laid it on the cool marble, then swirled the chocolate on top by twisting the candy fork over it. He did the same with five more truffles until he had a tidy row laid out.

On another slab were pieces of what would be dark chocolate raspberry coconut bark drizzled with white chocolate.

Earl Grey tea truffles coated in cocoa powder were resting alongside white chocolate lemon blackberry bonbons. The last offering was a dark chocolate ganache infused with Sumatran coffee—Ethan's favorite—and orange liqueur.

The samples were flavorful and beautiful, as Jeff

concentrated now on decorating each piece until it shone.

"The chef I was going to have you use would have made the bark white chocolate with dark chocolate drizzle. To showcase the red of the raspberry." Pam sniffed a little.

Gabe slanted her a puzzled look. "Jeff's creations look perfect."

"Oh, they're very nice." She shrugged. "I just think a more experienced chef might have done an even better job."

Okay, he thought, she'd been a little off ever since their first fight about the chef and she was still off tonight. Not really angry, but not herself, either. He'd wanted her there with him because it had really all started out as Pam's idea. The two of them together, facing down Ethan. But ever since Gabe had decided to use Jeff, Pam had been…different.

"What's going on with you, Pam?" Gabe asked. "Jeff studied with master chocolatiers in Belgium. He's been with Heart Chocolates for four years. He's worked his way up to being an assistant chef and he wants this almost as badly as I do."

"All true," she said with a shrug, "but you never even gave my guy a tryout."

"I didn't need to," he said, impatient now. After all, this might have started out as her idea, but this was his life. His company. She didn't have a horse in the race, so she had nothing to lose.

She flashed him a hard look and interrupted him. "I keep telling you, I thought we were in this together, Gabe. *We* were making decisions, and then suddenly, you changed the rules and I'm cut out. How do you think I should feel?"

He blew out a breath and tried to see it from her point of view. Gabe guessed he would have been pretty pissed if the tables were turned. But bottom line, this was his life. Not Pam's.

"I know you wanted to help," he said, striving for patience. He loved Pam, But damned if he understood her. "I do trust you. But this is my company. I've got to do what I think is best for it."

"I know, Gabe. Really. And I love you. I'm just..." she shrugged again. She shifted her gaze to Jeff.

Gabe watched as the man used an airbrush pencil to dazzle the white chocolate with rainbow colors in swirled patterns. As those colors began to set up, Jeff switched cartridges to paint a stylized red heart on top of the dark honey-infused caramels coated in a thick layer of milk chocolate.

"They all look great," Gabe said.

Jeff paused to glance up at him and smile. "Thanks, boss. The dark chocolate raspberry and chipotle chili are going to be coated in an extra layer of dark, then streaked with the milk in a heart pattern." He glanced around at his creations. "Then I think we'll be ready."

Ready to face down Ethan and demand he take a chance on the future. Hell, Gabe was betting everything on this as a win. Ethan's head would explode when he found out Gabe had taken the family recipe from the safe. So these chocolates had better damn well convince Ethan that Gabe was right, or working with his older brother from now on was going to be a living nightmare.

"When will you take these to Ethan?" Pam asked.

"Tomorrow," Gabe said firmly, nodding to himself. "You ready for it, Jeff?"

"So ready," the chef said, concentrating on the last of the chocolates he was creating. "I've got the boxes here. When they're finished setting up, I'll box them for tomorrow."

"In the morning. Be at my office at ten. With the chocolates. We'll face Ethan down together." He turned to Pam. "Are you going to be there?"

"Sure." She lifted her chin and met his gaze. "I told you before, Gabe. I'm with you."

Gabe dropped one arm around her shoulders. She was tense and stiff for a couple seconds, then she moved into him and leaned her head against his shoulder. He smiled to himself. Whatever was going on, they'd get past it. Once this was settled, he'd sit down with Pam and not let up until he found the answers he wanted. But for now, he had to focus on the plan he'd put everything into. He knew this was a step toward the future for Heart and damned if he wouldn't find a way to convince Ethan.

Gabe believed that. He had to. Because if he failed, he wouldn't lose only this chance at making a mark on the company. He might lose his brother.

Ethan was already in a crappy mood when Gabriel walked into his office the next morning. He hadn't slept all night because he hadn't had Sadie with him. For the first time since moving in with him, she'd slept in the guest room. Annoying to realize how much he'd come to count on having her there beside him.

She'd been right across the hall and yet she might as well have been hundreds of miles away. He knew what it would take to get her to come to him. And he couldn't give it to her.

Wouldn't, he corrected silently. She wanted a relationship. Something permanent. A family. A commitment.

Hell, he'd changed enough lately, hadn't he? He'd taken her into his house, into his bedroom. He'd been with her now longer than he had been with anyone else other than his ex. Ethan already knew he hadn't been a good husband. Why would he even *think* about trying that again? He liked Sadie. Liked being with her, so why would he risk making her miserable by marrying her? No. She might think he was being a selfish bastard by pulling away, but the truth was, he assured himself, he was doing this for her own good.

Let her find another man. His insides twisted at the thought. One who would hold her at night, make her belly swell with a child. He gritted his teeth and fisted both hands helplessly. Some other man would be the one to get her smiles, her kisses, her—

"Ethan," Gabriel said, splintering his thoughts, "we have to talk."

"Looks like more of a meeting than a conversation," Ethan observed. He looked from his younger brother to Sadie, to Jeff Garrett, one of their top chocolate chefs. A cold, suspicious feeling snaked along Ethan's spine and colored his tone when he demanded, "What's this about, Gabe?"

"Jeff and I have something we want you to try." Gabe motioned to the chef, who stepped up and set three small candy boxes on Ethan's desk.

His temper bubbled, but Ethan kept it tamped down. Gabe had done it. Gone behind his back and made up samples of the candies he wanted to incorporate into the company's product line.

Standing up behind his desk, Ethan looked at Sadie. "Did you know about this?"

"Nope," she said, and shot Gabe a hard look.

"Don't give Sadie a bad time. She didn't know a thing," Gabe said, and faced off against Ethan. Bracing his legs wide apart as if readying for a fight, he folded his arms across his chest and said, "This was my idea. Well, mine and Pam's."

He turned to hold out one hand toward a woman hovering near the doorway. "Come on in, honey. It's game time."

Ethan watched her walk to his brother and he frowned slightly. "Who's this?"

"Pam Cassini," Gabe said. "She's with me."

Amazing. He'd brought his new girlfriend in on this? Ethan studied the woman. She looked familiar somehow, but he couldn't put his finger on why. Frowning, Ethan set that niggling worry aside a second later because damned if he didn't have bigger issues at the moment.

Sadie walked up and stood beside him. Thankful for the support, he gave her a quick nod, then looked back to his brother.

Gabe was standing in a slash of sunlight pouring through the tinted windows at Ethan's back. He stood like a man waiting to hear a sentence pronounced. Well, he wouldn't have to wait long. "What the hell have you done?"

Nine

Gabe lifted his chin and met Ethan glare for glare. "I rented a professional kitchen and Jeff made up some samples of a few of the flavors I was talking to you about."

Ethan's gaze shifted to Jeff, who looked a lot more worried than Gabe did. As he should. "You know I could fire you for this," he said tightly.

Jeff swallowed hard. "Yes, sir, I know. But I agree with Gabe. It's time to push outside the box."

Astounded, feeling cornered, Ethan lifted his eyebrows. "In a box? You think Heart Chocolates is boring? Is that it?"

"No, he didn't say that," Gabe interrupted. "And don't come down on him, either, Ethan. He can't fight back."

"But you can," Ethan said, and his voice was so controlled, so quiet, Gabe should have been wary. Instead, his brother looked defiant, rebellious. Situation normal as far as Gabe's attitude went.

Sadie caught Ethan's reaction, though, and silently slid her hand into his and gave it a squeeze. With that single touch, she dialed down his temper, his frustration, and helped him focus.

"What exactly did you do?" Ethan asked, and thought he was remaining remarkably calm, all things considered.

"I told you."

"Yes. But how did you make up the chocolate?" Ethan studied his brother. "For these 'samples' to be a true representation of Heart, you'd have to have access to the recipe."

The minute the words left his mouth, Ethan saw the truth on his brother's features. And his calm dissolved into a pit of white-hot fury. "You *took* the recipe?"

"I'm a Hart, too, Ethan," Gabriel argued, meeting fire with fire. "Yes, I took *our* recipe. I made a copy of the one in your safe."

Ethan actually saw red. That recipe never left the safe. It had been copied and protected and kept in a separate place, but the original... "How did you—"

Sadie tugged on his hand and he looked down at her. "I ran into Pam and Gabe here in your office the night Emma arrived. I didn't mention it because I didn't think anything of it."

Could his head actually explode? Ethan stared into Sadie's big blue eyes and read a plea for patience. She was asking a lot. But for her, he'd try. He took a long, deep breath, glared at his brother and demanded, "What did you do with the original?"

"What do you think I did with it?" Gabe sounded offended now, which was astonishing to Ethan.

"How the hell do I know?" Ethan shouted, and when he heard himself he made a valiant effort to lower his voice. "I didn't think you'd take our heritage out of the safe and make a copy, so for all I know, you sold the original on eBay!"

"Don't be ridiculous." Gabe went to the safe, hit the dial lock, spun it a few times, then swung the door open. "There's the recipe. Right where it belongs. Do you really think I'd risk everything we are to prove a point?"

"Isn't that exactly what you did?" Ethan shouted again.

Sadie squeezed his hand once more, but this time he barely felt it. This was over the top. He felt betrayed by his own damn brother. He and Gabe had argued a lot over the years, but this was something he hadn't expected.

"Hell no!" Gabe went toe to toe with his brother, and met him glare for glare. "I used the recipe, but the chef involved already works for us. I trust him as you should, too, since he's one of our top guys."

Ethan gritted his teeth so hard he should have had a mouthful of powder. "Jeff isn't the issue here."

He heard the man's sigh of relief.

"Fine." Gabe threw both hands out in supplication. "I'm a traitor. Have me drawn and quartered tomorrow. But today, try the damn chocolates."

Stunned, Ethan could only stare at him. Gabe was still pretending this was no big deal. "Seriously? You expect me to go along with this when you went behind my back?"

"You didn't give me a choice, Ethan." Gabe pushed

both hands through his hair, looked over at Pam, then back to his brother. "I wanted to do this with your approval. Hell, your involvement. But you're so damn stubborn. So resistant to change—"

"So really it's all my fault," Ethan said wryly.

"Well, I wouldn't have put it that way, but since you did…"

"You're something else, Gabe."

"Is it so hard to see my point of view, Ethan?" Gabe's voice was low and tight, filled with frustration that Ethan could sympathize with, since he was feeling it, too. "I'm not trying to wreck the company. I'm trying to make a difference and fighting you every damn day to do it."

"But you don't see it from my side, either. I don't want to change with the times," Ethan said. "Forever trying to figure out which way the wind's blowing in this business. It doesn't pay to chase trends."

"It doesn't pay to ignore advancements, either," Gabe argued.

"You guys…" Sadie tried to intervene, but neither of them acknowledged her.

"I'm not ignoring anything," Ethan said. "And I won't risk everything we are, either."

"I wanted him to use a chef I know," Pam said, speaking up for the first time. "But Gabe refused. He wouldn't risk that recipe. Instead, he insisted on using a Heart chef to protect it."

She still looked familiar to him and it was irritating to not be able to identify why. Still, she was emphasizing the point Gabe had made earlier. Mollified a bit, Ethan nodded and took a deep breath. He folded his hand around Sadie's and didn't even question why he was using her as a touchstone of sorts.

Gabe seemed to sense that the worst was over. He gave a signal to Jeff, who cautiously moved closer to the desk. Deftly, the man opened up the boxes, displaying the candies he'd personally created the night before.

"They're beautiful," Sadie whispered.

That they were, Ethan admitted silently. The variety of chocolates were artistically presented—everything from cocoa powder to the white chocolate bonbons decorated with a rainbow of colors.

"Thank you." Jeff grinned, pleased at the response.

"They're not just pretty," Gabe said, with satisfaction. "They're delicious."

Ethan scowled at him and Gabe grinned. "Admit it. You want to know what they taste like."

As angry as he was, Ethan also felt a ripple of pride in Gabe. He had his own vision and wasn't afraid to follow it. His brother had believed in something and found a way to make it happen. Not that stealing the family recipe was the way to do it, but Ethan admired that his brother believed in his own vision enough to risk everything.

"What if I don't like them?"

Gabe grinned even wider. "That won't be an issue."

"He seems sure of himself," Sadie said, with a wink for Gabe.

"Always has been," Ethan muttered.

Gabe walked to Pam and dropped one arm around her shoulders. He watched as Jeff laid out a white cloth napkin on the desk, then stepped back to wait. And watch.

"All right. Moment of truth." Ethan looked at Sadie. "I want you to try them, too. I trust your opinion."

She gave him a smile that lit up her eyes and Ethan's breath caught in his chest. Then he turned to the candy. He took one of the rainbow-decorated, glossy white chocolates.

"That's a lavender truffle," Jeff provided, then looked at Sadie as she chose another piece. "And you have a dark chocolate raspberry coconut bark drizzled with white chocolate."

"Interesting," Ethan murmured, and carefully broke the white chocolate piece in half. Satisfied at the sharp snap of the chocolate coating, he then inhaled the scent, approving of the precise blend of spice and sweet. But the proof was in the flavor.

He bit into it and let the ganache melt on his tongue while flavor exploded in his mouth. He really hated that his brother had been right. The candy was perfect.

He shifted a look at his brother and saw the triumphant gleam in Gabe's eyes. "It's great, right?"

Chewing, Ethan nodded. "It is. Better than I would have thought."

Again, Jeff heaved a sigh of relief and Ethan couldn't really blame him. The chef had risked a hell of a lot, too. He'd worked his way up at Heart and he'd gambled his job on these samples.

"Sadie?"

She swallowed the bite she'd taken and shook her head in amazement. "This bark is terrific. The raspberry is sweet but not overpowering the chocolate, and the coconut gives it a slightly salty, savory flavor. Really amazing."

Jeff smiled and Gabe looked proud enough to burst.

Ethan couldn't blame him. They went through the other chocolates one by one, with both Jeff and Gabe explaining the process and how they'd chosen the different flavors they'd blended into the ganache.

"This last one is a Sumatran coffee, orange liqueur blend," Gabe said slyly.

"Clever," Ethan murmured. "Hit me with a flavor I love."

"I'll pass," Sadie said, and took one of the lemon blackberry bonbons instead.

Pam was strangely silent, but Ethan assumed it was because this wasn't really her business. She had nothing riding on this gathering; she was simply there to support Gabe.

"You did a hell of a job, here," Ethan ruefully admitted when the tasting was completed.

He'd been backed into a corner so neatly the only way out was Gabe's way. Ethan hated change, but he'd been dealing with nothing *but* change over the last couple weeks and it hadn't killed him. And really, the damn chocolate was *good.* Maybe Gabe had a point, after all, and it was time to branch out. To test new waters, before he—and his company—became so comfortable, neither of them could grow.

"That means what, exactly?" Gabe asked warily.

Ethan looked from the candy to Sadie to Gabe. "It means we should talk privately. Pam, would you and Jeff mind stepping out of the office for a few moments?"

"She doesn't have to go," Gabe argued.

"It's okay," Pam said with a weak smile. "I'll wait outside."

When they were gone, Ethan perched on the edge of

his desk and said, "You made your point, Gabe. I don't like how you did it, but you were right about the candy."

Gabe clutched his heart. "Hold on a second. I might need an ambulance."

"Keep it up," Ethan promised with a quirk of a smile, "and you will."

Suddenly all business, Gabe asked, "So we'll go forward with the new line?"

"That depends," Ethan said, drawing Sadie over to his side and taking her hand in his.

Gabe's eyebrows lifted and a quick smile came and went. "Depends on what?"

"I don't want to start another line with only five or six offerings," Ethan said. "Can you and Jeff come up with a full dozen new flavors?"

"Oh, hell yes. Jeff's got a million ideas and—" He broke off. "You're making Jeff head chef on this project?"

"He earned it, don't you think?"

"I do. Between us, we'll come up with flavors that'll blow away the competition." Gabe was excited now, his eyes shining and a wide smile curving his mouth.

"Then go," Ethan said. "Be brilliant. But we decide together which flavors we're going to push."

"Agreed, Ethan. Thanks." Gabe went to pick up the candy boxes.

"Leave the candy," Ethan said, making his brother laugh.

Gabe walked out to tell Pam and Jeff the good news, leaving Ethan and Sadie alone in the office.

"That was well-done," Sadie said, and cupped his cheek to turn his face to hers.

"He pushes every button I've got, but he came up

with some great new tastes, textures." Shaking his head, he sighed and said, "He went about it the wrong way, but I guess he was right about something else, too. I didn't really give him any other choice."

"Wow, self-realization," Sadie mused, smiling. "I think we're having a moment here."

He caught her hand in his again. "It happens."

"You didn't have to put him and Jeff in charge," she said. "That was well-done, too."

He gave her a quick smile. "Are you kidding? He wanted this new line—now he can be in charge of making it happen. Seems fair."

Sadie laughed. "So you give him what he wants and punish him for it all at once. You're devious."

"Yeah, I know." He pulled her in close. "I missed you last night."

"I missed you, too."

"I didn't want to," he said.

"I know." She smiled wistfully.

He looked into her eyes and found himself drowning in that deep, cool blue. "I can't be who you want me to be, Sadie. But do we have to leave each other before we leave each other?"

She tipped her head to one side, those blond curls of hers sliding across her skin. "No, Ethan. Let's be together while we can."

"Good call," he said, then he kissed her.

Gabe left the meeting ready to take on the world.

Hell, if he could convince Ethan to make changes to the company chocolate line, he could do anything. He expected to find Pam outside the office waiting for him, but he spotted her with Jeff by the elevators. And it looked like they were having a conversation spiked by hand gestures and angry expressions.

Frowning, he hurried toward them, ignoring the phones ringing, the clack of keyboards and the low, muttered conversations rising and falling all around him.

"I told you I can't do it," Jeff was telling Pam as Gabe walked up. "That's proprietary information."

Pam looked desperate, furious. "For God's sake, it's not like it's a secret. You saw it last night. I'm just asking you to tell me—"

"What's going on?" Gabe looked to Pam for the answer, but shifted his gaze to Jeff when the chef spoke.

"Pam wanted me to give her the Heart chocolate recipe."

"What?" Gabe looked at her, shocked. That made zero sense. She knew that recipe was the best-kept secret in the company. Hell, she'd just been present when his own brother had reamed him for copying it. "Why would you do that?"

She took a breath and blew it out. Her gaze shifted from side to side before finally meeting Gabe's. "Because I need it for my father's company."

"What the hell, Pam?" He kept his voice low, to prevent anyone else from listening in. Jeff slipped away and Gabe barely noticed. Suddenly, a lot of things were making sense. How eager Pam had been to make up those samples. How quickly she'd suggested using her own chef to make the candy. How furious she'd been when Gabe had used Jeff for the project instead of the chef she'd suggested.

God. He felt like an idiot for trusting her.

The elevator arrived with a loud ding and Pam turned for it, but Gabe grabbed her upper arm and held her in place. "You owe me, Pam. What the hell were you doing? Was any of this real to you? Was I just a means to the recipe?" He snorted a harsh laugh as reality crashed down onto his head. She'd never been into him. It was all about Heart chocolate. "Damn, I've got to admire you. You went all out for what you wanted. Pretending to love me just to make sure your plan worked. Must have been a bitch when I didn't use your guy."

She yanked her arm free and shot him a hard look through flashing brown eyes. "Yes, it was hard. My brother's a chocolate chef. He could have made your candy and then kept the recipe for us to use against you."

Infuriated, confused, Gabe demanded, "Why? What have you got against the Hart family?"

The elevator started to close and she slapped one hand out to hold the doors open. "Because my last name isn't Cassini, Gabe. It's *Donatello*."

"What?" Everything Gabe thought he knew went right out the window. Stunned, he thought back to all the times he'd discussed business with her. How he'd told her about the Donatello buyout and how his brother was eager to take over the shop in Laguna and introduce a new venue for Heart Chocolates.

Hell, he'd *trusted* her.

Gabe looked at her as if seeing her for the first time. And still he didn't know who he was looking at. The woman he loved? Or an industrial spy? "You lied to me this whole time?"

"It wasn't all a lie," she countered, voice breaking as the first tears filled her eyes. "Cassini is my mother's maiden name."

"Oh, well then. That's okay." Shaking his head, Gabe

fought down the fury clawing at his throat as he looked at the woman he loved. The woman he'd thought was with him. A partner. "Are you even really in PR?"

"No. I make chocolate. With my family. Just like you."

"Of course you do," he muttered thickly. No wonder she'd known so much about the chocolate industry. "And you wanted to ruin Heart Chocolates as what? Payback for us buying your father out?"

"Your brother is ruining my father's life," she said, her voice urgent, desperate. "Dad can't stand up against a company the size of Heart. He has no choice, he *has* to sell because the great and powerful Ethan has decided he needs a street location and he's focused on my dad's." A hot rush of tears spilled from her eyes and streamed down her cheeks unchecked. "The Donatellos have been running that shop for forty-five years, Gabe. It's just as important to us as your company is to you. My brother and I grew up in that shop. It means everything to us."

Her tears shook him to the bone. He wanted to reach out to hold her, tell her everything would be okay, but he wasn't sure it would be. Hell, he didn't even know what he was feeling at the moment.

He loved Pam Cassini. But did that woman even really exist?

"I do love you, Gabe," she confessed. "I didn't mean to, but I do. I wasn't pretending about that. But this is about my *father*. I had to do whatever I could to help." She jumped into the elevator and kept her gaze on him as the doors slid shut. "I love you…"

"Damn it, Pam…" He lunged for her, but the doors shut him out. Then she was gone.

* * *

A few hours later, Sadie sat in the front passenger seat of Ethan's car while Gabe leaned forward from the back, still talking. They'd *been* talking for hours. Ever since Pam had dropped her bomb on Gabe.

"It's her father, Ethan," he was saying, not for the first time. "We can understand family loyalty."

"Agreed," Ethan said, giving his brother a quick look before shifting his gaze back to Pacific Coast Highway. He was just as shocked as Gabe by Pam's revelation. But at least now he knew why the woman had seemed so familiar. Ethan had met personally with Richard Donatello, and his daughter resembled him quite a bit. "She went about all of this the wrong way, but at least you two have something in common."

Sadie said, "Ethan, that's not really fair. Yes, Pam lied, and okay, I guess Gabe did, too…"

"Hey."

"Well, it's true," she said, and patted his hand. "But you both had good reasons for it."

That was surely true. From the moment he'd charged back into the office to tell Ethan exactly who Pam Cassini really was, Gabe had been like a man possessed. He couldn't stop talking about the woman. Ethan glanced at Sadie and didn't miss her wistful expression. Was she envious of what Gabe felt for Pam?

"I didn't expect you to take it this well," Gabe admitted. "I thought you'd be supremely pissed that Pam had used me to get to the recipe."

"I have to admit, I'm with Gabe. You surprised me, too, Ethan." Sadie was watching him, and even with his gaze on the road, Ethan felt the power of her stare.

He understood why the people closest to him were

shocked at his reaction. As little as a month ago, he'd have been furious, with Gabe *and* Pam. But it was impossible to be too angry with Gabe when Ethan himself had been allowing his emotions to guide his actions the past couple weeks.

"Let's just say that there have been a lot of changes lately and maybe I'm still responding to them." Ethan shot her a quick look and saw the smile that curved her mouth. "I'm not happy," he admitted, "but I can understand what she did."

He made a turn onto a side street in Laguna and pulled up outside a Craftsman-style bungalow. The house had a big tree out front, a wide porch boasting twin rockers and a small table between them. The winter flowers in the pot by the front door were a cheerful spot of color on a gray day. He turned off the engine and half turned to look at Gabe. "That's why we're here. I want to talk to Pam's father—her family—about this."

"Right." Gabe scraped one hand across his jaw. "What did he say when you called?"

"Richard already knew before I could tell him. Apparently," Ethan said, "she'd confessed the whole thing to her parents when she left you at the office. Richard's eager to talk it all out."

"That's good, right?" Gabe scrambled out of the car and stood in the street, staring at the house as if he could see past the walls to the woman he loved.

Ethan climbed out, too, and looked at his brother. He hoped this was going to end well, but he didn't have a clue what would happen when both families talked. As Sadie got out of the car, Ethan's gaze naturally drifted to her. It felt good to have her with him. Too good, really, because he was depending on her now even more than he had when she was simply his assistant. But that was a problem for later.

Ethan took Sadie's hand and she held on, glad that he automatically reached for her. She wondered if he even realized how often he did it. And she wondered how she would get along without his casual touch.

Richard Donatello opened the door for them and welcomed them inside. His daughter looked a lot like him, which was why Ethan had thought Pam seemed familiar, Sadie figured. The house itself was cozy and a lot bigger than it looked from the outside.

Richard led them through the house to the dining room, where his wife, son and Pam were waiting for them.

"Thanks for seeing us," Ethan said.

"No problem. Please. Sit." Richard took the chair at the head of the table and waited until they were seated before speaking. "Thanks for not having Pam arrested."

"Dad!"

"You could have been," her father said, his features stern.

The woman winced and gave Gabe a furtive look.

"This is my wife, Marianna, and my son, Tony." Richard paused and said sadly, "Pam told me what's been going on and I'm offering you my apology."

"Dad—" Pam interrupted, but her father shut her down with a single look.

Sadie sympathized. She knew Pam loved Gabe. And she could guess at how Pam had felt, torn between two loyalties. But of course she'd stood for her family. What wouldn't a person do for family?

"Your apology isn't necessary," Ethan said, and gave Sadie's hand a squeeze. "My brother and I were just saying that if there's one thing we understand, it's family loyalty."

"Thank you." Richard nodded, then looked at Gabe before turning to his daughter. "You were wrong to do it, Pam. And Tony, you shouldn't have gone along."

His son nodded. "Yeah, I know, Pop. We were only trying to help," he said. "To save the shop."

Sadie watched the people around the table, waiting to see where this would go. There was tension in the room, but over it all were threads of love so thick and interwoven she half expected to actually *see* them, like golden strands linking the Donatello family together.

"This isn't a hostile takeover," Ethan put in, but before he could say more, Pam interrupted.

"Of course it is. You're Heart Chocolates. Donatello's doesn't stand a chance in a fight against you."

"Pam," her mother said softly. "It's not a fight. Ethan came to us a couple of months ago with an offer to buy the shop. We talked about it—" she sent her husband a smile "—and after more negotiations, we decided together to accept."

"But why?" Pam asked, looking from one parent to the other. "Because you couldn't afford to fight back. That's why I wanted the recipe. I thought maybe we could barter for it. They get it back and we keep the shop."

"So blackmail?" Richard asked, dumbfounded. "You would do something like that?"

"To help the family, yes. I'm not proud of it, Dad," she said, and looked straight at Gabe. "I didn't want to. Didn't want to lie. But I didn't know how else to help you save the business."

"We don't want the shop," her father said, loudly enough to get everyone's attention.

Sadie was startled by that and it appeared everyone but Ethan was, too. Silence dropped onto the table in the wake of that announcement until Richard's son spoke.

"What do you mean?" Tony asked, obviously stunned. "It's ours. We've been working it together my whole life."

"And enough's enough," their mother said, smiling at her husband.

"I'm confused," Gabe muttered.

"You're not alone," Pam said, and gave him a sheepish smile.

Sadie squeezed Ethan's hand in solidarity. He looked at her and smiled, apparently knowing exactly where the rest of this story was going. He leaned in closer and said, "Remember when you suggested I talk to Richard myself instead of sending the lawyers?"

"Yes…"

"Well, I did." He winked at her and Sadie was more confused than ever. "Just listen," he said, and they both turned back to the others gathered around the table.

"I'm retiring," Richard said, letting his gaze slide around the table. "Your mom and I want to do a little living while we still can."

"But you're not old enough to retire!" Pam was clearly shocked.

"That's what makes it even better," Marianna said with a smile for her husband. "Why wait until we need someone to push us around in wheelchairs? No. We want to enjoy ourselves, Pam. It's past time for your dad to stop working so hard."

Richard nodded, smiling at his family. "Your mother's right."

"But the shop…" Pam simply stared at her father.

Richard shrugged that aside. "It's been good for us. Made us a decent living. Put you two through school and I enjoyed it, too. We both did. Working together, side by side, to build something special."

Marianna and her husband shared a secret smile that Sadie envied. This couple had what she dreamed of having. A real partnership. They'd worked and lived and loved together for decades.

"With the money Heart Chocolates is paying us for the location and our customer list and website, well…" Richard winked at his wife. "I can take your mother on all the trips she's wanted to take for years. We're going on a cruise, in May. First-class. To Europe. For our thirtieth anniversary."

"Europe?" Tony was astonished.

Sadie sighed at the romance of it all. How wonderful must it be to still love so fiercely that you wanted *more* time together, even after all those years.

"That's right," his mother said with a bright smile. "We're going to have some fun for a change. And stay up late every night, since your dad won't have to get up at three o'clock in the morning…"

"Looking forward to that," Richard said, grinning at Ethan.

"So this was all for nothing," Pam whispered.

This was such a private moment, if not for Ethan's tight grip on her hand Sadie would have felt like an intruder. But for now, anyway, she and Ethan were united. He wanted her there and that meant everything to her.

"I feel like an idiot." Pam looked at Gabe. "I'm so sorry. I didn't mean to betray you. Or lie to you."

"I know," he said, pushing up from his chair to walk

around the table and pull her to her feet. "I love you, Pam Cassini Donatello."

She gave him a watery smile and leaned into his chest, sighing when his arms came around her. "I love you, too, Gabe."

"Isn't that lovely?" her mother said. "Maybe we'll get a wedding to plan, too."

"Mom!" Mortified, Pam turned her face into Gabe's chest as he laughed.

Ethan shook his head at his younger brother and Sadie could almost hear him thinking *Not love, Gabe. Anything but that.* And her heart hurt as she realized there was no happy ending in this story for her. She and Ethan would part ways and all she'd have were the memories she'd made over the last weeks. That sounded unbearably sad.

Ethan turned to Richard. "So the deal's still in place? No more negotiating?"

"It better be in place," Marianna said. "I just made reservations for the cruise today."

"We have a deal," Richard said, and held out one hand. "I know better than to disappoint my wife. But if you don't mind my saying, you should hire my son, Tony, there. He's a hell of a chocolate chef."

"Dad!"

"Done," Ethan promised, as the two men shook hands.

A half hour later, Ethan and Sadie left the house together. Gabe stayed with Pam and Sadie had a feeling that Marianna was going to get the wedding she was hoping for. Sadie felt a pang of envy she tried to bury. Just because she wouldn't end up with her hero didn't mean she couldn't be happy for someone else.

"I'm glad that all worked out," she said, as Ethan held the car door open for her.

"Yeah." Ethan glanced back at the house. "Me, too. Gabe's in love. Never thought I'd see that."

Sadie took a breath and held it. She could let this go, but what would be the point? "It can happen to anyone, Ethan."

He looked down at her and shook his head slowly. "No, it can't. What you and I have is different, Sadie. I don't want to hurt you."

God, she felt cold. "Then don't."

Pulling her into the circle of his arms, Ethan held her close for a long minute. Sadie inhaled the scent of him, wrapping it around her like a cloak. She held on to him, luxuriating in his strength, his warmth, for as long as she could, because she felt like this was already a goodbye. He was letting go of what they had. Even if she wasn't leaving yet, a part of Ethan already had.

When he stepped back suddenly, his eyes were shadowed, like a forest in twilight. "Sadie, it's not that easy."

"I wonder why you're looking for the easy way, Ethan," she said softly. "Nothing worth having comes easy."

She couldn't keep looking into his eyes, watching as the shutters came down and the walls went up. So she slid into the car and he slammed the door after her. A couple seconds later he was in the driver's seat, turning to fix a hard stare on her.

"I'm not looking for easy. None of this is easy." It was a demand that she understand, and she'd heard that tone so many times over the last five years, Sadie didn't even blink in the face of it.

"It is," she said flatly, and watched a flash burst in

his eyes. "It's much easier to walk away than to stay and work for what you want."

"I'm doing this for you," he said, clearly angry and just as obviously trying to control it.

"Doing what, Ethan? Turning away? Shutting me out? Thanks, but I didn't ask you to."

"You didn't have to," he countered. "You think I don't see what's happening between us? What you're hoping for? I already know I make lousy husband material, Sadie. I made Marcy miserable. I don't want that for you."

Under her breath, a short, sharp laugh escaped her. "And it's all about you, is that it?"

"In this, yes." He snapped his seat belt, fired up the engine and pulled away from the curb with a squeal of tires. "You should be thanking me," he muttered.

"Right." Sadie turned in her seat and glared at him. "I should thank you for breaking my heart."

"Damn it, don't you get it yet? That's what I'm trying to avoid."

"Well you're too late," she snapped. "See, I already love you, you idiot."

Ten

Ethan swung the car to the side of the road, turned the engine off and said tightly, "Don't. Just... Don't."

"You don't tell me what to do, Ethan," Sadie said. "FYI."

"Damn it, Sadie. What're you thinking? I didn't want you to love me."

"You don't get a vote in everything," she said, shaking her head in complete amazement. Of course this was how he would take being told she loved him. Most men might feel a little surge of panic and then be happy about it. But not the man *she* loved. Oh, no. He fought like a caged wolverine.

"This is exactly what I was trying to avoid with you, Sadie." His voice was so low, she almost missed the words, and she really wished she had.

"Contrary to your own belief system, Ethan, you don't actually control the universe."

He turned his head to look at her. "You're making jokes about this?"

"Would you rather I cry?"

"God, no."

"Then laugh it up. I intend to." Eventually. At the moment it was taking everything she had not to give in to the tightness in her chest, the burning in her eyes. But damned if she'd cry in front of him. That really would be a cherry on top of the humiliation sundae.

"Really." It wasn't a question, but that's how she took it.

"Yes, Ethan." Sadie tipped her head to one side to stare at him. "I'm going to laugh at the absurdity of me loving a man for five years and he never noticed."

"Five…" His shocked expression would have been funny if it hadn't been so damn sad.

"Or how about the fun of telling that man I love him and having him order me to stop."

"Sadie—"

"I'm going to laugh because it's ridiculous." Her heart hurt, but damned if she'd let him see it. Whatever tears she would shed, she'd cry them in private. And maybe she wouldn't cry at all.

She'd known going in that loving Ethan was futile. She hadn't been able to help herself, so she was willing to accept the pain that was the inevitable result of being a damn fool. Sadie had seen today that it wasn't *all* Hart men who were incapable of loving. Just the one she wanted. And maybe it was time she simply accepted that and moved on.

"Look, Ethan, we've already agreed that I'll be leaving when we find the right nanny." She took a deep breath. "So let's just find her fast and pretend we didn't have this humiliating conversation, okay?"

"Damn it, Sadie…"

"Seriously, Ethan," Sadie said, giving him a hard, steady look. "I'm so done with this. I don't want to hear you're sorry or you're angry or whatever, okay? These are *my* feelings and I don't need you to tell me what to do with them."

"Fine." His jaw was tight and his green eyes were on fire, so situation normal.

"Good." She turned in her seat, faced the front and said, "Now, let's get back to the house. I want to see Emma."

That tiny girl wouldn't be in her life much longer. As hard as it was, Sadie was going to make finding a nanny her top priority. She couldn't stay with Ethan now that he knew she loved him. Because the one thing she *never* wanted from Ethan was his pity.

She loved him.

Ethan felt twin jolts of differing emotions—both pleasure and panic, with a little guilt tossed in. He shrugged his shoulders, trying to drop the burden. Hell, he hadn't asked her to love him. This wasn't his fault. Yes, she was wounded now and that pained him more than he wanted to admit. But her pain was far less than she would have felt if he'd tried to make a relationship work.

Ethan nodded, silently reassuring himself that he was doing the right thing as he stared out the office window at the steely sea. Sunlight pierced the clouds and slashed at the surface of the water like a golden sword. And the beauty of it all should have been enough to clear his head. But it wasn't.

It had been two days since her confession. Two days

since they'd solved the Gabe and Pam problem, only to fall into one of their own. They'd lived like polite strangers ever since and the tension in the house was so thick Ethan could hardly breathe.

Emma was the only bright spot in his life and he didn't miss the irony in that. The baby girl was the reason all of this had happened to his once orderly life in the first place, and now that everything was turned upside down, it was Emma alone who could make him smile.

He'd interviewed four nannies in the last two days and Ethan felt the pressure to find someone fast. The sooner he did, the sooner Sadie could leave and they could try to get past this mess.

Sadie. Leaving. It was the right thing, but it didn't feel that way.

A knock at the office door had him turning. "Yes?"

Sadie stepped inside and Ethan's heart gave a hard jolt in his chest. He ignored it. That was hormones. Lust. He hadn't touched her in days and his body missed hers. Hell, the sex had been great, so why wouldn't he react to her? It had nothing to do with her big blue eyes. Or the way she sang to Emma first thing in the morning. Or how she smelled. Tasted. The sound of her laugh, the touch of her skin.

"What is it, Sadie?" He sounded gruff even to himself.

One of her blond eyebrows arched. "Rick's taking over for me this afternoon. I'm going to the house to get Emma. Take her to a doctor appointment."

He straightened at that. "What's wrong with her?"

"Nothing, Ethan," she said, tipping her head to one side, and he knew she was doing it on purpose now. "She needs a checkup."

His heartbeat settled down as he nodded. "All right. Can Rick handle your desk?"

She lifted her chin. "I've been working with him. He can do the job if you're patient with him at first."

Since Ethan and Gabe weren't at war any longer, there'd been no reason why Rick from Marketing couldn't take over for Sadie. He wasn't as good at it as she was, but then no one would be.

"I'm not going to slow walk him, Sadie," Ethan grumbled. "If he can't do the job find someone else."

"He can do it, Ethan. Just don't be a jerk and you won't scare him into paralysis."

Shaking his head, he said, "Still feeling free to say whatever you're thinking, huh?"

"Freer than ever," she said with a sharp nod. "I've got to go."

She left and Ethan was alone again. Damn it.

They found the nanny that afternoon.

The woman was impeccably qualified and Sadie was trying very hard not to resent her for it. Teresa Collins was perfect. Her résumé. Her references. She'd been trained at a world renowned nanny academy, for heaven's sake, and Emma had taken to her instantly. Not to mention that at forty plus, Teresa wouldn't be leaving to start a family of her own. In other words, the woman was everything they'd been looking for.

Standing out in the backyard, where she could be alone and think, Sadie noted the finished fence—four feet of terra-cotta-colored brick topped by another two feet of wrought iron. Emma would be safe, she told herself. And happy.

She'd grow up in this beautiful house with Julie and

her daughter, with a perfect nanny and with Ethan. The only one missing would be Sadie. And since she was so young, Emma would never know that someone else had loved her, too.

Instead, the nanny would get all Emma's smiles and hear her first words and see her first steps. At that thought, Sadie had to wonder if Ethan would stay involved with the baby. Would he back away and leave it all to the nanny because it was easier?

This was Sadie's own fault, of course. She never should have stayed the extra time. Never should have moved in here with Ethan and absolutely shouldn't have had sex with him. But that part was really hard to regret. In fact, the only thing she was sorry for was that he hadn't touched her in days.

Not since the night she'd told him she loved him and he'd reacted like a vampire to a rope of garlic.

"Sadie?"

Speak of the vampire... She turned from the ocean view to watch Ethan walk toward her, and her heart did a spin and jolt just looking at him. She really needed to go. Soon. For her own sake.

"What're you doing out here?" he asked, when he was close enough.

"Just looking at the fence." She glanced at it again. "They did a nice job."

"Yeah. The view's screwed, but the baby will be safe."

Shaking her head at that, she faced him and scooped windblown hair from her face. "What did you want, Ethan?"

"I've given Teresa the bedroom beside Emma's so she'll be close."

"That's good."

"And I asked Julie to pack your things."

She sucked in a gulp of ocean-scented air and swallowed the knot of pain lodged at the base of her throat. "Well, that's…abrupt." But not surprising. Looking into his green eyes now, she didn't see the slightest hint of the man she'd spent the last nearly three weeks with. Ethan had tucked that man away and maybe he'd never escape again. He was back to being the all-powerful, distant CEO. The man who never let emotion touch him. And it was clear to Sadie that he'd already said goodbye to her and what they'd shared.

"It's best this way."

"Your way, you mean," she said softly. "The easy way."

He tucked his hands into his slacks pockets and his expression went blank, giving away nothing of what he was feeling, thinking. "The deal was you'd stay until we found a nanny. Well, Teresa's here now, so—"

"Time to get things back to normal, is that it?" Well, she'd planned on leaving today, anyway.

"It is." His jaw was tight, the only signal to her that he wasn't completely at ease with this. Funny how it was such a small thing that could ease what she was feeling.

"You're right, Ethan. It's time for me to go."

He nodded, clearly relieved, and she laughed shortly.

"What's so funny?"

"This whole situation. I've loved you for a long time, Ethan."

He winced at the words and she couldn't help the sharp jab of pain in her heart. But she ignored it to say what she had to say. "I know you and I know you're going to try to hide from Emma like you've been hiding from me."

Scowling, he insisted, "I haven't been hiding."

She held up one hand for silence, because she wanted to finish this before she did something ridiculous and cried. "Yes, you have, but that's not what I'm worried about."

"You don't have to worry about me." The wind tossed his hair across his forehead and somehow that simple thing made him seem more approachable. More vulnerable.

"I probably will, anyway, but that's my problem, not yours." God, just looking at him made her want to cry for what they could have had together. "What I want you to do is promise me that you won't ignore Emma."

"Why would I—"

"Because it'll be easier," she said, and she knew he was remembering when they'd talked about taking the easy way before. So was she. "Easier to turn her over to Teresa and tell yourself it's better that way. But it's not, Ethan. Don't cheat Emma, and more importantly, don't cheat yourself."

"Sadie…"

She shook her head. She didn't want to hear whatever he might say, because she was certain it wouldn't be what she most wanted to hear. That he loved her. That he needed her. That he didn't care about past failures and he wanted only her.

"Good luck, Ethan," she said, and started walking. Sadie really hoped that Julie had finished packing her clothes because she needed to get out of there fast—before her heart convinced her to stay and fight for what she wanted.

* * *

For the next week, Sadie slept in late, painted the living room in her condo, bought new plants to kill and visited her nephews and new baby niece. She drank with Gina, cried on Gina's shoulder, then came home to her empty place and told herself that it would get better.

Soon, she hoped.

Because sleeping was almost impossible. She worked in her garden, moved furniture around and played with her nephews, all in an effort to exhaust herself, and still she didn't sleep. How could she when her bed was as empty as her heart?

"Okay, this is enough already," Gina said, pouring another glass of wine for each of them.

Sadie took a sip and looked through the sliding glass door to where her brother was shrouded in thick smoke from the barbecue. His sons were on the trampoline and with every jump, the springs shrieked.

"Agreed," Sadie said, chuckling as Mike waved an oven mitt, trying to dissipate the smoke. "I say we go out for tacos."

"I'm not talking about Mike's latest attempt to be Gordon Ramsay," Gina told her. "I'm talking about you and the pouting fest."

Sadie sniffed in insult. "I don't pout. I sulk. It's much classier."

"Well sure, but I'm tired of it, so I'm doing something about it."

Sadie took a sip of wine, shot her sister-in-law a sidelong glance and asked, "What did you do?"

"I fixed you up with Josh. The firefighter on Mike's squad that I told you about?"

"Right." Sadie did remember talking about the

possibilities there, but how could she be interested in someone else when her mind and heart were focused on Ethan?

"You're going to meet him for coffee tomorrow afternoon."

Dread settled in her stomach. This was not a good sign. She was in no shape for a date. She hadn't slept. She had bags under her eyes deep enough to pack for a month-long vacation and she wasn't finished sulking. "Oh, Gina, I don't think so."

Gina scowled at her. "Sadie, you've been...*sulking*—"

"Thank you."

"—for more than a week now. You're in love with Ethan, but you're not doing anything about it."

Shocked, she demanded, "What can I do?"

"I don't know, fight for what you want?"

Hadn't she said something like that to Ethan not so long ago?

"I thought you were anti-Ethan," Sadie said.

Gina waved that off. "I'm anti-you-being-hurt. But if you love him, fight for him."

Shaking her head, Sadie said, "If you can't win, what's the point in fighting?"

"If you give up before you start, what's the point of anything?" Gina stopped and said, "Sorry, sorry. I told Mike I wouldn't butt in."

"Fat chance of that," Mike shouted from outside.

"Ears like a bat," Gina muttered, then said louder, "Here's the deal. If you're not going to fight for Ethan, then it's time you let yourself see that there are a few million other men out there. I told Josh you'd meet him at CJ's Diner in Seal Beach for coffee tomorrow afternoon."

Why did everyone think they could order her around? "Did you tell him what to order for me?"

"Sure," she said. "Coffee. Weren't you listening?"

Sadie laughed. She couldn't help herself. Gina was a force of nature. "Fine. What time am I meeting him?"

"Four," Gina said. "I told him if coffee goes well, you'll have time to get dinner."

"There, or are we going somewhere else?"

"Oh, I'll leave that up to you two."

"Hah! She gave Josh a list of restaurants!" Mike shouted, and slammed the barbecue lid down, trying to smother the flames erupting from the grate.

"Just suggestions," Gina shouted back.

"I appreciate it, Gina," Sadie said, and it was true. It was nice to be loved so much. Her family was her rock. Knowing that Mike and Gina had her back made what she was going through more bearable. But in spite of her good intentions, Gina couldn't know just how far out of "dating" mode Sadie really was. "But—"

"Don't say no, sweetie." Gina leaned in and squeezed Sadie's hand. "Just give Josh a chance. Meet him for coffee. See what happens. What could it hurt?"

Ethan was fine.

No problems here. He could concentrate on work again now that his world was back in order. He didn't have the distraction of Sadie to keep him from concentrating. It was only the memory of her that haunted him now. He sensed her all over his house. Her scent lingered on the pillow she used. Her shampoo was still in his shower—he should toss it out, but he hadn't. He heard the phantom echo of her laughter and when he closed his eyes, he saw *hers*.

And the office wasn't much better. Hell, he could hardly stand to sit at his desk because of the memory they'd made *there*. Plus, as much as he tried to focus, he kept half expecting Sadie to briskly knock on his office door and poke her head inside. Instead, it was Rick manning the desk outside his office, and he wasn't nearly as good at the job as Sadie had been. In the man's defense, though, nobody would be.

Hell, two days ago, they'd lost an entire shipment of chocolates when a train derailed in Denver. Sadie would have had the whole situation taken care of in an hour. This time, it was Ethan himself who'd had to handle the crisis because Rick was out of his depth.

It was only natural that Ethan would miss her, wasn't it? She had kept his life, his office, running smoothly for five years, so it only made sense that her absence would throw everything off-kilter.

"And just who're you trying to lie to?" he muttered, and tossed his pen onto the desk. "It's not Sadie's efficiency you're missing. It's everything else about her."

"Talking to yourself is never a good sign."

Scowling, Ethan looked up at Gabe. "It's traditional to *knock* before you come into a room."

"I'm a rebel," Gabe said affably as he crossed the room and dropped into the chair opposite Ethan. "So, I'm here to let you know Jeff's come up with several more candies we'll have ready for you in another week or so."

"Good." Ethan picked up his pen again and pretended to read the papers in front of him. "Great. Goodbye."

Gabe laughed. "Nice talking to you, too. You know,

you used to be easier to get along with. Wonder why that was. Oh. Maybe it was Sadie's influence."

"You want to stop talking now." Ethan lifted his gaze and gave his brother a hard glare.

"No, I don't."

Ethan tossed the pen down again. "Damn it, Gabe, this is none of your business."

Gabe shrugged. "Yeah, but you helped me out when the Pam situation got so screwed up. Thought I'd return the favor."

"I don't need help." And even if he did, he wouldn't ask for it. He'd been fine before that insanity with Sadie and he'd be fine again. At some point.

"Pam and I are engaged."

Surprising, but not. Ethan was happy for his brother, but he really didn't want to hear about love or marriage. Didn't want anything else to remind him of Sadie. "Congratulations. Get out."

Gabe laughed and settled in for a chat. Irritated, Ethan wondered what it would take to get rid of him. Probably dynamite.

"Pam's brother, Tony, has been working with Jeff on the new line."

"I know."

"He's as good as Richard said he was. Of course, Jeff's still in charge, but Tony's really pulling his weight." Nodding, Gabe added, "And we've contracted for the rehab on the Donatello shop."

"I know that, too." They'd agreed to use Donatello's storefront in Laguna to launch their new line. Gabe and Pam were in charge and Tony and Jeff would be the chefs. It would be a good test spot and if it worked, which Ethan was sure it would, they'd think about opening up more specialty stores. He wanted to tell Sadie all about it. Hear her thoughts, ideas and suggestions. She had a sharp mind and wasn't afraid to give her opinion, and damn it, he missed that, too.

"I saw Sadie yesterday."

Ethan's head snapped up and Gabe grinned. "Got your attention with that one, didn't I?"

Yeah, he had. It felt like years since Ethan had seen her. "How is she?"

"She's doing great. Looked happy. She was out with her sister-in-law, shopping at Bella Terra. You know, the Huntington Beach mall."

"I know what it is," Ethan grumbled. So Sadie was out shopping and having fun and probably dating. Why wouldn't she? Who would she be going out with? It wasn't as if she'd had a lot of time to meet anyone. Or had she already met this mystery man before she left Ethan's life? How? When? Most importantly, *who*?

The thought of her with another man was enough to send ice through Ethan's veins. But he'd let her go, right? So he'd just have to live with that decision.

How did Sadie think that walking away was easy?

Nothing about this was easy.

"When are you going to admit you miss her?"

"When are you going to butt out of my life?"

"When you stop making a mess of it." Gabe leaned forward. "Sadie's not Marcy."

Ethan drew in a deep breath and settled the blast of anger he felt at Gabe throwing his past at him. He was right, though. Sadie was nothing like Marcy. Sadie would stand up and tell him what she was thinking. Marcy had kept her resentments to herself. Hadn't told him that she was unhappy. Not that their marriage's failure was her fault. He hadn't put the time in and he knew it. What he realized now was that a woman like Sadie wouldn't have put up with him ignoring her.

But Sadie wasn't the problem, was she? It was *him.* Ethan was the same man who'd made a mess of his marriage, so how could he know this time would be different?

"And you're not the same, either," Gabe said, as if reading Ethan's thoughts. "Sadie changed you."

Change. Used to be Ethan hated that word. Now, he could almost see the good in it. He had changed. For the better?

How was he to know?

"I'm just saying," Gabe added, as he stood up, "you might want to try to fix this before the chance gets away from you."

"I think it's too late already," Ethan murmured, re-membering the look on Sadie's face before she'd left his house. Not only had he let her go, he'd practically shoved her out the door. Why would she be willing to walk back in?

"Yeah," Gabe said, "but you won't know until you try."

Eleven

Josh was nice.

At any other point in her life, Sadie would have really enjoyed him. The man was gorgeous, seriously built, and he had a great smile and a wonderful sense of humor. In short, he was everything she should have wanted. Sadly, the one thing he was not was *Ethan*.

Sitting across from him at the diner, Sadie listened while he talked about the fire station and the guys he worked with. But instead of *hearing* him, she was thinking of Ethan. Wondering what he was doing. How he was feeling. Did he miss her or was he counting his blessings to be rid of her? God, that was a horrible thought.

"Hey," Josh said, distracting her. "Are you okay?"

"I'm sorry," she said quickly. "Yes, I'm fine. I'm just…tired, I think."

Sunlight slanted through the window and lay across the bright red Formica tabletop. Just across the street was the ocean, shining in the winter sun, and the crowds on Pacific Coast Highway belied the winter cold. Nothing stopped Californians from enjoying the beach.

Sadie just wished she was in the mood to enjoy *anything*. Maybe Gina was right, she told herself. Maybe she'd done enough sulking. How long could she mourn a love that hadn't happened? Was she going to wither up and spend her life sulking? Wind up alone with a houseful of cats? The best way to forget a particular man was in seeing another one, right? Well, Josh was a good place to start. She didn't even like cats.

"We can do this another day," he said with a shrug.

"No, really. I'm okay." She shrugged off her dark thoughts, pushed Ethan completely out of her mind and focused on the man opposite her. "And I'm interested. Tell me why you decided to become a firefighter."

He grinned. "It's always dangerous asking a man to talk about himself. We could go on for hours."

Sadie laughed. "I'll risk it."

Josh started talking then, and this time she really tried to pay attention. But less than a minute later, Ethan walked into the diner, carrying Emma against his chest, and Sadie was lost.

Following her shocked gaze, Josh looked over his shoulder, then back to her. "What's going on? You look like you've seen a ghost or something."

"Or something," she said, wondering what was going on. Her heartbeat was racing and her mouth was dry. Her stomach did a quick spin and flip, and she had to fight to keep her coffee down.

Ethan strode up to their table and completely ignored Josh as he said, "Honey, don't do this."

"What?" Sadie blurted.

"I know we've had some problems," Ethan continued, as if she hadn't spoken. "But we have a *baby.* You can't just walk away. We need you."

Horrified and embarrassed, Sadie stared up at Ethan. She couldn't believe he was doing this. And how had he found her? Groaning internally, she thought *Gina.* It was the only way. But *why* was he doing this?

"What's going on?" Josh gave Sadie a hard look. "Who is this? Gina didn't say anything about you having a baby. Or a husband."

"He doesn't know about us?" Ethan looked wounded as he stared down at her. "Even if you're mad at me, you can't forget about our child. Sadie, we need you. Come back home."

"Oh, for heaven's sake." She snapped a furious look at Ethan, then shifted her gaze to Josh. "This isn't what it looks like." She choked out a strained laugh. "Really. That's not my baby—"

And right on cue, Emma crowed in delight and threw herself at Sadie. Defeated, Sadie instinctively caught her and cuddled her close. She was warm and soft and smelled so good, Sadie smiled while the baby patted her cheeks with both tiny hands. Oh, how she'd missed this baby.

"Okay," Josh said, "I don't know what's going on here, but I'm out." He slid off the bench seat, tossed a ten dollar bill on the table and said, "Good luck with whatever this is."

When he left, Sadie looked up at Ethan and scowled

at the wide grin on his face. "Why would you do that, Ethan?"

He shrugged amiably. "I needed to get rid of him and I was afraid you wouldn't let me." He dropped onto the seat opposite her.

"Well, you're right. I wouldn't have." Sadie tried to be angry, but it was hard, with Emma cuddling in as if she were right where she belonged. "Gina told you where to find me, I'm guessing?"

"Not without telling me exactly what she thought of me first," he admitted. "The woman has a creative vocabulary."

Sadie laughed helplessly. Of course Gina would tell him off and then lead him right to Sadie. Beyond all else, her sister-in-law was a hopeless romantic.

The waitress came up with a fresh cup and poured coffee for Ethan, then refilled Sadie's. She left with questions in her eyes and Sadie couldn't blame her. She had plenty of questions herself.

"Why are you here?" she asked, keeping her voice down. "Why did you bring Emma?"

"When you're going to fight, bring all of your ammunition," he said, and Sadie was more confused than ever.

"Fight for what? What do you mean?"

"It means I want you to come back."

His gaze met hers. Sadie held her breath. "Come back to what?"

"To work."

She let the breath out and felt disappointment wash over her in a wave so heavy it weighed her down. "No."

"I thought you'd say that," Ethan said, cupping both hands around the mug of coffee. "So I'm offering you twice your old salary."

Sadie's heart sank even further. The minute she'd seen him, her foolish heart had hoped that he was there to confess his love. To ask her to marry him. To live and love with him. But he only wanted her back at the office and that, she couldn't do.

"No. I don't want to work for you anymore, Ethan." She scooted off the bench seat, snatching up her purse as she moved. It was hard to give Emma back to Ethan, but she did it, in spite of the fact that the baby reached up both arms to her and screwed up her tiny face to cry. "If that's why you came, you wasted a trip."

"It's not why." He stood up, too, tossed another ten on the table and led her out of the diner. "Not completely. Come on. We're not doing this here."

"Doing what?" She came to a dead stop on the sidewalk and refused to be budged until she knew what he was up to. Traffic hummed past, the wind howled in off the ocean and she had to squint up at him because of the sun.

He glanced around and frowned at the crowds and the noise before turning back to Sadie. "This isn't the place I would have picked, but screw it. This needs saying."

Sadie couldn't take much more. Tears were threatening and her throat was so tight she could hardly breathe. She had no idea what he wanted now, but she wished he'd just get it over with so she could go home. She had more sulking to do.

"Hold the baby," he said, and held her out so Sadie's only choice was to take the tiny girl.

"Okay, I offered you double your salary and you said no."

"I did," she said, "so don't throw more money at me."

"What if I offered you something else instead?"

She sighed heavily and smoothed Emma's wispy hair back from her forehead. "Like what?"

"A side job." He reached into his pocket, pulled out a blue velvet ring box and flipped it open.

She went perfectly still. Sadie was nearly blinded by the sun glancing off the enormous diamond nestled inside. Her heart actually stopped before it jumped into a wild gallop she had no hope of easing. She looked from the ring up to him and saw light and passion and love shining so brightly in his eyes it almost dimmed that diamond's gleam.

"Marry me, Sadie," he said, and the world seemed to suddenly fade away.

She couldn't hear the traffic or the people around her; all she could hear was the man she loved saying the words she'd never thought to hear him say.

"I know I'm not a good bet," he said. "And I admit, I was too scared to tell you how I felt because I didn't want to make another mistake. But I do love you. I love you so much it's making me crazy not being with you."

Sadie took a deep breath and held it. Emma leaned her head on Sadie's shoulder as if she was watching the show and cared about the outcome.

"I realized something last night, Sadie. The only mistake I was making was in *not* marrying you. You make me laugh. You make me think. You made it impossible for me to live without you. You made me love you."

"Oh, Ethan…" Tears filled her eyes and she blinked frantically to clear her vision.

"I can say the words now," Ethan told her. "I should have said it before. But if you say yes, I'll tell you how much I love you every day until you're sick of hearing it."

"That would never happen," she whispered.

His eyes speared into hers, and it was as if he was willing her to see inside him to the truth shining there. "Marry me and take your old job back, too."

She laughed wildly.

"Seriously. Come back to work, too." He grinned at her. "That way I can kiss my assistant anytime I want to. And you'll save me from Rick. He's terrible."

Still laughing, Sadie shook her head and tossed her hair out of her eyes. She didn't want to miss a moment of this.

"Marry me, Sadie," he said. "I fired Teresa."

Surprised, she held Emma a little tighter. "What? Why? She was perfect."

"No she wasn't," he said. "She wasn't you. I only needed a nanny because I was going to be alone with Emma. If we're married we can take care of Emma and all of our other kids together. And Julie's there to help, right?"

"Right…" Together. *All of our other kids.*

"If we're married—"

"Stop," she said, and stepped into his arms. She didn't need to hear anything else. He'd already said everything that mattered. Everything she'd dreamed of hearing for so long.

When he held her, pulling her tight and close, Sadie's heart started beating again. His warmth enfolded both her and Emma, and Sadie knew that this was the absolute best moment of her life.

"Is that a yes?" he asked, smoothing her hair back and out of her eyes.

"It's a yes. To everything." Sadie went up on her toes and kissed him. "Oh, Ethan, I want you and Emma and more kids, and my job."

"Thank God."

"It won't be easy," she teased, as he slid that diamond onto her ring finger.

"Who wants easy?" He scooped Emma up, then dropped one arm around Sadie's shoulders, turning to walk toward the parking lot. "You know, when we tell our kids about how Daddy proposed, we're going to have to come up with a more romantic story."

"Oh no, we don't," she said, leaning into him as they walked through the crowded streets. "This was perfect."

He kissed the top of her head and said, "I swear I'll be a good husband and father."

"I know you will," Sadie said, smiling up at him. "Because I'll be with you every step of the way."

* * * * *